P9-CEP-414

STILETTO JUSTICE

DURHAM COUNTY LIBRARY

Mar 13 2018

DURHAM NC

STILETTO JUSTICE

CAMRYN KING

KENSINGTON PUBLISHING CORP.
www.kensingtonbooks.com

To the extent that the image or images on the cover of this book depict a person or persons, such person or persons are merely models, and are not intended to portray any character or characters featured in the book.

DAFINA BOOKS are published by

Kensington Publishing Corp.
119 West 40th Street
New York, NY 10018

Copyright © 2018 by Camryn King

All rights reserved. No part of this book may be reproduced in any form or by any means without the prior written consent of the Publisher, excepting brief quotes used in reviews.

All Kensington titles, imprints, and distributed lines are available at special quantity discounts for bulk purchases for sales promotion, premiums, fund-raising, and educational or institutional use.

Special book excerpts or customized printings can also be created to fit specific needs. For details, write or phone the office of the Kensington Sales Manager: Kensington Publishing Corp., 119 West 40th Street, New York, NY 10018. Attn. Sales Department. Phone: 1-800-221-2647.

Dafina and the Dafina logo Reg. U.S. Pat. & TM Off.

ISBN-13: 978-1-4967-0216-6
ISBN-10: 1-4967-0216-6
First Kensington Trade Paperback Printing: March 2018

eISBN-13: 978-1-4967-0217-3
eISBN-10: 1-4967-0217-4
First Kensington Electronic Edition: March 2018

10 9 8 7 6 5 4 3 2 1

Printed in the United States of America

PROLOGUE

"Is he dead?"

"I don't know, but seeing that lying trap of a mouth shut is a nice change of pace."

Kim Logan, Harley Buchanan, and Jayda Sanchez peered down at the lifeless body of the United States senator from Kansas, Hammond Grey.

"I agree he looks better silent," Kim mused, while mentally willing his chest to move. "But I don't think prison garb will improve my appearance."

"Move, guys." Jayda, who'd hung in the background, pushed Harley aside to get closer. She stuck a finger under his nose. "He's alive, but I don't know how long he'll be unconscious. Whatever we're going to do needs to happen fast."

"Fine with me." Harley stripped off her jacket and unzipped her jeans. "The sooner we get this done, the sooner we can get the hell out of here."

"I'm with you," Kim replied. Her hands shook as she unsnapped the black leather jacket borrowed from her husband and removed her phone from its inside pocket. "Jayda, start taking his clothes off."

"Why me?" Jayda whispered. "I don't want to touch him."

"That's why you're wearing gloves," Harley hissed back. "Look, if I can bare my ass for the world to see, the least you can do is pull his pants down. Where's that wig?"

Kim showed more sympathy as she pointed toward the bag holding a brunette-colored hair transformer. "Jayda, I understand completely. I don't even want to look at his penis, let alone capture it on video."

Harley had stripped down to her undies. She stood impatiently, hand on hip. "I tell you what I'm not going to do. I'm not going to get buck-ass naked for you two to punk out. It's why we all took a shot of Jack!"

"I'm too nervous to feel it," Jayda said as she wrung her hands. "I probably should have added Jim and Bud."

"Hold this." Kim handed Jayda the phone and walked over to the bed. After the slightest of pauses, she reached for the belt and undid it. Next, she unbuttoned and unzipped the dress slacks. "Jayda, raise him up a little so I can pull these down."

Harley walked over to where Kim stood next to the bed. "Don't take them all the way off. He looks like the type who'd screw without bothering to get totally undressed."

Kim pulled the pants down to Hammond's knees. The room went silent. The women stared. Kim looked at Harley. Harley looked at Jayda. The three looked at each other.

"Am I seeing what I think I'm seeing?" Jayda asked.

Harley rubbed the chill from her arms. "We're all seeing it."

"*Star Wars*? Really, Hammond?" Kim quickly snapped a couple pics, then gently lowered the colorful boxers and murmured, "Looks like his political viewpoint isn't the only thing conservative."

She snapped a few more. Harley donned the wig, looked in the mirror, and snickered. "Guys, how do I look?"

"Don't," Kim began, covering her mouth. "Don't start to laugh . . ." The low rumble of muted guffaws replaced speech.

The liquor finally kicked in.

"Come on, guys!" Jayda harshly whispered, though her eyes gleamed. "We've got to hurry."

"You look fine, Harley. As gorgeous a brunette as you are a blonde."

Harley removed her thong and climbed on the bed. "Remember . . ."

"I won't get your face, Harley. What the wig doesn't cover, I'll clip out or blur. You won't be recognizable in any way."

"And you're sure this super glue will work, and hide my fingerprints?"

Jayda nodded. "That's what it said on the internet."

"I'm nervous." Harley straddled the unconscious body and placed fisted hands on each side.

"Wait!" Kim stilled Harley with a hand to the shoulder. "Don't let your mouth actually touch his. We don't want to leave a speck of DNA. I'll angle the shot so that it looks like you're kissing."

"What about . . . that." Jayda pointed toward the flaccid member.

"Oh, yeah. I forgot. Look inside that bag." Harley tilted her head in that direction. "With the condom on, it looks like the real thing."

Jayda retrieved a condom-clad cucumber and marched back to the bed as though it were a baton. "He won't like that we've filmed him, but he'll hopefully appreciate that we replaced his Vienna sausage with a jumbo hot link."

The women got down to business—Jayda directing, Harley performing, Kim videotaping. Each job was executed quickly, efficiently, just as they'd planned.

Finally, after double-checking to make sure her work had been captured, Kim shut off the camera. "Okay, guys, I think we've got enough."

Harley moved toward the edge of the bed. "Pictures and video?"

"Yep. Want to see it?"

"No," she replied, scrambling into her jeans. "I want to get the hell out of here."

"That makes two of us," Jayda said, walking toward the coat she'd tossed on a chair.

"Three of us." Kim took another look at the footage. "Wait, guys. I have an idea. Jayda, quick, come here."

"What?"

"No time to explain. Trust me on this . . . please?"

Five minutes later they were ready to go. "What should we do about him?" Jayda asked, waving a hand at his state of undress.

"Nothing," Kim replied. She returned the phone to its hiding place in her pocket. "Let him figure out what may or may not have happened."

They'd been careful, but taking no chances, they wiped down every available surface with cleaning wipes, which they then placed back in the bag that once again held the condom-clad cucumber. Harley almost had a heart attack when she glimpsed the wineglass that if forgotten and left behind would have been a forensic team's dream. After rinsing away prime evidence, she pressed Grey's fingers around the bowl, refilled it with a splash of wine, and placed it back on the nightstand. After a last look around to make sure that nothing was left that could be traced back to them, the women crept out of the bedroom and down the stairs. Harley turned off the outside light and unbolted the side door.

Kim turned to her. "You sure you don't want to come with us?"

Harley shook her head. "I have to leave the way I came. Don't worry. The car service is on the way. See you at the hotel."

After peeking out to make sure the coast was clear, Jayda and Kim tiptoed out the back door as quietly and inconspicuously as they'd arrived. A short time later Harley left, too.

Once down the block, around the corner, and into the

rental car, Jayda and Kim finally exhaled. The next day, as the women left the nation's capital, hope began to bloom like cherry blossoms in spring. Until now their calls for help and cries for justice had been drowned out or ignored. Maybe the package specially delivered to his office next week would finally get the senator's attention, and get him to do the right thing.

1

A Year Earlier . . .

We the jury in the above titled action find the defendant, Kendall Aaron Logan, guilty . . .

Kim sat straight up, pulling in a gasp of air as she awakened from the recurring nightmare.

Guilty . . .

She checked her watch and looked around, momentarily confused as to why she was in bed with the sun still out. Then she remembered. The other nightmare. The one that happened today, that crushed her heart completely and sapped her strength to the point where lying down was all she could do.

Her son's last appeal, the one to the Kansas Supreme Court, had been denied.

Denied . . .

Head in hands, she squeezed her eyes against another onslaught of tears.

Guilty. Denied.

The words echoed and repeated in her head, like a silly song you hated but later found yourself singing. Only this wasn't a song, it was her real life, with a melancholy melody that made breathing difficult and dancing impossible.

Pulling the cover over her head, she squeezed her eyes shut again to hold back the tears. They leaked out anyway. Tears of sadness mixed with ones of bittersweet joy. Cries for her son, her miracle baby, the result of a pregnancy doctors had said would never happen. It did, after years of trying. A difficult one, but Kendall came out as six pounds, eight ounces, and twenty-one inches of perfection. Kim never got pregnant again. All the more reason the sun rose and set on their now six-foot-two, one-hundred-ninety-pound angel. The one who'd been in prison for two and a half years. The one whose final appeal the Kansas State Supreme Court had just denied.

"That's it. Get up, Kim." These mumbled words accompanied a determined push off the pillows as she rolled herself out of bed. "Aaron!"

Silence.

"Honey, are you here?"

She trudged down the stairs of the lovingly restored American Foursquare located in Kansas City, Missouri's historic Hyde Park neighborhood. When her husband had suggested they purchase it fifteen years ago, she had thought him mad. It had been in shambles, empty for more than a decade. Where she saw dilapidation, he saw potential. Over time, she saw it, too. They bought it for a steal, and over the next five years restored each room to its turn-of-the-century glory, with modern touches for convenience and a blended sense of style. Now, however, she didn't see any of that. Or Aaron. A quick check of the rooms confirmed that she was alone. When troubled, her husband of twenty years either sought solitude, buried himself in work, or combined the two. Solitude was the last thing she needed. Back upstairs, she picked up the phone to call her mom. It rang in her hand.

"Hi, Harley."

"Oh, no, Kim. Don't tell me . . ."

Kim knew she didn't have to, that her somber greeting had

more than answered the question for which her good friend had called.

"What reasons did the judges give?"

"None, if you ask me. They wrote a bunch of legal jargon, yada, yada, that made about as much sense as his conviction." She heard Harley's heavy sigh.

Exactly.

"Kim, I'm so sorry."

"Me, too."

"How are you holding up? Stupid question, I know, but . . ."

"At the moment, not too good."

"Is your husband there?"

"Nope, it's just me. And the quiet isn't helping. I feel like I'm going crazy."

"I'm coming over."

"You don't have to do that."

"Did that sound like a question? I'm not letting you deal with this by yourself."

"I appreciate that. But I've got to get out of here."

"Fine. We'll meet somewhere then. How about Johnny's, where I used to work? The portions are large and the drinks are strong."

"I don't have much of an appetite, but I could sure use a drink. That's downtown, right? Near Twelfth and Main?"

"Tenth and Main."

"Got it. How soon can you get there?"

"Give me fifteen minutes."

"From Olathe? Slow down, girl. That trip should take half an hour at least."

"Okay, thirty minutes then."

Kim experienced her first laugh of the day. "All right, Mario Andretti. See you then."

Thirty-seven minutes later, Kim pulled into a space just a few doors down from Johnny's Steakhouse in downtown

Kansas City. It was Tuesday, a beautiful May day, and were it the lunch hour finding a parking space near this popular haunt would have been impossible, let alone a table. But at four in the afternoon, one could sit almost anywhere. Though she lived twice as far from the restaurant, Kim wasn't surprised to see that Harley, a fiery millennial with Jack in her glass, ice in her veins, and a heart of gold, had beat her there and was sitting at the bar. Shocking Kim, though, was who sat beside her. Jayda, Kim's other best friend from WHIP, as sweet and easy-going as Harley was tough. WHIP, Women Helping Innocent Prisoners, was the organization Kim had founded soon after her innocent son was wrongfully convicted. It was this organization that had brought Harley Buchanan and Jayda Sanchez into her life, and helped save it.

Kim gave Harley a big hug and then turned to Jayda with a stern look. "You're supposed to be at work."

"I got sick," Jayda blurted before Kim could continue to fuss her out. "As soon as I heard what happened, I felt the beginnings of a fever and my throat got scratchy."

Kim's eyes narrowed.

"You needed me more than the pharmaceutical department did," Jayda whispered as she pulled Kim into a heartfelt embrace. "I'm sorry."

"Kim, what do you want to drink?"

"I could use a shot of your favorite, Harley, but since I'm driving it's probably better to stick with Merlot."

"Go grab a booth," the bartender told Harley. "I'll have the server bring over her drink, and freshen up your Jack and Coke."

"Sounds good." Harley slid off the barstool. "Come on, guys. Let's head to my office."

It was said lightheartedly enough, but heaviness joined them at the table, an uninvited, unwelcomed guest that settled in with the cocky confidence of an entity that knew it had every right to be there.

Kim looked between the two women almost young enough to be her daughters and stretched her hands toward them. "Thanks for being here, guys."

Each took a hand and squeezed. "Where's Aaron?" Jayda asked.

"The office, probably." Kim took a sip from the full glass of wine the waiter brought over, ready to take their order until Harley waved her away. "Or the golf course. Maybe the gym. We handle stress in polar opposite ways. He shuts down. I go off. He buries himself in work. I scream from the mountaintops to whomever will listen."

"I don't understand how the case was denied. I mean what . . . how could he . . . what happened?"

Kim shrugged. "I don't know. I haven't known much about anything since June twenty-seventh three years ago when Aaron and I got the call that changed our lives."

She clenched her jaw, rapidly blinked back tears, and looked beyond her friends into the nightmare that had become her life. "How did Kendall get a ten-year prison sentence on drug possession charges with no evidence, no witnesses? Just testimony from plea-bargained cronies that was corroborated by police officers who just happened to be friends with a district attorney blatantly building a political platform by being tough on crime?"

"Political platform. Who, Grey?" Harley's crystal-blue eyes widened in staunch disbelief.

"You didn't know?" Jayda asked. "He announced, what, a couple months ago? He's running for senator. I didn't see the announcement, but my mom did."

"You've got to be kidding." Harley's face showed disgust.

"The incumbent had a stroke," Kim continued. "With elections six months away the party had to scramble to find a 'suitable' candidate, one they thought could beat Jack Myers." She used air quotes to emphasize the adjective used by the papers to describe the district attorney, but Kim's expression made it clear that she found nothing suitable about him.

The waiter who'd been shooed away earlier came back bearing gifts. "You're going to need something to soak up that alcohol, girlfriend," she said to Harley with a wink, as she removed spicy wings, spinach avocado dip, and tortilla chips from a large, round tray and placed them on the table.

"When it came to taking care of customers, you were always the best. Guys, this is Lisa. Lisa, my friends Jayda and Kim. Right after getting hired, she took this clueless green thing under her fairy wings and taught me everything I know about giving good service."

"I taught her the basics," Lisa said. "Her naturally flirty nature and Midwestern charm did the rest, brought out the big tips and kept customers coming back."

"You gave me the lowdown on the cute new customer in my station. Jesse," she explained to Jayda and Kim. "Now *that* was a tip, my biggest and best by far. I always say if we get married, both she and my mother will give me away."

"How's he doing?" Lisa's voice lowered and was filled with concern.

"He's in prison," Harley deadpanned. "So despite his attempts to convince me otherwise, he's pretty fucked up."

"Of course. That was dumb. Sorry."

"No, it wasn't. It was a perfectly legitimate question. But hearing some news about the man who helped put him there just put me in a really bad mood."

"Well, food always makes me feel better. So what can I get you ladies? It's on the house. And don't say salad. This is a steakhouse. We serve real food here."

"I'm fine," Kim said.

"This will do for me," Jayda added, picking up a wing.

Harley looked at Lisa. "I think we're good."

"Got it." Lisa dropped the order pad into her pocket. "Three porterhouses coming up."

Kim watched Lisa walk away, then looked at Harley. "I like her."

Harley crossed her arms as vibes of all kinds of pissed off transmitted from her person. "What are we going to do?"

"About what?"

"About Grey, the judge, the denied appeal, our guys rotting in prison, the fucked-up system, take your pick. We've got to do something, Kim! What?"

"She's tried everything, Harley," Jayda said, with a calming touch on Harley's arm. "Formed WHIP, organized our protests, kept this fight in the media, hired great lawyers. What else can she do? What else can any of us do?"

Harley wouldn't back down. "We've got to fight. I waited a lifetime for somebody like Jesse, and I'll be damned if I let an A-hole like Grey ruin my happily ever after. And I'll be double-damned if I sit back while Grey climbs the political ladder on my boyfriend's back."

"Harley's right, Jayda. We can't quit." Kim ran a weary hand through the new pixie haircut she'd had cut extra short and was still getting used to. "I don't have the energy for it right now, but give me a few days, maybe a week. It didn't work for Kendall, but I'll talk to my attorneys about working on your guy's appeals."

"Pro bono?" Harley asked. "We sure as hell can't afford an attorney. Mom's medical bills take every penny I have, and a few that I don't."

"I don't know if our family could afford them, either," Jayda said. "Maybe we can write to one of those nonprofit groups, like the Innocence Project, or work with a public defender to get our guys a new trial."

"Fuck that," Harley spat, throwing back a shot of Jack, or Mr. Daniels, as she sometimes called her liquor of choice.

Jayda frowned. "But you just said—"

"That we've got to keep fighting. I know. But not through

the system. It's broken. It doesn't work. We've got to try something else."

Kim's expression was a mixture of wariness and weariness. "Okay, Harley the Houdini. What do you suggest?"

"I don't know. But the three of us need to put our heads together and figure out how to *whip*, pun intended, Grey's wannabe senator ass."

"But how?" Jayda echoed. "He's got money, power, status, everything! What do we have?"

"Each other," Harley retorted.

"The truth," Kim added, renewed strength in her voice.

"Determination," Harley continued. "My mom says that where there's a will, there is always a way."

Jayda's eyes lit up. "My grandmother Alma changed the phrase 'hell hath no fury like a woman scorned,' to 'earth has no blessing like a woman born.'"

Kim smiled at Jayda. "Your grandmother sounds like a wise woman."

"Yes, very wise. Wisdom we sure could use right about now."

"I say we toast to continuing our fight, getting justice for our men by any means necessary." Harley held up her glass. "To justice for Jesse."

Jayda raised hers, too. "To justice for Nicky and Daniel."

"To justice for Kendall!" Kim lifted her glass. The women downed their drinks.

When Kim had arrived at the restaurant, she felt the fight was over. Upon leaving she knew one thing for sure: it had only just begun.

2

Kim, Harley, and Jayda left the restaurant with full stomachs but with no real plan to do what the courts had not: get justice for all. However, the next day Kim read about a Saturday rally planned for Grey in Edgefield, Kansas, his hometown. A few phone calls, text messages, and several emails later a protest had been thrown together to coincide with the event. That morning Jayda, her mother Anna, aunt Lucy, sister Teresa. and sister-in-law Crystal headed to the community center where every second Saturday of the month WHIP meetings were held. Though they'd eaten breakfast, she carried a container of mini *gorditas de huevos*, masa cakes stuffed with chili-spiced eggs. *Abuela* had insisted.

"We're only going to Kansas City, Grandma," Jayda laughingly told her. "Not El Paso."

To which her grandmother responded, "A hungry stomach will growl in either place."

"Ha! So true, Grandma. *Te amo.*"

The women piled into Lucy's roomy Ford Expedition and headed toward Interstate 35 and the State Line Community Center, just over the state line from Kansas into Missouri. They all wore bright yellow cotton t-shirts with the WHIP acronym across the organization's logo, a whip breaking open handcuffs on the front, and the spelled-out acronym on the back— Women Helping Innocent Prisoners. The group had voted on yellow as their color based on an old long-lost love classic from the seventies by Tony Orlando and Dawn.

"What are we going to be doing exactly?"

Aunt Lucy's stereo was programmed to her favorite Tejano music but when Lucy's sister, Anna, asked the question, she turned it down.

Even though the music was low, Jayda leaned forward so the two up front could hear her clearly, pushing thick locks of shiny black hair away from her heart-shaped face as she perched on the seat's edge. "Making protest signs for the rally."

"How many do you think will show up?" Crystal, Jayda's sister-in-law, asked the question while scrolling through her cell phone.

Jayda shrugged. "Hard to say. There's over a hundred members in the group, but we only average around twenty or thirty at the monthly meetings. Some members are like you guys, depending on someone who goes regularly to keep you informed."

"I work most Saturdays," Lucy said in defense.

"I'm usually helping Rick," Crystal said. "Or visiting Daniel."

"I know, guys. Just kidding."

Jayda knew how hard her family worked. Lucy and Anna's company, Great Housekeeping, had allowed for the purchase of homes and put kids through school. Crystal had been a stay-at-home mom, babysitting Jayda's daughter Alejandra while taking care of her three, until her husband, Daniel, and Jayda's boyfriend, Nicky, had gotten locked up. Without them, her husband's successful auto detailing business floundered. Crystal was forced into the workforce; began working part-time for her older brother, an ex-Marine with a private catering business, who had honed his skills while serving in Iraq.

"Crystal, are you working with Rick full-time, now? His business is really taking off."

"Not officially, but yes, lately I've been working a lot. Guess word on his strong work ethic and skills as a chef is getting around. He catered a dinner party fund-raiser a few months ago, for a city council member. Since then he's gotten several calls from political figures and organizations wanting him to cater their events. He wants me to go full-time, but I don't want to burden Alma with all of the kids."

Alma, the seventy-five-year old Sanchez family matriarch, was the undisputed boss and resident babysitter-in-a-pinch.

"Mama raised seven kids by herself," Anna responded. "I'm sure she can handle yours."

"Maybe, but right now I want to stay part-time. So he's looking for another part-timer to pick up the slack."

"To answer your question, Aunt Lucy, I don't know how many will be protesting with us today. I'm expecting a good crowd, though. Most of the time we feel so helpless, with our hands tied and nothing we can do. So even holding a sign in protest feels good, because at least we're doing something."

"*Mi Dios*," Jayda's mom, Anna, whispered as she peered out the window at the graying sky. "I hope it doesn't rain."

"Pray to the patron Saint Medard for good weather," Lucy replied. "There's a rosary in the glove compartment."

"Gosh, Aunt Lucy," Jayda exclaimed. "You know a patron saint for everything."

"Almost," was Lucy's quiet reply.

Yes, almost. Jayda knew exactly what her aunt meant and imagined the others did, too. In the months leading up to the trial of her boyfriend and brother, everyone in the family had prayed. It hadn't helped Daniel and Nicky.

A short time later they arrived at the center. The parking lot was fuller than usual. For Jayda, this was a good sign. The larger the crowd of protestors, the better the impact. They walked into a room filled with excitement and smelling like coffee and freshly baked pastries. Two long, rectangular tables were set flush against a wall on the right side of the room. They held materials for sign-making: cardboard, paper, markers, industrial staplers, strips of plywood, and hammers and nails. White pieces of paper with slogan ideas were taped above them. Below the table were stacks of t-shirts in cardboard boxes. On the left side of the room another rectangular table held two coffee machines, boxes of donuts, and a tray filled with condiments and an assortment of teas. That's where Kim stood, sipping from a yellow cup emblazoned with the WHIP logo as she talked to Faith Brockman, one of the group's earliest members, especially passionate for the mentally ill who, like her son, found themselves behind bars. Jayda ushered her family over to meet them.

"Let's get you guys started," Kim said, after Jayda had reintroduced the family, whom Kim had met at one of the earlier meetings but hadn't seen since. "Why don't each of you join a group at a different table? That way, you can meet someone new and socialize while you work."

After thirty minutes, Kim interrupted the group's focused creativity.

"Everyone, may I have your attention? I hope you all have completed your signs. We'll roll out in about five minutes. There are slips of paper by the door with the rally address along with our code of conduct. We don't want anyone getting arrested while protesting about people in jail. We also have about twenty umbrellas bearing our logo. Feel free to grab one. Hopefully the rain forecasted won't come until later. But those who choose to can be prepared if it does."

Several of the cars formed an unofficial caravan from Kansas City to Edgefield. Once inside the city limits, "Vote Grey" signs and ten-foot-tall cardboard brooms were seen everywhere, along with his campaign slogan, "Clean Up Kansas The Grey Way!" Jayda

didn't see any for Myers, his opponent, and wondered if anybody in town besides WHIP and the inmates housed in
Edgefield wanted Grey to lose. *Edgefield.* Home to her husband
and brother for more than a year. Just being close to the facility
gave Jayda chills. Or was it being this close to Hammond Grey
for the first time in almost two years, since shooting daggers
with her eyes in his back at the Jones County courthouse? She
didn't ask Lucy, but Jayda silently wondered what saint could
help a face-to-face encounter with the devil.

The size of the crowd surprised them. Jayda guessed it to be
at least a thousand, easy. Once the protestors parked and gathered the group, they walked in a loose formation, two abreast,
one message on their t-shirts, a second on their signs. The gray
skies actually worked to their advantage. The yellow shirts
stood out, were eye-catching, even among the dense throng. A
mixture of expressions followed their progress from the sidewalk to their target destination, as close to the main stage as
possible. Many were simply curious. Others, after reading
their t-shirts, signage, or both would voice the displeasure that
showed on their faces. It was impossible to get in front of the
makeshift stage, but the women managed to get about ten
yards away, close enough, they hoped, to be seen by Grey.

If he was at all aware of their presence, the crowd couldn't
tell. His demeanor was as relaxed and easy as the jeans he wore,
as though assuring a thousand old friends that he'd bring back
the security felt in the good old days and make the state great
again.

"A few short years ago I vowed to take on the gangs, illegal
immigrants, and others determined to turn America the beautiful into a lawless, godless nation. I promised to take criminals
off the street, your streets, and make our neighborhoods safe
once again. I vowed that with your help, and that of law enforcement and the justice system, I'd get things back to how
they used to be in the good ol' days of the Sunflower State.

How they were when I was a young boy growing up right here in Edgefield. Where we slept with our doors unlocked and left car keys in the ignition. In this small, God-fearing town, not much has changed. Well, after this speech, you might want to grab those keys."

He waited as the audience chuckled, and he flashed his killer-watt smile. "During my time as district attorney, the crime rate dropped by over twenty percent. My office imposed some of the toughest penalties and longest sentences in the history of this state. We decreased crime and built state-of-the-art facilities to put these thugs in and at the same time increased the job market and this area's economy with job opportunities at these prisons for law-abiding citizens like you!"

A few boos were sprinkled between the cheers. From some of the WHIP members, Jayda supposed. One with differing views from that diatribe could be quiet for only so long.

"But don't put down those brooms just yet," Grey continued. "With your help and support, we've made Kansas a safer state in three short years. But we're just getting started. There are forty-nine states to go. We have a safer Kansas. Now, let's work on a safer America in all fifty of these United States!"

One of Grey's staffers, a tall, handsome blonde standing close to the candidate, raised his broom and led a chant. "Clean up Kansas. The Grey way!"

The crowd enthusiastically joined him, waving their brooms. The WHIP protestors tried to counter with a mantra of their own. "*No witnesses! No evidence! Grey locks up the innocent!*" A couple dozen voices were no match for a thousand equally boisterous ones. The WHIP members were quickly drowned out, and almost as quickly ignored and forgotten.

Kim turned to Jayda. "That's an hour we'll never get back," she said, observing the crowd. "I guess we should have thought twice about fighting a bully in his own backyard."

Jayda saw a reporter making his way toward them, a photographer in tow. "Not so fast," she mumbled discreetly. "It looks like a photo op is headed our way."

Kim turned to see a middle-aged, harried-looking reporter coming toward them. She returned the smile he offered and held out her hand.

"Mark Carson, *Olathe Republic*," he said upon shaking it. "What group is this?"

Before she could answer, a commotion ensued behind them. Kim's head jerked around in time to see a WHIP member being pushed. The scene had trouble written all over it. Like a mama bear protecting a cub—eyes blazing, hands outstretched—she rushed toward the fray. "Stop!"

Another cameraman on her opposite side snapped several pics and landed a mouth-wide-open money shot. The reporter rushed to meet his paper's Sunday deadline. The girls didn't know it yet, but they and the WHIP organization were about to be headline news.

Jayda saw it first. Awakened by Alejandra before five a.m., she'd gotten her daughter back to sleep, crawled back into her own bed, and seeing her message icon lit, lazily reached over for her cell phone. She clicked on to her email host's website. A familiar face—eyes glaring, mouth wide—jumped off the screen.

WTH?

Rubbing sleep and disbelief out of her eyes, Jayda scooted into a seated position and leaned against the headboard. She tapped the screen and read the heading:

Angry Protestors Disrupt Peaceful Rally

"No way!" Jayda scrolled down and continued reading, a look of incredulity spreading across her face. Halfway through the short piece she tapped the phone icon, then after noticing the time on the phone's face, tapped out a message instead.

You're not going to believe what I saw online. Call me ASAP.

Jayda reread the brief piece, then whipped back the covers and got out of bed. The blatant misrepresentation of the facts gave her unexpected, eerie chills. It was early, but any chance of more sweet dreams had just been dashed by a nightmare happening with her eyes wide open.

3

Harley had planned to attend the WHIP protest rally. But after arriving home from work at two-thirty in the morning and getting forty winks of sleep, she awoke to a battle that was totally different than the ones the girls had faced. Even now, hours later and on her way to work once again, she was oblivious to the WHIP brouhaha. Which was probably a good thing.

She pulled into the parking lot across the street from a large, nondescript five-story building where she had begun working after Jesse's arrest, when the steakhouse check was no longer enough to cover her mom Shannon's rising medical costs and household luxuries like electricity and gas. Though it was only one o'clock in the afternoon, the lot was three-quarters full. An award-winning chef was the reason why. The membership included unlimited access to a beautifully appointed dining room and impressive menu, from noon to two a.m. For the dining shift, Harley worked as part of the skimpily clad dining room waitstaff. Not as lucrative as dancing or "cocktails and conversation," as private shows were called, but it was less stressful and always a lot of fun.

Harley exited the car, gathered her outfits from the trunk for back-to-back shifts, and hurried across the street. Tiny drops of rain mingled with the tendrils whipping against her flawless porcelain face. She grabbed the heavy brass handle and pulled open the door. A gush of cool air enveloped her as she entered the lobby, empty save for a security guard at the front desk and Bobby, a police officer who patrolled the area and protected the girls, chatting with him. With mere minutes to spare before her shift began, she waved a quick hello to them as she bypassed the sometimes slow elevator and took the stairs two at a time up to the second floor.

Bursting through the dressing room door, she announced her presence by almost killing a co-worker.

"Shit, Harley!"

"Kat! Oh, my God! Are you all right?"

Katherine "Kat" Lowe, the premiere diva of divas within the group of girls, was crouched and hunched over, mumbling curses while holding her hand. She'd danced at the club for almost ten years and had been around the block a few times. Many would assume that, like Harley, she was in her twenties. But good genes, Botox, and carefully placed implants belied the forty-seven birthdays Kat had counted.

Harley took tentative steps, with hand outstretched. "What can I do to help?"

"Slow the heck down," Kat spat through gritted teeth.

Harley could have explained that the accident was as much due to limited sleep as exceptional speed, but neither was an excuse. "Where are you hurt? Did I hit your face?"

Kat shook her head as she slowly straightened her body. "Thanks to quick reflexes learned during a volatile relationship when I was nineteen, you only broke my hand. That I can live with. Had you damaged my B's or scratched my face, we'd have a situation."

In spite of being mortified at having possibly caused injuries, and the battle she'd helped wage at home, Harley smiled at Kat's reference to an exotic dancer's moneymakers—boobs and butt.

She gingerly reached for her hand. "I didn't mean to run you over. Sorry about that."

Kat gave a playful swat with said "broken" hand and scooted around her. "You'll have two shifts to kiss up to me. I plan to milk my injury, so get ready to sweat."

"No problem."

Kat stopped and turned around, really looking at Harley for the first time. "That was a joke."

"Oh, okay."

She walked over to where Harley stood in front of a locker. "Are you okay?"

"I'm fine." Harley's mouth smiled. Her eyes didn't.

"Bullshit. What's going on with you, girl?"

Harley looked at the clock on the wall behind them. "We'll talk later."

She shimmied out of her clothes and threw them in the locker, then squeezed into the waitress "uniform," a skintight mini-dress with a V-navel cut (normally called V-neck but theirs went much lower) to show off the goods. She slipped fishnet-covered feet into four-inch heels, tossed her hair back and forth to fluff it up, touched up her mascara, and ruby-red lipstick and strutted to the dining room. Showtime!

For the next two hours she hid abject pain behind smiles, laughter, and flirts that helped her sail through an extended lunch service and make more than two hundred bucks in tips. At four o'clock, the dining room shut down for one hour to make the transition from lunch to dinner service. Harley and Kat took their break, grabbed some chow, and headed to an empty first-floor office for private time and gossip.

Kat kicked off her shoes as soon as they shut the door. "I thought that lunch service would never end. Why do all of the good tippers have to be ugly?"

"And old."

"And gnarly!" Kat plopped down on a love seat, pulled out

a cigarette, and after lighting it blew a stream of smoke at the no smoking sign. "Mr. Johnson always wants to slide a hand up my dress and feel my butt. But he's a long-time customer who's always treated me well. So I let him."

"Seriously?" Harley opened her salad container and moved the lettuce around. "You let him feel your ass?"

"That's the least I can do for the poor old codger. Every squeeze probably adds a month to his life." Harley smiled. "But enough about work. We didn't come in here to talk about that. What's wrong?"

Harley set down the uneaten food. "Mom had another reaction."

"Oh, no, Harley."

"We ended up in emergency."

"Oh, honey." Kat leaned over and gave Harley a hug. "I thought she was in remission and doing better?"

"She was. But ever since we ran out of the herbs Jesse got from that center in California, the chemo and radiation have taken a toll. She definitely responded better to the conventional treatment when using the alternative approaches as well. Now the nausea is back, along with headaches and insomnia. A month ago they changed her meds. She started feeling a little better, and I thought we were out of the woods. Then came this morning when I walked into her room and found her hugging the porcelain god. When blood came up, that was it. Loaded her into the car and headed straight to ER."

"What'd they say?"

"Nothing much. Checked her vitals, ran some tests. I guess they won't know until the results come back."

The women fell as silent as the deadly cancer that had lurked undetected just beneath Shannon Buchanan's rib cage until it reached Stage IV.

"Guess that's why they call it practicing medicine, huh? Doctors keep trying until they get it right."

Harley sipped her tea, deep in thought. "Sometimes I don't know whether Mom is sicker because we don't have the herbs or because of how guilty she feels about Jesse being in jail. She blames herself for him being there every single day."

"Why? She didn't ask Jesse to do what he did. I know the money was for her but still, it was his decision. And as unwise a decision as it was, even that didn't put him there. We both know who's to blame for your man being behind bars."

"I hate that motherfucker." Harley held out her hand. Kat passed her the cigarette without a word to the fact she'd given up smoking after Shannon got sick. "How can you prosecute somebody when the very people who brought the charges wanted them thrown out?"

"I remember you telling me that. How when the bank president found out why Jesse had stolen the money—"

"Borrowed."

"Okay, *borrowed* the money, they just wanted restitution."

"And if it hadn't been for Grey he would have paid them back by now. The irony was that six months after they slapped on the cuffs, his grandmother's estate was finally settled and the money he'd planned to pay them back with became available. Money that were it possible to access could be used to hire better attorneys, add to the cash on his card. Money that could buy Mom's herbs. Money that's sitting in a fucking bank and that because of the legal bullshit around him being a felon he can't get to right now."

She squashed out the cigarette. "Can I have one?"

Kat shook her head. "No. Eat your food. You're already as skinny as the pole we dance on."

Harley picked up the salad and took a bite.

"What about his family? Can't they get it?"

"They won't try, have basically cut him off."

"Because he's in jail?"

"That's part of it. They're ultraconservative and live in a

small town. Jesse being arrested put a spot on what they considered an unblemished name. So when he sinned, as they put it, they cut him off. Haven't visited him one time. Won't take his calls. I personally think they're just mad that he was the favorite. His grandmother left most of her money to him.

"He considers Mom and me his family now. She loves Jesse as much as I do. He's like the son she never had, and the first boyfriend that she approved of completely. He's been pretty depressed lately, and even though he tries to hide it when he talks to us, we both pick up on it, can feel the hurt in his heart. Jesse's a country boy. He hates being cooped up, and that Mom was forced to give up the holistic treatment. Even with the chemo, she'd started gaining weight. Her hair was growing back, her face was filling out again, and her skin had lost that pasty look."

"Damn shame your insurance doesn't cover it."

Harley made a sound of disgust. "Insurance doesn't even cover all of the traditional treatment. Having to come up with almost three thousand extra dollars a month is why I'm in here dancing my ass off. Even with all the extra shifts I'm working, there's barely enough."

"There's always 'cocktails and conversation.'" Kat used air quotes. "Emphasis on *cock*."

Harley rolled her eyes. "I do my share of lap dances. But that's where I draw the line. Cocktails, not cocks."

"You could write your own ticket, Harley. Look at you! Those long legs, big doe eyes, face of innocence, that pouty mouth that women pay for—albeit one that curses like a sailor. Where'd that come from?"

"That's Grandpa Wendt coming out. I learned from the best."

"You'd have to curb that, especially around the southerners. They like their women dainty and sweet." Harley snorted. "But seriously, that killer bod. And look at all that thick, long hair! You're a blue-eyed blond fantasy. The men would eat you up, literally. I'm telling you what I know, darling. The real money comes out after the talking's done."

Harley side-eyed her fiery-haired friend. "You haven't."

Kat calmly checked her nails. "Haven't I?"

"Shut up!"

"Don't judge me. Men will do anything to stroke the kitty. It's the most powerful weapon women own. Any woman worth her salt knows that, and if more of us did, we'd rule the world."

"Maybe, but sex for money is different than sex for love."

Kat rolled her eyes. "Society creates acceptable parameters to make it more palatable, but at the end of the day sex is sex, no matter the scenario or the motive, and when dealing with the opposite sex there is always, *always* some form of exchange."

"Wow, Kat. That's a pretty callous outlook."

"Maybe. But it's an honest one, too." Kat reached for her cigarette case, but after a glance toward Harley, she picked up her soda and took a drink of it instead. "A few months ago you asked why I'd stopped dancing and now only work in the dining room, remember?" Harley nodded. "I told you it was because my youngest had graduated high school. That was true. She did graduate. But it isn't the whole story." Kat took a bite of her filet mignon wrap with pickled vegetables, homemade mayonnaise, and shaved white truffles. "You remember the older gentleman who came in about six months ago, the silver fox I said looked like Pierce Brosnan?"

"Yeah." That's all she said but there were all kinds of questions in the look on Harley's face.

"I gave him a C and C. He gave me his card. On his next trip to town he invited me to dinner. I invited him home for dessert. We were both open and upfront about what we wanted. He's married. Thirty-five years in. Grown children. No sex. But a good reputation in his community that he wants to maintain. So for him it was discreet meetings, an occasional travel partner, a good listener, and good sex. For me it was money, and lots of it. He bought me a condo, set up a college fund for my daughter and a bank account for me. We've been having private cocktails and conversations ever since."

"Wow, Kat. That's . . ."

"Crazy? Probably. But you have to remember I'm almost twice your age, twice married, and too set in my ways. It works for me. Last month I met him in Washington, DC. We went to this private, swanky club where all the power brokers and politicians come to network and hobnob. It's also where they display their side chicks. Wives not allowed. It was one of the most luxurious places I've ever seen. He was stunned that I didn't recognize anyone in the room, said they were some of the most influential people in politics." Kat looked at her watch and stood. "I've never been into that scene, but if things go south with me and the mister, I know where to go for my next companion . . . that club near Capitol Hill."

The hour was up. Kat headed for the door, Harley up to the second floor dressing room to change into the dancing costume for her second shift. She didn't take any C and C's that night, and while she gave a good show on stage, it was all body; her mind wasn't there at all. Her thoughts were back in the empty office they'd made a private breakroom and on what Kat said about power brokers, politicians, and side chicks. Her thoughts were on whether or not a sleazeball like Hammond Grey fit anywhere in or around that world.

That day at Johnny's Steakhouse the women had all agreed to keep their eyes and ears open for how they could turn the tables on the DA-turned-candidate and get the upper hand. Kat had caused Harley to take Grandma's advice and rephrase her gaze. Not that she wanted to sleep with Grey. The mere thought was enough to make her gag. But if doing so would free Jesse and help save her mom's life, she'd not only sell her soul to the devil for fifteen cents, she'd fuck him, too.

4

Plumes of bluish silver smoke from double-aged vintage Perdomo cigars wafted above the heads of the six men enjoying after-dinner drinks in the stately appointed home of Hammond and Sunnie Grey. The seating area was designed for conversation—two square tufted leather chairs faced a chenille-covered sofa. A solid oak coffee table handcrafted by Hammond Grey's wife's great-great-grandfather and passed from one generation to the next was set in between the attorneys who sat on the couch and the businessmen who occupied the chairs. A judge and former college roommate of one of the businessmen sat to the right of the couch while Hammond reclined in a bonded leather Godiva rocker, his favorite place in the house. A library wall anchored the room. It was mostly filled with law books—case books, legal citations, law dictionaries, treatises. But there were a number of books on history, religion, politics in America and the state of Kansas, as well as a section dedicated to biographies on those political, religious and civic leaders Grey most admired. One day, he planned to write a few books. But only after a few had been written about him and the indelible mark he planned to leave on the political landscape. He was nothing if not confident, and not the only one to think so.

Thaddeus Stowe, a long-time senator, influence peddler in conservative circles, and personal mentor to Grey, peered at his charge from beneath bushy eyebrows as he relit his cigar. "I'm glad yesterday's rally was such a success. Of course it's no surprise. You're the logical choice, Hammond." He paused to take a few puffs and make a smoke ring. "You're smart, ambitious, come from a good family. A handsome enough fella,"— he paused as the gentlemen reacted with humor—"and the wife's a looker, too. Great, well-mannered kids. The perfect all-American snapshot. Your family will be a nice addition to this state's political force, and you have the tenacity and demeanor that a position of power and influence like this requires. Most importantly, you can crush Myers. You're made for Capitol Hill, my boy. This is the first rung of what could be a very high-reaching ladder."

"Those words are especially meaningful, Stowe, coming from you. And all true, of course." Hammond made this comment only slightly tongue-in-cheek. "As you know, I'm all about justice. I've long been a proponent of tough laws and have very little tolerance when it comes to the criminal element in our society. They've been allowed to run amuck for far too long. I'm equally committed to rebuilding the economic viability of this state, and setting up a framework that will ensure profitability for years to come. I've had my eye on politics for years. Dad's wanted me to run for mayor of Edgefield for years. Almost stopped speaking to me four years ago when I didn't. Was mad as a hornet, wasn't he, Tom?"

Thomas Jefferson Ward was chief judge in Division Twenty of Kansas's Tenth Judicial District, the division that included Edgefield, Hammond Grey's hometown. Like Grey, Tom was smart, cunning, and ambitious. At forty years old, he was one of the youngest judges in the state.

"He was pretty upset, until we laid out the plans for Edgefield Correctional." Said with a conspiratorial wink in Grey's direction. "That's when he got the big picture and realized that

Grey holding any job in that town, governmental or otherwise, could be perceived by his detractors as a conflict of interest.

"Besides, being mayor of a town that size would be too small a stage for somebody like Ham. The senator role is much more appropriate."

Grey's attorney and long-time friend Geoffrey Sullivan knocked back the rest of his Scotch. "I don't know, Tom. I think governor fits him more closely."

"Well, shoot," Grey said. "Why don't I just run for president and be done with it?"

Retired judge Clarence Dodd, the oldest member of this curious brotherhood and legal consultant to the Guardian Group, the multi-billion-dollar corporation that owned and operated the Edgefield Correctional facility and dozens of others like it, removed a bogwood pipe from between thin, chapped lips. "Let's not get ahead of ourselves," he droned, in the same slow, deliberate speech pattern he had used when on the bench. "There's a hell of a lot of work to do between here and the White House."

"Work that I can do without running for office," Hammond said. "The political machine is more ruthless now than ever. I can handle it. But I don't know about Sunnie. Seeing those protestors at yesterday's rally upset her. And I'm concerned about how the children will fare in the glare of a spotlight that can sometimes be hot and unforgiving. Make no mistake. My goal is the White House. I just hate climbing these rungs in between."

"That's why I'm here," Thaddeus said. "To make that climb easier. I've been down the road you're traveling and have dealt with my share of villains. Though I must admit, not many of them wore a skirt."

The group laughed.

Clarence chuckled, too. "What'd you do to piss off that group of fired-up fillies?"

"The group is called WHIP," Tom answered. "Women

Helping Innocent Prisoners," he added, with sarcastic emphasis on *innocent*.

"Ah, yes," Clarence said. "The innocent prisoner scenario.
Every son-of-a-bitch I locked up was innocent. Hell, everybody in any jail, if you asked them. They're the same kids who
lied about eating the cookies while wiping crumbs off their
faces."

Grey swirled the ice in his drink. "Just a bunch of mothers who
don't want to believe their sons are fuck-ups. I'm not worried
about them, especially with papers like the *Eagle* doing its job."

"Don't be," Thaddeus said. "We don't want you to get your
hands dirty. That's what a fixer is for. I've got one in mind that
I want you to meet."

"A what?"

"A fixer. Someone who flies in on one of those 'Clean Up
Kansas' brooms you hand out and sweeps trouble out of your
path. If that group needs to be handled, she'll do it."

"You know, like Olivia Pope," Tom offered.

"Who's that?" Hammond replied.

"Seriously?" Tom shook his head. "Never mind."

Hammond looked at Thaddeus. "How does one do that, fix
it, as you say?"

"Very carefully," Thaddeus answered. "Takes contacts, insider info, smarts, guts. But trust me. Caroline's got all of that
and then some."

"A woman?" Hammond asked.

"A beast," Tom corrected.

Hammond's gaze shifted. "You know her, too?"

"Since she was knee-high to a gnat. Her grandparent's farm
was next to my uncle's spread. We grew up fishing and shooting together during summer vacations, her brothers and sisters
and our clan of cousins. Then she went to off to college—"

"Cornell," Thaddeus interjected. "Under and grad. Main-
tained a near four point oh."

"Real dumb chick," Hammond teased.

"She was always a tomboy, but when she came back from college she'd totally transformed. I hardly recognized her. She looked like a young Elizabeth Taylor, only ten times better. But she could still best me with an over and under, shoot a tin can off a fencepost from seventy-five feet."

Hammond whistled. "Okay, now I'm impressed."

"Wait until you meet her. Although I had no idea she was involved in politics until Thaddeus happened to mention her name to my dad."

"She's not into politics," Thaddeus said. "She's into winners, and winning. You'll see.

"What I want you to focus on, what all of us want your sole aim to be, is winning the election." Thaddeus tapped the ashes from his cigar and placed it in an iron ashtray shaped like a horseshoe. "For our long-term plans to proceed, we need you in that prominent position, reiterating what you emphasized in the role of DA—that crime is out of control and steadily rising. People not being safe in their homes. If that windbag Myers has his way, we'll have no way to protect ourselves because owning a gun would be against the law. We need bigger, better prisons and more of them, run by people who know how to handle both people and business."

"People like the Guardian Group," Clarence said. "The Edgefield Correctional Facility is the first of hopefully three new prisons in Kansas and four in Missouri. Over the next five years that's a growth rate of forty-two percent. That's why Jack Myers can't win. If he does, trust me, soon Tom will be out and so will the new DA. We can't have that. The bleeding hearts get in and our plan is as good as dead."

"What's so great about our plan is that it benefits Kansans in two ways. One, making neighborhoods and communities safe. Two, increasing state revenue, which means more jobs, higher income, and a better quality of life." Jim Hartwell, a former warden at one of the country's most notorious prisons, was the founder and CEO of the Guardian Group, the largest private prison owner in the country. He was largely credited with creating the model that turned incarceration into a privatized industry worth more than seventy billion dollars.

"Everyone wins." He held up his tumbler. "More prisons. Less crime."

"More revenue. Less unemployment," the attorney, Geoff, said.

"More allegiance. Less rebellion," Clarence intoned. "Cleaning up Kansas, and all of America. That's what this is about."

"And improving everyone's quality of life," Tom cheekily admitted, as he snipped a fifty-dollar cigar with a diamond-encrusted cutter.

"Nothing wrong with that," Hammond added.

The men clinked their glasses. "Hear, hear."

5

"I am so pissed off right now!" Kim said with conviction as she slammed down her fist. "That they can report a lie as the truth is simply not right. And I will not stand for them maligning my name and misrepresenting what WHIP is about."

More than twenty-four hours had passed since the rally. Kim was still livid about how her shout of concern as the WHIP protestor fell was turned into a propaganda piece for Grey's senatorial campaign. As if WHIP were the problem and his winning was the solution.

"It's a terrible thing they did." Betty's voice oozed with concern for her daughter. She'd called soon after returning home from her church's afternoon program, retrieving the Sunday edition of the *Kansas City News* from her front porch and seeing Kim's face splashed on the front page. "So dishonest."

"Can't believe this is happening," Kim mumbled.

"That's politics, baby. That Grey fella is running for office now. That's a filthy, dog-eat-dog world. Anybody who lived through the last presidential election knows how dirty it can be. It's as though politicians dug down below low and found a lower level.

"Maybe you should take a step back, lay low, until this

whole thing blows over. Did Peter call you? He's worried about you; suggested a weekend trip to Chicago might do you good."

Peter was Kim's older brother by three years, and how she met Aaron. Peter was friends with Aaron's older brother, and when he was invited to Peter's twenty-first birthday party, Aaron tagged along.

"If only it were that easy. After getting Jayda's text, I opened a voice mail box that was full with messages. Reporters calling from all over the country. Which tells me the story got picked up by the Associated Press, putting me in a defensive position for something that didn't even happen. But not responding isn't an option so . . . I'll have to figure it out."

"Just tell them what happened, Kimberly. Tell the truth. That's all you can do. Folk are going to believe what they want." Betty cleared her throat. "What did Aaron say?"

Aaron. Her husband. A whole other story.

"We haven't talked about it. He left first thing this morning to visit Ken, so there's a chance he hasn't seen it. All the more reason I need to see if he's back and have the conversation." Kim swung her legs over the side of the chaise in the master suite's sitting area, stretching as she stood. "I'd rather he hear the truth from me before he reads what's basically a propaganda piece. Thanks for calling me, Mom. You always make me feel better, whether things actually are or not."

"Life always gets better, Kim. No matter what it looks like. Remember that."

"I'll try. Love you."

"I love you, too. And I'll be praying for you and the other women."

After using the bathroom, Kim slipped a robe over the pajamas she still wore and walked downstairs to the smell of freshly brewed coffee. A good sign that Aaron was home and not at the gym or somewhere else avoiding her. She poured a cup, took a couple fortifying sips, and then headed toward the sounds coming from the theater room.

"So you are back."

A short pause and then, "Yep."

Aaron sat in the first row of eight recliners, each strategically placed to give guests an unobstructed view of the ninety-six-inch smart screen.

Kim sat down in a recliner beside him. Took a sip of coffee. "How was Kendall?"

This time the pause was long enough for the receiver on the screen to run a deep cross route, down the field and over, as her quarterback son scrambled out of trouble, dodged linebackers, planted his feet and threw a perfect spiral pass. The receiver ran the remaining twenty yards for a touchdown. A play that took seven, eight seconds. Maybe more.

"All right."

Kim had been married to this man for twenty years, had loved him for twenty-two. She could read his nonverbal signs like a neon poster. Spoke "Aaron" fluently. He didn't want to talk. Lately, that was nothing new. A naturally quiet, introspective man, he'd grown increasingly more so with each passing year of Kendall's incarceration. They'd become distant. Or maybe with their son gone she'd finally recognized what already existed. Maybe their marital cracks had been covered by a Band-Aid named Kendall. In the early days of their marriage Kim and Aaron shared everything. She wanted to feel that intimacy again, and while she didn't think her husband's constant viewing of their son's high school football highlight reels was particularly therapeutic or beneficial, it worked for him. She decided to meet him where he was.

"Wasn't this the night we met his agent?" No response. "I think this was the game. I remember it being so cold that night. Unseasonably cold for September. The guy showed up in a windbreaker. Remember?"

A sigh signaled Aaron's annoyance. "Yes, Kim. The regional championship game with KC Tech was the night we met Chad Grainger."

"Obviously you're not in the mood to talk. But there's something I need to discuss with you." Aaron continued to watch the game. "An incident that made the front page of the Sunday paper, along with my picture."

Can you hear me now?

He did; he turned to look at her for the first time since she entered the room. Paused the tape. Turned to her—eyes questioning, accusing, concerned—all at once. "What happened?"

She told him. "That's what actually happened. It's not what you're going to read in the paper, but it's what really took place."

Aaron thought about it, nodded, and picked up the remote. "Okay."

Kim watched, stunned, as he pressed play and resumed watching the game. "Okay? That's it? You don't have anything else to say?"

"What do you want me to say, Kim? It is what it is."

"No, it isn't! It's nothing like what the paper is saying it is!"

"What do you want me to do about it?"

Kim took a breath, tried to stay calm. "I want you to communicate, Aaron, and act like you care. 'I'm sorry that happened to you' would have been a good response. I want to not have to knock down a wall or crawl over an emotional barrier to reach the destination of your opinion. We were out there protesting the man who put our son in prison. I want to feel like I'm not in this by myself."

"What, you're saying I'm not doing my part? That just because I'm not out there being all loud and high-profile that I don't care?"

"That's not what I said and you know it."

"Maybe not exactly. But the implication was in every other

word." He grabbed the remote, angrily punched the off button, and stormed out of the room.

She jumped up and rushed behind him. "Aaron, wait! Let's talk about this. Running away solves nothing! Aaron, wait! I want to—"

"I don't." Had the curtly delivered words not stopped her forward progress, the scowl on his face would have done the trick. For good measure, he put up his hand, as if splayed fingers could stop her harsh words from piecing his soul. "I can't do this with you. Not right now."

Kim watched him ascend the steps, his footsteps sounding as heavy as her heart felt. She wanted to call him back but knew it was no use. Where she quickly lashed out when angry or hurt, her husband retreated, needing time and space to ponder and process. A moment later she heard the garage door opening. Headed to his office, no doubt. As a tenured college sociology professor, Aaron often worked on weekends. But where before Kendall's incarceration he'd grade homework and create school outlines from home, now he spent more time at his school office.

Perhaps it's just as well. I don't feel like fighting, either. Just as she began walking up the steps, she heard a message indicator ping.

"Oh, shoot. His phone," she mumbled as she raced into the theater room and grabbed the phone partially hidden in the chair crease. She ran up the stairs and through the rooms, reached the door leading to the garage and jerked it open. "Aaron! Your phone!"

She thought he saw her frantic waving, but if he did, her actions were ignored. She sighed, walked back into the house and set his phone on the table just inside the door where keys, sunglasses, and other accessories were deposited. When she did, the message indicator caused the face to light up. Normally Kim wouldn't have given this a second thought. But lately, nothing had been normal. So Kim picked up the phone, tapped the icon, and read the message.

Hey Aaron. It's Jessica. Just reaching out to check on you and make sure you're okay. You know I'm a good listener. If you need me . . . I'm here.

The words sent her reeling. She fell back against the closed door. The hand holding the phone shook slightly. Rereading the message, Kim searched for an innocent, harmless, non-threatening interpretation of the text. Tried . . . and failed. Who was Jessica? A new teacher? An administrator? A student? A chick on the side? The phone number's area code read 707. The Atlanta area, Kim knew, because of friends who lived there. Could this be some random woman he'd met online? How did he know how good a listener she was? Because they'd talked before? And if so, about what? Was he able to share the feelings about Kendall's incarceration that he'd not shared with her? She returned to the den, plopped into the roomy theater seat still warm from Aaron's presence, and contemplated the unthinkable. All this time she'd thought the distance in her marriage was due to the strain of Kendall's absence, the virtual loss of their only child. Undoubtedly that was part of it. But could it also be the presence of a stranger named Jessica? Kim was determined to find out.

6

Kim had never been a snooping wife. No sneaking into Aaron's emails, skimming his phone contacts, or sniffing shirts for a perfume she didn't wear. Aaron had never given her a reason to question his fidelity. Until now. Armed with a first name and the number she'd copied from Aaron's phone, she went upstairs and retrieved her laptop. Before she could begin her internet sleuthing, her phone rang.

She noted the caller, frowned, and tapped the call's speaker button. "Tanya?"

"Hi, Kim. Sorry to bother you on a Sunday."

"Oh, no problem. Sorry I answered that way; just surprised to see your face pop up on my screen."

"Probably about as surprised as I was to see your picture in today's paper."

"Oh. That." Kim picked up the laptop and headed downstairs. "It's not what it looks like."

"It looks pretty bad, and given my visceral reaction to seeing it, I can only imagine what Gary's will be."

Gary Young was chief operating officer and part-owner of Fletcher Young, the public relations agency where Kim worked as an account executive and reported to Tanya. The office was in an affluent area called Mission Hills; its clients were largely conservative and rich.

And probably Grey supporters, Kim deduced, as she felt tension grip her shoulders and a headache rev up.

"What happened?"

Kim bit back a sigh as she retold the story for the third time in one hour. "One of our protesters was pushed," she finished after a quick narrative of what led up to that point. "I reacted, reached out to stop the fall, even though I was too far away to do so, and yelled for them, it, whatever was happening to stop. That's what I was saying when the pic was snapped. And yes, it makes me look crazed and angry and all kinds of wrong, when in truth, I wasn't even involved in the actual altercation."

"I believe you, Kim. Even if you had caused a ruckus I'd understand. Your son is in prison for a crime he didn't commit, for God's sake! I've met Kendall. I know that young man, and what a travesty it is that he's in a jail cell instead of a college dorm right now. From one mom to another? They're lucky that a sign is all you were carrying.

"Those are my feelings. Gary, however, is unlikely to share them, let alone some of our top clients. It's why I called, Kim. To suggest you brace yourself for work tomorrow. There might be fallout."

"Why? What I do on my own time should be my own business."

"You know better than that. An AE for a PR firm is always repping the company, officially or no. These are buttoned-up citizens who abhor any kind of scandal, even indirectly. Even more, they may take an attack against their candidate of choice as a personal affront."

"Are you sure you haven't talked to Gary? It sounds like you might know something that I don't."

A sigh spilled from the speaker. "Okay, I will share something, but it can't be repeated. Promise me that you won't."

"You have my word."

"In a managers' meeting a few months ago, Grey's name came up. I can't remember how the conversation turned to politics, but I do remember how pleased Mr. Fletcher was to have him as a candidate."

"The jerk who tore up my home now invades my workplace. That's just great."

"Sorry."

"It's not your fault."

"Hey, maybe I'm overreacting. We could get to work tomorrow and nothing happens. But just in case that isn't the case, I placed the call so that you would be prepared."

"Thanks, Tanya. I appreciate it." She ended the call and was pacing the floor when the cell that she clutched in her hand rang again.

"Hello?"

"Kim Logan?"

"She speaking."

"Bryan White, *KC News.*"

Too late Kim realized she should have let the unknown caller go to voice mail.

"Yes."

"I'm calling about the story that hit the paper this morning, about your organization, WHIP, and the run-in with Grey protestors."

"There was no run-in. The picture you saw was taken totally out of context, and rather than get the story confirmed and print the truth, newspapers like yours just snapped the story off the Associated—"

"I believe you."

"Press. Instead of double-checking and getting the facts, people like you took it and ran, when if instead you'd done your homework and called before . . . wait . . . what did you say?"

"I said I believe you." She could hear the smile in his voice.

"Had it been up to me, the *News* wouldn't have printed that story."

"Oh. Then why'd you call?"

"To get to the truth. Like many other sports lovers, I was familiar with your son's name and followed his trial. Through that I became aware of your organization, WHIP, and learned more about you, a professional woman who doesn't strike me as one likely to start a fight. So . . . what really happened yesterday?"

Kim launched into the true story. Take four. This version was the shortest one of all. "I just learned what was implied in the article may affect my job. Is there anything I can do to fix this?"

"Sure. Have your attorney contact them, threaten to sue unless they print a retraction or at the very least a clarification that you weren't directly involved in the altercation. Beyond that, though, it's your word against the guy quoted in the article."

"The one who conveniently wanted to remain anonymous?"

"Makes sense, especially if he somehow twisted the story for his benefit."

"What kind of benefit could come from his remaining anonymous?"

"Painting WHIP in a bad light, silencing detractors, advancing Grey's cause. Whoever the reporter talked to may not have been an innocent bystander, but someone planted to deliberately start trouble with your group."

Kim slowly sank to the living room sofa as she absorbed the information. "Bryan, you might be right. That this was instigated never entered my mind but makes total sense. Even more of a reason for me to speak up. First thing tomorrow, I'm calling my attorney."

"Keep in mind any retraction or correction may only happen in the *Edgefield Eagle*, the paper that broke the story. It got picked up by the AP, and while they too can make a correction, there is no guarantee that the dozens of other papers who ran the story will do the same."

"Getting the *Eagle* and other local papers to do it will be a small victory, at least, for me and the group. Thanks for the info and for calling to hear my side of the story."

"You're welcome. But that's not the only reason I called." As she remained quiet, Kim's defenses snapped back into place. "I wondered if you could tell me about your son, beyond the highly publicized facts of him being a star quarterback for a championship team, courted by colleges across the country to join their program. Who he was before the arrest, before he became known as a convicted felon?"

The unexpected question brought on unexpected tears.

"Kim? Ms. Logan? Are you there?"

"Yes, I'm here." Kim cleared a throat gone raspy with emotion. "Sorry, your question caught me off guard. In the three years I've been interviewed about him, no one before has asked me who he really is.

"He's amazing. Of course as his mother you'd expect that answer. But he really is a special kid, always was. Kind and considerate, with a goofy sense of humor. Competitive like his dad, who placed a football in his crib to welcome him home. Kendall studied hard to do well in school. On his own, not because we forced him. Football was the same way. He'd work out with his dad before and after practicing with the team at school. Threw perfect spirals at fifty, sixty yards, and that's before he tried out in junior high. By the time he hit high school, he'd probably thrown tens of thousands of passes.

"He's not perfect, and got into his share of mischief. We caught him sneaking either in or out of the house a time or two, pics of naked girls on his computer, teenage stuff."

"Did he use drugs? At least, that you or your husband knew of?"

"He drank beer with his buddies, maybe got drunk a time or two. After being arrested he admitted to having smoked weed. But hard drugs like they found in the house? Never. He wouldn't have put anything harsh into his body, wouldn't think about selling drugs or any other type of criminal activity. As a young Black man in America, his father and I stressed the microscope he was already under; emphasized the importance of a stellar reputation. Kendall received over a dozen scholarship offers and had just accepted a full-ride to the Ivy League's University of Pennsylvania. His bags were all but packed and loaded. He wouldn't have risked his future like that."

"Sounds like a very unfortunate case of wrong place, wrong time."

"You have no idea."

"I'm beginning to. Kim, for the past couple months I've been conducting research for a *KC News* piece, a four-week series on the privatization of prisons. It's a pretty hot-button item this election season and I'd love to get your thoughts. Are you familiar with the topic?"

"Private prisons? I think I've heard the term before. Didn't the president pass some type of federal law regarding them?"

"No law was passed. The administration put a plan in motion to phase out the federal government's use of them. But they explained the policy shift as one due to declining numbers and safety concerns. I'm researching the topic from another angle."

"What's your angle?"

"Money, the one that makes the world go round."

"I read somewhere that it can cost three times as much to incarcerate someone as it does to put them through college. Other than the fact that a campus is where Kendall should be right now, I don't understand how I can help you with an article like that."

"I'm not talking about the money taxpayers spend. I'm talking about the money that Wall Street and big business make from the prison system. I'm talking about mass incarceration. I'm talking about free labor. And I'm talking about Hammond Grey, the former district attorney for Jones County, possibly being a cog in this lucrative machine who benefits financially as well."

"Well, if you didn't have my attention before, you definitely have it now."

Bryan chuckled. "I thought I might. Listen, the prison industrial complex is one of the fastest growing industries in the United States. Private prisons are a seventy-billion-dollar business, and counting. Ten years ago, there were only five private prisons in the country. Today there are over one hundred. Edgefield Correctional, where your son and many other WHIP family members are housed, is a privately owned prison. Edgefield, as you well know, is Grey's hometown. I find it interesting that this prison was built right after he became district attorney and that under his watch prosecutions and convictions for Jones County, the county that includes Edgefield and feeds its prison, rose by over thirty percent. What do you think?"

"I think I need to know more about these prisons for profit."

7

Jayda pulled into the driveway, surprised not to see her mother's car parked there. She walked inside. The house was quiet, not a frequent occurrence at the Sanchez residence. Up the stairs and a sniff later, Jayda knew there'd been no cooking, either. Downstairs was empty. She went upstairs. Daniel's son and oldest, Rafael, was on his bed in the bedroom he shared with another cousin, playing video games.

"Where is everybody?" He shrugged, eyes fixed on whatever opponent he was trying to beat. "Mom hasn't been home?"

"No."

Jayda left the room, a scowl on her face as she pondered what could have happened to upset normal. A year ago, a break in routine wouldn't have been given a second thought. But ever since that day the call came that Daniel and Nicky had been arrested and were being held in county jail, any change to the regular routine caused a knot to form in her stomach.

Before she could work herself into a panic attack, the front door opened. Anna walked in, obviously fatigued, followed by Jayda's aunt Lucy.

"Mom! Aunt Luce! Hello, baby." Jayda reached toward

Alejandra's outstretched arms and relieved Anna's burden as she planted kisses all over her daughter's face. "Not finding anyone home almost scared me to death."

"Why? You think you're the only one who works around here?" Lucy threw over her shoulder as she too left the room.

"Because you're normally here cooking by now. And where's Grandma?"

"With Crystal. Rick was training two new hires so she was able to leave early. She took Mama to the city for a friend's birthday."

Breathing heavily, Anna walked over and plopped on the couch. Jayda joined her. "You should have called me. When I came home and nobody was here I thought all sorts of possibilities on why that was, none of them good."

"Sorry, *chica*."

"So . . . you worked all day?"

"Yes." Anna yawned. "We got a call for an emergency cleaning, a big house in Edgefield."

"You mean mansion," Lucy yelled from the kitchen.

"Edgefield?" The mere mention of that town made Jayda's blood boil. "And you went?"

"Hey, don't knock it," Lucy said. "They might bleed red, but their money's green."

"As long as it wasn't what's-his-name," Jayda said.

"Oh, please," Anna replied. "I wouldn't clean his plate, let alone his house."

"I would," Lucy answered, returning to the living room and reaching for the purse she'd tossed on the coffee table. "And while there I'd find his drink in the refrigerator and pour in some antifreeze. Oops, did I say refrigerator? I meant radiator." She winked at Jayda, hugged Anna, and ruffled Alejandra's hair as she played on the floor.

"Couldn't do that," Jayda joked back. "Might kill the whole family."

"Good point. That might be an assignment for Rick. He

could make the DA a special 'plate.'" Lucy emphasized plate with air quotes.

"Stop, you two," Anna said. "It's not funny to joke of killing someone, even a bad man like him."

"Who's joking?" Lucy asked. Anna gave her a look and shook her head. "All right, sis, I'll stop. You still cooking on Sunday?"

"That's the plan."

"Okay, guys. See you then."

Shortly after Lucy left, Crystal and Alma came home. While Alejandra played with her cousins, Jayda went upstairs to help her mom with dinner. Anna elaborated on the grandiose beauty of the home they'd cleaned. Jayda listened half-heartedly, her mind on the conversation with Kim and Harley at Johnny's Steakhouse. About what they could do to get justice for their guys. And here her family gets a client in Edgefield? Was this one of Anna's saints come to their aid, perhaps St. Jude, who was known to aid impossible causes? Could she fight the money and power Grey had with a mop and furniture polish?

Later that night, Jayda had put Alejandra to bed and was watching TV when her cell phone pinged. Unknown number. She let it go to voice mail. A few seconds later, it pinged again. Jayda looked, picked up the phone, thought about answering, set it back down. Less than a minute later her message indicator beeped. She tapped the screen, tapped the speaker icon, and was shocked at the voice that whispered into the bedroom.

"Jayda, where you at? It's Nicky. Pick up next time."

She did, almost before the phone rang. "Nicky! How are you calling me?"

"Shh! You trying to get me busted? Stop yelling?"

"How are you calling me right now? It's late."

"What, you got somebody there? Am I interrupting something?"

"Yeah, Ally and I are really turning it up! Drinking

Coronas. Smoking blunts. Who else do you think I'd have in here with me?"

"You're questioning why I'm calling so late, I don't know."

"Because it's outside of the normal calling hours is why. Is something wrong? Or did they just change the hours?"

"Nothing's wrong. The hours are the same. Friend of mine let me use his cell phone."

"Nicky!"

"Don't start, I already know you're scared for me and don't want me to get caught."

"You know how hard Edge comes down on anybody caught with contraband! Thirty days in solitary."

"Look, I didn't call you to talk about what I already know! Just forget it. I'll talk to you—"

"Nicky, wait! You're right. I'm sorry. I'm just so surprised to hear from you. But twice as happy. You know how much I love you, it's why I worry so much. Can we start the call over?"

"Yeah," followed a lengthy pause.

Jayda lowered her voice. "Hey, *papi*."

"*Mi novia . . .*" he whispered.

His sweetheart heard Nicky swallow, could imagine he fought back tears. Tattoo-covered arms and a strong jawline gave him a tough-guy look, but she knew the truth. He was a closet romantic with a heart of gold, whose daughter had him wrapped around her finger from birth. The gentle quality that made him such a great brother, boyfriend, uncle, and lover, and an amazing artist, was why she worried so much. Opponents saw the tough guy as a challenge they often wanted to use to gain street cred. Nicky was more of a lover than a fighter, but behind bars it was a side he could never show.

"You okay?"

"Better now. I never was one for hanging out with the guys. Spending twenty-four seven surrounded by ego-filled, anger-fueled testosterone, it's sometimes too much. I miss my girls."

"I miss you, too, so much, Nicky."

"Ally's probably sleep, huh?"

"Yeah, but I can wake her."

"Naw, let my baby girl sleep."

"That's probably best. Keep her from having another tantrum."

"What do you mean?"

Shoot! Jayda hadn't meant let slip how Nicky's absence had led to Ally acting out, often waking up screaming and crying, wanting her dada.

"She misses you," Jayda said simply. "Everybody does. Both you and Daniel. How's he doing?"

"It's rough, baby. You know how he is, don't take stuff from nobody. Plus he's still angry at being in here. Almost two years hasn't taken away any of that, and for some jacked-up charges? That gang bullshit! But wait, I don't want to talk about stuff like that, remember? What are you wearing?"

Jayda giggled at the way Nicky asked the question, his voice low and raspy, making her feel sexy even in sweats.

"If I were there, you wouldn't be wearing nothing."

"I can't wait until you're back. We can get married, make a baby brother for Ally. We're doing everything we can to get you guys out of there."

"Yeah, I heard about that group you're with causing trouble at that fool's rally."

"It didn't even happen like they said it did. But we do plan to cause trouble, though. We're not going to be quiet, not going to stop until we get justice." Jayda worked to push strength through the words as she wiped away tears.

"Hey, what's that I hear? Are you crying?"

"No."

"Liar. Don't cry, baby."

"I'm not," she repeated, with bass in her voice. It elicited the laughter she sought. "But you shouldn't be there, though. You should be here with me and your daughter."

"There's nowhere I'd rather be. It is what it is. Don't cry, baby. Everything's going to work out all right. What day are you coming?"

"I was planning for Saturday."

"As early as you can. I can't wait to see y'all and hold my little girl."

They talked a bit more before a guard neared Nicky's cell, and he rushed off the phone. A message had come through while they'd chatted, Kim asking if Saturday was a good day for lunch. She texted back her plans to meet Nicky that day and suggested a later time, or instead on Sunday. Jayda definitely felt a powwow with Kim and Harley was in order. After leaving the steakhouse, she had doubted she could be of any real help in freeing their guys and showing Grey for the scoundrel he truly was. But who knew? Maybe their prayers to the saints were working after all, and with a little great housekeeping . . . justice could be served.

8

Harley fought back a yawn as she sped down the highway in her trusty Mustang. At twenty-three years old, her world revolved around work, sleep, and Shannon. While grateful that life was as good as it was, especially that Shannon was still in remission, she still couldn't help but ponder, *How did this humdrum existence become my life?*

Eighteen months ago, it was totally different. She had Jesse. Shannon was healthy. Life was good. Then Shannon got sick and Jesse got busted. Even though the victim declined to prosecute and asked the court to consider the circumstances and exercise leniency, Jesse was given a sentence of ten years. Jesse had told her to go on with her life. Harley had vowed to wait for him. She loved him; there was no doubt about that. But could she really put her life on hold for ten years? People on the outside saw criminals get locked away for crimes without realizing that their families got locked up, too.

I've got to do something to get my life back. This routine has got to change.

She cranked up the volume. There were few situations that a good dose of rock couldn't fix. The sound of her cell ringing through the speakers interrupted the impromptu concert.

"Kim, what's wrong?" Harley turned down the stereo.

"Nothing. Sorry if I frightened you by calling so late. I expected to get your voice mail."

"No, I'm actually leaving the club before midnight for a change. What's up?"

"Jayda and I wanted to meet on Sunday, maybe grab brunch or lunch, something early. You available?"

"Later would probably work best for me. Tomorrow's going to be a late night for sure and I work Sunday, too. Maybe we can meet before my shift, an early dinner?"

"That works for me. Better actually, now that I think about it. I can use the morning to visit Kendall."

"Tell you what. There's a restaurant close to work. I'll text you guys a time and the address. Cool?"

"Perfect."

A short time later, Harley arrived back at the two-bedroom apartment she shared with her mother and their two cats, Pepper and Sage. The lights were off, the blinds still wide open. Not a sound came from inside. Despite her resolve to think positively, fear jumped into her chest and hampered her breathing. Shaky fingers placed a key in the lock. She opened the door. Her mother lay on the couch—Sage at her feet, the TV on mute, a remote dangling from her hand.

Is she breathing?

Harley took a step toward her and then stopped. What if a touch found her mother cold? What if . . .

"Mom!"

Shannon's eyes fluttered open.

Harley released a ragged breath, angry at the fear that had so quickly engulfed her. "Why are you watching TV with your eyes closed?" she joked, grabbing the remote and turning up the volume, as if sound could chase away the worry that was born in silence. She perched on the edge of a cushion, by Shannon's side. "Why are you here on the couch and not in the bedroom?"

Shannon reached out and placed a hand on Harley's arm. It felt bony and cold. "I was waiting for you, Harley. The hospital called earlier. The results from the tests we took last week came back, from when you drove me to emergency. They requested a consultation as soon as possible."

The fear Harley saw in her mother's eyes increased what Harley felt in her heart. "I'm sure it's fine." *Liar.* She didn't believe it, but she really wanted it to be true.

"I don't know, Harley. I feel pretty weak."

Harley leaned over and hugged her mother, squeezing her eyes against the tears that threatened. All her life Shannon Buchanan had been Harley's rock. Now it was the daughter's turn to be strong for the mom.

Can I do it?

Harley had her doubts, wondering if there was enough strength in all the world to weather the potential storm heading in their direction.

What am I thinking? Of course I can do it. I've got to do it.

She reached for Shannon's hand. "What about food? What did you eat today? Come on, let's sit you up."

"I don't know if I can, Harley."

"If I can do this, then you can do that."

"What does that mean?"

"Hell if I know, but in the moment I thought it sounded prophetic, like a saying that could go on a poster or t-shirt. Come on. Wait, let me go get some pillows. We'll prop you up like a puppet and let them do all the work."

Harley grabbed every pillow on her mother's bed. Her trying to carry them all at once produced a smile from Shannon. As weak as it was, Harley's entire world brightened. While helping her mother to the chair and ottoman that would make sitting up easier, her mood slipped again. Shannon had never been a big woman. But the sharpness of her bones emphasized the dramatic weight loss. Harley pushed the thought into a mental "no go" zone and then put a cheery tone into her voice.

"What about the soup Mrs. Hastings made? If I warm it up, can you eat some?"

Shannon allowed her head to fall back against the chair. "I can try."

"In the meantime, let's bring out your heartthrob. Our man Lenny can always get our pulse racing, right?" She went over to the stereo, pulled out some Lenny Kravitz, and cranked the volume. Soon the handsome rocker was asking them and probably several of their neighbors if they were going his way.

Harley nuked a large bowl of soup, grabbed a sleeve of crackers from the pantry, set both on a tray, and brought it into the living room. Her mother's head still rested against the chair and her eyes were closed. But her fingers tapped a light beat against the afghan. Harley saw her mother's body giving out but knew a strong, bright soul still lived inside of it. She placed the tray on the ottoman, and after walking over to tone down Lenny, she tucked a large napkin under Shannon's chin. Their neighbor, Mrs. Hastings, had brought over a hearty chicken and vegetable soup. Harley scooped up a soup spoon of the broth, blew on it, and offered it to Shannon.

"Here you go, Mom," she said softly, fighting tears yet again. "Open your mouth." The napkin got most of that first spoonful. No matter to Harley. Her mom was trying.

"It's good," Shannon said, her voice breathy with the effort to talk. "You worked a double yesterday. Are you eating, too?"

"Sure am; got a bowl big enough for the two of us."

For the next several minutes she fed Shannon, who even managed to eat a bit of the chicken and vegetables and a cracker. The soup, *or maybe Lenny*, energized her mom to the point where she pushed some of the pillows away and sat up mostly on her own. A household favorite began to play. Harley leaned over, pulled Shannon into her arms, and rocked back and forth in a seated slow dance. The song, "I Can't Get Over You," was appropriately haunting, even melancholy, and expressed Harley's feelings completely.

"Babe," Shannon said softly, once the song was done. "That was beautiful. I love you so much."

"I love you too, Mom."

Shannon continued, her speech halting, but increasingly clear. "Before we get the test results tomorrow, there's something I want us to talk about." She squeezed Harley's hand. "I want to talk about . . . what could happen . . ."

"No." Harley snatched her hand away. "I don't want to talk about that."

"I know, honey. I know. But it's inevitable. Both the conversation and the topic. Hey, the last chapter of everyone's life is the same. None of us get out alive."

There was no stopping the tears now. "Mom, I can't . . ."

"Harley." Shannon's bony hand, veins prominently displayed beneath translucent skin, reached up to wipe the tears. "I'm not trying to go anywhere. I'm going to keep fighting. But it's a battle I might lose. And if that happens, I don't want there to be one thing left unsaid between us. Shh, just listen, honey. It's hard for me, too.

"I can't even think of the words to describe how incredibly proud I am of you. Not only for how hard you've worked to take care of me, and how you've been strong for the both of us. But because of who you are. You were such a precocious kid and at times so incredibly annoying."

A chuckle slipped beyond the tears.

"You've always had such a sense of who you are, even when the neighborhood girls were jealous and made fun of you, wouldn't let you in their clique. You ran in, cried just a little, and then remember what you told me?"

"That you were my best friend."

"Let me tell you something. I never felt so special as in that moment."

"It's still true."

"I don't know. I think Jesse is giving me some stiff competition."

Harley shook her head. "No one can compete with my love for you."

"I think Jesse's a good man, baby. I think you two can be happy for the long haul. I give you guys my blessing."

"Mom, stop talking like that. You're not going to die, okay? I won't let you."

"That's another trait I admire. You were always stubborn, too." Shannon paused for a while. She turned toward the window, but it seemed her eyes looked far beyond the scenery. "I had a dream about Chris last night. I think your daddy might still be alive." She turned back to Harley. "I want you to try and find him, honey."

"Why?"

"Whatever his reason for being absent all these years, he's still your father. I want you to get to know him. You guys are so much alike that in knowing him you'll learn a lot more about yourself."

"I'll only look for him if you're here with me. So if you want that to happen . . ."

"Ha! So you're trying to bribe the angel of death?"

"Whatever it takes."

"I admit I'm a little scared about tomorrow. And the mere thought of leaving you breaks my heart. But you'll be okay."

"No, I won't."

"Yes, you will."

"Not unless you stick around until I'm eighty."

Shannon's eyes brightened. "And I'm a hundred? Okay, we'll see."

"That's what I'm talking about. The only way I'm thinking about you, Mom, is alive."

"Harley Christina. My sweet, sweet baby. I love Lenny Kravitz, but make no mistake. You're my rock star."

The next day, at one p.m., mother and daughter sat together and received the test results. The cancer was back.

9

Kim was the first of the three women to arrive at the place Harley had suggested, a secluded restaurant near where Harley worked in Kansas City, Missouri's West Bottoms. Though Kim had lived in the city all her life, she'd rarely visited this historically infamous area where mafia had gathered and, according to history buffs, from where Tom Pendergast operated the political machine that helped usher Theodore Roosevelt into the White House. Waving away the hostess's suggestion of a front table next to large-paned windows that faced the street, she walked through the near-empty dining room to a partially hidden booth along the far back wall.

"It gets a bit chilly back here," the waiter informed her, while sitting a glass of water on the table and pulling out a pad. "Right under the air vent."

"I'll be fine."

"Would you like something to drink?"

"Not yet. There will be two others joining me."

Kim's eyes wandered from the retreating waiter's back, over to where the bartender yakked it up with a customer, and around the old building's brick-and-plaster-covered walls, intermittingly broken up by columns of dark wood. Red candles in clear glass holders were set atop worn checked tablecloths.

Flames danced to the beat of ventilated air. The subtle aroma of stale cigarettes defied the "no smoking" sign that hung over the bar, next to another that read "Bartender's Bucket List: Ice, Beer." Hanging fern and philodendron cast eerie shadows on the ceiling. She shivered, easily able to imagine a group of black-suited mob bosses wearing fedoras and smoking cigars, discussing illicit activities and planning hits. Given how these three women had come to know each other, it was a fitting location.

Her eyes stopped at where Jayda nodded a thanks to the man who'd held the door for her as she chatted on the phone. Once inside, she scanned the room. Kim stood and waved. Jayda walked toward her.

"Hey, Kim!"

"Hello, Jayda. How are you?"

"Good." And into the phone, "I'm at the restaurant. Let's talk later, okay?"

Jayda rubbed her arms as she looked above her. "Why'd you choose the table right under the air vent? It's freezing!"

"You're cold? I thought it felt good. Good Lord, could that mean I'm menopausal?"

"You're not old enough for that."

"I'm forty-two. My mom went through hers before she reached fifty. It might be that I'm wearing this suit jacket. Here, put this on." She took it off and handed it to Jayda.

"You sure?"

"Positive."

"Thanks." She pulled on the jacket and then reached for a menu. "So, Harley's not here yet."

"No."

"Can't imagine how she found this place," Jayda said, checking out the surroundings. "I'm glad we're here early. I don't think I'd want to be in this area at night by myself."

"Me, either. I'm such a creature of habit. I grew up in this town, yet there are dozens of communities that I don't know about."

"You live in Kansas City, Missouri, yet your son got tried in Jones County."

"Because that's where the young man who got busted lived."

"Oh, right. At least Kendall has someone on the inside that he knows."

"Not really. The guy was Kendall's cousin's friend. It was the first time they'd met. Kendall had no idea he sold drugs and had them in the house."

"That is really jacked up."

"Tell me about it." Kim looked at her watch. "Maybe I'll call Harley, see how close she is to being here."

"That's a good idea."

Kim pulled out her cell and tapped Harley's number. Her pleasant face immediately scrunched into one of concern. "Harley? What's wrong?" She looked over to see a worried look on Jayda's face.

"Oh, no, Harley. I'm so sorry. No, I completely understand. Is there anything Jayda and I can do for you? Is there anything you need?"

Jayda mouthed, *What?* Kim held up a "just a sec" hand.

"We'll definitely pray for you, girl, and Shannon, too. Are you going to work today? Do you need someone to go check on her? Mrs. Hastings? Good. Bless that woman for being such a friend to you guys. We've got your back, Harley. Don't forget that, okay? And don't hesitate to reach out if there's something you need. You're not alone, okay? All right. Love you."

Kim sighed as she ended the call. "Shannon's cancer has returned."

"I had a feeling that's what happened. That poor girl. Harley must be beside herself."

"She sounded pretty upset, and she's so fearless. It was hard to hear her sounding that way."

"What can we do?"

"She said nothing right now, except pray."

"If I feel helpless, I can only imagine how she feels."

Kim got the waiter's attention and waved her over.

"Decided not to wait on your other friend, huh?"

"She's not coming," Kim said. The two ordered drinks. "You know what, I'm not that hungry. I'll just have the spinach salad."

Jayda handed her menu to the waiter. "I'll try the kale salad, with chicken."

"Okay, ladies. Drinks coming right up."

Jayda watched the waiter walk away. Then she said, "I can't believe what came out in the paper, how they took that picture of you totally out of context and slammed WHIP."

"Me either, at first. But my mom made a very good point about it. Grey's running for senator. This is politics, one of the dirtiest games in the business. As bad as that was, I'm kind of glad it happened."

"Why?"

"Serves as a wake-up call. Reminds us of the seriousness of what we're doing, the ruthlessness of who we're dealing with. Cautions us to be careful in how whatever plan we come up with is carried out."

"Speaking of which, I learned something this week." Kim arched a brow in question. "My mom's cleaning company is now doing houses in Edgefield."

"Really? You mean—"

"No, not his. Ha! I thought the same thing. But it was a rich person's home, a mansion is how Aunt Lucy described it. Chances are whoever lives there knows Grey, probably even supports him. I don't know if it means anything for what we're trying to do, but I thought it interesting that one of the company referrals led them to Edgefield. Crazy timing, huh?"

"Or divine intervention."

"Maybe! My mom and aunt are always praying to their saints, and lighting candles."

Kim smiled. "Sounds like my mom. She's had Kendall's name on her church's prayer list since the day he was arrested."

They paused as the drinks were delivered.

"I learned something interesting this week, too, from a reporter, Bryan White, with *KC News*. He called to ask me what happened in Edgefield, and to tell me about a series he's working on." She gave Jayda the short version on privatized prisons she'd learned from Bryan and her research online. "What if Bryan's hunch is true? What if Grey is somehow profiting from the prison in Edgefield, and was doing so at the time he served as DA? It could be the evidence we need to get new trials for all of our guys."

"Oh, my God, Kim. I'd love to find something on that arrogant asshole. Let him sit and rot where our guys have been for the past few years."

"Or at the very least throw a wrench in his political plans, possibly even ruin his career. That and seeing my Kendall come home would be considered a job well done."

"What can we do?" Jayda asked, with animated excitement. "How can we help this Bryan guy?"

"I don't know. But just thinking about the possibilities has cost me sleep." Jayda pulled out her phone. "What are you doing?"

"Texting Aunt Lucy. I want to find out whose house she cleaned so we can do a search and see if the name comes up."

"Great idea, Jayda. But then what? Finding out who lives in the house would be one thing. Gaining access to any relevant information within the house is quite another."

"It wouldn't be so hard. Get in there, do a little cleaning, and while we're at it leave behind a video camera or recording device in a few key places. Could learn something, could learn nothing, but anything is worth a try."

Kim was delightfully taken aback. "Excuse me. Who is this duplicitous mastermind, and what happened to my sweet, compassionate friend afraid to break laws?"

"Grey killed that bitch."

The women laughed and high-fived. Jayda's phone pinged. She tapped on the message icon to open it.

"Dodd. That's the name of the owner."

Kim's eyes narrowed. "Clarence Dodd?"

Jayda looked up. "Yeah. How'd you know?"

"I remember that name from the other night." Kim's thumbs skimmed across the phone's keys. "Don't remember the site, but it had to have some relevance to prisons or the justice system.

"Clarence Dodd, retired judge, Jones County." She gave Jayda a knowing look, kept scrolling.

"What does it say about him?"

"I don't see anything related to my search. Hold on." She clicked the link to an article and began reading.

"Friends and colleagues of Judge Clarence E. Dodd will attend a party being held in his honor to celebrate his retirement after more than forty years on the bench. The celebration will take place at the Edgefield Country Club," Kim enunciated, "located at blah, blah, blah in Edgefield, Kansas, where Dodd now resides."

The women's eyes met. Jayda pulled in a breath. "No."

"Yes. Jayda, my *señorita*-soon-to-be-spy, you just might be on to something."

She continued to scroll. "After several years in private practice and a stint on the Kansas City, Kansas city council, Dodd was elected as the district judge in Wyandotte County, where he served for forty-two years. While not a political event, the party will be attended by elected officials, including former mayors of Wyandotte County. Also present will be several current and former judges, attorneys, and members of the law enforcement community."

Eyes widening, then narrowing, Kim quickly continued as her voice lowered and hardened. " 'He is a true embodiment of the American ideal,' said Hammond Grey, a district attorney in Jones County and an Edgefield resident. 'He stands for good morals, great family values, and a fair and strict interpretation of the law. On the bench and in our courts, he will be sorely missed.'"

Kim looked up to see Jayda busy scrolling on her phone. "Did you hear what I just read?"

"Yep." She kept scrolling.

"What are you doing?"

"Checking out surveillance shit. You know, the kind you can plant and it won't get detected. She doesn't know it yet, but if they're ever called to clean his house again, Mama's cleaning company is about to get another part-time employee . . . me."

During lunch, Kim learned more about spyware than she ever thought possible. Video cameras that looked like regular pens, eyeglasses, watches, clocks, keychains, books, even inside a necklace cross. There were GPS devices to track one's prey and recording equipment hidden in what looked like a regular quarter.

"Whew, my head is spinning," Jayda said, as she finished off the rest of her plate.

"Who are you telling? I might know too much information. Now every time I see someone with a ballpoint pen, I'll get paranoid. Think they're taping our conversation or snapping a pic!"

"Right?!"

"How soon will you know when or if your mom will be back in Dodd's house?"

"I don't know, but as soon as I find out you'll be the second to know. It's going to be tricky, though."

"What, planting the devices?"

"No, talking my way into a temporary job at Mom's company. Just asking her about it will throw up a huge flag. Not only because I hate the Mexican domestic stereotype but because Mama and *tía* always told their children that they cleaned houses so we'd never have to."

"Ooh, I agree then. It's going to be a hard one to explain,

and there's no way you can tell her the truth about what you're doing."

"*Dios*, no. You think I'm scared to break the law. My mom would faint if she knew. But don't worry. I'll figure something out, because right now this educated, second-generation little Latina has never wanted to clean a house so much in her life."

10

Feeling restless and hyped after having lunch with Jayda, Kim turned her car opposite of the direction home and headed to the mall. Nothing to buy in particular, but some of her best thinking was done while browsing racks and window-shopping. Would it really be possible for Jayda to plant a video recorder or listening device in the judge's home? If so, would they hear anything that could actually help their cases, or even Bryan's news story? Something incriminating about Hammond Grey, something scandalous that if revealed would send voters fleeing from him and straight to his rival Jack Myers? What if they got caught? What if the device was discovered and the finger could be pointed back to Jayda? What would happen then?

She reached Crown Center and after parking joined hundreds of others passing time and spending money in the upscale two-level midtown shopping center. Browsing the shelves of a favorite store got her thinking of how long it had been since she and Aaron had enjoyed a wonderful meal together. When Kendall was home, she'd cooked almost every day. They'd sit in the dining room and be regaled with Kendall's latest sports feats or academic achievements.

So much of their world had revolved around their son.

Experiencing how empty the marriage felt without him was a shocking wakeup call Kim hadn't expected, a call further exacerbated by how differently the two had dealt with the arrest. She'd thrown herself into the public eye, demanding to anyone who'd listen that he be freed. Aaron had retreated inside himself, feeling the courts were too powerful to fight. She'd not been overly empathetic to his position. Had he found a listening pair of ears that belonged to a woman named Jessica? The woman who'd texted Aaron last week? The one she'd planned to Google but hadn't? She loved Aaron and had no doubt he loved her. But neither liked each other much these days. It was like they were headed down the same highway but on opposite sides of the road. One thing was for sure: Kim wasn't ready to toss in the towel on their marriage.

What are you going to do?

While she perused the juicer aisle and seeing the latest blender options, a plan formed. Putting it immediately into motion, Kim approached the cashier with the same fancy spiralizer she'd seen advertised on TV and left the mall to implement Operation Seduction.

After a trip to the spa for a bikini wax usually done only near Aaron's birthday, Kim stopped at the neighborhood gourmet grocer and the bakery two businesses down that made Aaron's favorite dessert—outside of his mama's sweet potato pie—a chocolate truffle torte. Once home, she texted him.

Did you hear my voicemail? Dinner ready soon. What time will you be home?

She placed the phone on the kitchen island along with the bags, and after taking a shower, splashing on a liberal amount of the perfume Aaron had gifted her with last Christmas, and changing into a form-fitting yet comfy stretch jersey maxi, she returned downstairs. Aaron hadn't returned her text so she called him.

No answer. She sent another text.

Hey babe. Call me when you get this. After a short pause she added, **Make it quick. I have plans for us. K**

A wave of suspicion swept across her like a gentle breeze. She forced herself to ignore it. Nothing could be gained from continued distrust. When he got home, they'd have the Jessica conversation. He'd allay her fears. She'd believe him. Simple and done. She opened and poured a small glass of wine, spiraled zucchini, placed it in a marinade, and transferred a salad from its plastic container into a decorative glass bowl. What next? Aaron liked his steaks medium well. Cooking the nicely marbled rib eyes on the stovetop cast-iron grill would take less than ten minutes. She set the table, lit candles, placed the house stereo on a channel playing smooth jazz and nineties R & B.

Back in the kitchen her cell phone screen lit up. She reached for the phone and read the text.

Sorry, Kim. Just now seeing messages. In Blue Springs, at Larry's. Invited over for BBQ and poker with the guys. Didn't know you had plans.

Kim read the message a second time. This time suspicion was less a gentle breeze and more a gust of wind. Aaron went out, just not that often. And since when did he play poker?

Unable to think of a non-confrontational, productive response, she set the phone on the counter, opened a glass-front cabinet door, and pulled out one of the larger wineglasses, not quite the size used by her secret shero Olivia Pope, but bigger than the size used when life was normal and all was well. She poured the remainder from the other glass, topped it off, and went into the home office. Shaking the mouse to wake up the computer, she scanned the university staff dictionary, located a woman named Jessica who worked in the same department as Aaron, then decided to make a bad night worse and typed "Jessica Smith" into the search engine.

More than a hundred fifty million results.

She would have to have a common name. Where was Shaniqua when you needed her? Just peachy.

Kim went to the college website and entered it there. Sure enough, a link came up for Jessica R. Smith adjunct professor of political science. She clicked on it. Seconds later she wished she hadn't. Pretty girl—thick, shoulder-length black curls, a flawless caramel complexion, perfect white teeth, confident smile. Feeling she shouldn't, Kim scanned the bio beside the pic. Gained her undergrad and master's from a well-known college in Atlanta, her undergrad year as summa cum laude. Should have heeded the gut check.

Smart and beautiful? I need more wine.

She drained the bottle, but instead of returning to the computer she turned off the oven, put the steaks in the fridge, and took wine, water, and an entrée-sized helping of salad upstairs. Nothing good could come from her fixating on smart and pretty. She grabbed the remote and channel-surfed, looking for a distraction. Hallmark? No, not in the mood for happily ever after. Lifetime? No, didn't need any ideas on how to kill her spouse. Kim continued surfing until a heading jumped out at her—Kids For Cash. She turned back to CNBC and *American Greed.*

The announcer described the upcoming segment about a newly built detention center, a spike in arrests, and the shocking identities of who was behind it. Just as she reached to turn up the volume, the opening garage door sounded. *Aaron?* She got out of bed and walked downstairs, reached the dining room as Aaron turned the corner into the kitchen. Silence bellowed as she watched him take in the scene: the set table complete with slightly burned candles, a vase of fresh flowers, low lighting, soft jazz playing in the background.

His eyes settled on her. "I'm sorry. I didn't hear your voice mail until the text came in."

Kim shrugged. "It was a last-minute idea, born in the aisles of Function Junction."

"That's where you were earlier, shopping?"

"I had lunch with two of my friends from WHIP, well, it was

supposed to be two. It ended up being just me and Jayda. Decided to stop by Crown Center on the way home." Awkward silence. "When'd you start playing poker?"

A sheepish grin. "Tonight, and badly."

"Hmm."

"That's one of the reasons I decided to quit and come home. Wasn't helping my partner much anyway."

Was your partner pretty, with a name that begins with a J?

"Larry's been bugging me to see his new house for months. Went over just for something to do, to get my mind off . . . things."

Noticing the empty wine bottle, he looked at Kim. "You drink all that?"

"About half of it. The rest is upstairs on the nightstand, along with the salad I'd just begun eating when I heard the garage door. Have you had dinner?"

"Snacked mostly; a few barbequed wings, chips and dip. What'd you cook?"

"Nothing yet. Steak and vegetable pasta was on the menu. Would take less than fifteen minutes to prepare." She rubbed her stomach. "I probably need to put something solid in my stomach to soak up the wine."

"That sounds good." He passed her, walked into the living room, and turned on the TV as she entered the kitchen and turned on the oven.

"Turn it to CNBC," she said from the kitchen. "*American Greed* is doing a piece on two corrupt judges who received kickbacks from a detention center for putting kids in there." When he didn't reply she added, "Only if you want."

As she passed the living room on the way to the bedroom to retrieve the uneaten salad, the somber voice of the *AG* announcer sounded from the speakers, repeated what she'd heard moments before. "Later in this episode of *American Greed* . . ."

Back downstairs Kim plated the reheated food and set one

on each of the two dinner trays Aaron had positioned in front of the couch.

"What do you want to drink?"

"Do we have any beer?"

Kim checked. "No. Your choices are tea, wine, or soda."

"Water is fine."

"Cold or room temp?"

"Cold, please."

She opened two bottles of water, poured them over several ice cubes and brought them into the living room.

"This should be interesting," Kim said, after turning up the TV volume. "I get the feeling that somewhere in that storyline may be the answer to why Kendall's in jail."

Aaron's eyes went from the TV to Kim's face, but he said nothing.

For the next fifteen minutes they mostly ate in silence while Kim learned about another facet of the privatized prison system that Bryan had introduced to her just two weeks before.

Mass Incarceration.

Lucrative kickbacks.

Mandatory minimums.

Corruption galore.

"Bryan told me about other incidents similar to this happening throughout the system," Kim said during a commercial. "Where certain groups are specifically targeted to exploit, or an opportunity arises where certain segments of our population can be victimized."

"Who's Bryan?"

"A reporter for *KC News*. He called to get my side of what happened at the campaign rally and suggested I contact an attorney, which I did, one who specializes in defamation lawsuits. He's sending an official letter to the newspaper requesting a retraction or correction. I need to call him for an update.

"We got talking—"

"You and this guy?"

Kim nodded. "Yes, the reporter. He knows a lot about the privatization of prisons, the laws that have been passed to make incarceration easier, quicker, and to make sentences longer. Babe, it's a seventy-billion-dollar industry."

Aaron gave her a long look as he eased back on the couch. "Sounds like you and this Bryan dude have done a lot of talking."

What about you and Jessica? She thought it but the conversation was going better than it had in a while. So she kept the comeback to herself.

"We talked for a while, well over an hour. What I didn't learn from him I found on the web."

They quieted as the commercial break ended and the show continued. Kim's heart broke for a woman whose fifteen-year-old wrestling star son had been arrested, charged with possessing drug paraphernalia, and sent to the detention center. He later lost a college scholarship and his girlfriend, the first love of his life. Unable to cope or get back on track, the young man committed suicide.

The similarities between his sports-centered life and that of her son scared Kim to death, and increased her determination to get Kendall out of prison before he too lost the will to hang on.

"Dinner was good, babe. Thanks."

"You're welcome."

The rest of the evening passed comfortably, almost like old times. Aaron helped clean the kitchen. The two retired to the bedroom and enjoyed cake and ice cream. A little time later, they enjoyed each other. It was the first time they'd made love in weeks and came back together with the ease and comfort of an old, worn shoe. It was a beautiful night, magical really. In fact, it might have been perfect had Aaron not mumbled a name in his sleep. And if Kim hadn't been awake to hear it. But she was. And she did. *Jessica.*

11

The next morning Kim woke to a chill in the room that had nothing to do with the early hour, overcast skies, or spring rain. She had to say something about last night, how Aaron had uttered another woman's name. After a quick shower, she headed downstairs for much-needed coffee. The hearty meal she and Aaron shared had helped cut through last night's wine. Strong java would erase the rest of the cobwebs. She sat at the dining room table, contemplating, when Aaron joined her downstairs.

"Good morning." Kim flinched. "Didn't mean to startle you. You were pretty deep in thought," he continued, passing her in the dining room and heading to the kitchen.

"Yes, I was."

"Still thinking about that show last night, that *American Greed* episode?" He stopped pouring coffee to turn and look at her. "Or what happened afterwards." He gave a knowing smile.

"What happened afterwards," she answered. No smile.

He frowned slightly. "Oh, okay." Coffee dressed, he reentered the dining room and sat down. "So what's up?"

"I think we need counseling."

Aaron's cup paused midway between the table and his mouth. "Counseling?" He took a tentative sip of the hot brew he held. "Where'd that thought come from?"

"From a lot of thinking." Aaron chuckled. Kim managed a smile. "We've been through a lot these past few years. Lost our son. Not to death, thank God. But still, he's gone from our daily lives."

"Is counseling going to bring him back? No. I don't need to talk to anybody about that."

"What about talking to someone about us?"

Aaron sighed, set down his cup. "Kim, what is this about?"

Seconds passed as she passed a finger around the rim of cup and gathered her thoughts. "About something that happened last night."

"What, missing your phone call? You're upset that I went over to Larry's?"

"It's not about you spending time with the boys. We both could probably stand to socialize a bit more often. Last night was wonderful. I've missed that man who sat with me, watched TV, and shared conversation. Who made such good love to me that my toes curled." Love-filled eyes met wary ones. "I've missed my best friend."

"You're looking like you lost your best friend. What's the matter? I'm right here."

"After we made love, as you were drifting off to sleep, you mumbled a name." Her eyes pierced him. "It wasn't mine."

Aaron frowned. "Who was it?"

"Jessica."

A nervous chuckle. "Naw, I didn't do that."

"Yes, you did." No chuckle.

He observed her serious expression, then shrugged. "It's no big deal, Kim. I was obviously half asleep."

"You don't think murmuring another woman's name after making love to me is a big deal?"

"Work must have crossed my mind before I dozed off."

Kim forced her body to relax. Reminded herself that she wanted a discussion, not an argument, and softened her tone. "That's never happened before. Fifteen years of teaching and I don't remember you mentioning any other teacher in your sleep."

"Maybe that's because I've never worked with one to create a class for the school's curriculum. Jessica and I were asked to create a lesson plan for next semester that focuses on the widening racial divide in this country from historical, economic, and psychological perspectives."

Kim's expression remained bland as she absorbed that information, while a million questions raced through her mind.

"How'd that happen?"

"The idea developed out of a conversation during a faculty meeting. I suggested we add more topics relevant to what our kids are dealing with. Jessica had taught a class on economics and race. It grew from there."

"Is that why she was texting you the other week? Something work related?"

"You checked my phone?"

"Only glanced at the message that came in when you left it. A message from Jessica. Was it about work, this class?"

"Of course. Why else would she be texting me?"

"I don't know. That's why I asked." She took a sip of coffee. "What else can you tell me about her?"

"What do you want to know?"

Kim shrugged. "Whatever you know."

Now, Aaron sipped. To the point where Kim wondered if he were going to answer at all.

"Her name is Jessica Smith. She's an adjunct professor from Atlanta; last taught at Clark University."

"What brought her here, to Kansas City?"

"Opportunity. Less competition here than in Atlanta."

"How old is she?"

Shrug. "You know how you women are about telling your age. I'd guess thirty-something."

"Hmm. Is she pretty?"

"Jessica's a beautiful woman."

He didn't lie. Judging from the picture on her faculty profile, Jessica Smith was stunning.

"Is she married?"

Aaron heaved an impatient sigh. "Why all these questions, Kim? I don't know about her personal life. You'd have to ask her that. What about the dude at the paper you're all friendly with. Bryan? Is he married?"

"Seriously? You're going to ask me about a news reporter with whom I've had one conversation, one that revolved around our son? Why are you being defensive? I'm not the one who murmured someone else's name after having sex. Because of that, I believe these questions are perfectly legit."

"I'm not fucking her, Kim. As far as I'm concerned, when it comes to Jessica that's all you need to know." Aaron left the dining room. The conversation was obviously over.

Kim refreshed her coffee and walked into the living room, her mind spinning with more questions than answers after talking with her husband just now. The situation with Kendall was all about politics, economics, and the racial divide. So was what got her picture in the paper! But Aaron had said nothing to her about that, which was obviously not the case with Jessica. Just because they weren't physically intimate didn't mean Aaron wasn't cheating. There were ways other than sexually to betray a spouse. An affair of the head could be just as dangerous. An affair of the heart could be downright deadly. As Jayda would say, *no bueno*.

12

A few days after her lunch with Kim, Jayda overheard a conversation between Anna and Lucy. When Anna went upstairs to chat with her husband, Bruno, Jayda joined Lucy in the family room. "Aunt Lucy, you guys cleaning houses in Edgefield this weekend?" Jayda tried her best to sound casual, even tossed in a fake yawn for extra nonchalant.

"Yes. Why?"

Jayda shrugged. "Just heard you and Mom talking."

"Our hard work at the Dodd house paid off. The missus was so impressed that she let go the people who'd been working for her and hired us full-time. Mentioned us to some of her friends, too. More business, more money, which is great because our thirtieth anniversary is coming up. Manny and I want to take a second honeymoon."

"Where'd you go on your first one?"

"Holiday Inn." Jayda laughed. "Hey, don't knock it. We were two young, broke kids glad to leave a houseful of Sanchezes if just for the night!"

"Where would you go this time?"

"Someplace that gets warm in the winter; Jamaica or the Bahamas, or a beautiful resort in Mexico."

"How much are you paying your PTs these days?"

Lucy's brow-raised look didn't surprise Jayda. It probably had something to do with a comment she once made about hell freezing over before she'd work as a domestic and that they were earthbound with a current temp of seventy degrees.

"Why are you really asking? And don't say it's because you need money. You make good money on your own with almost no expenses since moving back home."

"How much do you think I get as a pharm tech? Last year I made thirty-one thousand dollars. After taxes, Social Security, insurance, and everything else I cleared less than twenty-five thousand dollars. A chunk of that goes to pay attorney fees and another chunk goes on Nicky's books. Not to mention the phone bill, and the money I give to Mom and Dad for living here. It's less than I was paying, Auntie, but I'm not rich."

"I know, honey. I was teasing you because of how much you've always hated that we clean houses for a living."

"That's when I was younger and feeling the peer pressure of being a teen. Going to school in rich Jones County where my classmates had executive dads and soccer moms. Today, I couldn't be prouder of you guys. Then I looked at you as domestics. My perspective is different now. You're successful business owners with a domestic business."

Both women grew quiet. Jayda remembered the shy, chubby Mexican girl who struggled for acceptance both from others and herself. Lucy's next question revealed what was on her mind.

"Are you really looking for a second job?"

"I was thinking it wouldn't hurt. Just through the summer while the cousins are home and can help Nana take care of Ally. Maybe earn a couple hundred to go toward Christmas gifts."

"We pay the workers ten dollars an hour. Tips are split evenly between the crew."

Jayda nodded. "I only want to work jobs in Edgefield."

Lucy crossed her arms. "Okay, Jayda, for the last time. What is this really about?"

"I told you!"

"No, you told me what you want me to believe. Do you forget I've known you since before you were born? There's another part to this story."

"After you talking about those fancy mansions, you think I want to clean an average house? I want to see how the rich folk live."

"I say being rich is overrated."

"Can I work on the weekends or not?"

"Sure. Starting this weekend, if you like."

"Morning or afternoon? WHIP meets this Saturday."

"We work early mornings."

"Okay. Next Saturday then."

When the day arrived, Jayda was ready. She'd caught up with Harley the day before, showed off her spyware and got last-minute tips.

Wear gloves to hide fingerprints.

And maybe a face mask, say you're allergic to dust.

Be careful!

Don't get caught!

It had been hard to convince Lucy of her reasons for working extra, but Anna was disappointed. "Why didn't you tell me you were struggling? You could stay here for free."

That she was being deceptive sent her on a guilt trip but she was back in time to wake up bright and early Saturday morning, don the white, button-down shirt with "Great Housekeeping" embroidered on the pocket, black slacks, and black shoes that made up the company uniform and head over with Lucy to the Dodd residence in Edgefield.

Just before reaching the gated community of Edgefield

Estates, Lucy pulled out a pass and placed it on her wind-shield. She stopped at the guard post. The elderly gentleman noted her pass, wrote down the number, and waved her through. Jayda was struck with the immediate transformation of their sur-roundings. The ten or so miles between Olathe and Edgefield were filled with strip malls, fast food chains, and unkempt grass. Inside these gates, the meticulously cut grass was so lus-ciously green it looked fake. Gargantuan houses with expan-sive lawns set back from tree-lined streets, some behind wrought-iron fences, others partially hidden behind leafy trees and ten-foot brick walls, all equally impressive in their archi-tectural design. Jayda had only seen houses like these in maga-zines and could not have imagined she'd ever clean one that looked like these did, let alone live in one.

Lucy pulled into a long driveway, one that curved around to the back of the house. She opened the trunk and retrieved a storage container on wheels filled with cleaning items.

"Here, Jayda. Leave your purse in the trunk."

"What? Oh, um, let me get my phone first."

"Leave it. No talk or texting while working is allowed."

So much for the idea of still shots of the house. Good thing she brought the video glasses and the recording device. She re-trieved them from her purse, slipped the coin-shaped recorder in her pocket and the glasses on her face.

"What are you doing? You don't wear glasses," Lucy said, suspicion lacing her voice as Jayda donned the cute frames.

"Just for fun," Jayda relied.

"You are up to something," Lucy said, a wagging finger em-phasizing this belief.

"Don't be paranoid, auntie. I'll do a good job." Jayda fol-lowed her lead as she walked to a back door and tapped lightly.

"Leave the talking to me," she whispered, as they waited for the door to be opened. "Only speak to the residents if they speak to you. Okay?"

Before Jayda could answer, the door was opened by an older woman wearing a crisp black dress with a starched white collar, an equally starched apron, and an expression as stiff as her attire. A lacy white kerchief adorned her head. She looked like an actor straight out of the movies. Jayda forced herself not to stare.

"Good morning," Lucy said. "Great Housekeeping, back again."

Miss Stiff's eyes slid from Lucy to Jayda. In a stern voice and slight accent as nerve-wracking as her demeanor, she said, "That is not the same girl as last time."

"No. This is my niece Jay—"

Jayda coughed and nudged Lucy at the same time. Lucy scowled. "You okay?"

"*Si pero yo*—"

"Is she sick? We have strict rules against anyone transporting contagious germs or viruses inside this home."

"No, ma'am, just nervous. She'll be fine."

"Come on in," Miss Stiff ordered. "Do not clean the family room at this time. And no vacuuming for an hour. The missus is entertaining."

"Yes, ma'am."

The subservient behavior of her take-charge aunt made Jayda sick for real. So much had been sacrificed for her and her cousins. It made Jayda proud to work alongside her aunt and even happier to do her part to expose any misdeeds that may be taking place inside this home.

Stiff turned on her heel and departed. Jayda breathed a sigh of relief. "Why do they hire us if they have a maid?" she asked in Spanish.

"Don't know, don't care. As long as the money's green, they can be a cleaning company hiring a cleaning company, and we'll do the work. And why are you talking to me in Spanish? What is up with you?"

"Just being careful."

"Stop being weird."

Luckily Jayda didn't have to request the downstairs. Lucy instructed her to sweep, dust, and shine the beautifully restored hardwood floors downstairs while she handled the upstairs bedrooms. Jayda placed her cleaning supplies at the end of a hall and began dusting. While working, she managed a quick scan of the large, airy kitchen and a formal dining room and living room. When she reached a hallway bathroom, she ducked inside and quickly turned on the video glasses. To do so may or may not come in handy, but she figured it good practice to learn how they worked. Back at the end of that hallway, Jayda reached an intersection. To her right was another hallway like the one she'd just cleaned, with a series of doorways. Straight ahead was an open set of double doors to a room from which hushed but animated voices drifted.

Mrs. Dodd? And if so, with whom? Jayda wondered whether to try and find the retired judge's office or take a chance on placing the recorder near the room now occupied. She swirled the mop in a circular motion over beautiful Brazilian cherry wood, weighing her options. She had only one recorder and maybe only once chance to plant it. Now. With that in mind, she dusted in the direction of the voices. The right choice, considering what she heard next.

"He'll make an amazing senator. When he sets a goal, he reaches it. He never gives up."

Grey?! It has to be him they're talking about. With a quick sign of the cross, Jayda quickened her movements toward what looked to be a parlor or family room.

"I think he's perfect," a cultured voice said. "Just what we need in today's climate. Someone who's determined to maintain our way of life while appealing to the masses needed to get him elected. He's just so handsome. And smart. A perfect combination."

"A blessing for sure."

"Part blessing, part curse. Money, power, and good looks are scallywag magnets."

The other woman chuckled. "Scallywag, Mary? I can't remember the last time I heard that word."

"That's what I call them, what I named the women who went after my Clarence, almost from the moment he won a spot on the bench. Women are drawn to power, you know. It will take a great deal of strength to remain dignified in the face of the kinds of whorish behavior he'll undoubtedly face."

"Hammond is a respectable man with good morals and solid Christian values. No matter how tempting the . . . traffic . . . he'll take the high road. The same as he handled those disruptive protesters the other day. Did you know that . . ."

Disruptive? Oh no she didn't! Jayda wanted to hear the rest or, even better, go in and confront the woman who thought the senator walked on water. But there was no time for that. After trading the dust mop for a melamine sponge and a spray bottle of oil soap, Jayda pulled the recorder from her pocket and crept as close as she dared to the open doors. She knelt down and after running her finger over the baseboard slipped the device into a groove between it and the wall, far enough that she hoped it would go unnoticed but with the thin wire attached still accessible enough for her to pull the device from the crevice. With a quick swipe of the cloth, she leveled the wire with the wood and, satisfied that it was hidden, stood, turned . . . and looked into the eyes of a scowling Miss Stiff.

Holy crap! Jayda's heart dropped along with her eyes. How long had the Dodds' maid been standing there? How much had she seen? With legs turned nearly wooden with fear Jayda quickly knelt and began cleaning the baseboards on the opposite side of the hall. She'd never cleaned a baseboard in her life but focused on the task as though they were mirrored and she sought her reflection. A life did hang in the balance. Her child's father's life. She scrubbed harder.

Snap. Barely audible yet clear, Jayda looked up once again to see Miss Stiff's bony finger directing her up and away from the family room. She hurriedly obeyed, bobbing her head subserviently much as she'd seen Lucy do. Reaching the end of the hallway, she picked up the container of cleaning supplies and dared to look back. Miss Stiff stood over the baseboard and the recorder, hands on hip, staring.

"Hail Mary, full of grace," Jayda rapidly uttered under her breath. "Our Lord is with thee. Blessed art thou among women and blessed is the fruit of thy womb, Jesus."

Stiff whipped around. Jayda almost peed her pants. Instinct took over. She raced forward with fear and anxiety etched on her face.

"Not clean?" she whispered, matching Lucy's earlier demeanor. "I clean again. Do good job."

The woman with straight A's in English slipped into a broken form with nary a thought.

Stiff's eyes narrowed as she viewed Jayda's face. "Go clean the toilets."

Almost two hours later, house gleaming, shining, and buffed, Jayda, assured that Miss Stiff wasn't snooping behind her, chanced one more walk down the ill-fated hallway by the now quiet family room. She'd downloaded the software that enabled remote listening to the recording device, but something told her not to chance leaving it there. If Miss Stiff found the recorder, it could mean big trouble for Great Housekeeping. She knelt down by the baseboard where she'd stuck the recorder, ran her hand along the groove. No wire.

Oh, God, no!

A bit more frantic now, she searched again, felt the breath of Miss Stiff on the hairs of her neck. Afraid to turn her head, she did it anyway. No one was there. Jayda clutched her heart, about to hyperventilate. Clearly illicit activity was not her forte. Fingers shook as she moved them along the top of the baseboard.

The wire! Found it!

Just as she snatched it from its hiding spot a voice hissed behind her.

"What are you doing?"

Jayda almost died. She swallowed her fear, slowly stood, turned around, and saw . . .

"Auntie!"

"What in the heck is wrong with you?" She pulled Jayda toward the hall from which they'd entered. "You look like you've seen a ghost."

"You scared me."

"Good. Because looking at you in those ugly glasses is scaring the hell out of me."

Jayda laughed. "Sorry." She took them off.

"Oh, since we're finished you can see again?"

"We're finished?"

"Yep."

Gracias, Dios mio.

Jayda was more than happy to leave. She only hoped that there was something on the recording that was worth the five years getting it had surely taken off her life.

Later, after she'd put Alejandra to bed and the house was quiet, she listened to what the device had captured. What was on it gave her the five years back.

"Hot damn," she quietly exclaimed, as she reached for her cell phone.

Emergency meeting, she texted to Kim. **ASAP. UNBELIEVABLE news!**

13

The next day Jayda, Harley, and Kim huddled in Kim's dining room turned detective agency, all staring at Jayda's cell phone.

"You ready?" Jayda asked, her eyes wide and sparkling with mischievous excitement.

"Was ready when you texted me," Kim said.

"Come on already," Harley added. "A working girl doesn't have all day!"

Jayda pressed the play button on the recorder app, then turned up the volume. Three sets of ears leaned closer.

"Wait!" Kim ordered. "Shut it off."

Harley huffed. "Why?"

"Bluetooth speaker," Kim replied, already heading to the office before either woman could further object.

Jayda hurriedly paired her phone with the speaker and pressed play once again. Scratchy sounds emitted more clearly across the airwaves with snatches of muddled voices heard in between.

Harley frowned. "I can't hear a thing."

"Shh, wait. I want to bypass their social chitchat and get to the good stuff." Jayda moved the bar on the recording, stopping midway. She tapped play.

". . . beautiful it is."

"The estate? Yes, breathtaking indeed."

Jayda paused the recording, tapped the bar a little farther to the right. "Hang on, guys. Almost there."

She pushed play again.

"Who needs Switzerland when you've got the Ozarks?"

A pause and then, "I do."

A duo of tinkling laughter ensued.

"Are you two joining me and Clarence for the ride down? The Wards have offered the use of their private plane, you know."

"Hammond hasn't said, and I've learned not to ask."

Kim's jaw dropped.

Harley sat straight up. "Is that—"

"Shh!"

". . . perfect for him, Sunnie. Clarence says so, too."

"I try. It isn't always easy."

"I know."

Small talk ensued as Mrs. Dodd poured more tea.

"Yes, to answer your question," Jayda told Harley. "Sunnie Grey. The devil's wife."

"Dinner on the third, it's a formal, correct?"

"Absolutely. Two potential investors will be joining us, heavy hitters. One is a bank executive. The other, an heir to a sizable manufacturing empire. It will be a catered affair; the chef comes highly recommended. He did several party fund-raisers during the presidential election. An ex-Marine. Very patriotic, respectful young man."

"I look forward to it."

"I wish you could stay through the weekend."

"Me, too. But duty calls. Hammond has three appearances on the fourth. He wants the family with him."

"As it should be. Now, dear, for dinner. Who will you be wearing?"

Jayda shut off the tape. "The rest isn't important," she said with the wave of a dismissive hand.

Harley looked up. "Is that it?" One couldn't miss the disappointment in her voice.

"I thought there'd be more, too," Kim said. "I mean it's good to have it confirmed that the two are friends but . . ." She shrugged, looked at Jayda. "You tried, and while I understand why you didn't, I wish you could have left the recorder. Maybe we could have gotten more."

"There's more."

Harley huffed. "Then why'd you shut off the tape?"

"There's more to what you heard than what you heard," Jayda told Kim.

Kim and Harley in unison, "Huh?"

"The best part isn't what they said. It's what I'm about to drop on you. My mom owns a cleaning company, but did I tell you that my sister-in-law's brother is a caterer?"

"No, but . . . what?" Kim crossed her arms. "Are you trying to tell us he's the one they're talking about?"

Jayda nodded.

"No way," Kim said.

"Quit bullshitting," Harley added. "What are the chances that your mom cleans the guy's house and your brother-in-law cooks his food?"

"It wasn't Grey's house, and he's not my brother-in-law."

"Same difference."

"Sometimes the truth is stranger than fiction," Kim offered.

"I think we're getting help from Aunt Lucy's patron saint. Probably got tired of being locked in the glove compartment."

"You've totally lost me now." Harley sat back and crossed her arms.

"Never mind. Inside joke."

Kim sat at the table. "You know the person catering this private dinner attended by retired judge Dodd and the Greys?"

Jayda sat, too. "Yes, he's Crystal's brother. Crystal is married to my brother Daniel. They're expecting about twenty people. It says so later on the tape. The Dodds, Greys, Wards, and whoever else, at a private dinner in a secret location? Probably discussing their plans for getting Grey elected and building more jails? Sounds like a huge opportunity to get some insider information, maybe even something incriminating."

"What about the glasses?" Harley asked.

"Glasses?"

"The video eyewear," Jayda told Kim. "I flubbed that up. Thought I'd turned them on when I hadn't. I know how to work them now, though. Sorry, guys."

"Don't apologize," Harley said, slouched against the wall. "You did great considering the circumstances. I just don't see how what we learned can be used on jerk-o. It's not like we can ask your, how did they describe him, ex-Marine patriotic brother-in-law to record for us."

"Can you go?" Kim asked.

"I want to." Jayda sighed. She dropped her head in her hands.

Harley pushed off the wall and sat down beside Jayda. "What? You don't think Crystal's brother will let you help out?"

"Rick, that's his name, would probably be glad for the help. I already kinda sorta set the stage when Crystal asked why I was working with Mom. Told her what I told Aunt Lucy, extra money for the holidays. But I'm scared. The Dodds' house manager hated me on site. I think she was born suspicious, and she nearly caught me planting the device."

"Oh, God, Jayda," Harley exclaimed as Kim's hand flew to her chest.

"Exactly," Jayda said. She nodded toward Kim's hand. "Almost had a heart attack."

"But the recording said Ozarks," Harley said to Jayda. "You think the house manager will be there?"

"I don't know. But if she is there and the girl who she knows as a housekeeper is now catering food . . ."

Kim nodded. "I get it. She'll think something's up for sure."

Harley sat down. "Jayda, it sounds like we could learn a lot from this party. If you can work it out and help him, I think this is a chance you'll have to take."

"We don't want to put you in harm's way, though." Kim placed a hand on Jayda's arm. "Is this something you feel you can do?"

"I don't know, but I'll try. I've got to."

Harley looked dubious. "You really think Grey is tied up with the prison, and somehow getting money from them?"

"I think there's some type of connection," Kim said. "Dodd is a retired judge from Wyandotte, a conservative judge known for being tough on criminals. Ward is the judge who presided over most of Grey's cases, and handed down sentences to all of our guys. There was reference on the tape to impressing investors. Investors for what?"

"Prisons would be my guess," Jayda answered.

"Exactly," Kim said.

"Sounds like this is our next move, then," Harley said.

Jayda pulled out her phone. "Might as well put the wheels in motion."

"Who are you calling?" Kim asked.

"Rick. The one whose growing business has him swamped. Time to see if he can use an extra set of hands."

14

Rick Weiss immediately accepted Jayda's request to earn some holiday money, and unlike Lucy, neither he nor his sister, Crystal, were suspicious of why she'd asked. Two days after the call was made from Kim's dining room table, Jayda and Crystal showed up at Rick's house.

"You guys are lifesavers," was his greeting when he opened the door.

Jayda gave Rick a hug. "Let's see if you're still saying that when you get my bill."

Rick Weiss was a stocky, brawny ex-Marine with a mean crewcut and a slew of tattoos. While serving in Iraq, he was assigned kitchen duty and made the ironic discovery that cooking relieved his stress. After two tours overseas he retired from the military, went to culinary school, and after a few restaurant stints and time on a cruise ship came home and started his business, the Seasonal Chef. Two years later, business was booming.

They entered a fully renovated gourmet kitchen with a pot on every burner and both ovens in use. Counters were covered with dishes in various stages of preparation. Ingredients for his planned menu were everywhere.

"Oh, my God, Rick," Crystal said as she took in the chaos.

"It looks crazy, but there's a method to this madness. Let

me get you guys started on what I call phyllo fingers." He quickly took the women through four easy yet precise steps to create the spicy appetizer. "Wash your hands and let me see you do it."

The women complied.

"These are easy," Jayda said. Her first phyllo finger having passed Rick's strict inspection, she was already on number three. "How many of these are we doing?"

"A hundred."

"Seriously?" Crystal asked.

"Yes, and that's just one appetizer. I've got two more."

Jayda placed her rolled phyllo in the pan. "What type of people can host a party needing this much food?"

"People who see more money in a year than most will in a lifetime. We're living in one of the richest counties in the nation. You wouldn't believe some of the stuff I've seen."

"Like what?" Jayda asked. "People living like rock stars?"

Rick smirked as he massaged a variety of spices into the huge pan of chicken wings. "Better than that. In the area I mostly work, about a seventy-five-mile radius, people are living in a way the average person wouldn't believe. A mile away folks are hungry, starving, but behind their high-tech security fences and strapped security forces . . . they don't see a thing."

Even though on a mission to get as much information as possible, Jayda was genuinely intrigued. She knew a couple people who'd cooked for extra money or catered a party or two. But none on this level, making enough money to hire folk or own a home. "How do you get your customers?"

"Word of mouth mostly, being referred by a satisfied client to a new one. These are very exclusive communities that you can't even stick a toe into without references or background checks. Once you're in, though, it's cool. As long as you know how to act and stay in your lane."

Crystal looked at her brother askance. "What does that mean?"

"Never forget that you're the help," he replied with a wink.

Before they knew it, four hours had passed. A lot of work, but it had been a fun night. Jayda couldn't remember the last time she'd laughed so much, had as much fun cooking, or eaten food as delicious as what Rick had made. The women dragged themselves to the car around midnight.

Jayda slumped into the passenger seat. "What time are we taking off tomorrow? Those four hours felt like eight at the store."

"He wants to be on the road no later than five. He'll be doing all the driving, though, so you can sleep on the way."

"Good. Tonight was fun, though. Rick is the only Republican I like."

"He's probably the only one you know!"

They laughed. "That's true."

"I'm glad you asked Rick to work this weekend. Otherwise, I'd still be rolling phyllo fingers and shaping meatballs."

"Ha!"

"We've all been under so much pressure. Tonight was a nice change of pace. How long do you think you'll do this?"

Until I can dig up some dirt on Grey. "Just long enough to ensure a good Christmas for Ally and the kids."

"Good. Having you there makes it not feel like work."

They arrived back home to find all quiet on the Sanchez front. Jayda took a shower and after checking emails and social media, and tiptoeing in to kiss her sleeping daughter good night, she went to bed feeling optimistic, excited even. She hadn't anticipated the Fourth of July this much since holding sparklers as a kid.

The next morning, a few hours after leaving Olathe, a jolt to the GMC Yukon she rode in shook Jayda from a sound sleep. She stretched and looked around her.

"How much longer until we get there?" she asked amid a

yawn, still checking out the scenery. "Why would anyone live out here in the boonies?"

"Good morning to you, too," Rick said.

"According to the GPS it's not much farther." This from Rick's top assistant, Sam, who rode up front. Three more assistants were also riding, all to help Rick pull off an amazing dinner for an important and somewhat persnickety client.

They arrived at a private road secured by a tall iron fence. Rick pulled over to an intercom, pushed the button, and announced his name. He was given directions to the employee entrance. After a few minutes the gates slowly opened, and Rick drove inside.

"This is amazing," one of the assistants said, echoing all of their feelings. Beautifully manicured lawns and majestic horses romping behind stark white fences, bright red barns contrasted against the cloudless blue sky. Around the last curve, on top of a hill, was a sprawling architectural masterpiece.

Jayda strained her neck forward to take it all in. "Is that a hotel?"

Rick laughed. "Big enough, huh? But no, that's one residence. And see those lights blinking over there?"

"Yeah."

"That's a tower connected to the landing strip for private planes."

Like the Wards' private plane that was mentioned on the tape. "Wow."

The main road ended at the base of the hill where the house stood, a formidable masterpiece of wood, rock, and steel. Rick drove around to the side of the home and the entryway for deliveries and employees. Several workers' cars were already there. The house manager directed them to a commercial-style kitchen rivalling any restaurant or hotel's. It wasn't Miss Stiff, for which Jayda thanked God. After unloading the van, the crew settled in to a day of cooking and serving a seven-course meal. Unlike the previous night, when Rick had joked and clowned around, today he was serious, focused, acting more like the disciplined military man and less like last night's laid-back cook.

Several hours later Jayda had changed into black slacks and a white top, the Seasonal Chef uniform for service. It was a long walk from the chef's kitchen to where the guests would soon arrive and mingle amid appetizers and drinks before the formal dinner, a room where everything—the floor, ceiling, and entire back wall—was made of glass. It was both architecturally magnificent and completely terrifying. Jayda walked on tiptoe, afraid she'd fall through to the exotic plant–filled solarium below. With each trek to the kitchen, Jayda became less enthralled with her surroundings and more focused on carrying out her tasks to the perfection that Rick demanded. Serving guests at a party had sounded easy enough, but in truth? Catering was hard work. By the time seven p.m. arrived and the procession of courses had begun, Jayda knew she'd already earned every penny of her paycheck.

Rick strode to the center of the kitchen with the intensity of a sergeant on the verge of leading troops into battle. "Okay, everybody. Over here. Now!" Snapped fingers quickened movements. The six-member crew stood at attention. "Now, listen up. The second course is going out in those tureens."

He pointed to a couple of elaborately covered dishes that appeared to belong in a museum or at the very least inside a locked glass case. Crystal looked from them to her brother. "We're putting soup in those?"

"Yes, and me and Wally will carry them. Not only are they heavy but the boss had to add pressure by telling me what they were worth—enough to put a kid through college. Jayda, Barb, trail us so you can get a feel for the seating. Don't come in with us, just check us out from the hallway and memorize how we serve the soup, the order. Every other course has to flow like that. Got it?

"One last thing, especially for you, Jayda, since this is your first time serving. Our goal when we're out there is to be as un-noticeable as possible. Plates go down gently, no rattling, no noise at all. The way we rehearsed last night. The only way they should know that we've even been in the room is the next plated course in front of them. This is a big client, so I'm counting on you to be perfect, all right?"

"Gee, Rick. Thanks for relieving the pressure."

If he thought her comment funny, it didn't show. He crossed the room and nodded at Wally The men lifted the priceless art pieces and began what at that point felt like a mile-long journey to the dining room. The girls stopped a few feet from the door and watched Rick in action. Jayda positioned herself nearest the door, video glasses in place, recorder in her pocket, close enough to see Rick's movements but still remain out of view. She looked into the setting of another world. The women looked elegant, the men refined, their conversation lively, joyful, constant.

Jayda counted twenty at the table. She recognized the retired judge first. Dodd, the name Kim recognized from what she'd read online. A comment by a woman with her back to Jayda told Jayda what mattered most.

"Everybody knows that Hammond plays to win," she said, reaching a hand over to give that of the man beside her a squeeze. "He always does. And makes it look easy."

The voice on the recorder! Sunnie Grey. Which meant the man in the center facing away from them was Hammond. Jayda let out a relieved breath, even as her body hummed with nervous excitement. Once back in the kitchen, service began immediately for the next course, bacon-wrapped scallops with a spicy aioli. After turning on her video glasses, Jayda balanced a domed plate in each hand and followed Rick and the others up the stairs and down the long hall to the dining room. She silently repeated Rick's instructions to the beat of her steps. *No noise. No eye contact. Left plate down first, then the right.* Her heart pounded, ears burned as she attempted to tamp down anger, to hold her tongue, and not curse out the man who'd ruined so many lives.

They reached the table. Though her hands shook, she set down the plates with the slightest of rattles and tried to keep her eyes downcast. Once on the side facing Grey, she lifted her head enough to make sure everyone on that side of the table was caught on tape. Like the other men, Grey sported a tux. His was black, paired with a white shirt and black-and-white-striped bow tie. His countenance was smug and commanding, his body relaxed, not a care in the world. Not an ounce of discomfort for the men he'd sent to prison. Men like Daniel and Nicky, spending their holiday locked in cells. She made it out of the room before her hands began shaking almost uncontrollably.

"It's okay." Liz, one of the other waiters, said, placing an arm around Jayda as they hurried back down the hall. "It's your first time. You're doing great."

Following a palette cleanser, Jayda became mesmerized as she watched Rick's brisk movements as he sharpened a seven-inch knife, then decoratively layered thin slices of chateaubriand atop a cauliflower puree. Once again, they paraded to the dining room. She carried the plates, but in her mind all Jayda could see was that knife—newly sharpened, neatly hidden—plunged into Hammond Grey's deceitful skin. *Set the left plate down, then the right.* Behind him, her eyes were drawn to a sliver of flesh visible between his tux coat collar and his expertly cut dark hair. Her hand went to the knife, fingers curled tightly around the handle. Her arm lifted. And then, just like that. A strike, cold metal plunged into soft, warm skin. Gasps. Screams. Spurting blood everywhere.

Are you hurting, Hammond Grey? Now you know how it feels!

Exhilaration, horror, and shame of what she'd done closed off her breath.

"Jayda!" Rick grasped both arms and gave her a good shake.

The act snapped her out of wherever she'd gone. She looked around, as though in a daze. Checked her hands. No blood. What had just happened?

That's what Rick wanted to know.

"What the heck is wrong with you?"

"I'm sorry. I—"

"Save it. Sam, can you handle three plates?"

"Sure, boss."

Balancing three plates as well, Rick headed out of the kitchen. He turned back to Jayda with a face in full scowl mode. "Get it together," he barked.

Her legs were jelly and refused to hold her. She slid down the wall to the floor, taking gulps of air to clear her head. When footsteps announced the crew's return, she jumped to her feet and swiped away angry tears.

"Sorry, Rick," she said as soon as he entered. "I got overwhelmed for a minute. Won't happen again."

"It had better not," he answered without breaking stride, the next course plating taking his attention from her lapse in poise.

Rick's stern warning was all Jayda needed. She got through the remaining courses without incident. She listened carefully each time she entered the dining room, but heard nothing important. Whenever the servers had entered the room, the conversation turned general, if anything was said at all. But on the way home she learned that one goal had been accomplished. Her video glasses had worked this time, had captured everyone present. That could be a big deal or nothing at all. At least it was something. It was said that a picture was worth a thousand words. But would they be the kind to win her loved one's freedom?

When Rick dropped her and Crystal off at the Sanchez

house, Jayda closed the door to her bedroom, opened her laptop, and connected the glasses to the computer with a USB cord. Clicking on the icon for removable devices, she held her breath as the AVJ files downloaded, breathed a sigh of relief as the clear video played. After saving certain paused images as jpegs, she attached them and a saved copy of the video in an email and sent it over to Kim. Hopefully her reporter friend could put some names to the faces that they could not. Crawling into bed, she fell into the best sleep she'd had in days. Nothing to do now but wait on the outcome. Her part of this mission was done.

15

The good news was that Harley was off on the Fourth of July and was on her way to see Jesse. The bad news was that with it being a holiday, other friends and relatives of the thousand-plus inmates at Edgefield Correctional were probably off, too, and on their way to the prison. Even starting this early, an hour before visiting time began, there would probably be a long wait to get through security.

A phone call interrupted her off-key but heartfelt duet with Dan Reynolds and Imagine Dragons. She tapped her Bluetooth headset and greeted the caller.

"Bet my life on you!"

"And mine on you, babe," Jesse replied amid laughter. "Why are you up and sounding so happy this early in the morning?"

"I'm on the way to see you."

"I told you not to. You worked last night, and need your rest."

"I'll catch up on some later. I'm off today."

A pause and then, "I hate that you work so hard."

"You're worth it. Plus if the roles were reversed you'd do the same. You've proved that with all you did for my mom."

"How is she?"

Weak. Listless. Suffering peripheral neuropathy, a condition brought on by the new cancer medicine she's been prescribed. Truths, but Harley didn't voice them. She hadn't told Jesse the cancer was back. He was already depressed. "Good days and bad days," she said instead. Truth, too.

"She was doing so much better under that California doctor. And all that money my grandmother left me just sitting in the bank. Shit!"

"I know, babe. It sucks, but hang in there. My friends and I . . ."

"What?"

"Never mind."

Harley had almost slipped and told him about her and the girls' plan against Grey. All incoming and outgoing jail calls were recorded. Not a good move.

"What were you going to say, Harley? Don't leave me in the dark. I can tell something is going on."

"Don't worry, Jesse, everything's fine. I'll give you a full update when I get there. I'm only ten minutes away and hope the line isn't crazy."

"You're in Edgefield?"

"Not quite."

"Then make it twenty, Lead Foot. We don't need to add a speeding ticket to the money we're giving this state."

Jesse always made her smile, so much so that when she reached the facility she almost didn't mind waiting in the already long line, didn't get as frustrated as she normally did at the search all visitors were forced to endure and the rules they had to follow, one of which was posted on the entrance walls:

All persons entering upon these grounds are subject to routine searches of their person, property, or packages.

She'd locked her purse in the trunk and only carried her driver's license as the required ID and her debit card for the vending machines and the peanut M&Ms that Jesse loved. No personal belongings were allowed. Or gifts or money for the inmates. Or outside, home-cooked food like what she and Shannon would enjoy later. The line was long, as she'd expected on a holiday weekend. Harley took her place in line, behind a mom trying to manage twin toddlers and a hugely pregnant woman who looked to have two on the way.

About ten people away from her turn through security, she felt someone come up behind her.

"Hey, beautiful."

A smile split her face as she whipped around and saw the police officer who looked out for her and the other dancers. "Bobby! What are you doing here?"

"Visiting an inmate, same as you."

"Haven't seen you by the club lately. They change your beat?"

"I was on vacation last week. Unlike you, I take one of those every now and then."

"What'd you do?"

"Took the family to Boston. Saw the folks. Ate too much. Drank way too much."

Harley gave him a once-over. "You look different without the cop clothes."

"Ha! More handsome?" He wriggled his brow.

"Less menacing. But since you're fishing for compliments, you're still pretty cute."

"Cute?" He clutched his heart. "You wound me. Babies are cute. Doggies are cute. I'm one hundred percent full-blooded Italian, darling, who'll take menacing over cute any day."

"Okay." The line inched along. They moved with it. "Why are you looking at me like that?"

"You're what I call an anomaly."

"How so?"

"You're this gorgeous woman who looks like she should be on a runway or lounging by the pool in some swanky hotel, yet you're dancing for lowlifes and connected with criminals. Life ain't fair."

"No, it's not."

"So who are you here to see?"

"My boyfriend."

"What got your guy locked up, if you don't mind me asking?"

"Grey's campaign slogan."

"I don't get it," accompanied Bobby's puzzled expression.

"The whole oversized broom thing? My boyfriend is one of the many who got swept up." Bobby nodded. "My mom has cancer."

"Sorry to hear that."

"That's not a change of subject. The medication is very expensive. My boyfriend worked at a bank and took out what you could call an unauthorized loan to help save her life."

"He got clipped for embezzling?"

"I prefer my definition."

"Ha!"

"He totally intended to pay it back. Unfortunately an audit occurred before that happened. The bank pressed charges."

"That's bad luck."

"The bad luck is that it happened in Jones County, where Grey was the DA. Because after explaining why he did it, the bank president tried to get the charges dropped. Grey wouldn't back down."

Harley watched as the toddlers were ushered through the metal detectors and the mother's diaper bag and stroller were searched. When the officer used a straw to check a jar of baby food, Harley turned back to Bobby, disgusted.

"What about you? Here to see your boyfriend?"

Even accompanied by a flirty wink, the comment got the reaction she expected. Bobby was a man's man who ate macho for breakfast and swagger for lunch. If she found out he was mafia, it wouldn't surprise her.

"A buddy of mine who lives back east has a son in here. I promised to check on him from time to time."

Harley noted she was next in line. "It's good he has someone like you watching his back. And that I had you to talk to while waiting in line. Made it go that much faster."

"No problem, beautiful. Your guy's a lucky man."

A few minutes after being groped by a smiling security guard she wanted to punch, Harley forced a smile on her face as she walked into the large room where visits were held. She went to one of several vending machines and bought Jesse's favorite candy and chips. Several pairs of eyes followed her movements, but hers were only on Jesse's as he came through the door, escorted by a guard who removed his handcuffs and motioned him forward. Harley put down the junk food and reached out her arms for the three-second hug they were allowed at the beginning and end of each visitation. Not enough time to feel her man's arms around her. Not enough friendly human contact for these lonely men.

They sat at one of several round tables, surrounded by the chatter of other visiting families, many with kids.

Jesse gave her a slow once-over. "You look good."

"I've lost a little weight. So have you."

"Don't like dog food. Hell, even that might be better than what they serve in here."

Harley pushed the stack of vending machine goodies to his side of the table. "Eat up."

"Thanks." He reached for the M&Ms, tore open the package, and poured out a handful. "So what are you keeping from me?"

"Nothing!"

"Nothing," he mimicked in her girly tone. "Don't give me that. What didn't you say on the phone?"

Harley started to move her chair closer to Jesse but stopped at a guard's quick head shake and frown. She lowered her voice, told him what they'd learned about private prisons, and admitted that they thought Grey was involved. "He got you locked up for taking money that didn't belong to you," she whispered. "And here that asshole might be doing the very same thing!"

"I wouldn't put anything past him," Jesse said. "Which is why I want you to stay as far away from him and anything he's doing as possible. The last thing I need is for you to get in trouble. It's already hard enough in here. Something happening to you would kill me."

Harley nodded and changed the subject. She didn't want to lie to Jesse, and she didn't plan to back away from any scheme to keep Grey out of office and get Jesse out of jail. It would turn out to be a promise she couldn't have kept. Harley would soon find herself closer to the man she hated and more involved in his future than she ever dreamed.

16

Fourth of July at Kim's parents' house had been about as
strained as her marriage had felt for the last month, since
Aaron had muttered Jessica's name in his sleep. They talked,
mostly when necessary, but hadn't made love again since that
night. The Kansas City Royals' baseball game was televised,
which pretty much kept the men entertained. Kim was thankful for her mom's invited church friends who supplied a steady
stream of humorous chatter as they tidied up her mom's
kitchen and put away the food. Her brother was there, too,
with his wife and their two kids. It had been a year since she'd
seen Peter. His work as a youth counselor kept him busy in
Chicago. Still, she was surprised when, after the Royals had
won their game, he asked her to join him on a booze run.
When together, he and Aaron were usually joined at the hip.

"It's good to see you, big brother," she said once they were
buckled in and on their way. "We'll have to do better about
getting together. A year is far too long."

"I agree, which is why I wanted you to come for a visit.
Mama said if she'd seen Cedric on the street she wouldn't have
recognized him."

"I'm not sure about that," Kim said, laughing, "but I get

what she means. My nephew has shot up at least six inches and he's just, what, fourteen?"

"Be fifteen in October and yep, almost six inches. He's going to get the height I wished I'd gotten."

"I remember that growing up. You were so hoping to reach six feet."

"Yep. Still wishing for those extra three inches. Damn short grandpa."

"Ha!" She watched as Peter searched for and found a station that played adult R & B. "Looks like you and Marilyn are doing well. You two look happy."

Peter nodded. "We're good. Wish I could say the same for you and Aaron."

That the remark was unexpected showed on Kim's face. "Did he say something?"

He gave her a side-eye. "Didn't have to. You may be able to fake it with the folk, but I've known you too long and too well to get the wool pulled over my eyes."

"Like our parents haven't known me longer? Like any other couple, we have our problems, but for the most part we're fine."

Kim had said this with conviction, but that she didn't trip all over the lie surprised her.

"Oh, you think so? Because that sure isn't what Aaron said."

"Aaron talked to you about our marriage?" This surprised Kim even more.

"Not directly. He talked about Kendall, how much he misses him, how helpless, frustrated, and angry he feels about what happened to his son."

"I'm glad he's talking to somebody about it, because it sure isn't me."

"Maybe he'd talk if you'd listen."

"He'd talk if I . . . what in the heck does that mean? Is that what he told you, that I don't listen?"

"First of all, sis, you need to calm down. I'm talking to you because I love you, because Aaron is like a brother to me and part of our family."

Kim clenched her mouth shut, wanting to defend herself against God only knew what Aaron had said but determined to listen, if for no other reason than to prove that she could.

"Aaron is hurting, Kim, really hurting."

"So am I! Sorry. I'm listening."

"It's different for a man, especially when it involves a son. Not worse or more painful, just different. We're wired to protect those we love, to be the savior, the rescuer, the one who makes everything all right. To not be able to do that for Kendall has killed a part of his soul. Watching you suffer and not being able to help that, either, has taken another part."

The weight of Peter's words pushed her back in the seat. "Right after it happened he tried," she said, her voice a whisper. "Sometimes I let him console me. Most times I didn't. I tried to be strong for him, because I didn't want him to feel worse than I knew he already did."

"I know you meant well. But here's the thing about us. We need to be needed. May not be right, but it's true. When there's a problem we're supposed to solve it, and every time we can't it chips away at our manhood.

"Take your organization, for instance."

"WHIP?" There was no question in the way she'd said it that Mama Bear mode came out once again.

"Don't get mad, Kim, this isn't about the organization or even you, really. It's about Aaron, and men, and how we feel, okay? He didn't say anything about WHIP. This is coming from my perspective. Let me ask you something. Before you started the organization, did you ask him what he felt about it?"

"I told him all about WHIP, everything, from the beginning."

"You told him, but did you ask him?"

"I'm a grown woman, Peter, and this is the twenty-first cen-
tury. I don't have to ask permission from my husband to do
anything."

"No, you don't, but had you shared your intentions, you
may have learned of his desire to be involved, too. What's the
name of your organization called? Women helping innocent
people, right? Where was the room for Aaron in that?"

"Wherever he wanted it to be. I've never kept Aaron from
participating in anything we've done."

Peter looked at her, his eyes a mixture of love and sadness.
"I believe you on that, Kimberly. But it sounds like you never
asked him, either."

"Did he tell you he felt this way?"

"He didn't have to. I'm a man, sis, who picked it up from
what said, and even more importantly, from what he didn't."

The conversation shifted then, to their parents, his kids, and
Kendall's incarceration. But what her brother shared about
Aaron stayed on Kim's mind. She wrestled with how to approach
her husband about it. Her brother suggested she not do it at
all, to wait for an opportunity to present itself during a conversation about Kendall that Aaron initiated.

They talked about Kendall that night, she and Aaron, on
the way home from her parents' house. Her husband's words
were guarded at best but once in bed, when she melded her body
to his, naked and wanting, his lovemaking was tender, his touch
heartfelt. When he rolled over and went to sleep, he didn't murmur anyone's name. The intimacy was needed and appreciated.
She decided tomorrow would be soon enough to speak with
Aaron about what Peter had said. But the next morning instead of Aaron, there was another man on her mind: the re-

porter, Bryan White, and his response to the text she'd sent with the pictures Jayda had taken attached.

Where'd you get these??? Show no one else. Call me ASAP. We need to meet.

Off that Friday because of the holiday, Kim made arrangements to meet Bryan right away. Because of what he'd said, and the way that he said it, everything else, even fixing her marriage, would have to wait.

17

Kim pulled into a fast-food parking lot near where Bryan lived. He saw her, waved, and was out of his car before she'd fully pulled in. He walked over and tapped the window. She pressed the button to unlock the car door.

He slid into the front seat clutching a manila envelope. His face was flushed, his breathing uneven. He turned over the envelope and unclasped it. Shaky fingers pulled out a group of pictures, the top one a blown-up copy of the dining room shot she'd sent him with Grey front and center.

"You okay?"

He shook his head. "Not really. Give me a minute." She watched as he worked to calm his breathing. When his chest moved up and down in a more normal fashion, he turned to her. "This is some serious shit, Kim. You have no idea what you've stumbled into—"

"Tell me!"

"You have photographed what I believe to be the inner circle to the moneymakers of Edgefield Correctional and quite possibly all the other prisons owned by the Guardian Group. The fucking 'our gang' of prison profiteers!" He continued, his voice low and conspiratorial. "I didn't tell you before, but what I'm involved in goes beyond writing a series of articles for a newspaper."

"How far beyond it?"

"I'm working with a private investigator who's been hired to look into the private prisons built in Kansas, Nebraska, and Iowa within the last ten years. It's believed there is a direct correlation between those prisons, mostly owned by the Guardian Group, and the continual uptick in arrests and convictions in those states, and, as a by-product, Hartwell's bank account."

"Who hired the PI, Myers?"

"He won't tell me, and quite frankly, I don't care. Knowing that these assholes will finally be exposed was enough to deal me in."

Kim studied Bryan's intense expression. "You know why I'm so passionate about this. I've got an innocent son behind bars. What's your story?"

"I'm allergic to injustice. Hate to see the big dogs eating up the little ones with no consequence. Maybe it's the way I was raised, with parents who always pointed out situations of unfairness or bias. It's just flat-out wrong, and when I found out how much money was being made off of families being destroyed . . ." The sentence died as he looked out the window. "Trying to fix the problem is just the right thing to do."

He turned back to face her. "Kim, you have to swear that what is discussed here goes no further than this car."

"No can do."

"There's been an ongoing—wait, what?"

"I can't promise not to tell anyone else. Others have a right to know, especially the person who took that picture. She took a big risk to do it."

"Who is she?"

"A member of WHIP."

"Whatever risk she took is nothing compared to what will happen when my series gets published and, hopefully, this picture along with it. The men shown here and probably some who are not will be out to have the heads of whoever exposed them. It will be hunting season, and anyone who can be attached to this will be fair game."

"If it's so dangerous, why do the series at all?"

"Because it's even more dangerous for what's happening to not be exposed. The more people who know I'm connected to this story, the more eyes will be watching, should anything happen to me as a result of printing it. I can't be naïve and think these guys are beyond murder."

"I agree that there seems to be no moral compass in that group, but going from putting people in prison to killing them is a pretty big leap."

"You think so? Look at all they've been willing to do so far. Change laws so that it's easier to convict people. Push through legislation to build more jails and then award contracts to those private companies like the Guardian Group, who guarantee a ninety-percent occupancy rate. How can you guarantee crime? By having people in place who, if necessary, can create a crime where none exists.

"As a reporter, I have a high profile. If I meet violence after the article is published, the public will automatically look at the subjects as suspects. But ordinary citizens like you and the other WHIP members? They can make your lives a living hell."

"Everything you've just said is true. With my son locked away, I'm already living there."

"At least you're still living. People have lost their lives for much less money."

"I know Grey is ruthless, but I can't imagine him killing anyone."

"He wouldn't kill you. He'd just order the hit." Kim rolled her eyes and made a sound of disgust. "This picture changes everything, Kim. The men around this table represent every aspect of the criminal justice system in the state of Kansas. Careers could be ruined. Criminal charges might follow. The stakes are high, life-or-death high. I want you and anyone else you decide to involve to be fully aware of the shark-filled waters in which you're about to swim. Private prisons are big business."

"I know. You told me. Seventy billion a year."

Bryan nodded. "As the CEO for the Guardian Group, Hartwell made over five million dollars in salary and bonuses last year alone."

"That's crazy. What's the average salary for his equivalent in federal prisons?"

"About three to four hundred thousand."

Bryan positioned the eight-by-ten glossy so that Kim could see it and began identifying those in the picture. "This is Hartwell, right here. That's his wife and this,"—he jabbed a finger at a portly man with a buzz cut and beard—"this guy heads up the Jones County sheriff's department and works closely with the chief of police. I believe this is the chief but it's kind of hard to tell from the back of his head. But this is the cog that makes the whole wheel roll." Bryan continued pointing, used his index finger and tapped the side profile of the man at the other end of the table.

"Sitting next to Tom Ward."

"Oh, so you recognized him, huh?"

Kim nodded. "Unfortunately. He presided over my son's case. Ward, Grey, and Clarence Dodd are the only faces I recognized."

"Dodd retired from Wyandotte County's judicial system after forty or so years on the bench. But not before he'd increased the prison population by almost thirty-five percent. Ward presided over almost every Jones County criminal case involving drugs or weapons, which is a high percentage of crimes done in this county and the state. Again, a number that tripled after Grey became DA. But this is the puppet master."

Bryan slid his finger to point out the man at the head of the table. "Thaddeus Stowe, one of the oldest and longest running U.S. congressmen and Grey's close friend and mentor; he has headed up the judiciary committee since the Reagan era, helped to rally enough support to the most conservative Supreme Court justices ever confirmed, and has been a part of some of the most sweeping changes in penal law in this country's history. You'd be better off inviting the Klan over for dinner before fixing a steak for this guy."

Kim took the picture from Bryan. She studied the faces. "I get that they all have roles within the judicial system, but how does it work? And the money? Where does it come from?"

"You, my dear taxpayer."

Kim thought she'd be sick.

"Basically, it goes like this. A campaign is announced waging war on crime, drugs, terrorism, pick your poison. The theme usually changes with each decade, but the results are the same. A larger prison population. In the Nixon era it was the war on drugs. Addiction went from being a medical situation to a criminal one. Reagan continued it in the eighties during the crack epidemic with 'just say no' and mandatory minimums. Bill Clinton upped the stakes in the nineties with the three strikes law and brought a new term, the 'super predator,' into the narrative, most often depicted as a crazed, unkempt-looking Black guy in handcuffs.

"Americans get scared. That's where people like Stowe come in. He's authored some of the more egregious laws passed, under the guise of keeping America safe. The truth of the matter is that since the nineties crime has been on a steady decline. But that stat doesn't line pockets. That's why the Dodds, Greys, and Wards of the world have to get creative to make sure the jail cells stay filled."

Kim was quiet a long moment. "That just gave me chills."

"It should." Bryan flipped to the next picture and held it out to Kim. "This hotel. Where is this?"

"The Ozarks."

"Where in the Ozarks?"

"I don't know. It's where the party was held that my friend helped cater."

"She doesn't know who owns it?"

"I don't know."

Bryan studied the pictures. "Looks like a pretty extravagant place. This friend who took the pictures. We need her help."

"I thought you said that we shouldn't get her involved."

"She became involved the moment she snapped these pictures. We need to find this exact address and determine who owns it. This photo is proof of the type of wealth being enjoyed by people who shouldn't be able to afford such luxury."

"Okay, I'll ask her."

"Do you believe you can trust her?"

"Absolutely."

"Then tell her you're asking because the information might help your organization and the people you're trying to free. Do not tell her about the Edgefield investigation. If word of it leaks, it could ruin years of work. Please. I have to have your word on that."

"She knows about the upcoming prison articles. But I won't mention the investigation."

"Thanks." Bryan looked at his watch. "Look, I gotta go."

"Yeah, me too."

"Get that information." He opened the door. "Oh, and get a burner phone. Matter of fact, from now on anything you say about this situation, including what has to do with your organization, should probably be done that way."

"A burner phone?"

Bryan chuckled. "Throwaway. Temporary. One that doesn't require a contract or ID. You can pick them up anywhere, any convenience or super store. Use cash, not a debit or credit card. Go to the library and set up a fake email using a name that can in no way be tied to you."

"Why?"

"So our interactions can't be traced."

"Are you sure that's necessary?"

"Positive. Don't worry, it's easy. The instructions are on the back of the package."

"How do you know so much about this? Are you sure you're a reporter and not a criminal?"

"My record is as white as I am. But I'm hooked on ID, the Investigation Discovery channel." He got out of the car, then stuck his head back in. "You need to start thinking like an investigator, too. Because whether you know it or not, or like it or not, you are now a part of a major investigation with huge political and criminal implications. Pay attention to who's around you. Watch your back."

Kim laughed off his serious expression as she started the car. Had she foreseen the chain of events releasing those pictures would cause, she would not have considered his parting words a laughing matter at all.

18

Since she had to go to the library to set up her burner phone (she felt all cool and hip using Bryan's slang), Kim texted Harley and Jayda to meet her there. It was also a location where Kim felt there wouldn't be too many cameras. Just in case, let's say, someone had slipped a listening device shaped like an ice cube into the soda Bryan held when he got in her car, placing Grey and his bogeymen on her trail. Not that she was paranoid much. Or frightened and excited at the same time. She was all of that and still cautiously optimistic that in the game of dirty politics her team might score.

While waiting for the girls to arrive, Kim set up her fake email. Tapping her nails against the keyboard, she struggled to do as Bryan suggested and come up with one that was innocuous, forgettable, that wouldn't draw attention to her or WHIP. Remembering her experience while searching Jessica's name, Kim went to the search engine, looked up the most common name in America, and then set up an email for SSmith1296@Zmail.com. She'd been warned against it, but there was one small, personal connection. Kendall was born in 1996. Hopefully replacing the nine with a two would throw any would-be greyhounds off her scent. That done, she went into the room she'd reserved, plugged in the burner phone's charger, then wandered around the front of the library. Moments later, a voice cut through the quiet.

"A library? What the hell?!"

Kim shushed a frazzled Harley as the worker behind the circulation desk shot them a warning look. Jayda was with her and wore the same question on her face.

Harley lowered her voice to a whisper. "Why are we here?"

"Come on. I'll explain everything." Kim motioned them to follow and led the way to the study room she'd reserved. "I'm sure you have questions," she began as soon as they re-entered the meeting room.

"Damn right," Harley huffed, whipping her thick blond mane behind her before sitting down. "Like why you'd suggest a place that doesn't serve alcohol, knowing that any news about Grey should come with a drink."

"This is a rather weird choice," Jayda agreed, with a look around. She joined Harley at the table. "Were all the restaurants booked? No tables at McDonalds?"

"Very funny." Kim took an oversize bag off a chair and set it on the table before she too sat down. "But what I'm about to share with you is as serious as a prison sentence."

Harley sat up. "That serious, huh?"

"Yes." Kim looked from Harley to Jayda. "Turns out the pictures you took at the Ozarks are game changers."

"Really? Cool!"

"Jayda, I know I told you about it, but I'm not sure about you, Harley."

"What?"

"About the reporter Bryan White and the series he's doing."

"About the stuff in that link I texted you last week," Jayda interjected.

Kim frowned slightly. "That's the last time you'll be doing

that. Hold on." She got up and walked over to shut the door. "I sent the picture to Bryan to see if he could identify who all was at the table."

"Who is it?" Harley asked.

"A virtual who's who of the Kansas judicial system and one of the top criminal policymakers on Capitol Hill. Working together, they're able to fill up the county prisons and make a bunch of money doing it."

"So he is making money off of locking folk up, just as we suspected." Harley sat back with a sound of disgust. "What an ass."

Jayda looked at Kim. "How is this a game changer? That's what I want to know."

"Bryan is doing a series on the private prison system, implying that the sizable profits they generate are why the incarceration rate soared while Grey was the Jones County district attorney and cases were heard in Ward's court."

"How can he prove it?"

"I'm not sure. But when the first installment of the series comes out, that picture will be printed alongside it."

"He can't do that!"

Kim looked at Jayda. "Why not?"

"They'll know the picture came from someone who was there that day."

Harley shrugged. "So what?"

"Were you the only workers there?" Kim asked.

Jayda slowly shook her head. "No, we weren't. There were people in and out for hours before the party. But during the party, and with access to the dining room, I'm pretty sure that was just us, the people helping Rick cater the event. If this brought on a scandal and Rick got pulled into it and then found out I was the one who took the pic?" She looked from Kim to Harley. "Scary thought, guys."

"I see what you mean." Kim eyed Jayda thoughtfully. "We wouldn't want you to get in trouble for this."

"Any more trouble than she's in already?" Harley asked. "With Ally's father and uncle thrown in jail by that jerk? Short of rolling video, there's no way they could ever prove who took the picture. If you got questioned, just take a page out of Grey's book and lie, lie, lie."

Kim agreed. "Or deny. How can they prove otherwise? How could you have been taking pictures while serving salad, or whatever the heck they ate?"

"I don't know, guys."

"Hey, I've got an idea."

Jayda looked at Harley. "I'm all ears."

"Why not send the pic over to what's his name, Jack Myers's office?"

"Grey's opponent." Kim's eyes lit up. "Now there's an idea. He'd be busy pointing fingers at Myers and trying to find a connection in his camp to how the pic got taken and leaked."

"I think involving Myers is genius," Kim said. "Send the picture to his office anonymously. Maybe even to a few different sources. Muddy the waters."

"But at the end of the day the fact will still remain that whoever took the picture was someone in his house." Jayda stood and paced the room. After a few seconds she spun around and faced the table. "To hell with it. I don't care. If this will help get Grey out of the running for senator and our guys out of jail, let's roll the dice and let the chips fall where they may."

"Aren't those two different games?" Harley asked, an obvious attempt to lessen a stressful conversation.

"Bryan made sure I understood that this is no game at all." Kim relayed what he'd told her. "From now on everything involving our guys needs to happen on these." She reached for the bag on the table.

"I bought one for each of you." She set down her phone, pulled out two identical ones from a plastic bag and set them on the table between them.

Harley picked up the nearest one. "A burner phone?"

"Oh, you know about them."

"They're hardly new," Harley replied with a chuckle.

Jayda picked up the other one. "Temporary phones have been around for years."

"I'd never heard of them referred to as burners."

"Wow, this is cool," Harley said. "I feel all *CSI* inside."

"I was thinking *Law and Disorder*," Kim replied.

Harley diddled with her phone. "So when do we send the pic to Myers and burn Grey's broom?"

"I think I should run this by Bryan first to make sure I don't indirectly sabotage his series. Which reminds me. Jayda, where was this party?"

"The Ozarks. I told you, remember?"

"I know, but where exactly?"

"Rick never shared the address, never needed to. Some lavish mansion is all I know, behind a locked and guarded tall steel fence."

"In the Ozarks?" Harley asked. "Doesn't sound like a house like that would be too hard to find."

"More like impossible. It's tucked into a valley far away from the main road, behind tall maple, dogwood, and red oak trees. You can't see it from any part of the road, would go right past it unless you know it's there.

"You wouldn't believe the display of wealth. The women were draped in silk and mink and huge diamonds and other semi-precious jewels. I swear they could have fit right in to a *Housewives* taping. The men all wore tuxes. And the house? I can't even begin to describe how beautiful it was. One of the rooms even had a glass floor!"

"That's why Bryan wants the address," Kim said, her voice lowered to a whisper. "To prove that those guys are living beyond their means. Do you think you can get it?"

"I can try."

"The sooner the better," Kim said.

Harley looked at her watch. "I agree. The faster we move, the faster our guys come home and the faster I can quit working at Bottoms and showing mine."

Jayda was nervous as she pulled up in front of Rick's house. Although he was Crystal's brother, the two didn't interact much outside his catering business. When she'd called earlier and asked to come over, the conversation was awkward. He wanted to know why. *Because I can't talk to you on my cell phone, and if I called you from my burner you'd be even more suspicious?* Knowing the true reason wasn't one she could share, she joked and said simply, "I want to see what you're cooking."

To her relief Rick was indeed in the kitchen. He was preparing for a wedding involving seventy-five guests.

After a few minutes of casual conversation he asked, "Did you just come here to chitchat or are you here to work?"

Soon Jayda was elbow deep in a tub of shrimp: clean, devein, butterfly, repeat. Over, and again.

"Feels like old times," she said after more time and chitchat had gone by. "Except instead of turkey it's shrimp."

"I personally prefer turkey," Rick said, his muscles bulging as he easily lifted a huge pot of rice and placed it on a cooling rack.

"I don't see why," Jayda teased. "I'm the one peeling all these shrimp. Hey, Rick. Have you been back there?"

"Back where?"

"That mansion in the Ozarks."

"No, haven't had the pleasure."

"That place was insane! I can't believe people really live like that. Even celebrity houses I've seen on television aren't that grandiose. It was in Missouri, right?"

"Yep."

"What highway were we on?"

Rick looked over his shoulder at her, his expression curious. "Why all the questions?"

"Because I want to know."

"Don't worry about it. You can't just show up there. You have to be invited."

"Ha ha. Like I'd try. Come on, Rick. Even knowing the highway, there's no way I could find that house. You can't even see it from the road."

"Yeah, that's true." They worked a short while in silence. "It's Fifty-four Highway," Rick said. "Lake of the Ozarks, Missouri."

"Oh, right. I do remember a lake. It was really pretty down there."

Jayda called her mom. After Anna agreed to watch Alejandra, Jayda stayed and helped Rick for another four hours and along with a general mansion location picked up an unexpected fifty bucks. Once in her car, she called Kim on the burner phone. No one answered. Before she could finish leaving a message, Kim called her back.

"Is this Jayda or Harley?"

"Jayda."

"Boy, I sure had an awkward moment. Imagine trying to tell the husband you think might be cheating why you have an extra phone."

"Aaron's cheating?"

"Freudian slip."

"I certainly hope so. What did you do?"

"Told him it belonged to a co-worker who'd left it in my car when we went to lunch. One thing's for sure. I'd be a horrible participant in a real affair. I'm not good at lying at all."

"Sorry about that."

"It's okay. I put the phone on vibrate."

"Good idea. Lock in my number, too."

"Okay. What's up?"

"I talked to Rick."

"Did you get the address?"

"Rick wouldn't give me the exact address. But he did say it was off of Fifty-four Highway."

"Sounds like that's close to Branson, Missouri. Anyways, thanks for the info."

"You're welcome. Hope it helps."

Back in her bedroom, Jayda opened her jewelry case and pulled out the silver-and-lapis rosary she'd received from her grandmother Alma as one of several *quinceañera* gifts. She ran her fingers over the cool semi-precious stones, traced the silver crucifix, and closed her eyes. She hadn't called on saints this much since graduating Catholic school, but she needed their protection. Because if Rick got pegged for that pic being leaked and he found out she did it? There'd be hell to pay.

19

All was quiet on "Operation Grey" for the next six weeks. The protests continued at various campaign rallies, but the *Edgefield Eagle* article had done what was intended, painted the women as no more than hurting moms with misplaced anger. Disheartened and emotionally depleted, Kim cancelled the August WHIP meeting and encouraged the women to do what she'd planned: focus on the family directly around them.

That's what Kim intended. That's not what happened. The week after meeting with Bryan, Kim scored a big account at work, a new company that wanted to launch in three short months. As thrilled as she was to get a large client, it had required long hours at work, including the past two weekends. Outside of conversations regarding Kendall and a little about work, she and Aaron continued to find little to talk about. Still, a mutual unspoken but obvious truce kept the atmosphere civil, even cordial at times. Most of their communicating happened in the bedroom, with their bodies doing the talking. Enjoying semi-regular sex again was a stress reliever, too.

Between caring for her mother, visits to Jesse, and extra work shifts, Harley's plate was full. Shannon's health didn't improve all that much, but the good news was that it didn't get worse, either. She and Jesse had discussed a prison marriage so that she could access the $20,000 he'd inherited through his grandmother's will. She'd been more excited about conjugal visits, until she learned that Kansas was not one of the six lucky states in America that allowed married inmates extended, private family visits. Then he learned that marriage licenses were granted solely at the discretion of the warden, and when and if approved included a ceremonial "fee" of five thousand dollars.

"For what, the concrete we'd stand on?" Harley had questioned, indignant. "The marriage license is less than one hundred bucks!"

Included in the fee was a six-month mandatory marriage counseling clause. Jesse knew for a fact that the prison chaplain was divorced, which made him question what kind of advice he could give them. Jesse was still willing to go through with it, though, just to get access to the money for Shannon. But Harley didn't have the five thousand, and she didn't know if Shannon had six months.

Surprising everyone including herself, Jayda continued her side hustles with Great Housekeeping and the Seasonal Chef, alternating the companies each weekend while maintaining her forty-hour week regular job as a pharmaceutical technician at CVS. The extra work kept her hands busy, built greater camaraderie with her sister-in-law Crystal, and kept her mind off Nicky and the prison gangs he'd mentioned in a previous call, the ones pressuring him and Daniel to join them. Plus she kept hoping a personal reference would land Great Housekeeping in the Grey household. The Dodds had signed an ongoing contract. That's where Anna and Lucy were at this very moment, but a spiking fever had forced Jayda to take the day off and see after her daughter.

She was just returning from a visit to Urgent Care when the message indicator dinged on her phone. She tapped the icon. **Check your phone.** It took her checking her email twice and texts three times to realize which phone Kim meant. She hadn't thought about the burner phone Kim had given her since the day she'd returned home from the library and buried it in her undies drawer. She carried Ally from the car to the family room, and after getting her settled in front of the television with a snack and her favorite video, Jayda went upstairs to the bedroom where the phone lay hidden beneath a pile of "period panties." She turned on the phone and clicked the message icon. There were three missed phone calls and two messages, all from Kim. The last one sent contained a website link that when clicked opened directly to the picture she took. The picture was crystal clear, almost in 3-D. Its clarity snatched her breath. She scrolled down and devoured the article's first paragraph:

Senatorial Candidate, Others Implicated in Kansas Prison-For-Profit Scheme

Are lawmakers and those who enforce them profiting from the criminals who break those laws? This week CFTG, Citizens For Transparency in Government, released a report with damning allegations involving several past and present members of the Kansas judicial system, including former Jones County district attorney Hammond Grey, now a candidate for the U.S. Senate. According to organization founder and president Don Matthews, these findings cap a two-year investigation into the Jones County police force, attorneys, judges and employees of what some refer to as the jewel of Jones County, the Edgefield Correctional Facility. "The players in this profitable scheme have consistently denied any wrongdoing," Matthews said during a recent interview. "Yet we believe that the rise in arrests, convictions and long jail terms issued in Jones County is in direct correlation to the approval for and building of the Edgefield Correctional Facility. We've long suspected there was a well-organized plan involving several Jones County officials and law enforcement to profit from this facility and the recently taken photo during a covert meeting in a secret location, a lavish ten-thousand-square-foot mansion hidden deep in the Missouri Ozarks, seems to bear this out."

Holy crap! Jayda didn't need to read more to know that if it hadn't happened already the feces was about to hit the proverbial fan. She scrolled to the two-name contact list and tapped Kim's burner cell phone number and placed the call on speaker. The call was picked up halfway through the first ring.

"Did you read it?"

Jayda imagined Kim's shiny brown eyes matched the excitement in her voice. "Yes, and I'm scared half to death."

"Why, because of the picture? Don't worry about that!"

"I can't help but worry about it. You don't know Rick, and if you did, you'd know why it isn't a good thing to make him angry."

"Just remember if he brings it up, deny, deny, deny. Until then, focus on the good news. Everybody is talking about this story. Especially the fact that one of the guys in the picture, Thaddeus Stowe, is the chairman of the subcommittee on crime, terrorism, homeland security, and investigations. The very committee who—hold on, let me find where it is in the article—sets up the rules regarding the Federal Criminal Code, drug enforcement, sentencing, parole and pardons, internal and homeland security, Federal Rules of Criminal Procedure, prisons, criminal law enforcement, and other appropriate matters as referred by the chairman, and relevant oversight. Think there might be a small conflict of interest that he's breaking bread with the CEO of the largest private prison corporation in America? The reporters are all over him, but so far his response has been 'no comment.'"

Jayda couldn't miss the excitement in Kim's voice but was having trouble finding hers . . . either the excitement or voice.

"So you probably haven't seen the latest commercial for Myers, either."

"You sent the picture to his office, too?"

"No, but only because Bryan asked me not to. Either he leaked the pic to them or they've got a fast and talented production team. Either way, the commercial cites some of the facts in the article and asks, 'Do you want a criminal tackling crime?' It's fantastic! We'll see what happens to Grey's numbers now."

"When was this article released?"

"Yesterday morning. I've been trying to reach you since then, and finally thought to leave the message on your phone to check your phone!" Kim laughed at her own joke. "I haven't been this happy since Kendall received a full-ride scholarship."

Jayda pushed aside her angst and allowed the excitement she heard in Kim's voice to infect her.

"What do you think will happen now that the word is out?"

"I don't know, but I think the truth coming out brings our guys one step closer to freedom. I've been contacted by several news organizations and Jack Myers's office to get my reaction to the article."

"And?"

"I reiterated what I've said from the beginning. That my son is one of several in Edgefield and other Kansas jails for crimes they did not commit, or are serving sentences in these jails that are longer than normally handed down. I added that I looked forward to the whole story coming to light and to seeing the real criminals put behind bars."

"Whoa, girl. You didn't hold back!"

"I've held back for way too long."

"Does Harley know?"

"Yep. We talked last night."

"What do we do now?"

"Cross our fingers and hope that Grey drops out of the Senate race, and that the federal investigation leads to the cases conducted by him being overturned. This couldn't have happened without you, Jayda. Getting those pictures was everything; proof that these guys were in cahoots all along. You rock, girlfriend. Next time we meet, drinks are on me!"

The phone call ended, but the smile the conversation had finally elicited stayed on Jayda's face. Kim's joy had been contagious. She jumped off the bed, did a little dance in celebration. Her heart burst with the need to share the good news. But on this last Saturday in August, except for her and Alejandra, the house was empty. Everyone was out working or visiting friends. Crystal was over at Rick's, helping him prepare for a Labor Day party. She'd taken the girls with her while her older son Rafael was gone, too. Jayda went back downstairs, picked her daughter off the floor from where she watched *Frozen* for the thousandth time, and hugged her tight as they twirled around the room.

"Mommy!" Ally cried, even as she laughed when Jayda's fingers tickled her tummy. "Put me down, Mommy. I want to watch *Frozen*!"

"And Mommy wants to hug you!" Jayda rained kisses over her daughter's face.

"Why, Mommy?"

"Because Mommy's happy."

"But why?"

Because your father may be coming home soon. She thought this but dared not voice it aloud. Not only because to do so would lead to Alejandra asking where he was nonstop, but because she didn't want to jinx the possibility that a little under two years from when it began, the family nightmare might be over.

20

A few hours later, loud voices jolted Jayda awake. She eased off the couch, careful not to awaken her daughter, who slept beside her, but fast enough to end the ruckus that was headed upstairs. She placed her daughter on a blanket, then ran to meet Crystal and the nieces.

"Shh! Quiet, guys! I don't want you to wake up Ally."

Crystal looked up in surprise. "Sorry about that! I didn't see the van outside and thought no one was home."

"Ally had a fever."

"She okay?"

"Yes. Doctor said it was some kind of infection. He prescribed antibiotics and told me she should be better in forty-eight to seventy-two hours. If not, I'll take her back." She turned to Crystal's daughters as they headed back up the stairs. "Sorry, girls, for shushing you like that. I'm getting ready to take her to the bedroom so you guys can watch television."

Crystal walked with Jayda and quietly asked, "You coming back down?"

"Maybe later. I'm giving Mom a break and making chicken enchiladas."

"What put you in the cooking mood? You normally only do that when getting paid."

"Just felt like doing something for the family."

"Yum. Can't wait."

"You won't have to, since you're going to help me make them."

Jayda took Ally to her bedroom and returned to the kitchen, engaging in small talk with her sis-in-law. After dicing a rotisserie chicken, Crystal made a simple salad while Jayda assembled the cheesy casserole. Once done, they grabbed sodas and sat at the breakfast nook.

"What's going on with you?"

"I told you. Giving Mom a break."

"No, not the cooking. You. You look calmer today, happy."

"I am happy."

"What? You hear from Nicky?"

"Not yet. I'm hoping to, though. Where's Rafael?"

"Soccer practice."

"What?" Jayda dragged out the word in disbelief.

"I know. It was actually Nicky's idea; said the boy had too much spare time on his hands. Needed a way to expend all that energy." Crystal took a swig of soda, casually swinging the leg crossed over her knee. "I think it's going to be good for him. Help him to be a part of a different kind of gang, one that wears uniforms, plays with balls, and is called a team."

"I agree. I think it's great. I didn't even know they had soccer here. But how can they play? It gets so hot in August."

"At a place called All-American Indoor Sports. Nicky found out about it from one of his friends who has a son in a league. They live on the other side of town, but the dad offered to give Rafael a ride to practices, the games too if necessary. They're on Saturday, so I plan to be there cheering my boy on."

"Heck, the whole family will go. Sounds like fun."

Crystal heard a sizzle from the oven and got up to check on the casserole.

"It's probably cheese piping over," Jayda said. "I put a ton of it on there."

Crystal opened the oven. "Yeah, that's it. I'll just put a pan beneath it."

While she was doing that, her cell phone rang.

Jayda looked at the screen. Her heart skipped a beat. "Want me to get it? It's Rick."

"Sure. Put it on speaker."

Hail Mary, full of grace . . . "Hey, Rick!"

"Jayda, is Crystal there?"

"Yes, she's right here. You're on speaker. You sound upset."

"Upset doesn't begin to describe how I'm feeling right now. I'm pissed off to the fucking nth degree! Which one of y'all did it?"

Crystal frowned. "Did what?"

"Don't give me that innocent act like you don't know what I'm talking about. Which one of you took the picture?"

Crystal looked at Jayda. "Do you know what he's talking about?"

Jayda slowly shook her head. *Deny, deny, deny.*

"What picture?" Crystal asked Rick.

"The picture from the dinner we catered on the Fourth. The picture that's all over the got-damn news. The picture that just got my ass chewed out. The picture that may cause me to lose a ton of customers, maybe even to be forced out of business!"

Crystal visibly shrank away from her brother's bellowing accusation. "Rick, I swear I don't know what you're talking about."

"It was you, Jayda, wasn't it?"

Jayda swallowed, tried to speak. Hard to do with one's heart in their throat. She couldn't meet Crystal's confused eyes, either.

"Jayda!"

"I'm right here, dude. Dang, calm down. I didn't take any pictures down there."

"Yes, you did. You took the one of the house, remember? Before I told you to delete it and put your phone away."

"And I did."

"So you're telling me that you didn't take any pictures when we were inside? You didn't take the picture that was clearly snapped the night we were there and served them dinner?"

"No," Jayda managed from a mouth gone dry.

"Me neither," Crystal said, concerned, even as questioning eyes observed Jayda's nervousness.

"You sure about that, Jayda?" Rick's accusatory tone cut through the room like a knife.

No. "Yes!"

"Then what was with all the questions when you stopped by the other night? Asking about the house, how to get there? Acting like you were interested in taking your family to the Ozarks when you were obviously snooping for some other reason."

Crystal stared openly at Jayda now. "You didn't tell me you went to Rick's house last week."

"She probably didn't want you to know what she was up to, what reporter or whoever she was working with to try and blackmail some politician."

Jayda grew indignant. "What? I'm not working with a reporter and I'm not trying to blackmail anybody. I wouldn't know the first thing about doing something like that."

That much was true.

"Well, somebody knows something, because I just got a call from my client's attorney, who accused me of violating the privacy and confidentiality agreement I signed by taking pictures and talking to the press. I just read the article. Saw the picture, too."

"What article?" Even though Rick had made the statement, Crystal's question was directed at Jayda.

"Are you talking about the article on private prisons and how much money they make?" Jayda asked.

"So you do know what picture I'm talking about!"

"I just figured it out since you mentioned our conversation about the Ozarks the other night." Crystal's eyes now looked as accusatory as her brother's voice sounded. Jayda jumped up from the table, partly for show, partly from nerves, but mostly to turn her away from her sis-in-law just in case a chunk of guilty grease was smeared on her face.

"So what! I asked about a stupid party. There's a long way from asking a simple question to taking pictures for a story, like I'm paparazzi or some shit. There were tons of people there that day. Not just us. Anybody could have taken that picture. Maybe even someone *sitting* at the table is playing foul. We don't know!"

Rick's voice became low, ominous. "I'll tell you what I do know. I've got Hartwell's attorney breathing down my neck and demanding I find out who took that picture, because no matter what you two say, he believes it was someone on the catering team, and from the angle of the picture, I can see why. This is a serious matter, guys. These men are not to be fucked with, not even by someone who's done two tours in the Middle East. Matter of fact, as someone who's ex-military, a Marine, and a damn proud American, it's a blemish on my character and a blotch on my reputation for it to even be assumed I'd do anything like this, anything that could be viewed as unpatriotic."

Jayda rolled her eyes. "What's unpatriotic about talking to a reporter? Isn't that considered freedom of speech?"

"So you did talk to them!" Rick yelled.

"No!" Jayda yelled back, no longer having to pretend to be angry. "I just don't understand how you could be accused of not being patriotic."

"Read the article and you'll know why. And get this. If I find out you had anything to do with this information getting out there, I will call this attorney back and give him your address. You too, Crystal. Because anybody who would break the law or make it look like I violated an agreement is no sister of mine."

The call ended abruptly, bringing a tense silence into the kitchen. The sound of a light sizzle sounded as more cheese dropped into the water-filled pan beneath the casserole dish.

"Did you do it?" Crystal asked her.

Jayda looked at her with a sullen expression. "I'm not even going to answer that question."

She'd better not, Jayda admitted to herself while leaving the room. If she did, the feces that had just hit the fan might blow back and smack her dead in the face. When she reached her bedroom, she closed the door, locked it, pulled her phone from in between the period panties and shot off a text.

Rick knows about the picture. He thinks I did it. What now?

As she pondered the possible repercussions from the article's release, Jayda felt that was a question best left unanswered. Now she had more than Nicky, her brother Daniel, prison gangs, and a sick daughter to worry about. Now she feared Rick and hoped he was still on the meds for his PTSD. Because she'd just become his enemy. The kind he'd been trained to kill.

21

They'd arrived separately, surreptitiously, a select group of men who were each powerful in their own right but who together had enough power to steer the wheel of justice in the state of Kansas and beyond, and had for many years. One by one some of the same folk who had broken bread together on the Fourth of July made their way to Clarence Dodd's hunting cabin just shy of the Oklahoma border. They came in nondescript cars rented by third parties, with fixed odometers and disabled tracking devices. On circuitous routes, too, to shake anyone who might be on their trail. With the week's firestorm of controversy brought about by the damning article, and the bright media light shining on all of the players involved, nothing, especially being seen together, was left up to chance.

Worries ended when they reached the judge's land. Dodd country. Over seven hundred heavily wooded, game-filled acres with a river running through the south end and a man-made lake up north. Secluded. Hard to find unless you knew where to look. The only ones who did were the folk the Dodds invited. The ones who didn't weren't likely to learn. Folks in this part of Kansas went back generations. A suspicious lot who kept to themselves, didn't take to strangers, and posted signs warning trespassers they'd be shot on sight. No smiley face. For the most part, they meant it.

Modest by comparison to Hartwell's Ozarks spread, the split-level log cabin–style home was just over twenty-five hundred square feet with an outdoor Jacuzzi and a shower to wash blood off game. Several hunting trophies adorned the walls—deer heads, an unfortunate elk, a turkey whose majestic wings were forever spread across the far end of the living room. A sandwich station had been set up in the dining room. So far no one had touched it. Everyone had, however, made good use of Dodd's top-shelf bar on their way to the den.

"So you think Jack was behind the article?" Clarence peered at Grey from under bushy eyelashes as he relit his cigar.

"Of course. Some of what's written are the same talking points being used on the campaign trail."

"Needless to say with the bill Ward is trying to get passed through the Senate right now, this is exactly the kind of attention we don't need."

Jim Hartwell spoke of the Accountability Act, a bill that would make those who committed felonies susceptible to the same kind of tracking as sex offenders by using a similar registry process.

"That and Obama's asinine move to close private prisons on the federal level, along with Operation Innocent's latest biased report and the ACLU constantly on our ass is definitely bad for business."

"Don't worry about that, Jim," Clarence said. "Now that we're back in control of the White House, every low-class move that asshole made will be repealed."

Geoffrey Sullivan, Grey's high-powered attorney, who had called Rick Weiss on their behalf, spoke for the first time. "It doesn't add up."

"What doesn't?" Grey asked.

"Any of it. Myers's involvement. The facts in the article.

The photo. Especially that. Rick Weiss was carefully vetted. The guy is a staunch Republican, a patriot, a Marine. Why would he help out Myers by offering up that photo?"

"How are you so sure that he did? There were a lot of people in and out of the house that weekend." This from Tom Ward, who checked his watch just as a light tap sounded on the door.

"About time," he mumbled.

If Grey was irritated, it didn't show. "Come in."

The door opened. The lone help on duty today, an older, somewhat scruffy looking gentleman who'd been employed by the Dodds for decades, stepped just inside the room. A woman followed behind her. "Excuse me, gentlemen. Your guest, Ms. Coker."

The woman turned toward her escort. "Thank you, sir."

She stepped farther into the room as the obviously besotted older man nodded and smiled at the lady before closing the door. The men scrambled to their feet.

"Hello, guys." Blue-violet eyes locked on Clarence as with hand outstretched she glided to his side. "Judge Dodd."

"Hello, Caroline." The elder judge's voice usually had a raspy quality but some leftover bass from years past found its way into his tone. "Looking lovely as always."

"And you're as handsome as ever. Sorry I'm late."

"Yeah, sure you are," Tom said, all smiles, no grumble. "Good to see you again." He held out his arms for a hug. She blew an air kiss from arm's length.

Judge Dodd introduced her around the room.

"I know who this is," Caroline said, when the judge turned to introduce the last man standing. "A pleasure to meet you, Mr. Grey. You're even more handsome than the pictures on your campaign poster."

Grey had never been speechless a day in his life, but along with the sexy smokiness of her voice Caroline's beauty had taken his breath away. Her raven black hair appeared even darker as it hung in loose ringlets against flawless porcelain skin that he longed to touch. He coughed in hopes that the air pushed through his larynx would be followed by audible sound. It worked.

"Ms. Coker." He held out his hand for a handshake and continued to hold her hand once enveloped in his. With the heels she wore, he was able to look her straight in the eye. "I've heard a lot of great things about you."

"They're all true." The men chuckled. Caroline didn't. "Please, call me Caroline."

"Only if you'll call me Hammond."

"Okay, Hammond. Agreed."

Grey finally released her hand and walked toward the bar. "What can I get you? A touch of sherry, perhaps? Or a glass of wine?"

"Scotch on the rocks, Dewars if you have it."

Grey raised his brow in surprise and admiration. "I have something even better." He reached for the tongs and dropped three cubes into a tumbler, followed by a healthy splash of whiskey, an exclusive premium brand. "A woman after my own heart."

Tom laughed. "I thought I told you she was just like one of the boys."

Grey rejoined the group, handed the glass to Caroline, and felt a jolt as their fingers touched. "I don't know what happened to your eyesight, Tom. Ms. Coker here, Caroline, is hardly just one of anything." He reached for his glass and held it up. "Welcome to the team."

"To the team," she echoed, holding up her glass.

"Hear, hear."

Caroline settled into the comfortable chenille sofa, exposing an expanse of thigh as she daintily crossed her legs at the ankle.

"Who wants to bring Caroline up to speed?" Grey asked.

"No need for that," Caroline drawled. "I began my research months ago, research that included all of the players involved in this latest development."

"All of them?" Grey questioned, a hint of skepticism in his voice.

"Jack Myers's team, CFTG, WHIP, Bryan White," she said to the rest of the room before her eyes settled back on Grey, "among others."

Tom's look was smug. He wasn't the only one who wanted to cast the net of guilt further than Jack Myers's camp. "So you think WHIP is involved?"

"I don't have proof, yet, but it's a reasonable assumption. Especially since Rick Weiss's sister is married to a man currently incarcerated at Edgefield Correctional, along with the father of his sister's child."

"Wait, what?" Tom shook his head.

"You lost me, too," Judge Dodd said. "Remember there's an old man in the audience. "Slow your roll.""

"It's all in the report I emailed you, Hammond, shortly before I arrived. It's why I was late. I wanted to finish it up before arriving in order to present you with the latest and most comprehensive information. Rick Weiss has a sister named Crystal Sanchez. She's married to Daniel Sanchez, who has a sister named Jayda. Crystal has worked with her brother for quite a while. A short time ago Jayda joined her, not long before the Fourth of July holiday, when the photo was taken."

Geoffrey set down his drink. "Can you prove she took the photo?"

"No. Unfortunately, there are no cameras installed inside the Ozark residence, a matter that should be remedied immediately, if it hasn't already been done. There were at least a dozen workers in and out of the house that day. Without video, it's impossible to know for sure."

"But the angle of the picture, and the time it was taken," Grey countered. "The only workers in that room during that dinner was the catering group."

"Did you see any of them take a picture?" Caroline asked.

"No, but—"

"No buts," Caroline interrupted. "The very fact that you didn't see a camera means one had probably been mounted earlier, secretly. Most likely a video camera, given the slight blur of movement I detect in the picture. From my angle who took the picture isn't as important as the steps we take to deflate the momentum being gained from this story."

"How do you propose we do that?" Grey asked.

"By redirecting the attention to something Americans will find more important."

"Like what?"

"Their safety, of course." Caroline leaned back in her seat. Her speech became less formal, more relaxed. "I unearthed an article from a few months ago involving a convicted felon, one you prosecuted, Grey, and one who was released four years ago due to prison overcrowding. He was rearrested recently, over in Missouri, after a child died while in his care; at least that's what's being alleged. Had Jack Myers not fought you and others on the building of prisons, that monster would still be locked up and someone's sweet little angel would still be alive."

"I could call my contact over at FOX News," Dodd said to Caroline. "Get them to do an interview."

Dodd's focus shifted to Grey. "You have the kind of look, intellectual acumen, and likeability to successfully divert attention away from the naysayers and remind everybody of the thugs, terrorists, and other criminals that on a daily basis you work to keep off their streets."

"Everything you said about me is true, Dodd." Hammond made this comment only slightly tongue-in-cheek. The men laughed and, seeing a solution to what could have become a public relations nightmare, relaxed a bit. "This will be a perfect segue into the Accountability Act. That criminal had a rap sheet long before he assaulted that little girl. Had he been forced to register the way sex offenders do, law enforcement would have known he was in the area, and he would have come up on our radar before he had a chance to strike again."

"That's the way to go, buddy," Tom said.

Grey continued, excited about the opportunity to shove his opponents' lame attempt to smear him right back down their throats. "I'll remind them how I've long been a proponent of tough laws and very little tolerance when it comes to the criminal element in our society. And since the Democrats have placed us in debt again, I'll say that I'm equally committed to rebuilding the economic viability of this country, using a framework that will ensure profitability for years to come."

"Brilliant, my boy." Clarence tapped the ash from his pipe and set it on a holder made from the ivory of an elephant Dodd had shot while on African safari. "That position further solidifies you as an authority on criminal justice and criminal law and also crosses you over into the economic arena, two areas most important to the American people—crime and money. If we keep going like this, we might shorten our plan by at least four years, bypass your run for governor, and reach straight for the brass ring."

Geoff looked at Hammond. "How does that sound, Mr. President?"

Hammond flashed a Colgate smile. "It sounds correct."

"Let's not get ahead of ourselves," Dodd droned, in the same slow, deliberate speech pattern he used when on the bench. "There's a hell of a lot of work to do between here and the White House."

"Work that will be made a lot easier with Caroline on our side." Grey shifted his focus. "Great work, Ms. Coker. Whatever your fee is, you've earned every dime."

"I don't know, Ham," Tom teased. "I think she should get a bonus."

Grey's eyes narrowed as he drank in Caroline's loveliness. "I think so, too. What would you like, Caroline?"

Caroline shifted her body toward Grey. "Surprise me."

"You're on."

Conversation turned more casual after that. Grey joined in, but his mind was elsewhere, on Caroline and how long it would be before he screwed her. *I'll give her a surprise, all right,* he thought with a smile. One that lasts all night long. Little did he know it, but there'd be a surprise for him, too. Only he wouldn't be smiling.

22

After reading the damning Grey article together, Shannon had demanded Harley leave her and that job for a day and take time for herself to do something fun. She had said the truth coming out was a cause for celebration. Harley had balked, but Shannon won. Not only had their neighbor, Mrs. Hastings, agreed, but she had practically pushed the woman she loved like the daughter she never had out the door. Harley had called Kim and Jayda and a short time later was headed across town to meet them at the mall. Figuring she was at least fifteen minutes ahead of either of them, she bought their tickets to the latest comedy her friend Kat had suggested and then went into TGI Fridays to wait for her friends.

"Thanks for getting me out of the house," Kim said to Harley after sitting down and placing a drink order. "I didn't realize how much I needed a break until halfway over here."

"Crazy work week?" Jayda asked.

"A strange one," Kim replied.

Harley put down her menu. "What do you mean?"

"I think it has to do with the article, and Grey being branded as the criminal he is."

"The true thug," Jayda murmured.

"Not to everyone, including some of my co-workers and the big boss."

"Did someone say something?"

"Not to me directly. I just noticed subtle glances, whispered conversations. I kept my head down and did my job. Didn't want to get into it with any Grey supporters."

The waiter brought over Kim's iced tea.

Harley lifted her drink and motioned for Jayda to do the same. "Okay, ladies. Here's the deal. After this toast to what will hopefully be Grey's demise and plans put in motion to free our guys, I'm putting down a hard and fast rule for the rest of the night."

Kim lifted her drink. "What's that?"

"No talk about Grey, crime, prisons, politics, none of that. Let's make this a true girl's night out. We're going to watch a chick flick and talk about what girls usually talk about."

"That would be men, and mine is in pri—"

"Hey! Jayda, what'd I just say? Talk about life before he went in or what you're planning for later, but tonight for the next, I don't know how many hours, all that other shit is off limits. Agreed?"

Kim nodded. "Agreed."

Jayda said. "Okay."

"How'd you meet him anyway?" Harley asked Jayda.

"Who?" Harley dramatically dropped her head to the table, splaying hair everywhere. "Oh, Nicky." Jayda laughed out loud.

"Duh," Harley said brusquely, but with a smile.

"He started working at my brother's auto detailing shop."

"Cleaning cars?" Kim asked.

"No, well, that too but mainly customizing them. You know like, *Pimp My Ride*."

Kim made a face. "Do your what?"

"Ha! That show with the rapper Xzibit, about customizing

cars with artwork, TVs, refrigerators, game consoles, everything you can think of."

"Kendall and Aaron probably know all about it, but I don't have a clue."

"Sounds like something Jesse would like."

"So Nicky started working for your brother . . ."

"Yeah. I saw him one day when my mom stopped by the garage. One look at those dimples and that shy, impish grin, and I was hooked. For the next six weeks I found one excuse after another to visit the shop, something that in the past rarely happened. I'd sit in the office, which had a window that looked out to the shop, and watch a Trans Am, Chevy, Impala, or whatever was brought in become his canvas. Nicky is an exceptional artist. His work has an almost 3-D effect and is known throughout the Midwest. He even created buzz on both of the coasts. Car enthusiasts would see a car he'd painted and say simply, 'That's Nick.' Finally I got tired of waiting and made a move, showed up on a Friday night looking the right kind of cute in skinny jeans, heels, and with tickets to a concert I knew he'd like. My brother was like, 'Go out already!'

"We all laughed. Then Danny's smile disappeared. He got in Nick's face."

"Why?" Kim asked. "What did he say?"

Jayda lowered her voice and adopted her brother's intimidating posture. "She's my sister. Remember that."

"Did he remember?" Harley asked.

"Sure did. He was a perfect gentleman, and naturally shy. We pretty much were inseparable after that. Until . . . well, we're still that way. No matter what."

Kim dipped a tortilla chip into the nacho mixture that the waiter had set down earlier. "What about you, Harley? How'd you meet your knight in shining armor?"

"On one of the worse days of my life, that because of him also turned out to be one of my best."

* * *

Lisa walked over to where Harley stood tapping an impatient foot as she waited to clock out.

"Hey, why don't we go for a drink? Take your mind off of everything for just a little while. The relief is only temporary, but it might help a little." Harley remained silent. "Come on, girl. I ask all the time, and you never say yes. We can go to Bar Louie's where the atmosphere is casual, the drinks are cheap, and the food is good."

Harley turned to her. "I know what you're trying to do, and I appreciate it, but—"

"No buts. Not taking no for an answer, I just decided. One drink, on me. And some food, too. Your skinniness is getting on my nerves. Where's your purse? I'll drive."

Against her better judgment Harley gave in. Lisa had been bugging her for over a month, ever since her mother Shannon's cancer diagnosis had turned her world inside out, upside down, and sideways.

It was just past seven-thirty when they walked into the crowded bar and restaurant in Kansas City's Power and Light district downtown. To Harley's surprise, the drone of happy chatter, glasses clanging, and dishes banging didn't depress her but gave her life. She actually meant the smile she gave to the flirtatious bartender and forewent her usual bottle of Bud or Jack and Coke for the "killer mojito" he suggested.

As she waited for her drink, there was a tap on her shoulder. She turned around, expecting to see Lisa back from the restroom. It was someone else.

"Well, hello there, stranger!"

"Jesse. Hi." She may never admit that seeing the sexy hunk who always sat in her station was a pleasant surprise, but some parts of her body reacted that way. "Haven't seen you at the restaurant lately."

"Ah, been missing me, huh? Is that why your eyes look sad even though your mouth is smiling?"

"Oh, it's not that. I'm having some personal challenges. One of my co-workers forced me to come here and feel better."

"Your co-worker was right. And I'm going to help you do just that."

"Well, howdy, Jesse!"

"Well, if it isn't the hostess with the mostest. Lisa, correct?"

"He remembered my name. I'm flattered."

"Ha! I didn't know you came here."

"I don't much, especially on a Friday. I'm more of the *Monday Night Football* or dollar burger Thursday type of girl."

Jesse nodded, but his attention had returned to Harley. "What do you say we find a place to sit, maybe order some dinner."

"That sounds good," Lisa hurriedly answered before Harley could object, ignoring her raised brow in the process.

The three snagged a table and, in large part due to Jesse's gregarious and infectious personality, Harley had her first enjoyable meal all week. Lisa was right. She hadn't been eating. Hearing that your best friend who was also your mother might die had a way of taking away the appetite.

Just minutes after finishing the appetizer she'd ordered, Lisa stood. "Jesse, do you mind giving Harley a ride back to Johnny's Steakhouse? I just remembered something important that I need to do."

"I don't mind at all, Lisa." He turned to Harley. "If that's all right with you."

"It's fine." It really wasn't, but to say anything else would have sounded ungrateful.

Their goodbyes to Lisa were followed by an awkward silence. Harley stole quick glances at Jesse as he signaled a waiter to order more drinks. He looked more relaxed, with his suitcoat off and his hair slightly tousled. And even cuter than she remembered.

"What's that you're drinking?"

"A mojito."

He sat back, eyeing her thoughtfully. "I don't know why, but I pictured you more as a Ford truck, Levi, Bud Light type of girl."

"Your instinct is spot on. This was the bartender's idea."

"Was it a good one?"

"It's all right. I still prefer my Jack and Coke."

"A girl after my own heart. Are you trying to drink away the trouble I saw earlier in your eyes?" She didn't answer. "It's okay if you don't want to talk about it. You probably came here to forget."

"You're right. I did."

"Is it working?"

"Not at all."

"My grandmother always said it was better to let things out than to hold them in, because most rooms are bigger than our stomachs."

Harley's smile was bittersweet. "Sounds like a wise grandma."

Jesse's smile was equally bleak. "She was."

"She's . . . not here anymore?"

Jesse shook his head. "Died two years ago. From cancer. I hate that disease."

"I do, too," Harley muttered, her eyes tearing up instantly.

The waiter returned with a second round of drinks. She reached for hers immediately and drank half right down. The alcohol began to numb her mind, but it didn't stanch her tears.

"I'm sorry, Jesse, but can we go? I just . . ."

"No need to explain." He quickly stood, tossed a couple bills on the table, and escorted her out.

It was a quiet seven-minute drive to the garage next to the restaurant housing Harley's car. She spoke only to tell him where her car was parked, until they were beside it. Then, instead of getting out of his car, she stared out the windshield at the concrete wall.

"My mom is sick," she began, her voice barely above a whisper. "Like your grandma."

"I am so sorry, Harley." He reached into the glovebox and handed Harley a napkin to wipe fresh tears. "How long have y'all been dealing with it?"

"Just a few weeks, but it's been intense. She's in Stage Four and they say it's . . . she's undergoing intense chemo to try and . . . give her as much time as possible. I want to quit the job to stay home with her. But we can't afford it, especially now that I'm the only one working and the medical bills are going to be through the roof."

"Is it just you and your mom?"

"As far as I know. Haven't seen my dad since I was nine years old."

Jesse reached over and gently squeezed her hand. "I know what you're going through, Harley. You don't have to face this alone. If you'll let me, I'll support you, in every way I can."

"Thanks, but I can't even think about a relationship right now."

"I'm not talking about that. I'm talking about moral and emotional support, and sharing everything I learned during the two years we battled for Grandma's life. I can maybe even help out a little financially."

"No, I couldn't."

"Don't be proud, Harley. I've got a little extra coming soon. Helping someone like you, who could really use a blessing, is exactly how I want to spend it."

"Needless to say, I fell in love with him. A man like that—kind, sensitive, giving—who wouldn't? About a month after meeting Mom he found the holistic center in California that boasted cures for incurable diseases and he started paying for Shannon's treatments. When questioned about the cost, he'd wave off the question and change the subject. But doing the wash one day I found a receipt in his pocket. That first visit had cost him over five thousand dollars. But the treatments worked. Mom got better. You pegged him, Kim," Harley finished, her eyes misty. "He's my real-life hero for sure."

"Your turn, Kim," Jayda said. "How'd you meet your hubby?"

Harley looked at her watch. "That'll have to wait until after the movie."

"What movie?" Jayda asked.

"The one I bought tickets for before you guys got here. Stars Kevin Hart, so it should be funny."

"Good," Kim said as she got up from the table. "I need to laugh."

The three friends walked arm in arm into the theater, and for the first time in a very long time, their troubles didn't follow them inside.

23

WTH? Something was wrong. Jayda knew it as soon as she turned onto the block where her family resided. There were at least ten cars in and around the Sanchez driveway. If Anna was cooking one of her big meals, that wouldn't be unusual. But she was still working when Jayda left to meet the girls. She wouldn't have come home and cooked after that. *Would she?*

She pulled up behind an unfamiliar Kia Soul that was parked askew. The knot in her stomach tightened as she remembered silencing her phone before going into the theater. It was still turned off. Unlike every light in the house, which appeared to be on. *What could be wrong now?* She thought about Harley and what had happened to Shannon. Urgency fueled her moves as she jumped out of the car, raced across the yard and up the steps. If something had happened to Anna, Jayda couldn't survive.

And then another thought. Daniel. Nicky. Had one of them gotten an early release? Had both gotten out?

Fear turned to excitement as she opened the front door and stepped inside. All was quiet. Too quiet. This was definitely not a happy occasion. The Sanchez family was known to be raucous, when celebrating even moreso. A party welcoming ei-

ther Daniel or Nicky back would have music going, Coronas
and tequila flowing, and the sound of laughter bouncing off
the walls. She heard none of that. Instead as she walked toward
the great room at the back of the house, she heard a murmur of
concerned voices and then something worse: crying.

She dropped her purse on a coffee table and rushed over to
her mom. "What's wrong?"

Anna sobbed harder.

"We've been trying to reach you for hours," Lucy said.
"Where were you? What happened to your phone?"

"I turned it off when I went to the movies with Kim and
Harley." She reached for her phone inside her purse and turned
it on. The message and missed call indicators went bonkers.
"What happened? Somebody tell me!"

"I want you to stay calm," Lucy said, walking over to Jayda.
She reached for her hand. "It's Nicky."

"What?!" The question came out in a high-pitched wail.

"Shh! Be quiet! I told you to stay calm. The kids are asleep.
Do you want Ally to wake up and see you hysterical?"

Her legs turned to jelly. Jayda plopped down on the couch
as tears began to flow like water. "What happened, Mommy?"
She looked at her sister Teresa, whom she'd just noticed was
here from St. Louis.

"Some guys jumped Nicky, cornered him in the cafeteria
and beat him up."

"Oh, my God, no!" Jayda jumped up. "When'd this happen? Where is he? Are you sure he's okay?" She reached for
her phone, then remembered she couldn't call him. "Tell me
what happened!"

"That's about all we know," Lucy said, walking over to
Jayda once again, this time to put a comforting arm around
her. "Daniel called us a little while after it had happened, beside himself, blaming himself."

Jayda angrily wiped away tears. "Why?"

"Someone set Daniel up, got him away from the cafeteria on the pretense of showing him something or I don't know what. That's when the guys jumped Nicky."

"Was it the gang members?"

"We think so," Anna said, reaching for a tissue to blow her nose. "Daniel wouldn't say much. I'm worried about him now. He's so angry, wanting revenge. Nicky is like a little brother to him. I don't want him to go after the guys who got Nicky and get beat up, too!"

Teresa leaned against the wall and crossed her arms. "Tell us about the picture, Jayda."

"Picture? What picture?"

"Crystal said you took that picture of Hammond Grey and those other guys, the one that ended up in the paper. She thinks Nicky getting beat up might have something to do with that."

Jayda looked around for Crystal, ready to get into a fight herself. "I'll show her about starting some bullshit. Where is she? Why would someone beat him up over a stupid picture?"

"She left a while ago, took the girls. Didn't say where she was going."

"Why would she say you took that picture?" Anna asked.

"Because Rick called and accused me, even though he was with me all the while I served them, every time I went into the dining room."

"I think it was some gang nonsense," Bruno said, walking into the living room. Jayda ran into her father's arms. "It's okay, *princessa*. We'll all go and visit Nicky tomorrow. Stop crying now. You gotta be strong for your man, no? And for your *niña*."

Bruno's comment shifted the conversation. Jayda was thankful Teresa's interrogation was short-lived. She didn't have the strength to withstand a lengthy attack. After making plans to travel to Edgefield the next day, Jayda escaped the crowded living room for the solace of her bedroom, where Ally lay sleeping. She pulled out the burner phone and sent a group text.

Some guys jumped Nicky. Beat him up. Don't know how bad. Some think it's because of the picture. Sorry, guys. I can't take this shit. I can't lose Nicky. Fuck WHIP. Fuck Grey. I'm done.

Instead of returning the phone to its hiding place, she put it in her purse. Tomorrow she'd find a hammer and smash its face the way she wanted to smash those of the men who'd beat up Nicky. The way she wanted to smash Hammond Grey's face.

I never should have taken that picture. I didn't want to do it. I knew if discovered there'd be a price to pay. I just didn't know Nicky would pay it. She swallowed a sob and crawled into bed, next to her baby. She'd had so much fun tonight with Kim and Harley, the best time she'd had in a while. It had felt good to talk about Nicky, made her remember the good times. She pulled Ally into her arms and remembered more.

Jayda waddled into the apartment she shared with Nicky, back aching and needing to pee. Teresa had told her the last month was the hardest. Jayda was only thirty-four weeks along, but having added forty-five pounds to her five-foot-two-inch frame, she was ready to reach up and pull the baby out with her bare hands. The pregnancy had been a surprise, though it shouldn't have. Both were sexually healthy and very affectionate. They made love five to six times a week, often without protection. For Jayda, it wasn't good news. At the time she'd been taking courses at a community college, the first step toward her goal of going from working as a pharmaceutical technician making thirty thousand dollars annually to becoming a licensed pharmacist able to make six figures a year. An EPT put those plans on indefinite hold.

On the other hand, Nicky had been ecstatic. He'd walked around with his chest puffed out as if he was the first man to perform such a feat. When a sonogram showed they were having a girl, he got even more excited, would go along with Jayda and her sisters to pick out baby clothes. He painted her baby bed a canary yellow with elaborately drawn angels and butterflies.

"For my *chica*," he'd quietly whisper, inspecting his handiwork. His joy was contagious; Jayda's sadness was soon replaced with joyful anticipation, until around the sixth month, when the weight seemed to literally jump on her belly. The last two months had added fifteen more pounds. Eight hours behind the pharmacy counter took the life out of her. All she wanted was a double turkey sandwich with extra pickles and mayo, a shower, and sleep.

Two sandwiches later she stepped out of the shower, dried off, and walked naked from the en suite into the bedroom.

Nicky arrived home from work and walked into the room at the same time. He saw her and halted. "Dang, *mami*. You are huge!"

"Gee, thanks."

"But it's beautiful, though."

"Don't try and clean it up now." Jayda crawled into bed and under the covers. "After so eloquently reminding me that I look like a cow."

Nicky lay down beside her, snuggled her close. "Your body looks amazing."

"Yeah, right."

"Nothing will ever be more beautiful to me than you carrying my child." He placed a hand on her abdomen. "It is the greatest gift anyone could give me."

"She's going to be here soon. We've got to decide on a name."

"I thought I told you. Whatever you choose is fine."

"No, it can't be just me. Let's both decide. So far I've thought of Sophia Maria, Anna Karina—and call her Karina so as not to be confused with her cousin or Mom—or Alexa Giselle. What do you think of those?"

"They're all pretty." A pause and then, "What about Alejandra? On account of she's going to be our little angel?"

"And we could call her Ally."

"That sounds cute, no?"

"The middle name could be after your mom."

It was a touching gesture. Nicky's mother had endured an abusive childhood and hard life, yet was one of the sweetest people one could ever meet. With fortitude and an unwavering work ethic, she'd saved enough money to give both of Nicky's siblings a college education.

"Alejandra Rose," Jayda whispered, liking how the name rolled off her tongue and sounded like music. "I like it."

That night, Nicky had added a spray of pink-and-purple roses to the sides of the baby crib bed. The next day he'd brought home a tiny little gold bracelet with their daughter's name stenciled across it. The night after that he'd gone out with his cousins and got arrested. The shock sent Jayda into labor. Instead of Nicky it was her mom, Teresa, Lucy, and Rose in the delivery room, and Anna who cut the cord.

Alejandra was almost three months old when Nicky first held her, almost a year old when the trial by judge was held and he and her brother Daniel were found guilty. Though just a baby, Alejandra had bonded with her father. When he first went away, she cried for days. After their first jail visit, she later found out, Nicky privately did the same.

And now her child's father was hurt and it might be her fault? Tonight it was Jayda's turn to drench the sheet with tears. Later, about two in the morning when she'd awakened with the girls on her mind, she pulled the burner phone out of her purse.

Didn't mean it about WHIP, just about Grey. Going to toss this phone tomorrow. Don't worry about me. Will be in touch.

The next day she awoke to a slew of messages on the burner.

Harley: **WTH? Nicky jumped? Call me ASAP. Will ride to jail with you.**

Kim: **No! I'm so sorry! Is he okay?**

Kim: **Call me as soon as you get this. I'm worried about you.**

Harley: **Me, too. I can come over if you want. Call me!**

Harley: **Jayda, turn your phone on. I just tried to call you. Wait, what's this fuck WHIP bullshit? Are you breaking up with us? J**

Harley: **Okay, it's 2 am. Going to bed. Will keep phone on. Call me if you need me, otherwise I'll call you mañana.**

Kim: **Jayda, don't throw that phone away. KEEP THE PHONE!**

Kim: **Are you up yet? Call me or Harley. Call someone. I've got to go to work but keep me posted.**

Kim: **Hang in there, Jayda. Love you.**

By the time she scrolled through all of the messages Jayda was laughing and crying at the same time. She sent a final group text: **Harley, shut the eff up. Kim, I'll keep the fon. You're still my girlfriends, crazy bitches! I can't break up with you!**

Then she called Harley. "Wake up and get ready to roll."

Harley spoke inside a yawn. "Dang, girl. What time is it?"

"Six o'clock. We want to beat the line."

"Is that all y'all want to beat?"

"Don't make me think about it. I'm already trying to brace myself to see Nicky beat up."

"If I can handle Mom battling cancer, you surely can handle that. Hey, I got a question. Think they'll find Jesse's twenty-two if I hide it in my heehaw?"

Jayda burst out laughing. "Gross, Harley! I can't unhear that!"

Harley laughed so hard she started coughing. "Just thought the visual of a pearl gun handle between my flip flaps would get your mind off of Nicky's bruised face."

"Mission accomplished. Now get over here."

"I'm on my way."

"Oh, and Harley?"

"Yeah?"

"Thanks."

"No worries. Love you, too."

24

It could have been worse, the beating. At least Harley thought so. It was her first time seeing Nicky, and even with a black eye, busted lip, broken nose, and rib fractures, a bit of the handsomeness that Jayda had described the night before came through. They'd stayed together throughout the relatively short line but parted once they reached the prison visiting room to loved ones who sat on opposite sides of the large, open space.

"Why do you keep staring over there?" Jesse asked, looking at the Mexican couple obviously in love.

"That's my friend, Jayda." Harley spoke softly so only Jesse could hear, although in the crowded room made noisy by multiple simultaneous conversations there was little chance of someone else overhearing anyway. "And her boyfriend, her child's father, Nicky."

"Yeah, too bad what happened to him."

"Did you see it?"

Jesse shook his head. "We eat at different shifts. I know one of the guys who jumped him, though. Not really well, only casual."

"Was it gang related? That's what his family thinks." *And Jayda hopes, instead of because of the picture that put Grey in the hot seat.*

"Kinda looks that way. Joe, the guy I know, runs with this white supremacist gang called the Sixth Reich. They're always feuding with the Mexicans, the Black dudes, anybody that don't look like them."

"Guess you don't have anything to worry about, then?"

"Hell, they tried to recruit me into that mess. I told them straight up that I didn't want anything to do with it."

"And they were okay with that?"

"I don't care if they were or not. I'm in here to do the time they gave me and get the hell out. Period. That's what I told them. And that's what I meant."

"What did you hear about the fight?"

Jesse shrugged. "Just that three or four guys cornered him and started throwing punches. It didn't last that long."

"There were guards nearby? Thank goodness."

"Hell, if the guards had their way, they'd still be fighting. At least that's what I heard, and I don't doubt it, either. They play favorites with the other White guys, use them as their muscle to dole out threats. I think some of those guys are part of the Reich."

"Are you serious?"

"As a blood transfusion. You wouldn't believe all the ridiculousness that goes on in here, babe. The guards are right in the middle of some of it. Instigating, threatening, doing stupid shit to make a bad situation ten times worse. They pick on the Black guys, pit them against the Mexicans. I don't even want to talk about it. When you're here, I want to talk about what's going on in the real world. Like how my second mom's doing and when you're going to quit working at Bottoms Up?"

Harley had answered that question with "either when Mom gets a miracle healing or I win the lottery." Since neither happened between comforting Jayda, visiting Jesse, and checking on her mom who lounged at Mrs. Hastings's, she found herself with the pedal to the metal, flying down I-35 for a shift that began at two-thirty. Several blocks from Bottoms and with less than five minutes to spare, she rolled through a stop sign and turned right. Seconds later, flashing red-and-blue lights were in her rearview mirror.

"Damn it!" she hissed, with a bang on the steering wheel for emphasis. She put her head in her hands, not even wanting to lift it up when a stern tap sounded on her driver's side window.

"Hey! You! Roll down this window before I arrest your ass!"

Harley jerked her head up, jammed her finger on the button to roll down the glass. "Got-dammit, Bobby! I'm late for work!"

"Good thing it was me that saw you break the law just then. Follow me."

He jogged back to his patrol car, got in, and zoomed around her. Adding a siren to the already flashing lights, he flew through two stoplights at fifty miles an hour. Harley floored her Mustang, hot on his trail. By the time they skidded and fishtailed into Bottoms' parking lot, they both were cracking up.

"You're in the wrong business," Bobby chuckled, his long strides matching Harley's as she hurried to the plain building's doors.

"You scared the hell out of me, just so you know," she huffed.

"Sorry, not sorry. You're one helluva driver. If you ever stop dancing, give car racing a try."

Harley gave him a mean side-eye as she reached for the door. "Thanks. I'll keep that in mind."

He followed her in. "What are you doing on your break? I'll make up stopping you by buying you dinner."

"Meet me back here at eight, and I'll take you up on that offer."

Harley quick-changed and reached the dining room. Kat was managing so all was well. In between customers Kat showed off the five-carat tennis bracelet from her Nebraskan friend with benefits. Harley joked how that single piece of jewelry could buy Shannon a month's worth of herbs, and then had to practically threaten Kat, after insisting she was joking, to put the bracelet back on. As the dinner shift died down, Kat came over.

"Want to take a break? We're overdue for a catch-up."

"Would love to but can't. I've got a dinner date."

"What the what? You stepping out on Jesse?"

"Yes, with a super hot Italian cop."

Kat's eyes gleamed. "Do tell, because I won't."

"I'm sure you can keep a secret, but it's not as juicy as you think." She told Kat what happened with Bobby, and with Nicky, too. "We ran into each other over there, once. He was visiting a friend's son. Maybe he has some advice on protecting Nicky that I can pass on to Jayda."

"Damn shame, kiddo." Kat shook her head. "What's a beautiful girl like you doing in an ugly mess like this?"

"Trying not to go crazy," Harley said.

Kat threw a friendly arm around her. "Yeah, well, good luck with that."

When Harley got off the elevator, Bobby was waiting in the lobby. He offered his arm when she reached him. "Come with me, doll. Dinner is served."

"Really?" Harley hooked her arm with Bobby's. "Where are we going?"

"A top-of-the-line bistro. Real upscale."

"My break is only thirty minutes, Bobby."

"I'll get you back in time." They reached his squad car. He opened the door with a flourish. Two boxed lunches were in the passenger seat. "Madam, your bistro."

She punched him. "You little shit."

"Hey, I'm pushing two hundred," he countered, walking around to the other side of the car. "That's a very big turd, thank you very much."

Harley opened the container. "Geez, Bobby. This sandwich is huge!"

"That's not a sandwich, my dear. That's a muffuletta."

"Did you just call me a motherfucker?" It was said with mock surprise and a smile.

He cracked up. "You're the one with the foul mouth, all those ugly words coming from such a pretty face." He nodded toward the sandwich half she'd picked up. "A muffuletta. Came over with the Sicilian immigrants who settled in New Orleans over a hundred years ago."

She took a healthy bite. "Ohmygoodness." She finished chewing and studied the dish. "This is delicious. What's all in here?"

"Ham, salami, mortadella, mozzarella. But what really makes it is the bread and the spread, the spicy olive paste."

"Where'd you get it?"

"One of my mob friend's mom."

"Seriously?"

"Naw, I'm joking. You never been to Sal's Deli over on Eighth Street? A friend of mine runs it. Best casual Italian cuisine this side of Rome." He unwrapped an identical sandwich and dug in.

"I haven't, but I will." For a while, they ate in silence. "So that's what you are, Sicilian?" Harley reached for the cola he'd brought her and took a healthy swig.

"Me? No. My people are from Salerno, by the Amalfi Coast. You heard of it?" Harley shook her head. "Beautiful people. Beautiful place. You never been to Italy?"

"I've never been out of the country," she answered around a bite of food. "Barely been out of Kansas."

"You thought I was mafia, huh?" He chuckled.

"I was hoping so. Might need some muscle."

His smile disappeared. "Why? Somebody bothering you?"

Harley thought she was talking to Tony Soprano. In that instant, it was how his East Coast accent sounded.

"A friend of mine's boyfriend got beat up yesterday. At Edgefield."

"Yeah, I heard about that."

"You did?"

He nodded. "My friend's kid is in there, remember?"

"Yeah, I remembered that. Guess the fight was big news all over the jail."

"Those White racist punks. They're not as bad as they think they are. Wouldn't stand a chance if the guards weren't there to protect them."

"You know about them?"

"I know about everything that happens over in Edgefield, just about." He slid her a cautious look. "Everybody I know isn't on the right side of the badge, if you know what I mean." He finished half the sandwich, brushed crumbs off his hands. "What's the guy's name who got beat up?"

"Nicky Romero."

Bobby nodded. "I'll put a word in for him. No guarantees, but maybe they'll cut him some slack."

"Are you friends with that gang?"

"Hardly. But they don't know that." He winked. "And the less you know, the better."

"If you say so."

The conversation meandered from there, to Boston, where he grew up, and him laughing at her descriptions of her childhood small town. While she'd known Bobby casually ever since she started working at Bottoms, this was the first time they'd had a lengthy conversation. She enjoyed it more than she thought she would, enough to know that if she weren't in love with Jesse and Bobby wasn't married, she'd give it a go. He wasn't the kind of guy you wanted to cross, but he wasn't as mean as he looked.

She finished her sandwich and closed the box. "Thanks for dinner. I'm going to have to check out your friend's shop."

"Tell him I sent you. He'll give you a discount."

"Whelp, it's about that time." She opened the door. "Thanks again."

"Your friend's name is Nicky, right?"

"Yep."

"And your boyfriend is Jesse. What's his last name?"

"Cooper."

"I'll put a word in to my boys over there. Don't worry about it."

"You're an angel, Bobby."

An angel who danced with the devil sometimes, as Harley would soon find out.

25

The workplace still felt weird, but Kim was glad the load kept her focused and too busy to worry about covert glances, whispers, and fake smiles. Earlier in the day she'd met with her new client, a start-up investment company. They'd loved her branding ideas, from the simple image of the dollar sign shaped like an anchor to the slogan she'd created: "Your Money: Secure. Protected. Multiplied." Tanya was thrilled that her client was happy. When Kim looked good, she did, too. But the president, Scott Martin, had barely spoken a word to her since the article on Grey had come out more than a week ago. At another time in her life Kim would have been worried, would have bent over backwards to try and impress her superior. But life had rearranged her priorities.

Her major meeting over and Tanya gone for the day, Kim responded to several emails, sent off a memo to the graphic designer doing her client's artwork, and placed a folder of filing into her assistant's inbox. Then she turned off the light, shut her office door, and headed home. It felt good to take off a little early, especially now as fall approached, her favorite time of the year.

Kim reached her car, opened the glove compartment, and

pulled out the burner phone. She was relieved to see a message from Jayda. Kim shot back a quick response, glad that her time with Nicky had gone well and reminding her of the upcoming WHIP meeting the second Saturday, as always. She pulled out of the parking lot thinking of Harley and Jayda, how different they all were, yet how invaluable both now were in her life. Remembering their fun time last night made her smile, especially hearing how both had met the men they loved. Could she and Aaron ever get back to the love they shared in the beginning? Kim thought counseling would help, but she'd recently broached the subject a second time. Aaron's answer had been the same. No. Kim made a mental note to call her mom and get the name of the church's marriage counselor. Their marriage needed some kind of intervention. If Aaron wouldn't go see a therapist with her, Kim would go alone.

She turned onto their street as her phone rang. Aaron's name flashed on the dash. She tapped the icon on her steering wheel. "I was just thinking about you."

"Oh."

"You said that as though headed for time out. They weren't bad thoughts."

"These days I can't tell." A sober comment, but she heard the smile in his voice. "What time are you getting off work today?"

"I'm off now and pulling into the drive. Why?"

"The neighbors invited us out to dinner."

"Connie and Phil?"

"Yep."

"Wow, that's interesting. A special occasion?"

"If so, Phil didn't mention it. He was outside when I pulled up, said he and Connie were going out for dinner and asked if we wanted to join them. Said it had been a while since we'd all gotten together."

"He's right about that."

Their sons were best buds and classmates. And both played

football, a fact that had made the Logans and Goodes close friends at one time. Until now Kim hadn't realized how far apart they'd drifted.

"So what about it? Should we join them?"

Instead of pressing the garage door opener, Kim parked her car in the drive. "Sure. You'll never hear about me wanting to cook when given the offer of someone else doing it for me."

"All right. I'll call Phil."

"Cool. I'm walking inside now."

Less than an hour later, the casually dressed Logans got into Kim's car. Aaron drove them to an area called The Plaza, a tony shopping and restaurant district in midtown Kansas City, not far from where they lived and from the college where Aaron taught sociology. The popular tourist spot was wedged between historical Westport, a major battleground during the Civil War, and the Rockhill district, another historic area developed by fortune seeker and *Kansas City Star* founder William Rockhill Nelson, whose estate was now the Nelson-Atkin Art Museum. For Kim's birthday three years ago, Aaron had taken her there. The date had lasted several hours, until the restaurant tossed them out, in fact, as the two art lovers held a hearty, slightly inebriated discussion on the award-winning work of six photographers and the civil rights era captured and for some experienced solely through their lens.

The museum held fond memories for the Goodes as well. Along with being members and regular donators to the gallery, Connie, a closet artist who forewent her career to be a full-time mom, had one of her works depicting New York's twin towers featured in an exhibit celebrating local creations, shortly after 9/11. The last time the couples were there together was just after Kendall received his scholarship, just before he had been arrested.

Wednesday night traffic was light. Aaron found a parking

spot just a few doors down from the restaurant Phil had suggested. The night air was perfect. A warm seventy-three-degree breeze brushed across Kim's skin as she exited from the door that Aaron had opened and joined him on the sidewalk. Taking her hand, he pulled her to the inside as he always did. Had the move come naturally, Kim wondered? Was his move a conscious decision, one of protection that according to her brother Peter made Aaron feel more like a man? The night felt like dozens of other evenings when they'd enjoyed casual walks together, and totally different at the same time.

They reached the restaurant and joined Phil and Connie, who'd already secured a corner booth. Dim lighting and dark woods created a comfortable atmosphere that was further warmed by the bottle of full-bodied Pinot Noir the couples drank as they munched on deliciously unique appetizers such as French onion dumplings, twisted bread, and a salad called The Goat. As often happened, the conversation centered around family and football. Since the Goodes were staunch conservatives and the Logans leaned Democrat and Independent, politics was something they usually avoided. But with the Kansas senatorial race and more specifically the allegations against Grey front and center in the local news, the topic rather quickly made its way to their table.

Phil swirled his wineglass, his brows scrunched in thought. "When it comes to your son's case, I agree he was wronged. I know Kendall. Love the kid. He's smart, respectful, and when it comes to throwing the football, there's no one better. Our sons are best friends, for heaven's sake. But he's one in a million. Fate dealt him a bad hand, and he got a bad deal. But that's not the case with most of them. Most people in prison deserve to be there."

Aaron looked at Kim, felt her rigid back and gave her thigh a comforting squeeze. It had been so long since she'd felt such a genuinely loving touch from him she almost stopped being mad at Phil and wanted to thank him for the comment. Almost. Not quite.

"I totally get why you see it that way," she said, her tone neutral. "Until what happened to Kendall, that was my thought, too. People did wrong. They got locked up. But through WHIP, I am working with over twenty-five families in this area alone who believe and in many instances have proof that their relatives are either innocent or have been given a much harsher sentence than the crime required."

Phil shrugged. "It's their loved one. They're going to think whatever sentence handed down was too harsh."

"That's probably true," Aaron agreed. "But you can't deny or argue the fact that when it comes to sentencing and incarceration, there is a huge racial disparity."

"Oh, here it comes. The race card."

"Honey," Connie warned, with a sympathetic glance to Kim.

"No, it's okay. It's Phil. Of course he's going to think that bringing up race is an easy out. But this isn't something you have to take my word for, or Kim's. Just look at the stats. Numbers don't lie."

Kim listened to Aaron and was somewhat surprised. He seemed unwilling to discuss Kendall's plight with her, at least in depth, but had obviously done research, just like she had.

"One can always find a set of statistics to support their position. I listen to FOX News."

"That's the first mistake," Kim interjected.

"And they spout statistics, too. Ones that fully support what Grey did in Kansas and what Miller is doing here in Missouri."

The mention of the former Tea Party member gave Kim the shivers. "What Miller, Grey, Trump, and others like them are trying to do is turn back time. Great for White America but for everybody else . . . not so much. There's a reason you didn't see us on *Leave It To Beaver* or *Father Knows Best*. To a very large segment of the country, we didn't exist."

"I believe I recall seeing an African-American once," Connie said, sincerely.

"*Once* being the operative word," Kim replied, and not unkindly. "And she was probably a housekeeper, or maybe a cook. Look, I get it. Out of sight, out of mind. It's something that unless you're around us is often never even thought about. Phil, you grew up in Montana. You probably didn't meet a Black person until you were grown, and Aaron is probably the first one you talked to for over ten minutes straight."

"I'll beg your pardon," Phil said, reaching for the wine bottle. "He was the second."

A moment of levity from Phil's wry, often sarcastic humor reminded the Logans why they liked him enough to forgive what Kim's father called his Archie Bunker ways.

"My dad was very prejudiced," Connie admitted. "As I've told both of you before, I was brought up with a certain idea of how Black people were, opinions that came from my father but weren't rooted in truth. Or not even necessarily in his experiences. So I do understand how judgments can be made about a person without good reason or actual proof. I had a good friend in college, at Emporia State. African-American, bright, pretty, her family had more money than mine did. But I remember going shopping with her and seeing how differently we were treated. We went into a clothing store once, a large, national department store chain, separately. On purpose. She had me watch, and I saw how they followed her, convinced she was there to steal. How they didn't extend the same customer service as they gave me. I'm only fifty years old. This was the eighties. I can't imagine how it was in the fifties and sixties, or before."

Kim offered Connie a sad smile. "Or now, in some instances."

"Now?" Phil asked. "I believe the country has made great strides and that prejudice is limited to a marginal segment of society. We've had an African-American president! We've had Oprah. Heck, we've even had a Tiger Woods in the whitest sport besides hockey."

"Give us a minute, we'll take over that, too."

Kim elbowed Aaron as everyone laughed. A server brought their entrées. After they agreed to disagree on prison corruption and whether or not Grey was involved, the conversation turned back to college sports. A difficult one for the Logans given the circumstances, but they were happy for the Goodes.

"Seems like just yesterday we dropped Wilson off in Columbia. Hard to believe he'll be a senior next year."

"I know he wanted to roll with the Crimson Tide," Aaron said. "But it looks like being a Tiger has worked to his advantage."

Phil dug into a rare steak. "The full scholarship they offered definitely worked to ours."

"You mean to your bank account?" Aaron clarified with a laugh.

"Absolutely."

"He's a natural center, and even in losing seasons has been able to shine. Any looks from the pros?"

Phil shook his head. "Not so far. But he's ready for tryouts if no one comes knocking."

Connie picked up her napkin. "We told him to concentrate on getting through his senior year. There will be plenty of time for him to do open tryouts. Just like Kendall will do when this awful wrong is righted and he gets released from jail." She leaned forward and dropped her voice. "You know we love our son, but he's never been the sharpest knife in the drawer."

"Don't have to be the sharpest, darlin'," Phil said. "As long as you can cut."

With freshly refilled glasses, the foursome toasted to that.

Dinner continued, leisurely, relaxed. At one point chairs were swapped so that Kim and Connie could discuss Connie's latest art project and a shared guilty pleasure: reality TV. The guys placed bets on the city's beloved KC Chiefs and whether this was the year they'd take it all the way to the Super Bowl. The couples parted with promises to go out more often and that they shouldn't act like strangers, given the fact that they lived side by side.

It was a perfectly normal evening, like it had felt with Harley and Jayda the other night.

"That was really enjoyable," Kim said, as she and Aaron walked into their home.

"I agree, maybe because it had been a while. Phil makes me want to punch him sometimes, but overall he's a good guy."

"Would give you the shirt off his back."

"No doubt. Oh, by the way, he wanted me to ask you about an account he believes you acquired . . . Anchor Financial, I think he said?"

They were headed upstairs. Kim stopped in midstep. She turned to face Aaron. "How'd he know about that?"

Aaron placed his hands on her waist and prodded her forward. Maybe it was the wine, but the take-charge act caused a tingle in her belly that quickly dropped to her heat and caused drops of perspiration along the unshaved lips.

"A friend of his started the company. When asked for a recommendation of someone to help them with marketing, he gave them your name."

"Really."

They'd reached the bedroom. Kim proceeded into the walk-in closet and began to undress. Aaron followed behind her, removing clothes, too.

"I must say I'm truly surprised, and pleasantly so. Makes me believe there's still hope for humanity, even with people who voted for Trump."

"Ha. Right."

"That was really sweet of him. I wonder why he told you and not me? I owe him a genuine thank-you, a card or gift even. It's a nice-sized account."

Dress, bra, and panties tossed into a hamper, she slid a short pink nightgown over her shoulders.

"I think a part of him liked being anonymous. But if he hadn't told me, it wouldn't be Phil."

Aaron left the closet in his black boxers. He sat on the bed and reached for the remote to catch the ten o'clock news on the local FOX affiliate station.

Kim sat beside him. "Is that one of those man things?"

A quizzical look followed. "What do you mean?"

"Peter and I talked over the fourth. He tried to help me understand how Kendall being incarcerated affected you differently than it did me."

She'd said it casually, conversationally, the way she'd responded to Phil's ignorance on racism. The evening was going well. Kim had no desire to spoil it. The statement had flowed naturally, and because it was a conversation long overdue, she'd chanced it. Now she waited. Would he tense up, close up, as per usual? Kim scooted back on the bed and got under the covers.

To her relief, Aaron did the same. He leaned against the headboard, muted the commercial playing. "What did he tell you?"

"That not being able to help Kendall was like losing your identity. Protecting, rescuing, guiding . . . it's what you guys do. And that you weren't able to help our son, he said was as if a part of you . . . died."

Her voice softened, lowered further. "I remember those nights right after Kendall got arrested. How you tried to comfort me, to make sure I was all right. I lied and said I was when I wasn't. Acted stronger than I felt, in control when inside I was falling apart. I meant well. Called myself doing it for you.

Thought that being strong would ease your burden. Focused on the broken system, and Grey, and took my frustrations out on him.

"Peter made me realize it hadn't helped matters when in your silence I became such a visible, boisterous advocate. Not that I regret it," she hurriedly added. "But in talking with him I realize that things could have been handled differently. I could have listened more, talked less, and asked your opinion about my plans to defend Kendall. Like starting WHIP, for instance."

"Or talking to reporters, like you did earlier?" He answered the question her face asked. "It's not that you shouldn't have. What you said was right on. But it would have been nice to know beforehand that my wife was going to be on the news."

In three years, two months, and eleven days, this was the most honest and defining conversation they'd had regarding the actions and feelings that created a chasm in their marriage.

"It's so hard," she whispered, leaning her head on his shoulder. "Made even harder by trying to get through it without you."

She wanted to ask more questions. Wanted to know if he talked to Jessica about their son, and how the other woman made him feel. Did she acquiesce to his lead and in the process strengthen his manhood? Was she a better listener? Was there anything happening between them, physical, emotional, or otherwise? She wanted to ask the questions, but Aaron had turned toward her and started using his mouth to do other things. So she took a point from her brother's advice and for once followed her husband's lead.

After several languid moments of dueling tongues and roaming hands, Aaron slid his body downward so his tongue could do the same. Across her neck and around her nipples. Over her quivering stomach and down to an exposed nub already swollen with desire. She hissed, moaned, lifted her head to see him in action, and opened her eyes.

There on the forty-inch screen just above Aaron's focused head and swirling tongue was the face of Hammond Grey with his wife, Sunnie, sitting beside him and the caption "FOX Exclusive" across the bottom of the screen.

"Baby, baby, wait." Kim grabbed Aaron's shoulder. "They're doing an interview with that asshole. Where's the remote?"

26

Thirty miles south, in Edgefield, Kansas, a small but efficient FOX-TV crew had set up in the Greys' elegantly appointed living room for an exclusive interview that would be nationally televised. A lit fireplace in the background gave the formal setting a cozy feel. On the fireplace mantel were two identically arranged vases of red and white roses, red and white gladiolas, vibrant blue delphinium and white lilies, with small flags artfully tucked among the flowers lest anyone miss the point that this was a patriotic household. Grey was calm, smiling; his movie star looks appeared born for a close-up. A lock of thick raven hair against his forehead added a boyish quality to the hardline jaw, accented by a dimpled cheek, preppy shirt, and navy sweater he wore in place of his usual tailored designer business suits. Cross pin on his collar. Check. American flag, too. Check. The room had clearly been staged to elicit feelings of American pride. Some viewers might conclude the only thing missing was background music of "The Star-Spangled Banner" and a picture of Betsy Ross.

As the AD counted down to the show's live broadcast, Taylor Fields, the award-winning, no-nonsense host of one of the network's top shows, smiled into the camera looking poised and confident.

"Good evening America. Welcome to *Keeping It Real*, the show that offers a clear, unbiased look at the stories you are talking about right now. I'm Taylor Fields. For the past several years there has been a lot of conversation surrounding crime, incarceration, and the growth of private prisons, a discussion that mushroomed following the recent release of a story in the *Kansas City News* that went national after being picked up by the Associated Press. An article implicating several top Kansas officials in what was rather blatantly called a moneymaking scheme. My guest tonight has a lot to say about these topics, since his career was largely built by fighting crime, prosecuting criminals, and putting them in jail.

"I am in Edgefield, Kansas, where one of the privately owned prisons named in that article is located, and have been graciously welcomed," she continued as the camera panned out, "into the home of the son of one of this quaint town's founding families, a senatorial candidate for the sunshine state, and the former Jones County district attorney, Hammond Grey. Attorney Grey, thank you for your hospitality, and welcome to *Keeping It Real*."

"Thank you, Taylor. On behalf of my wife, Sunnie, and myself, it's a pleasure. And please, call me Hammond. We're just regular folk around here."

"I'm sure there are those in Edgefield and elsewhere that would disagree with that statement, Hammond, but thank you nonetheless. Let's jump right in to what everyone is talking about. Describe for me and those watching the term 'prisons-for-profit,' one that is often associated with privatized prisons and is used repeatedly in the article that quite frankly brought us here tonight."

"Taylor, that term, prison for profit, is an unfortunate misnomer coined by reporters and naysayers with no experience and very little credible information on the operations of this country's extensive, overburdened, overcrowded, underfunded, and undermanaged penal system. Crime doesn't pay, and the fact of the matter is housing criminals doesn't pay, either, at least not much." His smile, charming and disarming, underscored the lie. "But when it comes to companies in the private sector helping to relieve state governments from some of that burden, there are benefits."

"Let's talk about those."

"First of all, it takes some of the huge financial responsibility off of the state, thereby saving law-abiding taxpayers their hard-earned dollars. It costs the state close to thirty thousand dollars per inmate to keep our citizens safe and have these lowlifes pay for their crimes. That's close to two hundred million dollars across the state. I don't believe that burden should rest on the backs of law-abiding citizens who go to work every day, obey the law, go to church, knock back a beer or two, and take care of their families.

"For a town such as Edgefield, where you are now, a relatively small, largely blue-collar community with good citizens wanting honest work for an honest day's pay, it provides employment opportunities, not only in the facility itself but in complementary vocations as well. Laundry services, lawn care, healthcare, entrepreneurial opportunities that can further add to a family's income and the city's bottom line. But most importantly, prisons like Edgefield house criminals that, under a bill pushed by my opponent Jack Myers, overcrowded state-run facilities released.

"Those of us here in Edgefield, and in all of the surrounding communities that make up metropolitan Kansas City, know what can happen when criminals are allowed to roam the streets. Jimmy Smith, an inmate with a long criminal history that included assault, burglary, and drug possession was released under the bill that Jack Myers authored and worked doggedly to get passed, and less than a year later he sexually assaulted a young girl whose life will now never be the same." Grey looked directly into the camera. "That wouldn't happen under my watch, guaranteed."

"Your record as DA seems to bear that out. It's one of your

opponent's points against you and was also highlighted in the article, how with you in the court and Judge Thomas Ward on the bench, prosecutions doubled and convictions went up by thirty percent."

"Absolutely, and I'm proud of that record. Prosecutors like me who put gang members, drug dealers, murderers, and scum like Jimmy Smith away do so to keep our neighborhoods and communities safe. For all Americans, but especially our children. I'll be damned if I apologize for that."

Taylor nodded her understanding. "There's not a parent watching who'd expect you to, or blame you for feeling that no apology is needed. But I have to ask you, Hammond, about the picture. The one showing you, Judge Thomas Ward, retired Judge Clarence Dodd, the Jones County sheriff, and other major players in the judicial system enjoying dinner at what can only be described as a mansion. A group who together are responsible for the Edgefield Correctional Facility holding at an occupancy rate of almost ninety-five percent practically from the time it was built. Seeing that picture does lends credibility at least to the possibility of some scheming going on."

"Let me clarify something for you and everyone watching. That dinner was a formal, private event to celebrate our wonderful country being founded and the birthday of one of our wives. That we're all friends shouldn't come as any surprise, or be seen as anything nefarious. As a DA I spent more time with those ugly mugs than I did with my beautiful wife." Taylor chuckled. "No offense, guys. Figure of speech.

"But seriously, and here's the hard, cold fact. Here's the truth. No one in that picture or in that room, or in any police cruiser, any court, or anyone in the world for that matter puts anyone in prison. Criminals put themselves there. By breaking the law. They do the crime. They do the time. And if I'm the prosecutor, they'll do lots of it. That's the bottom line."

Taylor was quiet for a couple beats. The statement hung in the air, crystallized, became almost palpable.

"At the end of the day," she finally said, voice lowered, body leaned slightly toward Grey, "isn't that what incarceration is about? Punishing the guilty and, as you said, making our neighborhoods safe for the overwhelming percentage of Americans who don't break the law?"

The shift was subtle and successful. With one powerfully delivered paragraph Grey took the attention away from private prisons and placed it on crime. After a commercial break he was joined by his wife, Sunnie, and their two children, a bunch of small-town Midwesterners with small-town values, as Sunnie described them when Taylor asked the question.

"I'm not from here originally, but as Hammond said, I'm a small-town girl. I grew up in Lake Bluff, Illinois, a suburb of Chicago. Growing up there were . . . maybe five thousand people. It was a lot like it used to be here and in almost every other small town across America. Everybody knew each other, every grown-up was your parent and could tell you what to do. There was very little crime, and even what happened was mainly vandalism, teenagers painting graffiti or drag-racing on the highway just outside the city limit. But I attended college in Chicago—"

"What college?"

"Loyola; majored in English, minored in French. My initial plan was to become a schoolteacher, but you know what they say. We plan. God laughs."

"Indeed. How was the transition then to life as a wife and mother?"

"Very challenging, to be honest. Motherhood is hands down one of the hardest positions a woman can fill. I really believe it should come with a salary and benefits." Sunnie's laugh was easy, her demeanor genuine.

The show never returned to the topic of private prisons, and the next day, when the new poll was released for the Kansas senatorial race, Jack Myers's numbers were lower than ever. Grey's numbers soared through the roof.

27

Six weeks passed between the airing of Grey's interview and the election. But for all intents and purposes Grey delivered his victory speech, his knockout punch, that night on *Keeping It Real*. Myers fired back with the truth about Jimmy Smith, how he was paroled as scheduled and not a part of the inmates released due to overcrowding. Families of prisoners believed to be innocent came forward. Bryan interviewed Kim two more times. Channel Nine News's Pat Tucker brought her into the studio during Pat's Saturday morning show on community affairs. Experts and statisticians spewed numbers and facts about the prison system, disproving Grey's claim that mass incarceration didn't pay. The CEO of America's largest private prison contractor, Jim Hartwell, came under fire when his annual, multi-million-dollar salary was released. But Hammond Grey was Teflon, a seemingly impenetrable force, where the slime of scandal slid off his bronzed skin, washed away by constant attacks on Myers's weakness toward criminals, America's safety, and Jimmy Smith.

On the first Tuesday in November, at about eight in the evening, it became official. Hammond Grey became a senator from the state of Kansas. The former get-tough prosecutor from Edgefield, Kansas, was headed to Capitol Hill.

In the Logan household, thanks to a high definition, LED-backlit, fifty-five-inch smart TV, the newly elected senator seemed to jump off the screen and into the Logans' otherwise darkened living room. All of Grey's hard work to fulfill his promise to the state's citizens had paid off. Aaron sipped brandy and watched Grey in all of his victorious glory, looking like a young Rock Hudson, his pretty, petite wife by his side, adoring eyes drinking him in like a Raider Nation member in a sold-out stadium. Two attractive, well-dressed children completed the politician's perfect family tableau—chip-off-the-old-block four-teen-year-old son with rich chestnut-colored hair and searing hazel eyes, cute-as-a-button twelve-year-old daughter, her mom's mini me, a spray of freckles across a Tinkerbell nose and reddish blond curls cascading down her back. The four-some waved flags and clapped their hands as the band played, the crowd cheered, and confetti fell.

After several minutes of sustained applause, Grey's family and supporters stepped to the side. He walked to the podium, held up an oversize broom. The audience went wild.

Seconds later, the rapid sounds of heels meeting mahogany reverberated down the hall. Kim walked into the living room, picked up the remote, and turned off the television. Placing the remote on the coffee table, she glared at him. Aaron threw back the rest of his brandy, set down the tumbler, and met her intense gaze. Seconds went by. She left the room. He stared into the darkness. No words were said. None were needed.

"Hey, Harley." No answer. "Harley!"

"Can't you see I'm busy?" Harley scowled at the bartender. It had been a long shift, but a good one. Exhausted but fo-cused, she counted what hopefully was enough tip money to pay the rent and put more cash on Jesse's books.

"Isn't that the guy who sent your guy to prison?"

Harley's eyes slid from the bartending friend who pulled

strings and helped her get the coveted job at Bottoms to the TV screen he watched.

"Yeah, that's him." She stalked over and turned up the sound.

"Clean up Kansas! Clean up USA! Clean up Kansas! The Grey Way!"

Harley, the bartender, and several patrons watched a sea of fluttering American flags as the auditorium packed with Grey supporters listened to the victory speech and chanted.

"As your senator and representative in Washington, DC, on Capitol Hill," Grey finished amid a lull in the noise, "I promise to do just that! Thank you!"

"I hate that motherfucker," she hissed.

Bobby, who was sitting at the bar nursing a cup of coffee, looked over and shook his head. "There you go again. The fine filly with the foul mouth."

"Sorry, Bobby. I forgot how my cursing offends you. He does look more like a sonofabitch." Her narrowed eyes continued to watch the celebration, now in the background as a reporter covered the scene.

"Hammond Grey?" Another patron turned to her. "He's one of the good guys." Harley snorted. "What could he have possibly done to you?"

"Got my man locked up."

"Now, honey, was that the DA's fault . . . or the result of your man's behavior?"

"He wasn't totally innocent. But he didn't deserve the sentence he got. Hammond Grey lied and got elected. My boyfriend lied and went to prison. It's not fair."

"If you don't mind my asking, what did your boyfriend do?"

Harley's sky-blue eyes began to water as she looked at the patron. Just before walking away, she whispered, "Fell in love with me."

* * *

Jayda Sanchez's parents' house was crowded. It had nothing to do with it being election night and everything to do with Crystal's son, Rafael, and the upcoming *quinceañero* to celebrate his fifteenth birthday. The ceremony was on Saturday, but today, Tuesday, was his actual birthday. So of course the family had been invited over for a "small dinner," consisting of Rafael's favorite food: *tlacoyos*, a fried masa cake filled with pork, cheese, peppers, and spice; *menudo*, a hearty soup, and all of the trimmings. Translation: the Sanchezes had prepared a feast!

No food would go to waste. By the time dinner was served, thirty-seven people mingled in and around their split-level dwelling. In Kansas, where last year in November there were six inches of snow, this night's weather was superb. The men were outside on the patio, drinking Coronas and telling tall tales. The women sat around the cozy living room and engaged in one of their favorite subjects—family.

"Just yesterday he was a baby!" Jayda's aunt, Lucy, exclaimed, her lyrical Spanish often effortlessly intertwined with English. "And already your youngest son is becoming a man. *Dios mío!* I can't believe it. Where does the time go?"

"I don't know, but it goes too fast," Anna answered.

"Not fast enough," was Crystal's subdued reply.

Just three words, but enough to dampen the festive mood.

Jayda walked over to Crystal. "It's going to be okay." She reached out to touch Crystal's shoulder.

Crystal jerked back. "No thanks to you."

The family focus shifted. Lucy looked between the two. "What's going on here?"

Crystal was tight-lipped.

Jayda was short. "Nothing."

"Doesn't look like nothing," Anna said. She turned to Jayda. "What are you two fighting about?"

Jayda knew it was a risk, but she jumped into the fire. "Rick thinks I took that picture of Grey and those guys, the one that made the paper months ago and got him in trouble."

Various comments came from around the room from those who thought such impossible. All except Lucy, whose eyes narrowed as she looked at her niece. "Did you?"

"What kind of question is that? Besides, it doesn't matter. Grey will probably win anyway."

Crystal jumped up and left the room. Jayda did, too. But she didn't follow behind Crystal. Instead, she went upstairs for an update on the election.

Once inside the bedroom, she closed the door and reached for the remote. As soon as she turned to Channel Nine, Grey's smiling face filled the screen, along with the caption: "Grey Wins Senate Seat." *He won?* Jayda couldn't believe it. She raced downstairs to deliver the news.

They were stunned and angry, but the party continued. It was a celebration for Rafael, the family jokester. They couldn't act too sad. It would ruin the evening. So the music was loud. The laughter, plentiful. The food delicious and the drinks non-stop. There were balloons and streamers and fireworks, too. But unlike the raucous celebration Jayda saw on TV, the revelers at this party hadn't won their fight. They'd lost, and everyone felt the pain.

Later, as the household slept, Jayda rocked a cranky, teething Alejandra and watched a recap of Senator Grey's victory on the late-night news. With everything WHIP and the girls had done, he still won. She had risked Rick's wrath and now had a sister who was still barely speaking to her for a picture that showed all the guys in cahoots red-handed, and the voters ignored it. They'd already been out of options. Now they were out of time. All she could think about was how her family's pain was this man's victory.

28

Now that he'd been elected to the Senate, Kim figured the approach in her fight against Hammond Grey would have to change. When she arrived at Fletcher Young the morning after Tuesday's election, she found out just how much.

"You know how sorry we are for happened to Kendall," her boss, Tanya, explained as they sat in her office. "We understand your frustration."

Unless "we" have experienced what I have, "we" have no idea. A thought carefully hidden behind a placid mask.

"You know our clientele makeup. Some of our biggest accounts are supporters of Hammond Grey. In the past we placated their concerns about your . . . visibility in the media . . . and while not necessarily agreeing with them, we helped them understand how to you these actions were justified, taken against a man you believed had your son wrongly convicted. But he's a U.S. senator now. His actions as the county DA are in the past. And while your grievance against him is still very reasonable, it is no longer justifiable from a corporate viewpoint.

"Any actions that place you in an unfavorable light shine just as harshly on us. That's why we have to formally insist that the public campaign against him by you be curtailed." She handed Kim a copy of the corresponding memo that would go in her personnel file. "Personally, I'm not saying to quit fighting for your son, but it has to be handled differently. Within the walls of justice, not in the public eye."

Even though the door was closed, Tanya lowered her voice to a near whisper. Her sparkly green eyes were direct and sincere. "As a mother and as your friend, I'm on your side. But the higher-ups are pressuring me. I'm sorry."

"It's okay, Tanya. I understand."

Kim didn't agree, but she really did understand. Throughout her son's ordeal Kim had shouted his innocence from the rooftop to anyone who'd listened and placed the blame for what she believed his unlawful arrest and wrongful conviction squarely on Grey's shoulders. Many of the company's clients had probably voted for him. Heck, if she'd only had the handsome attorney's polished commercials, rousing stump speeches, and tagline promises to go on, and had she been a Kansas citizen, she might have voted for him herself! But life pushed her behind the PR curtain, allowed her to see the fallible man behind the tough-talking wizard, and revealed that there was no yellow brick road. Life had caused her to form the organization that brought Jayda and Harley into her life. The weekend after her meeting with Tanya, she headed to a restaurant to meet with them.

"What are you going to do?"

That was Harley's question after Kim explained why she was stepping down from chairing WHIP and taking a less active roll.

"I'm going to keep doing what I've always done, fight to get our guys' names cleared. Just not as openly and visibly as I've done in the past."

Harley slumped against the restaurant booth. "This is bullshit."

"I agree. But it's what has to happen now. I'm still just as committed to our cause, Harley, even more so."

"What about Grey?" Harley banged her fist on the table. It shook. Plates clattered. Water sloshed from her glass. Kim and Jayda jumped. Conversation ceased, and all eyes turned toward their table.

Harley was too angry to notice any of it, or if she did, to care. "He's messed up so many lives!" she hissed between clenched teeth. "Way too many to get away with it. What are we going to do about him?!"

"I don't know," Kim said with a sigh. "We'll think of something."

Harley's normally cornflower-blue eyes turned nearly navy with anger. "We'd better. Because there's no way I'm going to stand by and let that son-of-a-bitch live out his political dreams after making all our lives a nightmare."

Jayda pulled a hand through thick black tresses and shook the hair away from her face. "It's a nightmare, all right. Great Housekeeping has obviously been blackballed or something, because after Nicky got beat up and the Dodds let them go, they lost all their other Edgefield clients. Some Jones County ones, too. The company had to lay off half the work force, Moms and grandmothers with kids and bills. It's not fair at all!"

Kim reached over and squeezed Jayda's hands as tears welled up in Jayda's eyes. "If I knew what problems that picture would cause, I never would have suggested you take it."

"Especially since it had no negative effect on Grey whatsoever," Harley added.

"It's not your fault," Jayda said. "I wanted to take the picture. I wanted to do whatever I could to expose him for the monster he is. I hear you, Harley. I understand why you're upset. I am, too. I don't want Grey to get away with what he did. But he got exposed and still won the election! He's on his way to Washington. I'm tired of every waking thought centered around Grey and getting revenge. Doing so has been like a cancer poisoning everything that's been touched.

"Sorry, Harley. That was a bad choice of words."

Kim looked at Harley's scowling face, knowing what she was about to say wouldn't be well received, but she said it anyway. "I know it's a hard pill to swallow, Harley, but Jayda might be right. Since the night I got that phone call from Kendall and hearing he'd been arrested, my life has been consumed with getting him out, and as an extension of that desire, of seeing Grey taken down. My kid's still in jail. My marriage has suffered. My job status is tenuous. Wanting justice for Kendall has made my life a living hell, too."

"So what, that's it?" Harley sat up straight, looked from Jayda to Kim. "You guys are going to give up, just like that? Throw in the towel? Too bad our guys don't have it that easy. That they can't just say to hell with this long-ass prison sentence and walk out of jail." She stood up abruptly.

"Wait, Harley," Kim said, standing up, too. "Where are you going? Don't leave upset."

"I'm not mad at you. I'm mad at the situation. You guys can do what you want. But I won't rest until he gets hurt the way he's hurt us. There's no way I can give up. I'm not only doing this for Jesse. I'm doing it for Mom."

She turned to leave.

Jayda called after her. "Harley!"

"Don't worry." Harley half turned, smiled slightly. "You're still badass bitches." She turned again and with a backward wave to the friends behind her walked out the door.

Jayda looked at Kim. "She's pissed. I hope she doesn't go off and do something stupid."

Kim nodded, still looking toward the door where Harley had exited. "At least she'll be doing something. If that makes her feel better, then as long as she's going for it, I'll be supportive. If she needs my help and there's something I can do, and still keep my job, I'm in."

"You bitches," Jayda said with a sigh.

"Badass bitches!" Kim laughed and called over a waiter. "Teamwork makes the dream work. We love you, too."

29

Angry strides ate up the distance between Harley and her Mustang. She didn't even notice the small droplets of rain that slid down her in strands, over her tan-colored suede jacket trimmed with fringe, that splotched her jeans and dampened her tan suede boots. Reaching her car, she cranked up the engine and peeled out of the parking lot—mad at her friends, mad at the world, mad at God. Sure, she was pissed off that Grey had gotten elected. But what had tears falling down her face like the rain that streaked her windows was that the doctors wanted to start up chemo again, and Shannon had said no.

She arrived at Bottoms with more than an hour to kill before her shift began. She wasn't working the dining room today, but since she'd skipped lunch with Jayda and Harley, she bypassed the dressing rooms and got off the elevator on the dining room floor. Kat was there, talking to a nice-looking, older gentleman who visited the club often. Kat waved her over. Harley wasn't in the mood for chitchat but short of ignoring her there wasn't much she could do. She sulked over.

"Harley, this is my friend, Bill, the rancher from Nebraska. Bill, this is the beautiful friend I told you about. Don't let that scowl fool you. She's a sweetheart."

"Hey there, pretty lady." Bill held out his hand. "Why the sad face?"

"Life. Nice to meet you," was all Harley could manage. And then to Kat: "Can you put in an order for me? A chateau salad with an extra roll? I'll come grab it in a few."

"Sure."

"Can I bum a cigarette?"

"Sorry, kiddo. Bill made me give them up. I stopped over a month ago and don't mind telling you that you not noticing kinda breaks my heart." A pause and then, "That was a joke, Harley."

"Okay."

Harley ignored Kat's questioning eyes and Bill's bright smile. She went into the kitchen, copped a couple Marlboros from the sous chef, grabbed a small box of matches from a utility drawer, and went back out into the weather that matched her mood. She was still out there ten minutes later when Kat came searching with a Styrofoam container of five-star food.

"Hey!" Kat shivered as she yelled from just inside the lobby to where Harley stood near the alley.

Harley took a last puff, flicked the cigarette, and walked to the door.

When she got within reaching distance, Kat yanked her inside the warm lobby. "What are you doing out there? Trying to catch your death?"

Harley shrugged. "Worse has happened." She reached for the container. "You didn't have to bring this to me. I was headed back up."

"I didn't want you to come back up. Not in the mood you're in."

Kat pulled them past the elevators toward the empty office they used as a private breakroom. They walked inside. Kat shut the door, crossed her arms, and watched as Harley set down the container, shimmied out of her jacket, and plopped into a chair. Opening the lid, she took the fork placed inside and mixed together one of the chef's signature dishes—a salad of mixed greens, thin strips of fennel, radish, and orange bell peppers, all topped with strips of marinated chateaubriand and a tahini-based vinaigrette. She took a healthy bite, then looked up to see Kat staring at her with concerned eyes.

"Are you going to stand there and watch me eat?"

"If you're going to keep stuffing food in your mouth to avoid a conversation then, yes, I'll wait until you're done."

Harley took another bite, and another one of a warm, buttered roll before setting down her fork and picking up an unopened bottle of water.

"Yeah, that's for you."

"Thanks, Kat." She opened the bottle, took a long swallow.

"Ready to tell me what's got your panties in a bunch?"

"Sure. Mom's going to die." She picked up the fork, stabbed a piece of steak and several leaves, and then threw fork and food against the wall before doing something she hadn't done since before getting her period. She burst out crying. Not a soft, ladylike whimper but an all-out, gut-wrenching boohoo.

"Harley!"

Kat raced over to the table, pulled Harley's head to her chest, and wrapped her arms around her. "Oh, my poor baby." Someone knocked on the door Kat had locked. "Everything's fine. Go away!" She rubbed Harley's damp, long locks, much as a mother would comfort a grieving child. "That's it, Harley. Let it out, hon. It's going to be okay."

The knocking started up again.

"I said leave us the hell alone!"

Harley lifted her head from where it rested against Kat's stomach. "I'm okay," she muttered between a hiccup and sob.

"No, you're not, and you have every right not to be."

The doorknob turned.

"What the . . . Bobby! I locked that door. How'd you get in here?"

"Really?" Bobby stepped inside, closed and locked the door. "I'm Superman. I can get in anywhere." He turned to Harley. "What's the matter, kiddo?"

Kat answered for Harley. "Her mother."

"Did she—"

"No! Shannon's fine."

"She's not fine!" Harley pushed away from Kat's embrace. "She's dying!"

Bobby looked out of place and a tad uncomfortable in this maelstrom of emotion, but he took a couple steps and placed a burly hand on her shoulder. "Life's like that, kid. Death and taxes, the only things certain. No matter how much you make or who all you know they're coming, death and taxes, guaranteed."

Kat scowled. "Gee, thanks, Bobby. Way to cheer her right up."

It was said so deadpan and laced with such disgust that a snort of laughter burst through Harley's tears, along with a glob of snot.

Bobby jumped back. "Ugh! You trying to hit me with a loogey?"

"Sorry," Harley managed, a hand to her nose,

He pulled a handkerchief from his pocket and threw it at her. "Geez!"

Harley blew her nose and wiped her eyes. "I bet I look like shit," she said, looking around. "Where's my, oh, crap. It's in my locker."

"What?" Bobby asked.

"My purse."

"What do you need?"

"My makeup. What time is it?"

"Why?" Kat asked. "You're not going to work today."

"Says who?"

"Says me." She walked toward the door. "Bobby, hold her

here until I get back. I'll take care of everything, Harley. But you're not working. You're coming with me."

Fifteen minutes later Harley was in Kat's pearl-white Escalade heading to Kat's three-bedroom condo in downtown Kansas City.

"You didn't have to do this, Kat."

"Yes, I did."

"But your friend is here. You should be spending time with him."

"I'll make it up to him."

"All this time and you didn't tell me that Bill was your sugar daddy? I'd never met him or talked to him. He always chose your station. But so do a lot of guys. But his face was familiar, I knew he was a regular."

"Yeah, I kept his identity hidden more for him than me. But now he's on one about being in love with me and wanting the world to know."

"But he's still married, right?"

"Yep." Kat shrugged. "His problem, not mine."

"How'd you get them to let me off? We were already short a dancer."

"Don't worry about it."

"Did you tell them about Mom?"

"No."

"What did you tell them?"

"I told them to kiss our asses. Now shush with the questions until we get inside and I fix you a drink. Then we can start up again. Only this time, I'll do the asking."

That's what happened. After Kat had given Harley the fifty-cent tour of her penthouse condo, jokingly referred to as the mistress mansion, and after she'd fixed two Jack and Cokes and set out a bowl of chips, they got down to business.

"Now, tell me. What specifically happened with your mom today?"

Harley told her about the doctor's suggestion and Shannon's answer. "She's tired of suffering," Harley finished. "And as selfish as it is for me to want her to do whatever it takes to stay alive, I can't say I blame her."

"Has she ever talked like this before?" Harley shook her head. "Then there's a good chance that she'll change her tune. Not guaranteeing it. But I have a cousin who's a breast cancer survivor. On her bad days she'd threaten to overdose on her meds. On good days she'd ask for her makeup bag. Hang in there, Harley. I can't say I know how you feel as I've never been in your exact shoes. I know it's not easy. But I do know that you are strong enough to make it through whatever happens."

"Really? I don't know about that. Seeing Grey's smug face after getting elected liked to have killed me. We got the dirt on him, proof that he, the judge, sheriff, police, everybody was working together, and he still got elected."

"You did? What proof?"

Harley's eyes widened. "Oops, did I say that? Oh, hell. I think I can trust you. I know who took that controversial picture, the one of all of them hanging out together that ended up in the national press."

"Wow, really?"

"We just knew that was it, the proof needed for the truth to come out, and our guys to get out. He's a criminal, Kat. I just know it! I'd do anything to prove it in a way that would make people stop and pay attention, really understand what a jerk he really is. If I could just find a way . . ."

"There's always a way, Harley. You've just got to keep looking."

The women continued to drink and plot. Soon the ideas flowed as freely as the Jack and Coke.

"I remember you mentioning a club one time, a men's club in DC. Your friend, Bill, that's his name, right?" Kat nodded. "You said you went there with him. Have you been back?"

"No. Why? You're thinking it's someplace Grey would go?"

"Who knows?"

"If it is, then it's likely he'd be there with someone other than his wife. Finding out he has a mistress? That would be a scandal."

"He'd just talk his way out of it by saying she was on his staff."

"Now that would be the money shot."

"What, one of him and a girlfriend?"

"One with a girl on his . . ." Kat looked down at her crotch and then back up with a knowing look. "Staff. Get it?"

Harley burst out laughing. "Unfortunately, I do."

"Hey, nothing goes viral like a good old sex tape."

"Kat, that's it. A sex tape!" Harley got excited. "That would be perfect. It would go against that good old boy, flag-waving Christian image that he showcased on FOX News. That's genius, Kat. How could we do it?"

"We?"

"Yes! Does Bill know him?"

"I imagine so. Or knows of him, at least."

"Get Bill to set something up with him, invite you, and bring me as your plus one!"

"You know I love you, right?"

"Right."

"And I'd do almost anything to help you. But my kid's got three years of college left. I can't mess this up. Besides, you're much too good for somebody like Grey. I mean, political viewpoints aside, he's handsome as hell. If he offered what Bill does, I'd do him. But not on tape. Remember the sex tape would show you, too. Imagine what Jesse would think if you put yourself out there like that. Or your mom."

"Yeah, I guess you're right."

Kat fell back against the couch. Since dating Bill she'd stuck pretty much to glasses of wine. Harley's friend Jack was kicking her butt. Then a thought sat her straight up.

"There just might be a way to expose Grey without exposing yourself."

"I'm all ears."

The two ladies plotted for another hour, after which Kat insisted on paying for a taxi to take Harley home, who was in no shape to drive. Harley left the key to her Mustang, per Kat's request, so one of the workers could drive it over later. The taxi arrived, and Harley crawled in the back. Kat thought five minutes and she'd be passed out, but the idea Kat had planted for getting to Grey kept Harley wide awake. By the time the driver turned onto her block, Harley's mind was made up. It was a crazy plan, but she was going to try and make it happen. If neither Kim nor Jayda wanted to be a part of it, she'd understand. But she'd still do it, all by her badass bitch self.

30

"You're crazy."

It was the Saturday following Thanksgiving and the first time Kim, Harley, and Jayda had seen each other since Harley stormed out of the restaurant more than two weeks ago. They were at Kim's house, enjoying the turkey salad she'd made from her mother's leftover bird. While munching, Harley had shared her idea about going to DC to get Grey on tape.

"Crazy," Kim repeated, looking Harley dead in the eye. "Preposterous. Insane."

Harley looked at Jayda. "What do you think?"

"Sounds kind of exciting if you could pull it off."

"Jayda! Don't encourage her!"

"She asked my opinion. That's my opinion."

"I think my idea is as crazy as Grey's was to have a straight-A student headed to an Ivy League school locked up for drug possession with the intent to distribute. Or two brothers convicted of gang-banging when they were actually trying to buy a car. Or refusing a bank's request to throw out a case and allow restitution. Crazy happens. Crazy got elected. And now crazy is about to expose his ass."

Kim pushed her empty plate away. "So let me get this straight. This friend of yours—"

"Kat."

"Kat, who's dating a married politician and spends time in DC, is going to take you with her and get you introduced to Grey, and then you're going to somehow get yourself invited to his house, seduce him, get him in bed, and whip out a camera."

"Yes." Harley didn't stutter. Didn't blink.

"How?" Jayda asked.

"Good question, Jayda," Kim said, eyes fixed on Harley. "How?"

"In getting to the heart of what makes a guy like Grey tick, we realized it came down to ego. Approaching him in a way that feeds, strokes, and expands his . . ."

"Cock?" Jayda offered.

"Self-importance," Harley corrected, with a laugh. "Though for a narcissist, feeling important probably does make him hard."

"With that in mind, what way did you come up with?" As crazy and impossible as the idea was, Kim found herself intrigued.

"A student journalist."

"A journalist," Kim deadpanned.

"Yes. One who believed in his campaign, helped vote him into office, and wants to do a midterm paper on his success."

"I don't know, Harley," Jayda said. "He probably talks to dozens of reporters, maybe hundreds. How is your being one going to guarantee an interview, and even if it does, how do you get from there to a sex tape?"

Harley's smile was slow and devious. "Very carefully." As she continued, her tone grew serious. "Look, any way we go about this, there's risk involved. But it's worth it. That being said, I think the idea we came up with has a real chance of working. And while I really do appreciate you guys' opinions and concern, the curtains have already gone up on this play."

"What do you mean?" Kim asked.

"Kat told Bill, her guy friend, that her friend's daughter was a journalism major who would be visiting Washington and wanted to interview Grey for a school assignment."

"How does Bill know Grey?" Jayda asked.

"He's friends with the senator from Nebraska. That's where Bill lives. When visiting either him or his other clients in Washington, they often meet at a super private club called Filibuster where politicians hang out, usually with their girl-friends. Wives aren't allowed. Bill has taken Kat there a couple times."

Kim's concern deepened, and it showed. "How well does she even know this guy, given she's the side chick and not the wife?"

Harley raised a brow. "Are you kidding me? Sometimes the side chick knows way more than the wife."

Kim couldn't argue with that. Even though Aaron had as-sured her that he wasn't having an affair with Jessica, Kim still felt the pretty teacher might know more about Aaron's true feelings, about Kendall and other matters, than she did.

Harley shared more about the private club where politi-cians hobnobbed and networked while enjoying adult enter-tainment and fine dining, often with girlfriends at their side. "I trust Kat," she finished. "She wouldn't have brought it up to him if she had any reservations about this being able to work. And it did. Grey's already agreed to it."

"Wait, wait, just . . . hold up." Kim gave her head a good shake as if that would somehow improve her hearing. "You've already set up an appointment to meet with Grey?"

"He's already agreed to meet with me, but don't worry. It won't happen until after the holidays, early next year."

"Now I feel all better," Kim said, in a way that showed she didn't feel better at all.

"You mentioned Washington," Jayda said. "Is he moving there?" Harley nodded. "Won't his family move, too?"

"It's unlikely. Kat says most senators, congressmen, what

have you, have an apartment in Washington but fly home on the weekends to be with their families."

"Are you sure you can do this? Interview Grey without punching him in the face? And you still haven't answered Jayda's question. How are you going to turn an interview into a sex romp?"

"Glad you asked," Harley said, looking from Kim to Jayda. "Because that's where you two come in."

31

January. The holidays were over, a new year had begun, and the newly elected senators and congressmen had reshaped their lives to fit their new calling. Grey placed a key into the lock of his Washington, DC, brownstone and hurried inside. At first he'd balked at the idea of living in a unit that was connected to another, but his wife, Sunnie, had convinced him that the fully renovated and updated interior, along with its ideal location—a one-mile straight shot down North Carolina Avenue to the Capitol—far outweighed his dislike of dense urban settings and his penchant for total privacy. As had often been the case throughout their fifteen-year marriage, she'd been right. The close proximity allowed him to walk to work, which he did as often as possible, even on this wintry day, with temps below forty. Those daily jaunts, along with thrice weekly workouts at the gym and a sensible diet, helped Grey maintain the toned, slender build he'd had since grad school. The home's locale also put him in the middle of a very powerful mix of DC elite—movers, shakers, and powerful deal makers—and in close proximity to a variety of restaurants and shops. That the neighbor who shared his wall was an elderly and somewhat eccentric retired professor who preferred his own company to that of others was the final aspect that had sealed the deal.

Inside, the residence was as meticulously organized and restrained as he was, most of the time anyway. Grey removed his coat, hat, scarf, and gloves and placed them in the hall closet. He removed his shoes and set them inside the closet as well. His watch, wedding ring, and Harvard class ring followed, and were set in the silver tray on the closet shelf. Unless he was with a colleague, this was the procedure every day. If company were present, he'd remove the jewelry later. After retrieving his cell phone from the overcoat pocket, he proceeded to the kitchen and poured three fingers of single malt Scotch, stopping in the living room to set down his briefcase and turn on a television usually tuned to C-Span or FOX News. Drink in one hand, cell phone in the other, he returned to the living room, eased into a recliner, and took a healthy swig from the crystal tumbler. He closed his eyes, fully in the moment as the liquid created a slow burn on its journey from mouth to stomach. Another swallow, then he opened his laptop and clicked on Shadow, the computer monitoring system to the home surveillance he'd had secretly installed in the family home last week while Sunnie and the children were with him in Washington. He trusted his wife completely, but felt better knowing he could have eyes on the home even when he wasn't there. The cameras had been discreetly placed in a way where even his electronics geek of a son could not detect them. The app came on and revealed a four-way split screen showing the rooms where cameras had been placed: living room, great room, master suite, home office. He imagined his children, Matt and Emma, were in their rooms. Sunnie was probably in the kitchen, which she often called her favorite room in the house.

From the moment they met, he knew she'd be perfect for the high-profile, successful life he'd planned. He'd been her first and only love. She was totally moldable, Grey soon realized, with a quiet, almost timid personality; one who'd not question his authority, who'd be happy in the traditional stay-at-home role, and would uphold her vows to honor and obey. Her wholesome, pious nature caused one minor flaw: an infrequent and mundane sex life. For handsome, successful men like Hammond, of course, there were a myriad of ways to get around that imperfection. Hammond had used them all.

Placing down his drink, he sent a quick text, then swiped the face of his cell phone to reveal his wife's smiling picture. He tapped the screen and speaker button to make his nightly call. This was his routine four days a week. On Fridays, unless they were in special session, he flew home.

"Hello, dear."

"Good evening, Hammond. How was your day?"

"I can't wait until Thursday."

Sunnie's light chuckle brightened his staid mood. "Long week already?"

"Yes. And very busy." He knew that Sunnie would assume this busyness consisted of meetings, networking, and handling the few legal clients he'd retained. He saw no reason to correct her as the assumption was partially true. "How are the children?"

"They're fine, dear. All of today's activities are outlined in the daily recap."

The daily recap was a report his wife sent to Hammond before she retired each night, normally just after the ten o'clock news. Along with brief rundowns of the children's activities, the report contained progress on assignments Sunnie had been given, mostly related to making him shine, quick parental updates if necessary, and snippets of local news. Those were the inclusions Hammond had mandated when he implemented the procedure before leaving for Washington. It was a way for him to maintain complete and total control over the household, as was his right and responsibility as the head of it. The scriptures and cutesy endearments added at the end had been Sunnie's idea. He assumed these moments of creativity gave her pleasure. He hoped so.

"Dearest, I got a call from Pat Hartwell today. She's planning a surprise fiftieth birthday party for Jim. His birthday is on the thirtieth, which falls on a Saturday. The celebration will be Friday through Sunday, the twenty-ninth through the first."

"That's some celebration. Where will it be held?"

"That's the best part. Her gift to him is an island on Moosehead Lake in Maine. Very secluded, she says, a big plus for the group considering, well, given the recent controversy. It includes a log cabin–style main house and several actual cabins for guests."

"That sounds like Jim. He's come a long way."

He sure had. James "Jimmy" Dewar Hartwell's present life was a far cry from his humble beginnings in Glencoe, Alabama, a small nearly all-White town about an hour north of Birmingham, where he grew up amid alcoholism, domestic violence, and poverty. Jimmy had no goals and gave little thought to the future, until a friend's late-night drunken dare landed him on the town's police force. Fueled by the respect, power, and fear that came with a badge and a gun, Jimmy climbed the ranks. Quickly tiring of long, slow nights due to the low crime rate, he took a correctional officer position in Birmingham's largest jail. Within ten years he'd become a head warden in Louisiana, with a prison population of almost 1,000 per 100,000, the largest prison per capita in the nation. It was there he first learned about private prisons. Just after his fortieth birthday, he started the Guardian Group, a corporation that last year surpassed the Corrections Corporation of America to become the largest private prison operator in the country, with almost seventy-five prisons housing more than one hundred thousand inmates. A dozen facilities had been built solely to house the growing illegal immigrant population. As CEO of this corporation, Hartwell enjoyed a plantation-style southern estate, a private plane, a lifetime membership in one of Alabama's oldest, most prestigious, and most expensive country clubs, and an annual salary of over three million a year. A long way from "the city of patriotism" and ghastly memories of experiences he'd vowed to never endure again.

Grey was introduced to Jim Hartwell seven years ago on a hunting and fishing trip arranged by Grey's mentor, Mississippi congressman Thaddeus Stowe. The idea to build a prison in Edgefield was born, and through Grey's connections and position as DA it quickly gained momentum, and finally, voter approval. Hartwell's primary residence was in Mountain Brook, a suburb of Birmingham; however, he'd secretly lent considerable financial influence to Kansas-based Grey's senatorial campaign, a powerful and profitable alliance for both men.

"Confirm us for the weekend, dear. Order a bottle of Jim's favorite Scotch. It's listed in his files."

"I thought a house-warming gift would be appropriate as well. Perhaps an exquisite bouquet of fresh flowers in a Baccarat vase."

"Sounds perfect. Thank you."

"Is there anything else I can do for us, hon?"

"Absolutely, but that would be hard to accomplish long distance."

She gasped. "Hammond!"

Her response amused him. He knew her face was flushed, and her beautiful green eyes were shining. A light tap sounded on Grey's front door. "Sweetheart, I have an incoming call. We'll talk later."

"I love you, Hammond."

"Me, too." Before he'd finished speaking, half the distance to the door had been covered in long, sure strides.

He opened the door.

"Hello, beautiful."

"Hello, Senator."

"That sure sounds good, especially coming through those delicious lips. Get in here."

"I thought you preferred being the cleanup king."

Caroline removed her coat and handed it to Grey before continuing into the living room toward the fireplace.

"I was just getting ready to light that." He came up behind her, whispered in her ear, put a hand on each side of her concave waist and squeezed. "But perhaps you'd like me to light another fire instead."

She turned within his embrace, initiated a languid tongue duel. "That flame now," she said with a toss of brunette locks over her shoulder. She slid her hand down the front of his slacks and squeezed his crotch. "This flame later."

They switched places. Grey took a fireplace match from its bronze holder and struck it against the exposed brick mantle. Caroline crossed over to where Grey's drink rested. "Freshen your drink?"

"No, thanks. Haven't had dinner. By the way, did you—"

"Of course." She continued on to the bar in the dining room, reached for a crystal tumbler, and poured a Scotch on the rocks. "I handle all requests, personal and professional, with precision, focus, and attention to detail. Dinner will arrive promptly at seven o'clock."

Grey crossed over to the bar for a glass of water and then joined her on the couch in the living room. She pulled off her heels and ran a hose-covered toe against his pant leg.

"How are you settling in, Senator? Developed a routine yet, or are you still feeling out the capitol?"

"I'm settling in surprisingly quickly, to be honest. That's due in no small part to Thaddeus and the invaluable mentorship he's provided. He's connected me with all the right people, many of whom I'd already previously met. Gotten me on the proper committees. Membership into the right clubs." He reached over, pulled Caroline closer. "Made sure I had the right people on my team." He landed a quick peck on her cheek. "I'd say my DC life is close to perfect."

"How does Sunnie feel about your DC life?"

"Sunnie's place is in Kansas. My DC life is none of her concern. I have a superwoman here taking care of my needs."

"That's right, tiger. Which reminds me. Your personal aides and assistants have all been vetted. As for the press corps, I believe you received a dossier on all personnel. Be sure and run anyone by me who is not in that report. We don't want another Bryan White/Ozark situation."

"Absolutely, will do."

Grey saw no need to mention the journalism student coming to interview him next week. A native Kansan minoring in political science, she'd followed the race, had voted for him, and had been referred by the girlfriend of a good friend Grey trusted. Very conservative, a loyal family man—girlfriend aside. No nonsense. Bill had forwarded a picture. Gorgeous girl. Young, blond, and probably dumb, just the way he liked them. Caroline was the exception, one who, given their hot and heavy romance, might take exception to his entertaining someone other than Sunnie in what was supposed to be their exclusive love nest. What she didn't know wouldn't hurt her, right?

"Your office has been swept for recording, video, and other devices," Caroline continued. She stopped, frowned. "Do we need to do that here?"

"I can hardly believe it, but I'm actually one step ahead of you there. The place was checked out for me before I moved in."

"By whom?"

"Dick Schroeder, a PI I've known for years. Since then, no one's been here without me present and watching except my wife." He swept a hand across the room. "Decorating. How'd she do?"

"Very well, actually. Surprising, given the country feel of your Kansas estate."

"That's Sunnie's taste. Here, it's all Grey."

"Mmm." She swept her tongue across his lips. "So does that mean outside the sunshine state you're all mine?"

Grey ran a hand below Caroline's jaw and lifted her lips to meet his. "I'm all yours," he said, placing kisses on her face and neck. "And you," he continued, nuzzling her neck, "all of you," he ran a hand beneath the hem of her dress to expose her thighs, "belongs to me."

They kissed, softly, delicately. Grey continued his exploration of Caroline's inner thighs. She spread her legs for easier access, loosened his tie, released the top buttons on his shirt and dropped her hand to his crotch to run French-manicured fingernails over the material covering his burgeoning hardness.

Their foreplay was interrupted by the clang of a brass knocker.

Caroline looked at her watch and sighed. "Seven o'clock, just as I insisted."

Grey answered the door and returned to the living room with the night's order—two dinners of baked Dover sole, rice pilaf, and gourmet salads of baby spinach and beets from a local, organic farm-to-table restaurant. He placed the sack on the hallway table, then returned to the couch and the act of counting Caroline's teeth with his tongue.

"Aren't you hungry?" she panted, even as she pulled at his belt buckle.

"Starved."

Soon the food was forgotten as another appetite was assuaged. Right there in the living room clothes came off, a condom went on, and groans filled the air during frenzied lovemaking on the couch, the floor, and the dining room table.

All the while, thanks to a surveillance device that had been surreptitiously placed in a living room lighting fixture, one of several located throughout the home, a pair of eyes were glued to a computer screen . . . watching it all.

32

For weeks, months, years, Harley, Kim, and Jayda had sought justice for their loved ones. When the legal system failed them, they plotted revenge. They'd vowed to not rest until wrongs had been righted, lies had been exposed, and the true criminal was put on trial, convicted, and sentenced. And they'd meant it. Now the stage had been set, the plot had been written, and Harley had snagged the starring role. In one week exactly, it would be showtime. Tonight, the three sat in a downtown Starbucks, going over their plan. As the oldest, Kim usually took the leader role and headed up these type of plans. Tonight, however, was all Harley.

"Kim, you've got your ticket, right?" Kim nodded. "What about you, Jayda? Were you able to get that buddy pass?"

"Yep. Thanks to Aunt Lucy's friend who works for Southwest. I couldn't have gone without it. Those last-minute ticket prices are outrageous."

"What about hotels?"

"I booked us one in Baltimore, close to the airport."

"Dang, Kim. Don't look so sad. This is going to work."

"I'm not sad, Harley. Just extremely concerned. There are so many components to what we've planned, any number of which could go wrong for a hundred different reasons at a thousand different times."

"Stop being paranoid. The hardest part is already over."

Jayda looked up, surprised. "It is?"

"Absolutely. He's agreed to do the interview at his DC townhouse. That was the last piece of the puzzle that needed to get put into place."

Kim did a casual look around. Convinced no one was within hearing distance, she said, "No, the hardest part will be making sure you don't kill him."

"Giving him just the right amount of sleeping medication will be tricky, no doubt. But if he dies . . . oops!" Harley laughed.

"That isn't funny," Kim sternly replied. "We're talking about a U.S. senator. A slipup like that and we're looking at federal murder, and probably any other charges that can be applied."

"I'm not going to kill him, Kim. I've administered those to my mom dozens of times. I'm only going to crush four pills. We'll give him half of the dose and if he stays awake and keeps yapping, I will give him the rest. I won't do more than that, okay? Feel better?"

"A little."

"I don't."

"Oh, God," Harley groaned as she looked at Jayda. "Not you, too. Geez, I can't believe the both of you are so concerned about the man's life."

"I'm more concerned about yours," Kim retorted. "And Jayda's. And mine."

Jayda idly strummed nervous fingers on the table. "My concern is about what happens afterwards."

"We've already discussed that," Harley said. "We send him the tape with a letter demanding our guys' release."

"Just like that?" Jayda asked.

Harley's eyes narrowed. "As simple as that."

"That idea is exactly what makes this whole thing anything

but simple," Kim said. "Once we send the letter, he'll know who's behind the video."

Jayda's expression conveyed that Kim's statement was one she hadn't thought of before. "What if he doesn't meet our demands? What will that mean for us, or for our guys in the prisons that are owned by his friends?"

"You thinking about Nicky?" Kim's voice was gentle as she broached the still touchy subject.

"I'm always thinking about him," Jayda replied. "And I'm still not convinced that his getting beat up right after that picture got printed was just a coincidence, or gang-related, as you said Jesse believed."

"Harley, Jayda makes a good point. There's no guarantee that he'll release them, or that he even has the power to do that. But he'll have evidence that we've tried to blackmail him. What happens then?"

"Look, guys. I can't answer what if this happens or that happens questions. But I can tell you this. If we sit on our asses and do nothing, then nothing will happen. That I know for sure."

"What if we add more names to the list we're demanding be released?" Kim asked. "Faith's son, for instance, who should be in a mental hospital instead of in jail. Or Mrs. Newman's son, the one who was tried in Dodd's court and has been in prison for almost fifteen years for a simple assault."

"I say put all the names from our WHIP family members on the list."

"I actually thought about that, Jayda," Harley said. "But that's too many people. He might be able to pardon three, or get their sentences commuted. But twenty-five? Fifty? That would likely start a massive investigation, and a bunch of eyes on this situation is what we don't need."

"A bunch of people don't have to know," Jayda countered. "He doesn't have to place an ad announcing their release. Just let them go."

Kim shook her head. "The public will find out. The moment Kendall gets out he'll contact his agent, who'll start contacting teams regarding his availability. Journalists will know he got out early. Too many news outlets followed his arrest. The subsequent conviction and sentence made the front page of sports sections everywhere. Reporters will come sniffing to find out why.

"You're probably right," Harley commented. "They're nosy like that."

"Or thorough is another way to look at it."

"We can maybe add a couple more people," Harley suggested. "That way he won't know exactly who did what. Except for me. He'll pretty much know I had something to do with it."

"You're not using your real name, are you?" Kim asked, aghast.

"Of course not," Harley replied calmly. "But I'm using my real face."

"Oh, Lord."

Kim covered her eyes with a hand. Jayda giggled.

"At least wear a wig, Harley, or some kind of disguise!"

"That wouldn't have been a bad idea, but it's too late now. Bill already sent him a picture of what I look like."

"Bill, your worker friend's boyfriend?"

"Yes, and even he was fooled."

"I thought you just said—"

"I did. But with a few precautions. When I dance it's in heavy makeup. To embody the nineteen-year-old I purported to be, the shot I sent was with a freshly scrubbed face that not even you guys have seen. I look totally different."

"You're beautiful, Harley," Jayda said, her voice sincere. "A natural beauty that can't be scrubbed away."

"No wonder he agreed to interview you," Kim said. "No matter the social, economic, or political status, all penises have the same IQ."

"I feel like I'm in a TV drama, and even though it's dangerous, it's kind of fun, too. So . . . who will you be in DC?"

"My name?"

Jayda nodded.

"Samantha Jones. Sam for short."

"Sam Jones." Kim slowly shook her head. "Three years ago I was a middle-class American professional with a son on the fast track to a football scholarship and a law degree. Tonight I'm in a Starbucks plotting a governmental scandal so dangerous an alias has to be used. What the heck happened to my life?"

Harley looked at her. "Hammond Grey. He's what happened to all of us."

"That's very true." Kim yawned, looked at her watch. "Sorry, guys, but I'm still that corporate professional who has to get up early. Meeting first thing tomorrow." She gathered her purse and the empty cup in front of her. "I guess this is it, until we meet in DC."

Harley nodded. "Yep."

"Wait." Jayda's expression was as grim as her tone.

Kim had started to rise but sat back down. "What's wrong?"

"The name."

"What about it?" Harley asked.

"It's fake," Jayda said pointedly to Harley.

"Yes, and . . ."

"Two seconds on a search engine and you'll be found out!"

Kim's eyes widened even as her voice went low. "She's right, Harley. Ohmygod! I never even thought about him doing a background check, and with everything that has happened it's almost certain he or someone who works for him will."

"You're right," Harley calmly answered. "Kat and I thought about that, too. Which is why we basically borrowed the identity of a real student attending a community college in Olathe. She resembles me, too, at least the version of me in the picture I sent."

"What if they contact her? She won't know what they're

talking about!" Kim asked, feeling all the anxiety she'd worked to eliminate come back in a rush. "Now here we have yet another person involved in this scheme. And she doesn't even know it!"

"It's the chance I had to take," Harley said finally. "Anyone who does a basic search will find a Samantha Jones attending a community college and majoring in journalism and media communications. Her social media posts are those of someone who could have easily voted for Grey. That's why we chose her. If the search stops there, I should be okay."

Kim raised a brow. "And if it doesn't?"

Harley shrugged. "Hopefully Grey will think with his dick as you claim most men do, and the thought of getting some virginal pussy will be enough to cloud his judgment."

Jayda's jaw dropped. "He thinks you're a virgin?"

"One who'd love to give that gift to Grey," Harley said, adopting the voice of an innocent. "That's what my friend Kat 'let slip' "—Harley used air quotes—"when she gave Bill the pic."

Kim stared at Harley as though seeing ET. "This. Is. Madness."

"I agree. But necessary when dealing with a lunatic."

"On that note,"—Jayda stood up and pulled on a heavy wool coat against the winter chill—"I've got to go, too. But let's talk again before then, maybe a conference call the night before leaving?"

"Definitely. At least." Kim looked at Harley. "You're leaving Tuesday, right?"

Harley nodded.

"What if something comes up and he cancels?" Jayda asked.

"My ticket is non-refundable," Kim said. "Out Tuesday, back Thursday. If your meeting gets canceled, we're all up a creek."

Harley stood up and reached for her coat. "It won't get canceled." She zipped up the leather bomber jacket and pulled on a knit cap. "Kat says Tuesdays and Wednesdays are politician play days. Most of them with families elsewhere go home Thursday night."

The ladies headed out of the coffee shop into the chilly night. "All right, Sam Jones," Kim said when they reached Harley's car. "Next week in DC."

"For sure." Harley hugged Kim and opened the car door.

"Be safe," Jayda whispered, hugging Harley a little tighter, a little longer than usual. She and Kim headed to their cars parked a short distance away.

Harley started the car, sat for a bit to let the fifteen-year-old engine heat up. It looked like the justice train for Grey had left the station. It had taken some convincing, but she was very glad that her girls were on board for the ride.

33

They took separate airlines at separate times. Harley left on the first flight to Reagan National, located just minutes from downtown DC in Arlington County, Virginia; she took a taxi to the Renaissance and the hotel room Kat had insisted on pre-paying with the credit card Bill had given her. On the way Harley texted Kim and Jayda, on separate flights to Baltimore-Washington International, about an hour away. Shortly after getting checked in, she called Shannon, as she had promised she would.

"Hey, Mom."

"Hi, honey."

"You sound sleepy. Did I wake you up?"

"Yeah, but it's okay. With all the medication and stuff, just about all I do is sleep. I wanted to hear from you. Your first time flying. How'd it feel?"

"Exciting. I always wanted to do it. Was a bit nervous at takeoff but once we leveled off, it was actually pretty cool to be up in the air like that. Only wish you'd have been with me. Then it would have been perfect."

"Ahh, me too, honey. It would have been great if your first trip had been for a vacation instead of a protest. I know you said it would be small and civil, but I'm worried. Please be careful."

"I will."

Harley felt a stab of guilt at the white lie she'd told her mother, that a few members of WHIP were going to DC to lobby for prisoner rights. Only a slight pang, though. There would be lobbying occurring, just not the traditional kind.

"I just got in, Mom, and need to get unpacked. Just wanted to let you know that I arrived safely. Will call you later, okay? I love you."

"Love you more."

Unpacking took all of five minutes. Going over the fact sheet on Grey that Kim had sent her, the questions she'd prepared for him, and "Samantha's" stats took ten more. Even going over them for one minute was unnecessary. She'd already done so a thousand times.

Now what do I do?

There were several hours between now and the time to meet Grey. Not wanting to be alone with her thoughts, she decided to keep the appointments Kat had also made for a manicure and pedicure, a facial and a massage. She balked at the prices but then heard Kat in her ear. "He can afford it." Until meeting Jesse, Harley hadn't known what it was like to be taken care of by a man, at least after age nine. So she decided to relax, stop thinking, and enjoy being pampered. Her body could surely use it, as much as her mind. Stress had given her a stomach ache and her nerves were shot.

Once done with the treatments, Harley returned to her room. She ordered room service, sat back on a king-size, pillow-top mattress that felt like resting on clouds, and enjoyed unlimited cable. For a moment, it felt as though she really was on vacation. However, minutes later a text from Kim reminded her that no matter how grand the surroundings or pleasant the bustling city view, this was a business trip.

* * *

After landing at Baltimore-Washington International Airport, about an hour from DC, Kim rented a car and drove to a nearby restaurant to wait for Jayda. She ordered a salad but for the most part just rearranged the leaves. It was hard to get even a piece of lettuce past the knots in her stomach. This was without a doubt the craziest thing Kim had ever done. Only someone like Harley could have talked her into it, or been stubborn enough in going through with the plan that she'd drag two friends along. So many things could go wrong. So many families could be affected. Aaron hadn't said much when she'd told him about the trip. For once she'd been thankful for this quiet side. Had he pressed for details on why she'd been invited to a forum for mothers with children in jail, she would have had to spin more lies, something Kim dreaded, so close to spiders named busted, caught, and exposed already lurking in her web. When Jayda texted to say she was at the airport, Kim was relieved. On most days she enjoyed her own company. Today wasn't one of them.

Jayda waited at the end of the passenger loading zone. Kim whipped the rented Hyundai over to the curb. Jayda was at the door before Kim could pop the trunk. She tossed her carry-on in the backseat and jumped into the passenger side. "God, I'm glad to see you."

They hugged, clinging to each other's shoulders like life vests in a churning sea. "Me too, girl. What are we doing?"

"Hell if I know. Asked myself that question the whole plane ride."

"Me, too."

"What if this doesn't work or, even worse, what if we get caught?"

"Instead of visiting our guys on Saturday, we'll be in there with them."

"Kim, I'm serious."

"Oh, sorry. My bad. We'd be in the facility for women that's currently being built."

"Maybe we should rethink this."

"Too late for that. The horse has already left the stables and is galloping toward the makings of a videotape."

At six o'clock, Harley arrived in the lobby to wait for the car Grey's assistant insisted Harley take to the appointment with Grey. She hadn't liked the idea of being in someone else's control, even for transportation over and back, but felt there was nothing she could do about it. It probably made him feel important to be able to do this. That's what Kim thought when Harley had texted her the townhouse address and asked her opinion on the car service. Eventually she'd replied to the email from Grey's assistant. All was a go. She'd wanted to ask the assistant if he'd be there too but thought the question would sound suspicious. While needing them had seemed unlikely at the time, she was now glad for the extra sleeping pills she'd packed. If it took her knocking out two people to get the tape, then tomorrow two very sleepy people would wake up in Grey's house.

The car arrived, a shiny black Town Car with a uniformed driver. As soon as he'd closed her door, she pulled out the burner phone and sent a group text to Jayda and Kim.

Harley: **On the way over. Nervous as hell.**

Jayda: **You got this.**

Kim: **We'll be right around the corner, awaiting your text.**

Jayda: **Spike the drink quickly. The sooner he's out, the better.**

Kim: **Just make sure you don't kill him.**

Harley: **Now there's an idea.**

Kim and Jayda: **No!**

Harley: **Ha! Just kidding. Thanks guys. I'm more relaxed now.**

Kim: **Good.**
Harley: **I'm ready.**
Jayda: **You'll be fine.**
Harley: **Oh God. We're here. Wish me luck.**

She walked up to the front door of the townhouse with a confidence she didn't feel. The way Grey ate her up with his eyes when he opened the door, though, showed that putting together an innocently seductive look had been spot on—black pencil skirt, white blouse, black pumps, minimum makeup, hair in a ponytail with a few loose tendrils brushing her neck and shoulders.

"Samantha?"

"Yes." She lowered her eyes, but only for a second. What came off as an act of shyness masked Harley's fear that the hatred she felt had turned her eyeballs red. Gritting her teeth, she held out her hand with as much of a smile as she could manage. The shaking she didn't have to fake. "Senator Grey, thank you so much for agreeing to meet with me."

He clasped her hand. Harley's stomach roiled. *I can now take touching a snake off my bucket list. I know what one feels like.*

"After receiving the picture of you that Bill sent me, did you think I had a choice? Come in." He offered a smile that showed off stellar genes or an excellent orthodontist. His teeth were flawless, Harley noted, as she passed by him and stepped into the townhouse. "None of your pictures do you justice."

Harley stopped midstride. Her head shot up, her eyes a question mark as they searched his face. Her heart beat so wildly Harley imagined he could see it, too.

"Didn't think I'd have you over without at least a quick check online?"

"I guess not. This is all so new to me."

Harley followed Grey down the short foyer into the living

room. "We can sit on the couch or at the dining room table, whichever you'd prefer."

"The table, please."

His eyes sparkled along with that megawatt smile as he beckoned her to the table with an outstretched hand. They were a deeper shade of blue than hers. Richer, mesmerizing. Even through her hatred, she recognized his charm.

They sat. His posture was relaxed, open. Her back was ramrod straight.

"Relax, Samantha. I won't bite you." Harley feigned a nervous laugh. "Not without permission first, anyway."

"Senator . . ."

"Just teasing. Tell me a little about yourself."

"Sure, but, could I get some water first. I am a little nervous, and it's making my mouth dry."

"Sure, pardon my manners for not asking." He walked over to the minibar. "Would you prefer a glass of wine instead?"

"Would that be okay? I mean, I am working, sort of, and don't want to appear unprofessional."

"Tell you what. I'll have one, too. Would that make you feel more comfortable?"

"Yes."

The relieved sigh Harley emitted was totally genuine. He was pouring part one of the operation into a glass. All she needed was part two, the opportunity to spike it. She pressed a hand against her stomach to calm the butterflies and focused on the décor in an attempt to calm down. The colors were beautifully put together, like she'd seen in magazines. Shades of navy and gray, with splashes of color through throw pillows and artwork. Everything looked high-quality and expensive. Hard to imagine being able to come home to beauty like this every day.

"Which would you prefer, Chardonnay or Cabernet . . ."

"Whatever you're having."

He poured two liberal glasses of red wine and brought them over. He held out the glass. She accepted it. Their fingers brushed. His eyes bored into hers. She dropped her gaze.

"Thanks." She took a healthy sip of wine, and then another, and started to relax.

"Careful. That's a really good wine. It can make you lose your inhibitions if you drink it too fast."

"Oh, okay." She took a smaller, daintier sip.

He laughed. "Quick learner, huh, Sam? I like that."

"Okay, where were we?"

"You were telling me a little about yourself."

"Oh, right." Having practiced this speech helped Harley relax further. "Um, my name is Samantha Jones. You know that, though. Friends call me Sam. I was born and raised in Kansas—"

"Whereabouts?"

She'd prepared for that question, too. "All over: Kansas City, Kansas, Olathe, Bonner Springs, a couple other places. We had to move around a lot because of my dad." After purposely rolling off a long list of cities that would make fact checking more difficult, or time-consuming at least, she held up her hand in a gesture that translated "don't ask." "I live in Olathe now, with my mom, which works out because it's close to the college."

"Johnson County Community College."

"How did you . . . oh, right. You checked online." A difficult test had just been passed. Harley relaxed a bit more.

"What would you like to do after graduation?"

"From college?" Grey nodded. "Continue on toward a bachelor degree, if I can. My goal is to work in TV news."

"Where? Say you could choose your dream job. What would it be?"

"That's easy. FOX News."

"Good choice. What kind of show?"

"Like *Keeping It Real* with Taylor Fields. She's like . . . my mentor. I mean, I don't know her, but she's who I aspire to be like, and who I pattern myself after. I watched her interview with you and your wife, and it was perfect."

"You saw that, huh?"

"Oh, yes. I followed your entire campaign, saw every interview you did. Read every article. I thought you ran a very good campaign."

"Why, thank you."

"I'm sorry, was that an inappropriate thing to say?"

Grey reached out, placed his hand on hers. "It was a totally appropriate comment, Sam. Thank you for your support, and for voting for me."

So great was the concentration it took not to jerk back her hand, her voice came out in a breathy whisper. "Thank you. I mean . . . you're welcome."

Grey's cell phone rang. "Excuse me." He looked at the face, frowned and stood. "Excuse me a moment. Hello? Yes, sir what can I do for you?"

Harley watched, held her breath as Grey walked through the living room to where they'd entered and across to more rooms on the other side of the hallway. She strained to hear his voice but couldn't. Didn't matter. Part two had presented itself. It was time for part three. Reaching into her purse's side pocket she pulled out the small vial containing the crushed high-potency sleeping pills stolen from her mother's stash. Her fingers shook as she unscrewed the top. She looked around, then stood directly in front of Grey's wineglass, Blocking the view of it should he come back in, she quickly poured in half the powder, then stirred the silky burgundy liquid with her finger until it had dissolved.

"No, not a problem," she heard Grey say as he re-entered the living room. "I just can't meet tonight. We'll talk first thing next week." She reached for her wineglass with two shaky hands and stared at a painting on the wall as she took a long sip.

"All right, Stowe. Have a safe flight," Grey finished as he eyed her. "You, too."

Harley's body was rigid with fear. *Why is he looking at me like that? Did he see anything? Has my cover been blown and Stowe revealed to Grey my real identity? Is the front door locked?*

"I was looking at the picture," she blurted.

"What?"

"The picture." She pointed to an oil painting on the wall by the table. "It's really nice. I've never seen anything like that. Before you sit down, can I have more wine?"

"Are you okay?"

"I don't know why I'm so nervous. Well, yes, I do. Can I tell you something?"

"Sure?"

"You're the first famous person I ever met."

Grey stepped toward her, placed a hand on her shoulder and squeezed. "You're doing fine. I'll freshen both our drinks."

No! What if I get back the one that's been spiked? Harley nervously toyed with the strap of her purse, wishing it was a string of those rosary beads Jayda talked about. *If there's a saint up there who can help me knock this man the hell out, please help me!*

He bought back the drinks. Held out the one in his right hand.

Harley chewed her lips as she studied the glasses. "Um, I think mine is the other one."

"Excuse me?"

She placed her finger against a telltale smudge. "Lip gloss."

"Oh, right." Grey laughed. "Definitely not mine." He gave Harley the glass she'd pointed to but instead of returning to his seat, he placed his drink on the table in front of her, stepped behind her and began to massage her shoulders. "I'm told I have magic hands," he said, kneading her shoulders and neck. "Five minutes should loosen you right up."

"Thank you."

"How old are you, Sam?"

"Almost twenty."

"Almost twenty, and you've never had a boyfriend?"

"I've had boyfriends before, but we never . . . I never . . . it's hard for me."

"Why?" He stopped massaging her shoulders, and stepped to the side to see her face.

She lowered her head, thoughts swirling. Grey had just thrown a curve ball. A question for which she hadn't prepared. "I was molested," she mumbled.

"Did you say—"

"It's hard to talk about." Or at all, as fear threatened to overtake her, and Harley worked to swallow past the lump in her throat. Then from the maelstrom emerged a second of clarity and calm as Harley remembered something from the FOX interview, the one she'd watched as part of her research, and to learn about her "mentor," Taylor Fields.

She steeled herself, looked Grey in the eye, her own wide and vulnerable. "It's one of the reasons I admire you so, one of many. The way you stood up for that girl against that lowlife Smith guy. The way you fight for children and . . . keep us safe."

Grey eyed her a beat longer, ran a finger down her cheek, and returned to the massage. He worked his fingers from her neck to the lower part of her head, running them through her thick, freshly washed tresses.

"You have beautiful hair, Sam." She said nothing. He leaned down, his breath hot against her ear. "You smell good, too."

Harley pulled away. She couldn't stand it. Another minute and she'd jump over the chair and beat the shit of him.

"I'm sorry. It's just that . . ."

"No, it's me who owes you an apology. I was way out of line." Obviously flustered, he took several gulps of Pinot Noir.

"No, please don't apologize. It's . . . I liked it." She took a step toward him. "Maybe a little too much."

The smile returned, one of satisfaction and triumph. "Sam, what do you say I start this interview by giving you a tour of the house?"

"I'd love that. It's the most beautiful home I've ever seen."

"Good. Let's start upstairs. In the bedroom."

"Okay." She said it slowly, her voice filled with uncertainty.

"It's all right, Sam." He took her hand. "I promise. This is exactly what's supposed to happen."

They went upstairs. Along the way he pointed out a half bath, an office, and a parlor on the other side of the hallway where a stairway led to the second floor. Beyond the stairs was a back door. There, the neutral, subdued color scheme continued. The master suite was masculinity personified: various shades of gray, mixed with black, white and navy.

Grey sat on the bed. He patted the space next to him. "Sit down, Sam."

She did. She looked over the rim of her glass as she drained her wine.

"I told you to go slow."

"I don't want to go slow anymore. Drink yours, too."

"Looks like the wine is bringing out your bolder side, Sam." He took a healthy drink. "I like that." He finished off the rest of his drink and reached for his necktie. "Let's get a little more comfortable."

His words slurred the slightest bit. Encouraged, Harley stood and slowly removed her skirt, stared at Grey as she slowly released each button from its hole on her blouse. One button. His eyes fluttered. A second button. A slight shake of his head as he tried to stay focused.

"Senator, you all right?"

"Yes, I'm . . ."

Third button. "Senator . . ."

He placed a hand to his head.

"Senator Grey, Hammond, what is it?" She stepped toward him, placed her hand beneath his chin and raised his face in time to see the balls of his eyes disappear into the back of his head. A slight push and he flopped back on the bed. Out like a light.

"Senator . . ." Harley shook him slightly at first and then harder. "Grey!"

A soft snore was his response.

Harley scurried off of him and grabbed her phone while racing down the stairs.

He's out! Come around back. Now!!!

34

Twelve minutes after seeing Harley waving them to the back of the house and stepping through the door, the three women crept out of Grey's bedroom and back down the stairs. Mission accomplished. Not a word was spoken. They reached the landing. Harley stepped around them and gently opened the side door. Kim blew a kiss, Jayda waved, and the ladies eased out the back door, their forms quickly enveloped in the darkness of a moonless night. Harley clicked the bolt into its slot. She jumped at the sound. Upstairs her bravado was front and center but now, alone but for the man she hated, the gravity of the situation hit her in the gut. She'd filmed a pseudo sex tape of a United States senator, one she'd drugged to the point that he almost appeared deceased. What if she'd poured a fatal dose of pills into his glass? What if Kim's fear came true and he died? Did they get the evidence they needed? Would it be enough to make a difference? If she got caught, who'd take care of Shannon? With each thought, Harley's chest tightened. It was hard to breathe. Her hands began shaking again. It was the onset of a full-on panic attack and then . . . *What was that?* A soft thud came from upstairs. *Grey! He's awake!* Self-preservation trumped panic. Harley grabbed her bag and hurried to the front door. She forced herself to slow down, took a quick look in the hallway mirror, and almost had a heart attack. *The wig! Shit!* Picking up a brunette when he'd dropped off a blonde would have been a tricky transformation to explain to the driver. She shoved the wig into her bag, took a deep breath, and opened the door. After turning to softly close it behind her, Harley forced a smile and waved to the friendly driver she'd called from Grey's cell phone. She was appreciative of his constant yet mindless chatter as he unknowingly aided her escape from the scene of the crime. By the time they arrived back at the hotel, her nerves had calmed. Her heartbeat had returned to normal. After pocketing the tip he refused to take, she exited the car, stopped by her hotel room to pick up her already packed carry-on, and then went straight through the lobby to a back entrance where Kim and Jayda waited in the rental car.

Jayda's head whipped around when Harley got in back. "Harley! What took so long? We were so worried about you!"

"I had to wait for the car service."

Kim had pulled out of the hotel parking lot and now headed toward the freeway. "How are you, hon?" She stepped back and looked into her eyes. "He didn't wake up, did he?"

"I honestly don't know. I heard a sound just as the car pulled up front and got my ass out of there."

"It's over now," Kim replied. "So just take a deep breath and try to calm down. It's over," she repeated. "We did it."

"That's right!" Harley's comment was punctuated by a fist in the air. "We frickin' did it! We've got that asshole by the balls now."

"Yeah, literally," Jayda said, with a nervous laugh. She looked at Kim. "And switching us up at the last minute? Genius!"

"Plus the wig actually looked cute on you."

She and Harley high-fived. Kim honked the horn. A plethora of emotions was released—joy, anxiety, happiness, fear, elation, and most of all, relief.

"Now, how are we going to get this to him? Should we mail it to his office in DC? His house? Have it delivered by messenger . . . What?"

"Let's think about that tomorrow," Kim suggested. "My nerves have had all they can take for one day."

Plotting continued early the next morning. No one had gotten much sleep. The ladies gathered in Kim's room, sitting cross-legged on the king-size bed. They crowded the burner phone as Kim cropped the video, alternately laughing at the nerve of it all and cringing at what they'd filmed.

Once they felt they'd gotten a great two-minute presentation, they saved the work and argued the next move.

"Why not just email it?" Jayda asked. "It's a burner phone that can't be traced."

"But they can ping it to get the location." Harley said. "And then look at the lobby's videotape and see us on it."

"How do you know that?"

"Investigation Discovery," Harley said with a grin.

"Impressive," Kim said. "And the second time I've heard that channel mentioned."

"One of Mom's favorite channels."

"Bryan, the reporter, watches it, too."

"How about downloading it to a CD?" Jayda said. "Oh, wait. We'd need a computer for that, and none of us brought a laptop."

"Even if we had, using it would leave an electronic footprint." Harley said. "Just like the phone's GPS."

"What about using a flash drive," Kim suggested. "Do they make those for smart phones?"

"I don't know," Harley said. "Check the internet."

They did and discovered that there were flash drives for cell phones. Harley's flight left early, so Kim dropped her off at BWI to catch a shuttle to DCA for her return flight. Kim and Jayda found an electronics store and, wearing the wig Harley and Jayda had used the night before and Kim's big shades, Jayda walked inside the store and paid cash for four flash drives: one for Grey, and one for each of them. They'd all agreed that once everything was over and their men were released they'd have a bonfire and destroy the burners and drives. The last piece of the puzzle was decided as Jayda and Kim returned the car to the rental company and took shuttles to the airport— getting the flash drive anonymously to Grey's office on Capitol Hill.

Kim took care of the final action when she returned to Kansas City. After taking the shuttle to a different terminal than where she'd landed, she made a bathroom pit stop and while wearing the wig one last time Kim walked into an airport convenience shop, purchased a padded envelope, and called a messenger service. A fifty-dollar bill and a motherly smile allowed her to send the package without showing a photo ID. Kim darted into a bathroom just long enough to lose the wig, then walked out of the airport, hailed a taxi, and texted the ladies that the package was on its way. The plan had gone off without a hitch. Now all they could do was wait.

35

Sunlight streamed through the partially closed blinds. Hammond squeezed his lids against the unwelcome intrusion. He turned his head away from the window. Bad move. Pain shot from one side of his head to the other. His eyes blinked open, closed, and then with effort were forced open again. Slowly he rolled over and perched on an elbow, trying to push thoughts through a mind still groggy with sleep.

What the hell happened?

Eyes drifted downward. Brow furrowed deep. He was naked down to the ankles, where his pants and boxers pooled just above his socks. Sitting up, his gaze slid to the nightstand, and two empty wineglasses.

Samantha!

He looked at his shriveled member, at the glasses, and back at the worm. Was it possible he'd screwed such a beautiful woman and didn't remember a thing? He slid his hand over and under the cover. *And did it happen without a condom?*

He crawled out of bed and walked to the bathroom, his mind still boggled from passing out. That had never happened from one glass of wine. Standing under the spray of a hot shower, his head began to clear. He remembered Samantha's platitudes, and how nervous she'd been last night. But after the wine, she'd loosened up, accepted the advances as he knew she would. He remembered watching as she shimmied out of that tight skirt and unbuttoned her blouse . . . but nothing else. By the time he'd finished the shower, he'd chalked up the deep sleep to how busy he'd been in the previous weeks. The attention that had been given to countering the prison article, the subsequent deluge of media attention, and maintaining the image he'd worked years to create. He'd invite her over again, no doubt about that. Next time would be better, if only because he'd remember it. He had only one rule for their next encounter, one he would arrange as quickly as possible, tonight in fact if she was still in town. He'd get her naked immediately and let her drink as much as she wanted, maybe hump her right there on the living room floor then go upstairs and fuck her in all the ways he'd imagined. For him only one thing was off-limits. *Wine.*

He hadn't been able to contact Samantha all weekend, but as he entered his Capitol Hill office Monday morning, Hammond still felt good. Life had never been better. He'd just finished talking with Stowe, who'd confirmed his selection to the subcommittee on crime and terrorism. Specifically, he'd focus on the Department of Justice's criminal and corrections divisions. He'd doubted Stowe's confidence that the damning article could actually work in his favor. Even after four hours with Caroline, who'd learned her skills from the talented spinmeister who'd helped Bill Clinton remain in office after being impeached, and restore the respectable image enjoyed after leaving the White House—Hammond hadn't thought that a feat worth touting—but the day after nailing the interview speech, Caroline had prepared to divert the attention away from private prison profitability to the reasons why they were needed, and he realized that everything Stowe and others had said about her was true. Caroline was a political wizard. The conversation changed completely, exactly as she'd predicted. Hammond had even gotten an email from a woman who thanked him for getting her son convicted, believing that jail had gotten him away from the drugs that were killing him and had saved his life.

He smiled, leaned back in his chair, and set his polished black Ferragamos atop the pristine, glass-covered mahogany desk. As a part of the subcommittee, he'd be able to influence law enforcement across the country. The prison population was about to explode! Which meant money for his backers, jobs for good citizens, and funds for what would surely be the campaign of his life in three to seven years—for president of the United States. The plan hatched just over four years ago was working just as the group had expected. Clarence Dodd was sure then, too. *That old codger is a got-damn genius!*

A soft knock interrupted his musings.

"Yes?"

"Senator, a package for you."

He reached out to receive it. "Thanks."

After cutting open the padded envelope, he upended it to dump out its contents—a small item encased in bubble wrap. *That's odd.* He examined the envelope, noted the return address. It was from someone named Manny Freeman, sent from the airport in Kansas City. His curiosity piqued, he reached for a pair of scissors once again and cut away the wrapper from the item inside. A flash drive, he discovered, with no other enclosures. No letter. No note. No information on Manny Freeman, whoever that was.

Hammond eased his shoes off the desk and connected the flash drive to his computer. The computer's security system ran with no virus found. He clicked on the temporary drive and opened the flash. On it was an MP4 file and a Word document. A warning chill crept down his spine. He dismissed it, sat up and pulled the laptop closer as he clicked open the document.

Before even reading the first line, the first word, that warning chill morphed into a very bad feeling about what it contained. A feeling that within seconds was confirmed.

> *This message comes to you on behalf of the follow-ing inmates currently being held at Edgefield Correctional Institution: Daniel Sanchez, Anthony Newman, Jr., Jesse Cooper, Steve Brockman, Nicolas Romero, and Kendall Logan.*

"That Logan bitch!" Grey growled, between clenched teeth. The one at the rally who ended up in the paper. He'd immedi-ately recognized the name, Logan, but none of the others. *What's she up to now?* He kept reading to find out.

> *These men, unlawfully arrested, falsely accused, and wrongfully convicted, must be released, their convictions pardoned and their records expunged. Don't say it's not possible. Use the same connections that came together to put them in jail. If this doesn't happen within fourteen days, the enclosed will be released to all interested media. Should the above-named encounter any problems in prison, between now and when they are released, the same will occur. The tape will be released.*
> *Signed, The Other Clean Up Committee*

Though the note made him angry, Grey laughed out loud. He'd almost pay to see Logan naked, figuring she probably had balls that were twice his size. To think that she could blackmail him into releasing not only her son but several oth-ers was a complete joke. Had to give it to her, though. She had chutzpah, and drive. He could admire those traits in a mother, even one who refused to believe her son was a drug-dealing thug.

He studied the envelope, again with a smile. *Manny Freeman. Many free men.* Balls and a sense of humor. *Too bad she went up against me. I could use a smart Black on my team.*

He reached for his cell phone to call his private investigator, Dick Schroeder. Once the evidence was gained to link Logan to the blackmail, Grey would have her crushed, convicted, and sent to prison, preferably the soon-to-be-completed Edgefield Women's Correctional. The letter had come from Missouri. That might not be possible. But it sure would satisfy Grey for her to help him reach the inmate quota required on GGI agreements.

Just before dialing, Hammond glimpsed the screen and, seeing the video file, set down the phone and decided to watch whatever Logan had sent him.

A close-up of his sleeping face was the very first frame. *WTH?* Following it was a slow pan-out of his shoulders and chest on down to a pair of *Star Wars* boxers. He straightened so fast the chair almost flipped over.

"Fuck!"

The boxers were slowly lowered, revealing a soldier at shriveled ease. Grey grew warm as embarrassment and rage crept from his neck to the top of his head. The next shot was of a woman lowering her head to his pelvis. *Samantha?* But, no. The woman was a brunette with a body that looked nothing like the one he'd seen unbuttoning her blouse. Her legs looked shorter, the skin darker. Clearly this was taken in his town-home bedroom. But who was this woman? How did she get in there? Grey was certain he'd never seen her before, least of all in his townhouse.

After watching the video a second time, Hammond made three calls. The first was to Schroeder. The second was to his mentor, Thaddeus Stowe. The third and most important one was to Jim Hartwell in Alabama. All three conversations were short, the message exact. "We need to meet. In person. Tonight."

* * *

By the time Schroeder and Hartwell had flown in, Stowe's meetings had ended, and the men gathered at Hammond's place, it was almost midnight. Hours had passed. Hammond's unflappable façade was back in place. But his anger had increased, along with his resolve to get revenge on everyone involved in the fucked-up attempt to force his hand.

Inside he boiled, but his voice was calm. "I want everyone involved locked up. I want the names of their family members. I want their lives destroyed."

"Who do you think is behind it?" Stowe asked.

"That Kim Logan bitch is the ringleader, but she didn't do this alone. Sam Jones was in on it, too. And at least one other person, whoever that is on the tape."

Thaddeus removed his pipe. "You don't remember who you banged, son?"

"I know who I took upstairs, a tall blonde. I've never seen the woman in that tape before in my life."

Dick studied the message. "Let's do a little process of elimination. Kendall Logan is Kim Logan's son. The woman in the video had an olive complexion, right? So she could be Hispanic, which would probably tie her in to Sanchez or Romero. That means Sam Jones must be connected with either . . ."—he paused to scroll the screen—"Newman, Brockman, or Cooper."

"How sure are you that the drive came from one of these women?" Stowe asked.

"I'd bet my badge on it," was Schroeder's confident reply. "Give me a couple days and I'll find proof."

"In the meantime, I'll get a hold of Caroline."

"Why?" Grey asked.

"She's a fixer. And this is a situation that needs to be fixed."

Seventy-two hours later, Grey was angrier than when the tape was first viewed. Schroeder had taken the evidence and opened an investigation. Hadn't taken him long to get back to

Grey with pertinent information. So now another meeting was taking place, this one a conference call with him, Hartwell, the private investigator Dick Schroeder, Grey's attorney, Geoffrey Sullivan, and the fixer, Caroline Coker.

"First thing I did," Schroeder said, "was obtain a copy of Edgefield's visitor list and do some checking around on all the visitors listed for these men. I narrowed it down by who came most often. We know about Logan. Steve Brockman's a nutcase visited most often by his mother, Faith; Newman by his mother, Diane; Sanchez by several women, but most often his wife, Crystal Sanchez, and a sister, Jayda, who also regularly visits Romero."

"So she's the girl in the video?"

"That'd be my guess."

Kimberly Logan. He remembered the case as if it were yesterday, got major press because her son was some hotshot football star. A great win for the DA's office. Raised Grey's profile and helped the PR rollout for his senatorial campaign. He'd read a couple articles where she'd been quoted, and he'd been briefed on other public appearances she'd made. He remembered hearing about an organization she'd founded, one that tried to free those that some, most often family members, felt had been wronged. He'd paid little attention. All talk. Little action. That's usually what blowhards were about. He'd underestimated her. But no more. From Little League until now he'd won every battle he'd ever fought. Yet he'd unintentionally let down his guard at the worst possible time, a mistake that could cost him everything. For the ambitious senator with his eyes on the Oval Office, that price was much too high.

"Got-dammit!" He banged his fist on the desk before standing to pace.

"Calm down, Grey," Hartwell said. "I know it's hard, but you've got to keep a clear head. Schroeder, anything else on these women?"

"Everything. Have extensive background reports on all of them."

"Anything to further narrow that list? Besides Logan and the Hispanic who we know was involved."

Schroeder reeled off facts about Faith Brockman and Diane Newman. "Law abiding citizens from the looks of it," he concluded. "Churchgoers. Newman's a grandmother. Sanchez's mother and aunt own a house cleaning business. They've done work in Edgefield, Grey. Cleaned the Dodds' house a couple times before getting fired for something or other I haven't dug up yet."

"After the article."

Schroeder looked up. "Huh?"

"The damning prison piece," Grey continued. "And the picture that got taken at the compound. The company hadn't been properly vetted, and they weren't recommended by anyone in the inner circle. So they got the axe."

"Makes sense," Schroeder said. "Don't see a connection with them to this, though, at least not directly. The last one's intriguing, though. Name's Harley Buchanan. An exotic dancer at Bottoms. Had someone cover a couple of her shifts last week. A manager named Katherine Lowe. Said it was to take care of her mother, who has cancer."

"What does this dancer look like?" Grey asked.

"Tall, blond, pretty girl."

"Sounds like Samantha," Grey said. A few seconds later an internet search confirmed it. "Looks older here with all of that makeup but yes, this is her. Which means the real Samantha Jones's identity was stolen. Good. Cut and dried case for identity theft. Good for at least ten years behind bars, long enough for her to think twice before drugging another politician."

"That's on top of the attempted murder charges, right?"

"Absolutely." Grey looked at Hartwell. He couldn't ascertain whether the king of incarceration joked or not. Didn't matter. Grey meant it. "What about the girl in the video?"

"The Sanchez woman comes closest in resemblance, although the way the video was shot makes definitive proof difficult."

"None of that matters," Stowe drawled.

"How do you figure?" Grey asked, indignant.

"Because we're not going to throw away ten years of work over five fuck-ups. We'll deal with the women later. Right now the only thing important is figuring out how to make sure that videotape never sees the got-damn light of day, and your rising star keeps on rising."

"Rising star?" Grey harrumphed. "Are you kidding me? There's no coming back from this. I'm done. Finished. And not just my career. I'll be damn lucky if I still have a family by the time this is over."

"Sunnie's a good Christian woman," Hartwell replied. "She'd never leave you. Matter of fact, that woman is probably the brightest spot in your life right now."

"This is a fucked-up situation, Hammond," Stowe agreed. "No one could argue with that. But we're not going to get trumped by three conniving women. We're smarter. More experienced. And have dealt with dogs carrying way more fleas."

"Sullivan," Stowe continued. "We need you to draw up an agreement that is ironclad. Make sure it spells out in no uncertain terms that this is a one-time deal for these five guys only. That every copy of the tape must be destroyed and that if the tape somehow gets released, no matter by whom and no matter the reason, all five guys go back to jail . . . for life. No chance of parole."

"I don't like it," Grey said.

"I agree," Hartwell said. "Sets a bad precedent."

"If the agreement is drawn up properly, the blackmail stops here. Our only concern right now is shutting this down as quickly as possible. God knows if the liberal media gets a hold of it they'll have a field day, and your political career will indeed be ruined. Once we're assured that this is behind us, we'll mete out some long-term justice on those troublemakers. We'll teach them who to mess with, and who to leave alone."

"What do we tell the press?" Grey asked.

Silence until Stowe's voice came through the speaker. "Caroline?"

"I'll need time to get up to speed on the players and work a positive spin. Hammond, when are you back in DC?"

"Tomorrow."

"I'll have something drafted by then."

"Start working on an agreement," Grey said with a sigh. "We'll give them this victory. But make no mistake. One way or another, I will be the one who wins the got-damn war."

36

The next day Grey arrived back in DC. Instead of heading to the Capitol as he normally would, he worked from the townhouse office, waiting for the meeting with Caroline. For the first time since he'd begun sleeping with her, he was not looking forward to the visit.

A quick tapping of the brass knocker signaled her arrival. He took what felt like the longest walk down the hall and opened the door.

"Hello, beautiful."

A slight roll of the eyes. "Senator."

"Aw, come on, Caroline."

"Save it," she said, a hand in the air as she brushed by him and into the living room. She slung off her coat and turned to face him. Five-inch pumps added to her already commanding height of five-nine, the formidable presence made even more so by a form-fitting navy dress with shoulder pads and a tightly cinched belt. Her hair was pulled into a high ponytail, emphasizing big, periwinkle eyes, high cheekbones, flawless milky skin, and kissable lips now drawn in a straight line. "This isn't personal. It's business. I'm here to clean up the mess you made by not controlling your penis."

"Caroline, please, let's sit down. This isn't what you think."

She kept standing. "Then what is it? How do you explain someone being able to come into your house and make a sex tape, with you in it, I might add, and you know nothing about it?"

"I was drugged." Hammond sighed, walked over to the bar and put two cubes in a tumbler. On second thought he reached for a water glass and filled it. "That's the only explanation that makes sense. Harley Buchanan, who introduced herself to me as Samantha Jones, a community college student, had to have put something in my wineglass when I left to take a call from Thaddeus."

"Why didn't I know about her?" She glared at Grey, waited, but there was no answer. "Had she been run by me, as is protocol, she would have been vetted, her false identity exposed in five minutes."

Grey sat on the couch. "You're right. I should have called you. But she was referred by someone I trust, and even then, I ran her name through a search engine. When Samantha Jones's information came up it seemed to correspond. I let my guard down. Big mistake. Won't happen again."

Caroline joined him on the couch. Grey continued. "It was a favor for a friend, an enthusiastic college student, an interview that would have taken thirty minutes tops . . ."

"But here, Hammond? In your home? In what's supposed to be our love nest, and not at the office?"

"That's what had been planned, initially. Until my assistant found out that her flight got in later and as a non-refundable ticket couldn't be rebooked. I was leaving for home the next day so we rescheduled it for six-thirty. Here, in the living room. No big deal. Or so I thought."

"The video I saw wasn't shot down here. It was shot upstairs, in the master."

"She requested a tour."

Caroline *tsk*ed. "So stupid," she muttered.

"I was. In hindsight, in a moment of weakness, I was a gullible fool." For a man like Grey to admit to a vulnerability of any kind proved the severity of their situation. That he'd use "I" and "weakness" in the same sentence was unprecedented. He reached for her hand. She didn't pull away. "I know this will be difficult to fix."

"Don't worry. Difficult fixes is what I do."

"Do you have anything in mind?"

"Yes." She looked at him and offered her first smile of the day, but not to him directly. "America is about to see the heart beating beneath that cool, steel façade. Your ability to believe in second chances, and to give them to a few men who, in reviewing their prison files, backgrounds, family support, and ability to contribute to society, you believe deserve it. None of this happens until I go over the agreement that Sullivan is putting together, and we get the women to agree to its very stringent, specific instructions."

She turned toward him. "Now, do you think you can show me something stringent and specific?"

Grey pulled Caroline into his arms. "Oh, baby. I need you so much right now. So very much."

They went upstairs and made love. This time, Grey remembered.

That evening, Sullivan faxed over the agreement he'd prepared for the prisoners' families. After a phone conference between Grey, Stowe, Hartwell, and Coker, a few modifications were made and then it was sent back to Sullivan. Later in the week, Sullivan planned to contact Kim Logan with the proposition for her son's release, and that of the other men mentioned in the flash drive letter.

The next day, after a round of meetings on Capitol Hill, including one with the subcommittee of which he would become a member, Grey called Sunnie on his way to Filibuster and dinner with Caroline and a few other guests. It was time for his daily check-in that happened when he was out of town, but he also wanted to alert her to the upcoming press conference. Caroline had advised that instead of with his wife and family, the conference be done with local Edgefield officials flanking him, along with the warden of Edgefield Correctional. She felt it would be beneficial for viewers to see the law enforcement community represented when the announcement was made on Friday, two days from now.

"Hello, honey."

"Hello, Hammond. I was just thinking of you, dear. Are you all right?"

"I'm fine, Sunnie. Why would you ask?"

"You were very tense this weekend, a bit testy if I may be honest. It's unlike you. I can only imagine the additional pressures that have been put on you there in Washington, being pulled in multiple directions and trying to handle so many situations at one time. It has to be stressful."

"It is, hon. But I'm handling it. I'm also taking the advice of good friends who advise that I relax a little, not be so rigid, to show America a softer, gentler side of Hammond Grey."

"Interesting. Who came up with that idea?"

"It was a joint decision with several of my peers, here. And Thaddeus."

"Well, if Thaddeus is on board, then I'm sure whatever you do in that direction will be fine. In all these years, he's never steered you wrong. Hammond, speaking of ideas, I have one. Why don't I have the nanny stay the weekend and I come up and spend it with you? Just the two of us. A nice change of pace. I haven't been there since you moved in. Haven't met any of the wives. It would be fun, don't you think?"

"Sounds excellent, honey, but now is not the best time."

A slight pause and then, "Why not?"

He told her about the upcoming press conference. "We'll be busy preparing for that until I fly out tomorrow night. I'll see you then, honey."

"Are you sure you've told me everything about this change of position on crime and the people who commit them?"

Grey turned stern. "What kind of question is that?"

"An honest one."

"Also one that doesn't concern you. Don't question me, sweetheart. I handle work and my career. You handle home and family. That's how we work best."

"Of course, dear. Whatever you say. I'll see you tomorrow night."

He didn't make it home on Thursday night. Instead, Grey spent both Wednesday and Thursday night at his townhome, with Caroline in his bed. He flew out early Friday morning, with Caroline beside him, courtesy of Jim Hartwell's private plane. By the time the press conference rolled around, the angry, vulnerable, humble Kansas senator had left the building and the confident, charismatic Hammond Grey had returned.

37

The Sanchez family sat in the living room, unusually quiet for such a boisterous bunch. Kim had called Jayda at work and told her that Grey was holding a press conference today, announcing the release of the men mentioned in their demand letter. Jayda had worked through lunch so she could take off early, and had told her mom that Danny and Nick were getting released.

"Por qué? Cómo?"

Jayda hesitated only briefly as she gathered herself from the mental faux pas.

"Through WHIP," she explained. "I don't know all the details, but the attorneys worked out some kind of deal."

Fortunately, that was enough of an explanation for her mom.

"Shouldn't have been locked up in the first place," her dad, Bruno, said. "They were innocent from the jump."

Rafael looked up from the game he played on his phone. "We should talk to a lawyer, sue them for putting our family in jail."

"That's a good idea," Teresa agreed. "Make them pay for all the pain and suffering they've caused, all that time away from the family."

Jayda's aunt, Lucy, made the sign of the cross. "*Dios Mio!* No more courts, or lawyers or lawsuits. Let's just be thankful they are coming home."

"What about dad's business? They lost a ton of money. The shop almost closed!"

"I get it, Rafe," Jayda said. "I'm angry, too. But I also agree with *tía* that right now the most important thing is welcoming your dad and Nick home and just enjoying each other."

"They took a lot," Jayda's mom, Anna, added. "But no amount of money can replace them being back in our lives."

"Shh, here he is." Jayda reached for the remote and turned up the volume.

"I don't even want to see that fool." Rafael got up from the floor and left the room.

Jayda, on the other hand, pressed the DVR's record button. She not only wanted to listen but also get the statement on tape, just in case Grey changed his mind. After all, he was a politician. Changing positions is something they were known to do.

When the commercial ended, the station cut to a smiling Hammond Grey, standing confident and looking handsome. He was flanked by law enforcement, and several other men Jayda didn't know. There was also a tall, beautiful woman in back of the group, wearing large black sunglasses and a serious expression. Grey made eye contact with several reporters, including the one Jayda remembered from the *Edgefield Eagle* who'd helped shut down the WHIP protests. Finally he placed a hand on each side of the podium. His back was straight, his voice strong.

"My fellow citizens of Kansas. I've called this press conference to share some exciting news, and to offer hope, a feeling all should experience from time to time. Our campaign to clean up Kansas is working! After ten years we've turned the corner. The crime rate has shown steady decreases for the first time in years. This is indeed promising news. Our streets aren't totally rid of human vermin, every neighborhood isn't totally safe. Homes are still being burglarized. Drugs are still being sold. Gangs are still forming, and people are still being killed. But not like before."

He went on, citing what Jayda felt was a bunch of gobbledygook statistics, political rhetoric, and straight-out lies. All this change occurred in the short weeks since he became senator? *Give me a break.*

She tuned out for a bit until hearing Grey say, "Now, for the hope part.

"In an effort to not only reduce crime but to reduce the prison population and begin the process for those we deem can be rehabilitated, the staff at Edgefield Correctional Facility have identified a select few individuals for whom they felt a second chance was warranted. They have been model prisoners and had no arrest records prior to their convictions. To respect the family's request for privacy we are not releasing their names. Nor is this going to be a regular occurrence. In Kansas if you do the crime, you will indeed do the time. But as a representative for all of the citizens who live in Kansas, even those who become prisoners, I do not want to only enforce the law but to inspire hope. That is all. Thank you."

Hammond smiled and waved as he exited the platform amid shouted questions from the reporters. Sunnie followed, but when a reporter shouted out her name, she stopped and turned.

"How do you feel about what your husband just did?"

"I'm proud of Hammond," she said sincerely. "You all are seeing the compassion that because of his tough stance on crime is often overlooked."

"So you agree with his decision to free lawbreakers?" asked another. "Even though they were found guilty and convicted for their crimes?"

"As a mother, I cannot imagine being separated from my children and am grateful that these families will soon be reunited."

An aide came and quickly ushered Sunnie away. As he did, Caroline stepped up and addressed the group with an unperturbed demeanor and cool authority.

"The senator has nothing further at this time. Any questions can be directed to my office. Thank you for attending."

An hour later, as Grey returned home, anger replaced the compassion Sunnie had earlier spoken about. He was angry at the women for winning. At the press for their probing questions. At the criminals who belonged in jail but were about to be released. But none of them were present. Only Sunnie was. So soon after entering their master suite, he took out his frustrations on her.

"What was that?"

"What was what?" Sunnie asked, not turning away from the mirror where she calmly brushed her hair.

"You speaking to the press like that." Hammond snatched off his tie, strode angrily into the dressing room and then right back out. "What got into you?"

Sunnie systematically stroked her shoulder-length hair for several seconds. "Why are you angry?"

"Because you got out of line tonight, Sunnie, and that's not like you. I talk. You listen and look good while doing so. That's the way it's worked for all my years in the public eye. That's the way it needs to continue."

"I'm sorry, darling."

Her airy tone caught Grey off guard. "Are you?"

She turned to him. "I'm sorry that you're angry, but not for what I said. I'm glad those men will get to go home to their families, that a mother like that of the football player will get to hug her son again."

"That's not a good thing." Hammond was disgusted. And it showed.

"It's not?"

"No! And as for his mother, she needs to be in jail, too."

"Then why did you orchestrate his release, and those of the other men?"

"Politics. Too complicated to get into with you."

"Why would you think that, Hammond? I'm not as versed in the law as you are, but I'm not an imbecile, either."

Seeing how hurt she looked, and remembering how much he needed her should the agreement not hold and that tape get released, Grey walked over and kissed the top of Sunnie's head. "You're right, darling. In fact, you're one of the smartest women I know."

"Who's smarter?" she asked, with feigned indignation.

"My mother."

Sunnie laughed. "I can't disagree with that." She rose from the vanity and crossed to the bed. "I know you said it was complicated, but I must admit my curiosity is piqued. You hate crime and detest criminals. You've said more than once that if given the chance you'd give all criminals a life sentence no matter the crime."

"Politics is like a game of chess," Hammond said, as he crawled into bed and wrapped a willing Sunnie in his arms. "Sometimes you have to lose the rook to get the queen."

She turned to him. "You already have a queen, Hammond Grey."

"You're right about that." He leaned over, kissed her passionately.

"Oh, Hammond. It's been such a long day. Can we just cuddle?"

"Sure, honeybunch."

"Hammond, I also forgot to ask you. Who was the tall, beautiful woman standing in the back of the group?"

"Her name is Caroline Coker. She works for Thaddeus, among others, in Washington and helped put the speech together."

"And she flew here just to hear you deliver it?"

"She flew here to do her job." Grey kissed Sunnie's shoulder. "Good night, hon."

Grey settled into a comfortable position. But he couldn't sleep. He wasn't the only one. Sunnie was awake, too. In time he would learn that she'd been awake, wide awake, for a very long time.

38

Two days later, between six-thirty and seven in the morning, happy families gathered in Edgefield Correctional Facility's large parking lot. Smiles were as bright as the sun that was just beginning to peer through the clouds. The mood was festive. Laughter abounded. Balloons and colorfully decorated posters reading "Welcome Home," "We Love You!" and "Free at Last" added to the celebratory atmosphere. The names had never been mentioned, but the release date had been leaked. Kim noted two television stations parked nearby and assumed the others huddled nearby represented radio, internet, and other media outlets.

"I can't believe this is happening." Harley's blue eyes sparkled brighter than Kim had ever seen them. She leaned in and whispered, "We actually pulled this off!"

Kim nodded, waving as Jayda approached. "I know. I keep hoping that this isn't a dream."

"Hey, ladies!" The three women shared a group hug. Like Harley, Jayda's eyes twinkled, though a hint of redness also belied the tears that had been shed. "Today's the day!"

Harley looked at her watch. "What time are they being released?"

"They didn't say," Kim answered. "I'm hoping sooner rather than later. They've been away from us long enough." Aaron, who'd been sitting in the car answering emails, got out and walked over.

"Jayda, Harley, this is my husband, Aaron." Kim turned to him. "These are two of the women from WHIP who've become more like sisters than friends."

Aaron shook each hand offered. "Nice to meet you. Thanks for supporting my wife."

"We're the ones who are thankful," Harley said. "Kim's strength and courage to speak out and not take no for answer inspired the rest of us to believe that we could change the situation."

"And here we are." Jayda motioned her arm to take in the crowd. "Guys, come over here with me. I want you to meet my family."

Kim and Harley followed Jayda over to where more than twenty people stood talking, laughing, and crying. There were hugs all around, with *gracias* and thank you punctuating the air.

Jayda turned to Harley. "Your mom's not here?"

Harley shook her head. "She wasn't feeling well enough to come, but she's super excited. Jesse's mom and brother are here, though. I'm still kind of pissed at them for cutting off their financial support while Jesse was in prison."

"Best not to hold on to that anger," Kim offered. "This was a difficult situation for everyone. I think we all did the best that we could."

Harley threw an arm around Kim's shoulder. "You're probably right."

Just then they were approached by a couple reporters, one with a cameraman in tow.

"Pat Tucker with Channel Nine News," a smartly dressed woman said to Kim when she reached her. "You're Kim Logan, right, founder of WHIP?"

"I am."

"Can I get a brief interview?"

"A brief one, yes."

"Great. Thank you."

She turned, amazing Kim with how smoothly she went from casual conversation to reporter voice and mode.

"I'm here at the Edgefield Correctional Facility, where today five prisoners prosecuted and convicted by the former district attorney of Jones County are being released. Hammond Grey, the Kansas DA who ran for and won a Senate seat on a platform vowing to clean up crime said in a recent press conference that while continuing to rid the state of 'vermin,' the word he used to describe lawbreakers, he wanted to inspire hope as well.

"With me is the mother of one of the men being released, Kim Logan, the mother of former high school football star Kendall Logan. Mrs. Logan conducted a high-profile campaign passionately proclaiming her son's innocence, and later formed an organization called WHIP—Women Helping Innocent Prisoners—to gain his release." She turned to Kim. "What are your thoughts as we wait for your son to walk through those doors?"

"Gratitude, joy, relief. But mostly gratitude. I'm just so thankful that Kendall is coming home."

"What part did WHIP play in your son's release?"

"I'd like to think that our shining a continual spotlight on what we feel are gross injustices played an indirect role, but there is no direct link between WHIP and what's happening today."

"How did you find out that Kendall was being released?"

"I received a phone call from the facility." This answer was part of the "official story" in the agreement.

"From someone here, at Edgefield?"

"Yes."

"What did they tell you?"

"I can't share all of that, for legal reasons. And right now it doesn't matter to me. I'm just here for my son. That's all I have to say right now."

"Just here for her son, Kim Logan says while feeling the gratitude and joy that I'm sure is shared by all the families who are here waiting for their men to be released. Some have decried the senator's actions, others have questioned, and a few, like these families, have praised them. No matter what any of us think about it, at least the families here are very, very happy. For Channel Nine News I'm Pat Tucker, reporting."

An hour later, a collective cheer went up in the parking lot as the smiling men walked through the facility's front door. A sort of pandemonium ensued as families rushed the group, followed by kissing, hugging, and lots of tears.

"Kendall!" Kim pulled him into a bear hug, tears streaming as she kissed his face. Kendall then hugged his dad, Aaron, who was crying, too.

"It's good to see you, son," he said, his voice gruff with emotion.

"It's good to be out here," Kendall replied. He took a deep breath. "Y'all have no idea right now how good it is to breathe free air."

A few steps away two released prisoners were hidden, completely surrounded by about twenty Sanchezes and friends, not a dry eye among them. Aunt Lucy kissed her rosary. Anna and Bruno stepped away from their sons so the wives could get a hug.

"Nicky," was all Jayda managed, before bursting into another round of sobs.

"Thank you, *mami*," Nicky whispered. They shared a quick kiss before he reached for his heart. "Hey, baby," he said to Alejandra. "Daddy's coming home. Are you happy?"

Ally nodded, and buried her head in Nicky's chest.

* * *

Across from the Sanchez family, Harley and Jesse seemed glued to each other. They kissed so long that after coming up for air, the crowd around them cheered.

"Now that's what I call a welcome home!" an older woman shouted.

A deep voice called out from the back of the small group gathered around the lovebirds. "Yo, bro, I think you just set a record!"

Jesse took a bow. "I'm just getting started! Going to try and break it later on."

Others called out goodnaturedly. Reporters worked to capture the moment as did everyone with a cell phone, or so it appeared, as dozens were out snapping pics and rolling tape. While each family would work to help their loved one forget these hellish past months, this was a moment everyone wanted to remember.

Jesse turned to Harley, threw an arm over her shoulder. "How did you do this, baby?" he whispered. "How did you get me out of here?"

"Didn't they tell you? Hammond Grey did it."

"That's what they told me. I saw the press conference, too. But I don't believe what he said for a second."

Harley didn't answer, and Jesse let it go, but Harley knew that he wasn't alone. There were others who didn't believe what Grey said, either, and a few who knew for certain that his spin wasn't true. But today was about celebrations, for all of the families. Who knew how long the happiness would last? For some in the parking lot, unfortunately, it wouldn't be long enough.

39

The Sanchez household was a cacophony of happiness, over forty family members and friends gathered to welcome home Daniel and Nicky. Everyone talked at once, the conversations as spicy as the food. Beer and tequila flowed as though it was midnight instead of midday. Jayda took it in with Nicky by her side, holding the daughter who'd not let him out of her sight since he walked out of Edgefield prison. Daniel seemed happy but was quiet, Jayda observed, making a mental note to talk to him later. He'd questioned the reason they'd gotten out "all of a sudden," had seen Grey's press conference and "didn't believe a word that came out of that lying fool's mouth." She wanted to tell him everything, to share the journey she'd taken over the past five months with the entire family. They were close, with very few secrets between them. This one, however, she would take to the grave. One of the terms of the guys' release. Jayda didn't know how she'd be able to live with the secret inside her. A part of her was so proud for being part of the team of women who took Grey's arrogant ass down a peg or two. There would always be two people with whom she could share the victory. No doubt about it, Kim and Harley were her friends for life.

"Everybody! Hey, quiet everybody, I've got something to say."

Jayda turned to see her father, Bruno, half standing, half leaning against an oversize cushion. "Careful, Dad! Looks like you've been hanging out a little too much with Jose Cuervo!"

"Don't you worry about it. Me and Jose are going to get real friendly today. Danny! Nicky! Guys, come here."

Amid joshing, teasing, and with a little prompting, the two guys walked over to stand by Bruno.

"Everyone got a glass?"

A myriad of answers bounced around the room. Even *abuela* Alma, Daniel's grandmother, held up a dainty crystal flute with three drops of wine.

Suddenly Bruno became strangely serious. He turned, clamped his gnarly hand on Daniel's shoulder. "The family wasn't the same without you two knuckleheads," he began. He tried to sound casual and nonchalant, but his voice caught. Fresh tears flowed. He cleared his throat and continued.

"I don't know how this happened and really don't give a damn. We're all just happy you're home. Daniel, I know you were complaining about working too hard, but the next time you want to take a vacation, do me a favor and consider Hawaii or the Bahamas, you know, somewhere more traditional."

The family laughed. The party began, lasting well into the night.

Kim sat in the back of Aaron's SUV. She couldn't stop smiling, or staring at Kendall. She'd dreamed of this moment so many times, often willing it to happen. While outwardly she never showed a shred of doubt or uncertainty that his release would happen, secretly she'd had moments of abject sorrow when entertaining the thought that Kendall might not be released early or even make probation and end up having to do the full ten years. But that hadn't happened. The nightmare was over. Kendall was home! As important and miraculous was Aaron's transformation. Her husband was happy, almost giddy. The same man whose words she felt she had to pry out with a crowbar hadn't stopped talking to Kendall since leaving the prison parking lot—about how good Kendall looked, and the shape he was in, how he'd kept in touch with Chad so that his son stayed on the scout's radar. *You could talk to Chad but not to me?* And how going into the NFL and attending college afterward was an option to explore. *Oh, really?* Kim felt anger on top of hurt. When she thought of the times she'd tried talking to her husband, getting him to open up about what he was thinking and feeling and getting silence in response, she could just about choke him right now! Her panties would have gotten in all kinds of bunches had she not noticed Kendall's out-of-character reaction to Aaron's words. The charismatic football star whose witty banter had often made him the center of conversation and who always got excited about anything football was quiet, stoic, his expression somewhat annoyed. Kim wondered what all had happened while her son was locked up, stuck behind those prison walls. Even more, could she handle it if he told her?

"Son?" She reached up and squeezed his shoulder. "You're rather quiet. Everything okay?"

"I'm all right. Just still in shock. I can't believe I'm riding in this car right now; keep thinking that at any minute the police are going to run up on us and put me back in jail."

"It'll probably take a while to shake that place off of you," Aaron said authoritatively, even though he'd never spent one night behind bars. "But this is real. Make no mistake. You're not going back there."

Kendall looked at him. "How did you do it, Dad?"

Kim held her breath, strained to keep a neutral expression. But her smile disappeared.

"It was your mom's doing, son."

"For real?" Kendall looked back at her. "How did y'all get the DA to drop the charges? And not just for me but those other guys, too?"

The official agreed-upon answer rolled easily off Kim's lips. "Remember the organization I started . . . WHIP?"

Kendall nodded slowly, his brow furrowed. "Women . . ."

"Women helping innocent prisoners. All of the men who came out with you have women very involved in the organization. The two I introduced you to, Jayda and Harley, have become really good friends."

"Harley, that's the blond girl?"

"Yes." Kim's smile returned, slow and easy. "Pretty, huh?"

"Yeah. Was it her brother locked up?" he asked glibly, a bit of sparkle returning to his eye.

"Ha, you wish! Jesse is her fiancé. Did you know him or either of Jayda's relatives?"

"I'd seen all of them from time to time but never interacted with them much."

"I guess prison really isn't the sort of place where one makes friends."

"My cellmate was cool, the closest to what you'd call a friend, I guess. I tried to get along with everybody, but other than the guys I worked out with, I kept to myself."

"You definitely stayed in shape, man. I know there was no football going on in there, but it won't take much to get your throwing arm back. This happened so quickly. I know you haven't had time to think about it, but we need to get back to the plan as quickly as possible."

"The plan for what?"

"Football, son. You forgot about that?"

"I tried to."

The car became quiet after that. Kim was still euphoric about Kendall's release, but it was clear that the boy led off in handcuffs that fateful day was not the same man returning to her home.

"Damn, baby. You look so good. You have no idea how much I missed all of this." It was said as hands roamed everywhere.

"Yes, I do, because I missed you the same."

Harley turned her body for Jesse's full kiss, loving the feel of his hungry tongue probing and swirling while his hands continued to reacquaint themselves with her skin. A nine-inch of plastic could never replace the muscle, sinew, bone, and skin under her hand right now. The kiss went on for minutes, or hours, she couldn't tell. Her panties grew wet, and in that moment if Jesse had wanted to fuck her right then and there in the parking lot, she wouldn't have turned him down.

Jesse abruptly pulled away. "Whew, girl, we'd better stop before I embarrass us both. Let's get away from this hellhole and head to the nearest hotel. Yahoo!"

Harley started the car and zoomed out of the parking lot, honking as both of them flipped off the building that had housed Jesse for sixteen months, eleven days, twelve hours, and fourteen minutes. Jesse turned on the stereo. One of his favorite artists was singing one of his favorite songs. He blasted the volume, rolled down the window, pulled out an air guitar, and belted.

"Thank God for all I missed . . ."

Harley jumped in and sang along. She loved all kinds of music, but since meeting Jesse had gained a special appreciation for the country he loved. They sang out of key, some words a little off the beat. But to her Jesse's voice sounded like heaven, her own private slice of paradise.

Jesse stopped abruptly. "There's one."

Harley glanced over. "What?"

"A hotel, darling."

"But Mom's waiting. She knows we're on the way."

"Do you know how long I've been waiting to stir the honeypot? My balls are blue, Harley. If we don't do it in the next ten minutes, I'm going to go blind!"

They checked into a hotel just inside the Olathe city limits. When Jesse registered them as Mr. and Mrs. Cooper, Harley's heart skipped a beat. They took an elevator to the third floor, then ran down the hall like teenagers on a first date. Harley could barely get the card in the slot she was so excited.

"Damn, baby, let's hope I can hit the target a little faster than you."

"Get in here!"

They peeled off their clothes and fell into bed, laughing, crying, enjoying the feel of being in each other's arms. Jesse, already hard and ready, directed his missile into the slick, hot target he'd teased her about. The first explosion came quickly. The second one, too. But on the third round, Jesse poked, prodded, sucked, and thrust Harley into an endless array of orgasmic ecstasy.

Sometime later, a light, featherlike something or other crawled up Harley's thigh. She swatted it away. It happened again, this time on her stomach. Another swat, before reaching for the sheet and turning on her side in search of more sleep. She was just about to walk into dreamland when it happened again. Around her ear and down her neck. Just as she was about to either kill the pest or slap the heck out of her neck, Jesse grabbed her hand.

Reality dawned. Harley turned over. "So you're the pest." Eyes still closed, she snuggled against him. Then her eyes flew open. "Shit! How long have we been sleeping?"

"I don't know, babe."

Harley hopped out of bed. "Come on, Mom's waiting. We've got to go."

"Chill out, girl," Jesse said with a yawn, following her into the shower. "Shannon knows I've been hand holding for almost eighteen months. She saw how you were dressed when coming to get me. If I know her she'll put two and two together and know what's up."

40

Hammond exited the Jetway at Kansas City International Airport and immediately spotted his driver. As they spoke, the young man reached for Hammond's carry-on and led them to the black Town Car located just inside the parking structure across the street. Once inside the roomy backseat, the senator stretched his legs and laid his head against the seat. All the recent activity involving the newspaper article, the unfortunate incident that led to releasing the prisoners, and the subsequent press conference had caused the past four weeks to go by in a blur. Everything about him felt tired—mind, body, soul, spirit. It felt good to be going home, where life was always perfectly predictable.

Usually he wasn't excited about returning to Olathe. Not that he didn't love his family. He just liked DC more—the excitement, prestige, challenge and, until recently, Caroline's constant companionship in his townhome. Until he'd unknowingly invited in a serpent named Harley under the guise of a pseudo Sam Jones. She'd put an end to those regular encounters, at least for now. Women. So possessive. It would probably take a few weeks, several gifts, and maybe even her own special key to repair the damage to his lover's pride. Then there was the matter of Sunnie's sudden and continued insistence on spending more time in DC. It was almost as if she knew that an affair was going on. But she couldn't. He'd been careful. Grey repositioned himself in the seat with a sigh. He had been absent quite a lot lately. His wife was probably due a special present as well. Maybe a quick weekend getaway to someplace romantic. Except for her uncharacteristic behavior of speaking out at the press conference, Sunnie had been a good partner, and an exemplary mother to their kids. He made a mental note to have his assistant arrange something special for them to do, something next month, around Valentine's Day.

Satisfied that the wife and mistress problems would soon be resolved, Grey's mind drifted back to his other problem: bad press. The day after releasing the prisoners, an article came out on the Guardian Group, Jim Hartwell, and alleged prisoner abuse in several of his facilities, including forced labor. Edgefield Correctional was mentioned. Coming so close on the heels of his releasing the prisoners, Grey's name came up, too. It put him right back in the spotlight. Reporters questioned whether or not he knew of the alleged abuse that had taken place there. They wanted to know more about his connection to Edgefield Correctional. His connection to Hartwell. Grey had stated at the press conference and reiterated in subsequent interviews that there was no correlation between what he'd done and anything that happened at Edgefield, and that unlike what the earlier article had tried to portray, he and Hartwell were personal friends, not business partners.

Edgefield Correctional. No doubt an extremely profitable venture, but was the money worth all the headache it had caused? Like the headache he'd gotten from being drugged, taped, and forced to release men he'd put behind bars? The thought of being so thoroughly duped made him see red. Or, more accurately, honey blonde. His hands balled into fists of their own volition, so strong was the subconscious thought to wrap his hands around the long, slender neck he'd flirtatiously admired a couple weeks ago and choke the very life from its owner, the one in cahoots with Logan, Sanchez, and whoever else. Had it not been for the specificity of Geoffrey's ironclad agreement, part of which demanded all copies of the tape be destroyed, and Caroline's quick thinking on how to give the release story a positive spin, her actions, along with those of that loudmouth Logan witch, could have cost him his present career and future aspirations, his goal of becoming president of the United States.

Grey gave his head a shake, forced the angry thoughts out of his mind. The problem had been solved. In due time, each and every one of the troublemakers would be dealt with. No need to get upset about a scandal that had been averted and would never happen. He took a deep breath and tried to relax. It obviously worked, because thirty minutes later he was awakened by his driver.

"We're here, Senator. Welcome home."

Inside the Grey home was the peace and calm he'd come to expect, an atmosphere carefully orchestrated and managed by Sunnie. When arriving home on Thursday nights she knew he'd be tired. So she always made sure the children had been cared for and were already in bed. She also kept something prepared in case he was hungry, and Grey knew she waited for him in the suite, dressed in a nice set of modest lingerie, prepared to service him should he get "frisky." Hammond was used to regular sex, and tonight he was ready for a round of loving, even if no more than missionary style from a woman whose lovemaking had the passion of a dead fish.

"Hi, honey," Sunnie greeted him as he walked through the door. She wore a lavender satin gown trimmed with pastel-colored flowers, and a matching robe. "You look exhausted."

"It's been a rough week. But seeing your beauty has given me a sudden burst of energy." He wriggled his brows, the meaning clear.

"You rascal. Are you going to take a shower, or should I draw you a bath?"

"I'll take a shower," Hammond said, already shedding his clothes and heading toward the en suite.

"I'll get us some tea," he heard her say. He turned on the shower and stepped inside.

A short time later, the deed was over. Not the shower, the sex. Foreplay and the actual act had taken a total of seven minutes.

Sunnie got up, took a shower, and brought out a towel to freshen up Grey. She then slid back into bed, but instead of going to sleep immediately as was the normal routine, she reached for the remote.

"What are you doing?"

"Usually mint tea makes me sleepy, but for some reason I'm wide awake. Will the sound bother you?"

"Give me five minutes and I'll be out." He gave her a quick peck on the cheek. "Good night."

Minutes later, he heard his name. Only the voice didn't belong to Sunnie. It was that of the Channel 9 News reporter, Pat Tucker.

"We have breaking news tonight after receiving a sexually explicit video sent anonymously and allegedly involving Kansas Senator Hammond Grey. The former Jones County DA has been involved in a maelstrom of publicity recently . . ."

Hammond sat straight up, turned to his wife with a look of horror. She glared back from an otherwise expressionless face.

"Whatever they think they've got on me isn't true," he told her. "You know that."

Sunnie said nothing, turned back to the television and increased the volume.

Hammond leapt out of bed and stormed into his office. This time he didn't call his attorney, Geoff Sullivan, the investigator Dick Schroeder, or Senator Thaddeus Stowe. He called someone he'd met years ago, someone for whom he'd once done a huge favor, and from whom he needed a big one now.

"Don't say a word," he demanded, when a quiet voice answered. "Just meet me tomorrow. The usual place. I have a job for you."

"What kind of job?"

"Some garbage that needs to be picked up and removed. Can you handle it?"

"Every job can be handled if the price is right."

"I'm paying top dollar. Half upon agreement and the other when it's done."

"All I need are the details: who, what, when, where, and why."

Grey relayed all the necessary information, then returned to the bedroom. Sunnie had found the story on another station and listened for a second time.

"Why are you watching that, Sunnie?" Sunnie didn't respond, kept watching. He crawled into bed. "Do you really want to hear the lies they're telling on your husband? I've been under constant attack, take daily beatings from the press, and then have to endure the . . . turn it off!"

Sunnie started at the barked command. She clicked the remote, then turned to him. "They showed your picture, Hammond. They broadcast a still shot from the video. It was clearly your face."

"Of course it's my face. There are thousands of images of my face on the internet, any one of which can easily be transposed onto the body of another man. That's what happens on these stations. They make up stories, honey, pure fiction. It's not like FOX News, where everything is fair and balanced."

"Then we'll sue them for libel, slander, character assassination. We have children, Hammond, with the internet at their fingertips. Maligning your name and reputation stains the whole family."

"You're absolutely right." Grey pulled Sunnie into his arms. "And whoever is behind this latest attack will be dealt with, to the fullest extent of the law. But I don't want you to worry your pretty little head about that. I just want you to keep being my sunshine."

He felt his wife's body relax and realized the tension in his own. Even with the cost as high as their family members spending the rest of their lives in prison, those bitches couldn't resist trying to take him down. They just couldn't stop trying to play in the big leagues. With this latest stunt, they were definitely in the game. Each one responsible would get her turn at bat. And Grey wouldn't need three tries to strike them out. He'd only need one.

41

Harley felt like a new woman. She walked from her car to the club but could have just as easily floated over on the cloud of happiness she'd experienced since that first kiss with a free Jesse. He was so happy to be out of what he called "the cage." The joy was contagious. When Harley left the house, Shannon was up and laughing. She seemed better just having him around.

"Whoa, look at you!"

"Hey, Harley, you sure seem happy."

Kat hugged Harley and whispered, "Looks like somebody got some."

Harley hugged her back. "Yep, Jesse came home."

"What?!" Kat grabbed Harley's hand and raced toward the talk. "Excuse us, ladies. Time for a little private chat." They left the room. Kat hurried them down the steps and into one of the spare rooms on the first floor. She shut the door and turned to her.

"Here I was referring to your tryst out east, and you tell me Jesse's home? I can't believe you didn't say anything!"

"It just happened."

"When?"

"Yesterday."

"And you didn't know?"

"I'd heard something might happen. Grey did a press conference. You didn't see it?"

"You know I don't watch TV." Kat's eyes narrowed. "You said Grey did it. Did his change of heart have anything to do with your trip to DC?" Harley remained silent. "You fucked the senator!"

"I can't talk about it."

"Come on, Harley. It's Kat you're talking to. I'm the one who set that shit up for you. What happened?"

"Really, Kat. I can't talk about it. There were certain conditions to Jesse's release and not sharing the details is one of them." Kat's face fell. "I'm sorry, Kat."

"No, it's okay."

"No, it isn't. In fact, it sucks. I'll say this much. Your connection and my trip were involved in the process."

Kim looked up through a shock of red hair covering one eye. "So you did fuck him."

Harley gave her a playful shove. "You're a trip, girl."

"That's why you love me." Kat looked at her watch. "Come on, let's go. It's time to show our asses." They walked back upstairs. "Hey, are you still going to be able to work here with Jesse around?"

"He doesn't want me to, understandably so. He wants to get a job, like, yesterday. But I don't want him to feel pressured. It's probably best to take it one day at a time."

"You're probably right about that. So let's talk about what's really important. How's the sex?"

"Beyond amazing," Harley said, grinning from one ear to the other. "And then this happened."

Harley held up her left hand to show off her engagement ring.

* * *

Everyone in the room had a smile on their face. Kendall joked with his grandfather while his grandmother beamed. Every so often she'd touch his forearm or pinch his cheek, checking, it seemed, to make sure Kendall was really in Kim's living room, that he was for real. Aaron had his arms around Kim, hugging her as she sat perched on his knees. She looked into his eyes. In them was something she hadn't seen in a very long time: joy.

"I've been thinking about the counseling you mentioned," he whispered in her ear." She looked up in surprise. "I didn't want to admit it, but we need it. I need it. And I'm pretty sure that Kendall could use it, too."

Kim turned all the way around and placed her arms around her husband's neck. "Have I told you lately that I love you?"

"I don't think so."

"Well, I love you, Aaron Logan. I'll get the counselor's number from mom and call her tomorrow."

For the first time since the phone call from her son in jail, Kim had real hope that not only could she get back the life they once had, but that the Logan family unit would be even better. Her world had light in it again. And everything was possible.

Later that night, back at home, the Logan house was quiet. Kendall was out with his best friend, Wilson Goode, their neighbor's son. The two picked up right where they'd left off, as though no time had passed. Kind of like the Logan marriage. With Kendall back home, everything changed. The atmosphere. The energy. Her heartbeat.

Lying in bed, Kim turned to Aaron. "Why'd you change your mind about the counseling?"

"Because I realized that Kendall's arrest and sentencing tore me up inside. I didn't want to face it. Didn't want to lose myself, when I'd already lost my son. There's something else, too. I want to tell you, but I don't want you to get mad about it."

"Okay."

Aaron hesitated, but only for a few seconds. "Jessica shared a story with me about what happened with her parents. How her mother had died without ever knowing how much her father loved her." He looked down at her. "I don't want that to happen with us."

"It seems you shared a lot with Jessica. I'm almost jealous that when it comes to your feelings she seems to know more than me."

"Talking to her was easier, for some reason. She was just a co-worker. You're the love of my life. The one I felt I'd failed when our son got locked up. I was ashamed, baby. And prideful. I see that now. Will you forgive me?"

"It's already done." They hugged, misty-eyed. The marriage had teetered on the brink, of separation or even divorce, but seemed destined to right itself.

"I've missed this, Aaron."

"Me too, baby."

Kim watched Aaron lick his lips. She closed her eyes, waiting for the feel of the soft, cushiness she loved so much make contact with hers. Her hands roamed his body, every inch, as if she was being introduced to it for the first time. He did the same, and after his tongue took the same trail his fingers had traveled, they came together in an explosion of thrusting, grinding, panting, fucking. Over and again, until Kim cried out with her release followed shortly thereafter by Aaron's deep groan. Within minutes she heard his deep, even breathing. Soon she was asleep, too.

It seemed she'd only been asleep a few minutes when an annoying noise broke into her dream. It was faint at first, and then got louder. She was downstairs in the living room with family and friends, all celebrating Kendall's release. The sound stopped. Started again. The party had started up again but now stopped, too. The sound grew louder. An ambulance? No. A siren. The police! Her son yelled, "No!" and ran toward the back door.

Kim bolted upright, her heart in her throat, the siren sound from her dream actually the ringing landline on the nightstand beside her. Other than her parents, few people called it. Mostly she got calls on her cell. Just as she reached for the receiver, the ringing stopped. A glance at the clock, and though the details were fuzzy, the fear she'd felt in the dream touched her in real time. Nobody called with good news on a Sunday at six a.m.

A yawn escaped her. She tried to relax, tried to remember the fun of last night, with family and friends enjoying dinner and celebrating Kendall's return home. Conversation had been lively then, too, just like in her dream. The wine never stopped flowing. Kim drank more than normal. *Maybe that's why I'm so groggy and the dream seemed so real.* She took a deep breath and prepared to lie back down. Before her head could hit the pillow, though, the phone rang again. She reached for the receiver, clearing her throat before picking it up.

"Hello?"

"Kim, sorry to wake you. It's Mason."

Mason Hodges? My attorney? Remembering the dream and her son running out of the back door to evade the police, she flew out of bed in a panic. The movement woke Aaron, who sat up in bed.

"What's wrong? Is it Kendall? What happened?"

"No, Kim. Your son is fine, at least as far as I know. At least for now."

"Mason, talk to me." She saw Aaron's puzzled expression and put the call on speaker. "What is going on?"

"I'm hoping you can answer that. There has been a very serious breach in the contract from Geoffrey Sullivan that you signed a week ago. The contract that allowed Kendall to walk free."

"What kind of breach? What happened?"

"The tape was released."

Kim gasped, fought to find air. Aaron got out of bed. "How did that happen?"

"That's why I'm calling you, Kim, because that's exactly what I, Geoffrey Sullivan, and Hammond Grey all want to know. I understand you and the other women's bitterness toward Grey for what he did to Kendall. But in allowing that tape to be leaked to the press, your son and their loved ones may very well be sent back to prison . . . for the rest of their lives."

An hour later Kim sat in her attorney's office, still stunned at the news she'd awakened to and now at the tape she'd just viewed.

"I swear to you, Mason. That is not the tape I filmed, it's not the one we sent to Grey."

"I don't understand."

"Neither do I!"

"This isn't from the night you snuck into his apartment?"

"I never said I snuck into anywhere."

"Okay, Kim. I understand your desire to not incriminate yourself, but as the attorney trying to keep your son and you out of jail, you need to be straight with me so that I have all the relevant and necessary tools to defend. I'm not here to judge you. I'm here to help."

"Everything's wrong about how that tape looks. The video was shot from the left side of the bed. At an angle, down and across. This video appears to be an overhead shot. I could not have gotten this type of footage from where I was."

"Do you still have the video you sent him?"

"No, destroying all of the evidence was a part of the requirement for Kendall's release."

"This is a tough spot, Kim. Because basically this will boil down to your word against Hammond Grey's. The agreement is ironclad and one clause very specific: if the tape was leaked, the men would return to prison."

"Yes, if the tape *we* sent was leaked. I don't know where this,"—she pointed at the laptop with Hammond's face frozen on pause—"came from."

"You're telling me that you did not make this tape, that this isn't what you, or whomever you enlisted, filmed that night."

"That is exactly what I'm telling you. I swear it on my son, Mason. I did not make that tape. I did not leak that tape. And I will see hell frozen over before Kendall returns to jail."

Mason sighed, eyed Kim intently as he sat back in his black leather chair. "Then all I can tell you is pull out your fur coat. Because unless I can find out who's behind this tape being made and sent to the press . . . it's about to get cold as hell."

42

Kim left her attorney's office, dialing Harley's number as she walked to the car. A scratchy voice told Kim that she'd awakened her friend.

"Hi, Harley. Sorry to call so early, but we've got a situation."

"Why, what happened?"

"Hold on a moment, let me conference Jayda into the call." As soon as Jayda answered the phone, Kim hit the conference button. "Jayda, Harley's on the call, too. I'm just leaving my attorney's office. Did either of you see the news last night?"

"I was working," Harley said.

"Not me," Jayda said.

"Someone leaked a tape of Grey having sex."

Jayda screamed, a quick, short burst of *WTF* from an astonished mouth.

Kim gave a quick run-down of what her attorney had said. "Harley, did you hear me?"

"I did, and that explains it."

"Explains what?" Kim asked.

"Why I got jumped last night."

"Oh, no!"

"Are you all right?"

"Yeah, but only because Bobby was there."

"Who's Bobby?" Jayda asked.

"A police officer who patrols our area. He's friends with all of us, our unofficial bodyguard. Walks us to the parking lot, keeps an eye on our cars, stuff like that.

"When I got off work, I headed to the parking lot looking around like I usually do. Being alert. Didn't see anybody. Got to my car and . . . boom! Guy comes out of nowhere, grabs me from behind. Before I could even process that I was being attacked, it was over. Bobby had him tackled and handcuffed in seconds flat."

"Thank God Bobby was in the right place at the right time."

"Turns out he'd seen the guy earlier, snooping around my car. After finishing his shift he decided to swing back around and hang out a minute, just on a hunch. When he saw the same guy lurking across the street from the club, watching the door, he knew something was up. I owe that guy my life. If it hadn't been for Bobby, I'd have been raped for sure, or worse."

"That's so scary, Harley," Kim said. "I'm glad you're okay."

"Did you get a good look at him?" Jayda asked. "Was he someone who'd been in the club?"

"Everything happened so fast, I didn't have time. Bobby snatched the guy, yelled at me to get out of there, and that's exactly what I did. Tried calling him later, when I got home, but he didn't answer and hasn't called me back."

Harley's news stunned Kim so much she was still parked in front of the attorney's office building, her car idling. She put it in gear and drove away. "Why do you think what happened has something to do with the tape?"

"I've been working at Bottoms for almost two years and nothing happened. What are the chances that the breaking news story and my attempted rape, abduction, whatever, would happen on the same night?"

"Just like the night Nicky got beat up," Jayda said. "Right after I took the picture. It probably wasn't hard to put two and two together and figure out that whoever made the tape was connected to the people being released. I think you're right, Harley. Somebody somehow connected you to Jesse and came after you."

"So here's my question," Harley said. "If what you watched wasn't the tape we made, who in the hell made it, and how in the hell did they do it?"

"There was another tape running somewhere in that room. Probably a surveillance camera. Whoever has access to it decided to make use of it. That's the only thing I can think of, the only thing that makes sense, given the angle of the footage."

"Oh, my God," Jayda moaned. "Then whoever that is saw everything. They filmed us filming Grey. They've got our faces, saw us clean up, they've got everything. Oh, my God!!!"

"This is unbelievable," Kim said. "We may get blackmailed the same way we blackmailed Grey."

"All I can say is good luck with that," Harley said. "Because short of my tips from daily dances, I can't give them a damn thing."

Kim reached her home and pulled into the drive. "Guys, what are you doing later? Want to meet and talk more about what we're going to do?"

"What can we do?" Jayda asked. "We don't even know who sent the tape!"

"I'm talking more about how we're going to defend our men. You remember the stipulation of the agreement we signed. That if the tape is released, our men—"

"Fuck that," Harley interrupted. "Jesse Cooper isn't going back to jail. We'll run before that happens. Pack up Mom and relocate to Timbuktu. I've got my man back in my life, and we're never going to be separated again."

"I'm busy, too," Jayda said. "Nicky and I are having family portraits done later on. Keep me posted, though, Kim, if you hear anything else."

Kim disconnected the call and went into the house. The same hip-hop music that used to get on her nerves was now music to her ears as well as Kendall's. She bobbed her head, smiling as she looked into the refrigerator and decided to fix a big breakfast for her men. She turned on the oven, pulled out ingredients for an omelet, then placed several strips of thick slab bacon on a cookie sheet. She put on a pot of coffee, then, wanting to hear the breaking news story for herself, she went into the living room and turned on the TV. The story played on every news station. She watched for a bit and then, hearing the preheat indicator, got up to place the bacon in the oven. As she passed the living room window, she saw a black van pull up in front of their house.

Kim was instantly on alert. The story Harley had shared ran through her mind as if it had been recorded on tape. Grey most certainly knew that she was involved in making the sex tape. *As vocal as I've been? With Kendall's name on the list?* Was this somebody who'd come after her? Right at the moment she started to panic, a man got out of the van carrying a large bouquet of flowers. Belatedly she saw Just Flowers on a car magnet attached to the van's rear right door. She breathed an audible sigh of relief. She watched him look down at a clipboard and then up to read the house numbers before starting up their walkway.

Probably from Aaron. Her heart smiled when she remembered their conversation last night, and his concern this morning when she left to meet Mason. The doorbell rang. She opened the door.

"Kim Logan?"

"That's me!"

He held out the flowers. "These are for you."

"Thank you."

"Just sign here."

She looked up to reach for the pen, but instead of a writing instrument, Kim found herself staring down the barrel of a gun.

"Don't scream. Don't say a word, or I'll kill everyone in here. Your husband, Aaron. Your son, Kendall. Back up slowly. That's it, just like that."

Kim heard footsteps on the stairs. *Oh, no. Please, Kendall, don't come down.*

It wasn't Kendall. It was Aaron. "Hey, Kim, I thought I heard—whoa!" Aaron raised both hands, bent at the elbow, as if defending himself against a bullet's path.

"Come on down, buddy. Join your wife."

"Look, whatever you want, you can have it."

"Shut up. Sit down." The gunman pointed the weapon at Kim. "You, too."

They complied.

"Turn off the TV."

Kim reached shaking hands toward the remote. After trying without success to pick it up, Aaron reached over her, grabbed the device, and turned off the TV.

Even though he was unarmed, Aaron glared at the gunman. "Who are you? What is this about?"

The gunman slowly removed his sunglasses and lowered the gun. "My name is Bobby Cavallo. I'm a police officer with the Kansas City Police Department. Last night I thwarted an attempt on a woman's life. A friend of yours, Kim, Harley Buchanan."

"That was you?"

"That was me. It took a bit of prodding, but I finally got enough information from the assailant to know why he'd jumped her, who'd sent him to kill her, and that you, Kim Logan, were next on the list."

"Why couldn't you have just told us that, man," Aaron said angrily. "Why'd you have to come in guns drawn, scaring both my wife and me half to death?"

"Because I didn't know if there was someone watching to make sure the job got done. I wanted this to look as authentic as possible, maybe even draw anyone out who might be around here. Two marked cars have casually circled your home and neighborhood since earlier this morning, after I got the information."

Kim was stunned speechless. Aaron's chest heaved with relief.

Bobby smiled and set down the flowers. "You're welcome."

"Oh, yes, thank you!" Kim said, finally standing and walking over to him. "What can I ever do to repay you?"

"If I'm not mistaken, I smell coffee brewing. You can start by fixing me a cup, black, two sugars, and then by telling me what the hell you girls did to piss off Hammond Grey."

43

A few days later Kim, Harley, and Jayda sat in a corner booth at a diner outside the city. Incidents of the past forty-eight hours had left them traumatized and paranoid. Even with no one around them, they barely spoke above a whisper.

"I can't believe he did it," Jayda said. "Actually putting out a hit on you guys? I mean, who does that?"

"The same motherfucker who'd line his pockets with money made at the cost of other people's lives," Harley said.

"What about your family, Jayda? Is everything okay?"

"I think so. Thanks to your friend, Harley."

"I can't believe what Bobby knew and didn't tell me!"

"It was for your own good. And my protection. He wanted to make sure that your assailant acted alone, as he claimed. Cops get a bad rap and some deservedly so. But your Bobby? I probably owe him a life or two myself. He's one of the good ones."

"If it hadn't been for him, all our asses might be dead." Jayda shook her head as she looked out the window.

"And Grey might have gotten off," Harley said. "But Bobby put it to him, made the guy give up all the information."

"What'd he do?"

"Jayda, when I asked him, he told me I didn't want to know. And that right there was enough to tell me that I didn't want to know."

"I'll tell you what I want to know." Kim crossed her arms and looked pointedly at Jayda, then Harley. "Which one of you did it?"

"What?" Jayda asked.

Harley eyed Kin with a frown. "The tape? I thought you sent it."

"Why would I do that, and jeopardize my son's future? Have him sent back to prison for the rest of his life?"

"Why would any of us do it?" Jayda asked.

Harley answered. "We wouldn't."

"You know we wouldn't," Jayda said. "We destroyed those drives together!"

"And the phones," Harley added.

"I know we did." Kim rubbed her forehead in frustration. "Which is why I'm drawing a total blank on how that tape got out there. Unless . . ."

Jayda sat back. "Unless what?"

"Unless someone in his camp leaked it."

"Like who?" Harley was clearly unconvinced.

"I don't know. His lawyer. An assistant. One of his sexual liaisons up on the Hill."

"Like his publicist," Jayda said, snapping her finger. "The tall, really pretty woman at all of his press conferences."

Harley gave Jayda a look. "You actually watch them?"

"Just the one where he announced our guys' release."

"I saw her, too," Kim said. "Now that you mention it, she does seem to be there whenever he's on TV."

"And maybe when he isn't on TV," Harley said. "Maybe she thinks that fool and I actually had sex and is making him pay. Ha! Serves him right. He deserves everything he gets."

"When are they going to arrest him?" Jayda asked.

"Any time now," Kim said. "Mason said the guy gave a full written confession naming Grey as the person who'd hired him to get rid of us. He's agreed to be a witness for the state."

"What about the agreement?" Jayda asked. "Is Grey's lawyer going to still come after us, even though it wasn't our tape that was leaked?"

"That's still a very sticky situation," Kim said. "He's hoping to get a modification on that as part of the plea deal they'll offer Grey. I almost wish we hadn't destroyed those flash drives. Having one would be proof that what was released and what we shot looked totally different."

"Wait a minute." Harley sat up. "Grey should have the drive. Or at the very least his attorney should have a copy of the video, evidence they'd need to bring us to trial, right?"

"I don't know." Kim ran a hand through her pixie do, causing it to spike in all the right places. "But that's a good point. I'll bring it up to Mason when he calls later on, hopefully with good news that can get us totally free and clear from this mess."

"Whatever happens is going to be without me," Harley said.

Jayda looked at her. "Why?"

"I'm leaving."

"Harley, don't run. I know you don't want Jesse to go back to jail, but—"

"I'm not running." A smile softened Harley's face, and her voice. "We're going to California, on Tuesday. Jesse got his money and is taking Mom back to the holistic center."

"Harley, that's great news!"

"Yes!" Jayda agreed.

"Besides Jesse getting out," Harley said, "it's the best news I've ever received in my life."

"What about your friend, Kat?" Jayda asked.

"What, that the club fired her? Cats have nine lives, didn't you know? She'll be fine."

Harley had been sworn to secrecy and couldn't share the details on what happened once it got back to Bill that Kat knew the woman who'd helped bring down his friend. He'd immediately broken off their friendship, cut Kat off financially, and had her fired from the club. But a smart woman was one who followed her own advice, as Kat had done. Shortly after she was canned, a padded envelope showed up at the Nebraskan attorney's office. Someone else had been caught on video with a flaming redhead who, unlike Harley, made sure her face was shown. A short time later, Kat received the deed to her condo, and her bank account got a healthy infusion. Who needed Bottoms when experiencing life at the top?

"What about you, Jayda?" Kim asked. "How's Nicky?"

"He and Daniel are back at the auto shop. People have been waiting on them, loyal customers who know they need the work. They're booked out for six months already, working fourteen hours a day and making up for lost time."

"I hope it's not all work and no play," Kim teased.

"Not at all. We're trying to have a little sister or brother for Alejandra, and are planning to get married next June. I hope everything's over by then so we can put this crazy chapter behind us and get on with our lives."

"That's what Kendall is trying to do," Kim said. "The whole family is going into counseling to try and heal from not only this situation but from cracks that were in the marriage before our son's arrest."

"Honestly," Harley began, "there were times I never thought I'd see this day. I'm proud to say we truly lived up to our names."

"What? Badass bitches?" Jayda asked.

"That, too." Harley nodded. "But I was referring to our other name: women helping innocent prisoners. Remember that day at Johnny's when we made a promise to ourselves to get justice for our guys?"

Kim smiled. "I sure do."

Harley held up her water glass. "To justice served."

"Justice served," Kim said, her orange juice held high.

"Justice served for all our men," Jayda added. She toasted with a sip from her cup of hot chocolate. "And hopefully more justice to come."

44

Hammond was teeing up on the Edgefield Golf Course's tenth hole when two suited men walked across the pristine green grass and quietly informed him that he was under arrest for solicitation to commit murder. He asked to not be handcuffed, and they agreed to allow him to accompany them freely but added that any rash move on his part would lead to a very public takedown. He complied, ambling beside them as if on a casual stroll, laughing and maintaining the same boyish megawatt smile that had accompanied him to Capitol Hill. His attorney, Geoffrey Sullivan, was called before the car carrying Grey left Edgefield Estates. Geoffrey fought to keep Hammond in Kansas, but because the attempted murder had taken place across state lines in Missouri, the prosecutor demanded that Hammond be treated like the many criminals he'd so vigorously prosecuted. His country club ride ended at the steps of Kansas City, Missouri's metropolitan jail where, because it was Saturday, he was forced to spend two days, and bonded out Monday morning.

In those two days the entire country speculated on who released the sex tape. There were plenty of possibilities, from former rival Jack Myers to former and current prisoners with a grudge. They'd even dug up an old flame with whom he'd had a short-term affair ten years ago. Unfortunately for him, this ex-mistress craved the spotlight. Rather than flat-out deny she was the one who sent the tape, she milked her fifteen minutes for all she could get, and in selling her suddenly relevant back-story to various tabloids made a little money as well. The idea that this somehow involved the prison-for-profit players also continued to be debated among political pundits on news TV. Then late Sunday night, prosecutors in the case involving Kim Logan released a statement that the hit man in the murder-for-hire scheme had agreed to be their star witness. Even more damning, said hit man claimed to have a recording of the phone call where Grey ordered her killed. So when the senator walked out of the tall concrete building on Monday morning at ten a.m. wearing a tailored black suit, *Men in Black* sunglasses, and his signature smile, there were almost two dozen local and na-tional media lining the steps, calling for statements.

"Did you order the killing of Kim Logan?"

"Senator, are you guilty?"

"What was it like to be in the place where you've put so many innocent people?"

"Did you hire a hit man?"

"Is it true that Debbie Stone was your mistress?"

"Senator, any comment on the charges?"

The small posse that included Grey's attorney, assistant, publicist, and a boulder of a man acting as his bodyguard stopped at the bottom of the steps. Geoffrey spoke into a gaggle of microphones stuck in his face. "My client, Senator Hammond Grey, has been falsely accused and wrongfully ar-rested, and will be fully vindicated when we have our day in court. That is all."

The boulder stepped forward and cleared a path to the lim-ousine that waited at the curb. Hammond and Geoffrey, his high-powered, highly paid defense lawyer who'd successfully represented mobsters, politicians, celebrities, and troubled athletes, climbed inside.

Caroline was there, too, had been holed up in strategy sessions with Geoffrey and Hartwell all weekend, discussing a situation that for the first time in her political career she wasn't sure could be fixed. Catching the door before they closed it, she held up the bag of personal belongings retrieved from Hammond's jail stint. "Senator, your personal items."

Hammond removed his sunglasses, looked at it and at her. "Trash, just like the people trying to bring me down," he muttered. "Toss it in the nearest garbage, where they belong."

The car pulled off. Hammond dropped his cool façade. He stripped off the suit jacket, pulled his tie loose, and reached for the bottle of Scotch he'd requested.

Geoff eyed his client. "You okay?"

"As well as can be expected, considering I spent the weekend in a hellhole."

"At least we got you segregated from the population. You haven't seen a hellhole until you experience a regular cell."

"As you have?" he asked with a cocked brow and drink offer.

"As I've visited," Geoff said, declining the offer for a tumbler of Scotch.

Hammond poured a healthy shot and took a long sip as he stretched his legs. "No one gets to the top without scraping the bottom. But there's no way this can be pinned on me."

Geoff pressed a button on the console and raised the privacy partition. "So that's what happened? You didn't have it out for that Logan lady, and there's no way your ordering a killing could be on tape?"

"You know me better than that. I'd never put something on tape so incriminating as a murder solicitation."

"So this news about there being a star witness . . ."

"Look, if someone heard me say something negative about

someone and then decided to take matters in their own hands, with no prompting from me, then that's on their back, not mine. I know a guy, okay? Did a favor for him ten years ago, as a young prosecuting attorney. We talked. I admit I talked about my contempt for those women. But that I asked him to kill them? No way."

Geoff stared out the window, took in the passing scenery down Interstate 35. Just twenty-five short years ago this land was basically tumbleweed. Now businesses lined every inch of land between Kansas City, Missouri, and Edgefield, Kansas, just a few miles southwest of the larger town of Olathe.

"We've navigated some dicey waters this year," he finally said. "This accusation is the roughest one yet."

"You're the Babe Ruth of the courtroom," Hammond replied with bravado that he didn't feel. "Their star witness is a rookie just up from the farm team. I have full confidence in your ability to fully discredit him, shift the focus of attention, and make this go away. I can get you started with some background information that might make the guy think twice about testifying against me. Some information that if made public would be not only damaging for him but for his family as well."

"What about the one claiming to be an ex-mistress, Debbie Stone?"

"What about her?"

"Was she your mistress?"

"For someone like her, that would have been a promotion."

"But you do admit to screwing her."

"Outside of our professional liaison, that's the most I'll admit."

"She's the easier of the two fires that need to be extinguished. I could come from the scorned woman angle, or an extortion angle perhaps, get her to stop yapping to the media."

"I'd rather we stay away from anything financial. Creating an interest in my money is the last thing we need."

Geoff chuckled. "Duly noted. Speaking of, you should probably get with your accountant and make sure there are no holes or weak links in the laundry room."

"Everyone in that chain was chosen very carefully, all money hungry and devious enough to keep their mouths shut. Plus it's diverse and nonsensical. That's an area where we don't have anything to worry about."

Or so he thought. Little did Grey know that at that very moment a plan was being put in motion that would collapse his carefully built house of deceiving cards and leave him all washed up.

The limo exited the interstate and after a short drive down Highway 77 took the Edgefield exit. A couple left and right turns, and they passed the Edgefield Golf Course and Country Club. It had been a source of pride for him since being part of the team that led its construction; Hammond turned away from the sparkling man-made lake near the area of the course he'd forever now think of as "handcuff hole," the tenth hole where his perfect, successful life was temporarily interrupted.

Just a little hitch in the giddyup. That's what Grey's grandfather would have said about the weekend's events. As they turned toward the majestic wrought-iron gated entrance and the sign in the stone façade announcing Edgefield Estates, Grey's confidence returned, his mood lifted. His own personal sunshine, the beautiful Sunnie Grey, waited just beyond those gates. His faithful family had never lost confidence in him, had always seen the very best of who he was or at the very least who he wanted to be. One second inside of his wife's waiting arms and everything would be all right.

The car pulled into the Greys' circular drive. He turned to Geoff with an outstretched hand. "All right then, buddy. Let's talk a little later when you've settled on a plan."

Geoff returned the hearty handshake. "Don't worry about it. Take today to relax, regroup, spend time with your family. We'll get through this, Hammond. Take care."

Hammond exited the limo, stood and breathed in the fresh smell of freedom, felt the cool breeze of a fabulously gated life. Forty-eight hours ago he'd been housed with society's bottom feeders. But right now with a stellar support team, killer attorney, and protective family, he felt on top of the world. Whistling a tune, he stepped through the solid mahogany double doors of his colonial estate. It was quiet and peaceful, as always, eliciting the subtle smell of gardenia, Sunnie's favorite flower. Belatedly he wished he'd thought to bring home a bouquet and made a mental note to have his assistant deliver one later. He glanced at his watch. Ten o'clock. The children were in school. The housekeeper had Mondays off. Sunnie would probably be in her scrapbooking room, or perhaps in the exercise room practicing yoga, her latest fad. He looked in each place. She was in neither.

"Sunnie? Hey, hon."

The smell of cooking food was absent, but Grey walked to the kitchen anyway. Empty.

He walked to the other wing of the house and up the stairs to the master suite. "Sunnie, darling. I'm home!"

Another set of double doors was at the end of the hall. They were open. Low light poured through them, filtered through drawn blinds. Sounds of a Beethoven piece floated into the hall. Hammond smiled, relaxed a little more, and increased his stride. "Sunnie!"

Sunnie wasn't in the main section of the large seven-hundred-foot suite. He walked into her dressing room and saw a note on the vanity. She knew he was on his way home. *No way would she have gone anywhere knowing of my impending arrival. Unless it was an emergency.* Hammond's brow furrowed as he walked over and picked up the single sheet of pink lined paper with a border of spring flowers. The page was filled with Sunnie's curlicue cursive scrawl. Grey's first thought was that whatever she'd written would have probably been easier to convey in a phone call.

My dearest Hammond:
After fifteen years of faithfulness, a year of careful
observation, and many years of soul-searching, I have de-
cided to leave you and end this sham of a marriage.

Reading the unexpected declaration hit Grey like a punch in the gut. He stumbled onto the petite, velvet-covered vanity bench, momentarily breathless, then lifted his head and continued to read.

I know this message catches you off guard. See, dar-
ling, during all of these years you've pretended to love
me, I've pretended, too. I am no longer the all-trusting,
easily beguiled, naïve girl you married. I am a woman
who after years of refusing to acknowledge the obvious
has opened her eyes and finally faced a lifetime of ugly
truths. Not only of our union but of who you are and
who by complacency I've allowed myself to become. For
that which has been allowed through that silence, I ask
God's forgiveness. Now, I must do what I can to absolve
my guilt and cleanse these sins. I pray that someday you
do the same.

Looking back, I'm not sure you ever were the man I
thought you to be. A small part of me holds out hope that
the upstanding, intelligent, and yes, driven man I
thought I met and married as a teenager will show up
once again, and present a different version of himself to
the world.

With all the love that remains in my heart, Sunnie.

Grey lifted tentative fingers to his face, touched the wetness of tears that her words had produced. Clarence had said this could never happen, that Sunnie would never leave him. He crumbled the pretty pink paper in his fist and prayed his friend and mentor was right. With strength from a determination to win back his wife, he pushed up from the vanity bench, strode downstairs to the garage, got into his car, and backed out of the driveway. His predictable Sunnie was either at her parents' house or that of her best friend since childhood. Grey had never lost anything in his life. He didn't plan to start now.

Admirable resolve, but as many have learned, life did not always go according to plans.

45

Specifics in the linen and gold-leafed invitation had been vague. Even suspect. But if genuine, the opportunity was too good to resist. Attend a ninety-minute luncheon presentation on a new, all-inclusive luxury hotel chain in the Caribbean and within the next twelve months receive airfare for two and a free four-day, three-night stay at any of their twelve locations. When Kim had called the number printed on the invitation, she'd reached a recording that basically reiterated what the card said, but added that the limited special had only been offered to a few select individuals. Why, of course. Weren't they all? She'd almost backed out but, just to be sure, she'd called The Raphael, an upscale hotel in KC's tony Country Club Plaza, and the luncheon had been confirmed. So she RSVP'd. If nothing else, she'd have a great lunch.

The presentation was to begin at noon. At eleven-fifty, Kim pulled into a parking spot and entered the lobby. When asked, the concierge directed her to a signature suite on a top floor. By the time she reached the double doors, Kim was totally intrigued. When she opened them, she was stunned.

"Harley?"

An equally surprised Harley turned around, a slight frown marring her perfectly made up face. "Kim?"

"You're here for the Caribbean presentation?"

"Yep. Invitation came in the mail a week ago. I almost threw it away but called the number and it sounded legit, so . . . here I am."

"Same here," Kim said, looking around the living area to the dining room beyond them. She walked toward it and was surprised to see an elaborate yet small table setting. The invitation mentioned that only a few had been invited, but only four people?

"Only four place settings," Harley said, joining her in the dining room. "Weird, huh?"

"I was just thinking the very same thing. What is really going on?"

"I've been trying to figure it out since I got here. But so far, you're the only other person that's arrived."

Both women heard the outer door open slowly. They turned in unison just as Jayda peeked inside.

"Hey, guys!"

Harley and Kim looked at each other.

"Jayda." Harley walked past Jayda to the still open door. She looked out into the hall, both directions. It was clear. She closed the door. "Now I'm starting to freak out a little bit."

"Let me guess," Kim said to Jayda. "You're here for a presentation on a new hotel?"

"Yes, and to get a free trip to the Caribbean." Jayda pulled out an invitation that looked exactly like the ones both Kim and Harley had received. "I'm assuming that's what brought y'all here, too?"

Harley nodded. Kim reached into her handbag's side pouch and pulled out the designer card. "All three of us got the same card."

"Why would someone pick out the three of us?"

Jayda walked breezily into the room, tossed her purse on the couch, and continued to the floor-to-ceiling windows overlooking the plaza. "Maybe it's coincidence. Maybe more people are coming. It's a free trip to the Caribbean with airfare included. So at the end of the day, who cares?"

"I do." Kim joined her at the window. "This very well could be some kind of setup."

"A setup for what?"

"To get us together," Harley answered, walking over to the window as well.

"And alone," Kim added.

The three women slowly looked at each other.

Harley then took in the large plate glass. "Guys, let's get away from the window!"

Jayda dove behind the curtain while Kim and Harley made a dash for the wall.

"What did you see?" Jayda's muffled voice asked through the thick curtain.

"Nothing," Harley admitted. "But if someone wanted to shoot us, standing at the window made us clear targets."

Jayda snatched away the curtain, her disheveled thick black locks half covering her face. "Seriously? You almost gave me a heart attack on a maybe?"

"It's just after twelve," Kim noted. "And no one else is here, no hotel employee bringing in lunch, no representative from this supposed luxury hotel. No one but the three of us."

"Make that the two of y'all," Harley corrected as she snatched up her purse from the table. "This is too crazy to be a coincidence. Someone wanted the three of us alone in this room. I'm not going to wait around to find out why."

After checking the peephole, she opened the door, turned to her right and—

"Oh, excuse me!"

"I'm so sorry," the classy-looking, well-dressed woman replied. "Couldn't see you for this big hat I'm wearing."

By now Kim and Jayda were also at the door. "Are you from the Caribbean hotel?" Jayda asked.

The woman shook her head.

"You're here for the presentation?" Harley asked.

"No." The slightest of smiles accompanied her answer.

"You're not pushing a tray, so obviously lunch isn't what you're delivering. Who are you?"

The woman removed her large Jackie Onassis–style sunglasses along with the stylish straw hat. "I'm Sunnie Grey, Hammond Grey's soon-to-be ex-wife."

In that moment, one feather could have knocked over all three women.

"I sent the invitations. May I come in?"

Jayda and Kim stepped back so Sunnie could enter. Harley followed her inside.

Kim was the first one to get her voice back. "Something about you felt familiar, but even after you took off the hat and glasses I had no idea."

"It's probably the hair," Sunnie suggested. "This deep auburn is closer to my natural color but"—she slid a quick glance to Harley—"my husband always did prefer blondes. After fifteen years I finally have the opportunity to take a break from bleaching." She twirled as if among three best friends. "What do you think?"

"We, um, I . . . it looks good!" Kim said.

"I like the red, too," Harley said. "Brings out the green of your eyes."

"Am I the only one who feels this shit is hella cuckoo and downright nuts? This is Grey's wife, y'all. And we're acting like it's a besties' brunch? You've been sleeping with the enemy," Harley continued, her focus on Sunnie. "And I for one don't give a good got-damn what color your hair is. The color of your last name is gray so you'd best get to explaining why you brought us here because I'm just about two seconds from knocking your ass out!"

Kim stepped over to the would-be wrestler, knowing Harley could definitely be a woman of her word. "We all want to know why we're here, and quickly."

"Perhaps we can all sit down?" Sunnie gestured toward the suite's sitting area. "I will gladly explain everything. I've been waiting to do so for a very long time."

After a few hesitant seconds Harley marched over and plopped down on a chair, folded her arms, and glared at Sunnie. Kim walked over and sat calmly. Jayda followed, choosing to lean against the wall.

"I'm a little nervous." Sunnie reached for her purse.

Harley snatched it even as Kim rose from the seat. "What's in here?" she demanded, opening the bag.

"Just a handkerchief," Sunnie explained, clearly taken aback. "Do you think I'm . . ." She melted into the chair cushion as the gravity of what the women thought became apparent. "I'm not here to hurt you, though I can understand why your thoughts would lean that way. I'm here to help you. I've been helping you. I have followed all of your journeys, and although you are just now meeting me, you have been more influential in my life than you know. In a strange way, I feel we are already friends."

Harley gave off a disbelieving snort as she tossed the purse back over to Sunnie.

Sunnie pulled a white lace handkerchief out of it and twirled it in her fingers.

"Let's let her explain herself," Kim said. "Obviously she has something to say that we don't know about, and need to hear."

Sunnie gave a silent thank-you to Kim, took a deep breath, and revealed her first truth. "I leaked the tape."

"What?"

"You?!"

"The tape?"

All of the questions were spoken at once. The women looked among themselves.

"The tape that came out in the news last week?" Kim asked. Sunnie nodded.

Jayda glanced at Kim before addressing Sunnie. "How . . . could you have leaked it? I mean, was it your tape?"

"Ha!" Sunnie's laugh was light and genuine. She relaxed for the first time since entering the room. "I think we are going to get along famously. But only if we're honest. I know how the tape was made. In fact, I observed its entire production."

Harley looked from Kim to Jayda and finally to Sunnie. "What do you mean?"

"I know that Kim filmed it, that Jayda worked as the assistant, and that you, my dear Harley, performed the starring role."

Amid open mouths and silent expressions of *WTF* came a door knock.

"One moment, ladies," Sunnie said, rising. "That's probably our first course."

While ushering the women into the dining room and plating individual helpings of Parmesan fried green tomatoes atop a wedge salad, Sunnie shared the secrets she'd kept for many years as calmly as if discussing the weather.

"Hammond's unfaithfulness began early in our marriage, just after Matthew, our firstborn, arrived. Men will be men, of course, and like many women in similar positions before me I turned the other cheek and bought a new bauble, piece of furniture, or designer dress with every indiscretion. I won't disclose his level of promiscuity, but with what I've purchased due to such liaisons, we could probably open up a secondhand store."

Kim laughed out loud and leaned forward as Sunnie continued. Jayda moved from the wall and sat next to Kim. Even Harley relaxed.

"I had no desire for the type of debauchery which he seemed to enjoy, being a good Christian girl and all. Hammond was a good provider, an attentive father, and in most ways a thoughtful if somewhat presumptive husband. All in all, given the state of some marriages I've witnessed, I considered myself lucky and was for the most part content.

"Do eat up, ladies. For the main course you'll have the choice of either salmon or strip steak. Not knowing your palettes, I went with the two most popular preferences."

Sunnie cut a dainty bite of the fried tomato and ate with relish. "I love the sautéed spinach puree. The creaminess is a perfect for the tomato's acidity. Don't you agree?"

Jayda nodded. "The first time I've had these, but it's really good."

Kim finally picked up her fork.

Harley's look had gone from distaste to disbelief. "I don't have much of an appetite for food right now but sure could use a drink."

"Ah, of course. I'll request the champagne I ordered be brought up as well. Please excuse me for one more moment."

She left the room. Jayda immediately reacted by mouthing, "Oh. My. God."

"I know, right?" Kim whispered.

"You ask me this is still—" Harley's comment was cut short when Sunnie re-entered the room. In turn, Harley cut short Sunnie's soliloquy. "Grey cheated. Big deal. What does that have to do with the tape and you saying we did it?"

Sunnie finished her bite and reached for the linen napkin. "I chose the townhouse in Washington where Hammond stays," she said, while dabbing her mouth. "I also selected the elaborate yet discreet surveillance system it contains."

"Whoa!" Harley jumped back in her chair. "Damn, Mrs. Grey. I had you pegged all wrong."

"So did Hammond." Again, that small, wry smile. "And please, call me Sunnie, because I'm leaving the gray days behind me, and heading for sunshine."

"All right, Sunnie." Harley held up her hand. She and

Sunnie high-fived. "Here I'm thinking you're this sadity soccer mom chick and you're straight gangster!"

Kim shook her head. "I can't believe this."

"I am shocked," Jayda said.

"Hell, that comment jumpstarted my appetite." Harley picked up her fork and dove into the wedge salad. "So you saw us that night, everything that happened?"

"I saw that and much more. Including the many nights his publicist Caroline Coker spent in the same bed where that tape was made. I observed snatches of their lewd trysts, and listened in on some very . . . informative . . . conversations."

"And one of those conversations included details of the nondisclosure agreement Grey made us sign."

"It did. By then, I'd gone back and watched the surveillance tape. I knew that Hammond was the man on that bed, even though he tried to deny it. I must say I watched the three of you in total shock and disbelief. I sat amazed at your audacity,"—she looked at Harley—"your strength,"—she smiled at Kim—"and your unwavering loyalty." She nodded at Jayda, whose eyes were suspiciously bright, and whose lip trembled.

"You got all that from watching the tape?" Harley asked.

Sunnie shook her head. "I'd seen or read about some of it before. I knew about your son, Kim, Kendall. Went online one day after reading your story in the paper. I knew what I'd heard, what Hammond had told me. But I wanted to look at you through my eyes, curious as to what I'd see."

"What did you see?"

"A mama bear!"

"Ha!"

"One who growled loud and long, just as I would have done. From that I became interested in the organization, WHIP, and followed you loosely, mainly online. I don't remember reading anything about you, Harley, but I do remember a story on your family, Jayda, and the auto shop business."

"You really did follow us?"

"Yes, Jayda. I really did. That's why in listening in on the meeting that followed Hammond's receipt of the tape, and hearing the decision to release your loved ones? I was over-joyed. Could have almost exploded with happiness, literally! It was as though someone I loved was in prison and about to get out. And you know what?"

Sunnie paused, looked at each woman with watery eyes. One tear, then another, rolled down her cheek.

"Just now, in this moment, I realize that was so very true. I was the prisoner, who in seeing all of your fortitude, found the courage within myself to break free."

Jayda cried openly now. She leaned over and hugged Sunnie, who dabbed her tears. Kim was clearly moved, but her eyes were dry. As were Harley's, but they were filled with com-passion as she reached over and squeezed Sunnie's arm.

"Thank you," Sunnie said to Jayda. She sat back in her chair. "I really needed that hug."

Sunnie paused, took a sip of water. "I would have bet my di-vorce settlement that y'all were going to leak the tape. I've loved Hammond for almost twenty years, and I'll continue to love him. But right is right, and wrong is wrong, and from what I gathered he'd done to you and your loved ones—taken their freedom, jeopardized their futures, splintered your families—you all were going to nail him to the wall as soon as your men were free. I just knew it. And I applauded the move. That was one I could never have made. But after hearing the terms of the agreement, the threat of your men spending their lives in jail if the video got out? An idea that came courtesy of a woman named Caroline Coker, by the way, and I must admit it was brilliant. She's brilliant and beautiful, two of the many things my husband loves about her. Anyway, I heard that and knew that Hammond had found a way to win once again, to walk away from a fight without so much as a scar to show he'd been

in battle. In all the years we were together, whether profession-
ally or privately, he never lost a fight."

"And that's when you entered the ring," Kim said softly.

"Yes," she said, just above a whisper. "That's when I decided to switch teams, and join your fight."

For the next hour Sunnie poured out her heart, apologized
for what she'd known about and not acted upon, and promised
to be a better woman in the future. While she said she couldn't
confirm that Grey had profited from the Edgefield facility, she
admitted that it was something that given the opportunity he'd
likely do. As they finished dessert and she rose to leave, the
hugs that were given were genuine.

"Ladies, while the invitation's contents were a ruse to get
you here, the Caribbean vacation is genuine. I'm sure to get a
healthy settlement from the divorce. With the ammunition I
have, Hammond is unlikely to fight me. You all helped me do
something that I'd not had the strength to do before now. You
helped me expose something that needed to be seen in the
light of day, before more lives were negatively impacted. You
fought for justice, and won. A vacation where the three of you
can take a break from all the stress my husband's actions and
those of his peers caused you is the very least I can do."

She walked to the door, waved as she exited, and then stuck
her head back in with a nod toward Harley's feet. "Been meaning to tell you as I've admired them since arriving. I absolutely
love your stilettos. "

EPILOGUE

One year later . . .

It was the last Sunday in August. The weather was perfect: eighty degrees and barely a breeze. The seventy-nine-thousand-plus seater Arrowhead stadium in Kansas City, Missouri, was a sea of cheering red. It was a preseason game, but one couldn't tell. The excitement and buzz felt like that of a championship playoff game. In section 118, at the fifty-yard line, a group of loud, proud supporters of Kendall Logan anxiously awaited the appearance of the Kansas City Chiefs and their recently signed backup quarterback. Most of them had been there for hours, participating in age-old tailgating tradition. The Logans' neighbors had been Chiefs season ticket holders for years and were tailgating pros. They'd customized a Chevrolet Explorer high-top van into a virtual chef's kitchen with pull-out burners, grills, and refrigeration. No burgers and franks for this group. They'd spent the afternoon feasting on barbeque ribs and chicken, roast beef, roasted corn, grilled veggies, and a variety of sides. Liquor had flowed as easily as the laughter and now, two hours later, everyone was in a very happy mood.

"This is so much fun!" Jayda exclaimed as the teams took

the field for warm-ups. It's been years since I've come to a Chiefs game, and I've never been able to party in this grand style. Thanks again, Kim." She leaned over and gave Kim a hug. Jayda was the type who loved everybody, especially when inebriated. She'd been hugging folks all afternoon, friend and stranger alike.

"You're welcome, sister. This grand style is courtesy of our neighbors the Goodes, and Kendall. They're the ones who pulled strings and got all of these seats together. They all belong to season ticket holders and, quite frankly, I don't know how the feat was pulled off. But I'm glad they did!"

She nudged Jayda. "Look at your guys. I think they're trying to get some screen time."

The women looked over as Nicky and Rafael, their shirtless chests showcasing Nicky's artistic prowess with an Arrowhead supertron, the word CHIEFS across their pecs and magnificently drawn jerseys stamped SANCHEZ, stepped into the aisle and executed a funky man dance. It wasn't long before the screen operator homed in on them and placed their image on the oversize LED screen. The guys loved it. The audience cheered.

Jayda turned to Kim, her expression suddenly serious, her eyes shining with tears. "I can't thank you enough for what you did for Nicky and Daniel."

"It wasn't me, it was Kendall. He was blessed to receive a large signing bonus and wanted to spread the gratitude. He had a little motivation from his grandmother, who reminded him about tithing and instructed him that at least ten percent of what he made belonged to God and should be used to help people."

"It certainly did. By being able to expand their shop, Nicky and Daniel are doing three times the business they were before and still have a crazy waitlist. But there's more. It just happened last week."

"What?"

"Those pictures that Kendall posted of Nicky's artwork on his car got viewed by a cable network who now wants to talk to him about having his own TV show!"

"You're kidding!"

"Nope. Totally serious. Reality television is big business these days."

Kim screamed, pulled Jayda into an exuberant embrace. "I'm so happy for you!"

A loud voice suddenly boomed above them. "Hey, wait! What's a celebration without me?"

Harley and Kim spoke together. "Harley!" They turned as Jesse joined his wife in the seats just above them and shared a hug with the third musketeer.

Kim pulled away for a closer look and then hugged her again. "You look terrific! Marriage and California obviously agree with you."

"I love living out there," Harley said after the women had greeted Jesse. She put her arms around Jesse's waist and laid her head on his chest. "And I love being Mrs. Cooper."

"Oh, hush." Jayda's feigned anger was in total contrast to the smile on her face. "We're still mad at you for eloping."

"How many times do we have to say we're sorry for that? We didn't mean to. We went to Vegas, got drunk, and ended up in a wedding chapel with Elvis officiating and Michael Jackson serving as best man!" This got a laugh from everyone who heard it, even strangers. "When you guys visit us in San Diego, we'll have another private, more serious ceremony. Okay?"

Jayda nodded. "You got it."

"Shannon came, too, right?" Kim asked, looking toward where the Coopers had entered. "Where is she?"

"She couldn't make it but sends her love. Nothing's wrong," Harley added when seeing her friends' concerned expressions.

"The holistic program she's on I swear is working miracles. She stayed behind for another reason." A pause and then, "My dad."

Kim was floored. "Your father is in California?"

"Yep. Chris Buchanan. Been there all this time, since I was nine years old."

"Oh, my goodness, Harley," Jayda said, offering a hug. "I don't remember your ever mentioning him? That had to have been mind-boggling, seeing him after all these years. How are you doing? How is he? What happened?"

"In three words? Sex, drugs, and rock and roll." Harley counted on her fingers. "Oops. That's actually six words. But the bottom line is he's back in our lives, more in Mom's than mine. I'm still pretty pissed at him for taking off. He's got several years in the dog house, at least."

"Don't spend a lot of time on him being gone," Kim said. "He's here now. And he's your father. For better or worse, you only get one."

"Yeah, whatever." Outwardly, Harley dismissed Kim's comment. But she tucked it away to chew on later.

"I'm just so happy Shannon is better," Kim said. "All from the herbs and vitamins?"

"That plus a raw food diet, energy healing, and a spiritual practice seems to have her on a path to where totally beating the cancer isn't guaranteed, but gives her the strength to put up one hell of a fight. I think the year-round sunshine is good for her, too. For the first time in years I've allowed myself to hope that Mom may see her grandchildren."

Kim's eyes widened. "Does that mean—"

"No, it doesn't, and no, it won't for another couple years. We definitely want children, but right now we've got an empire to build."

With Kendall's financial gift and her mother as poster proof, Jesse and Harley had relocated to California to partner with the company that designed the program that had helped restore her health and produced the medication that led to her continued improvement. A natural salesperson, Jesse's southern charm was a perfect southern California fit that made his idea of packaging the nutritional herbs for a national retail market successful from day one. Harley's beauty and small-town down-home ways drew clients in and made her honestly delivered pitch totally believable. Over the past year she'd grown the company's clientele by thirty percent.

Beside her, Kim's husband, Aaron, talked to the neighbors who'd somehow schmoozed their fellow season ticket holders into forgoing the season opener and giving Kim, Jayda, and Harley's family these premium seats. Connie and Phil Goode, along with their son, Wilson, Kendall's best friend, chatted among other families they'd gotten to know well over the past ten years. A roar tore through the stands as the Chiefs took the field and warm-ups began. Aaron turned to Kim and squeezed her hand. She smiled, thankful for the genuine love that once again shone in his eyes. With a little counseling and lots of prayer, they'd gone through the storm of their lives, weathered it, and come out on the other side a stronger couple.

That Jessica had taken a job at another school had undoubtedly helped matters, too, even though Kim now believed Aaron when he said nothing physical had happened between them. As part of her therapy Kim had dug deep and found forgiveness, and Aaron learned that while he'd not had sex with Jessica, he'd developed an emotional intimacy with the coworker that should have been shared with his wife. He was encouraged to forgive himself for hiding his feelings of vulnerability and fear behind his knight armor, and Kim to do the same for the part she'd played in the helpless feeling that eventually led her husband to the comfort of a woman he felt was more understanding. There was still a ways to go toward total restoration. In some areas life was still partly cloudy. But both had faith that their marital forecast called for more sunshine than rain.

After the national anthem was sung, the crowd settled down

as the announcer began introducing the teams. A few minutes passed before the moment came that Kim had waited for. She stood and tried to hold her phone steady as she caught it on film.

"Wearing number two, tonight's starting quarterback for the Kansas City Chiefs . . . Kendall Logan!"

Forget a clear picture. The phone shook and was turned this way and that as Kim jumped, screamed and tried to capture the reactions of all around her.

When Aaron's face came into view, he was uncharacteristically outgoing, the stadium excitement contagious. "That's my son out there!"

They hugged and joined the others, who danced to the music of Queen blaring from the speakers. "We will rock you."

No doubt life had rocked these three women, and thrown their families for a loop. But here they were still standing—happy, cheering, and if need be, ready to fight again for justice, in whatever shoes they had on.

DON'T MISS
Collusion
by De'nesha Diamond

Framed for a high-profile murder, Abrianna Parker finds
herself hurtling down a conspiracy rabbit hole in a desperate
attempt to clear her name. Her only way out is to go after
the most powerful man in the country. But the powers
that be play dirty. . . .

Enjoy the following excerpt from *Collusion*. . . .

The Bunker . . .

In an unknown place in an unknown location along the bowels of Washington, DC, Douglas "Ghost" Jenkins, lifelong political hacktivist, pulled open the metal door of his underground bunker to see his old friend.

"Well, if it ain't Bonnie and Clyde," Ghost said, blocking the entrance to his hideout. "Or should I say Clyde and Clyde?" He cocked his head at Abrianna and took in her outfit. "Nice disguise."

"Thanks."

Ghost's gaze darted to Julian and Draya. "Damn, if every time I see you, man, your ass don't multiply. What kind of place do you think I'm running here?"

"Really? You're going to do this now? I have an injured woman. She's been shot."

Ghost straightened and glanced at Abrianna. "What? Again?"

"Not me this time."

Draya raised her good arm. "It's me."

Interest lit Ghost's eyes. "Well, hello."

Draya frowned.

"You're hitting on an injured woman?" Kadir asked.

"Is it my fault that women are always getting shot around you?" Ghost stepped back, allowing the small group to enter.

Hunkered down behind a row of terminals sat a skeletal crew of millennial hackers. Ghost introduced them as *the fellas* to Draya.

"Uh, nice to meet you," she said and then looked to Abrianna like *Who is this clown?*

"C'mon." Abrianna led Draya toward the bunker's back cot room. "I'll fix you right up."

Ghost smiled as he watched them walk away.

Arms crossed, Julian stepped forward to block Ghost's view.

"Oh. My bad." Ghost looked to Kadir. "Just how many people are you planning to tell about this place?"

"Chill. They're cool," Kadir said. "So what happened to you the other night? I thought you'd still be waiting to post bail."

"C'mon, playa. Am I the sort of person to give the cops my *real* ID?"

"They were putting you in the back of a squad car."

"Just some rookie busting my chops. You know how they do. Of course, I hope you got rid of the van. I had to report it stolen."

"Yeah. We traded that one in for another one and then filled that one with bullet holes, too."

Ghost chuckled. "That straight and narrow path that you swore that you were on isn't looking too damn straight, if you ask me."

"You don't know the half of it." Kadir looked around and leaned in close. "What do you know about . . . telekinesis?"

"What?"

"You know . . ." Kadir shrugged, inched closer. "The ability to move shit with your mind. Have you ever known anyone who could—"

"KADIR!"

At Abrianna's shout, Kadir and Ghost took off toward the back.

In the cot room, Draya and Abrianna stood in front of a nine-inch TV.

When the guys couldn't see what was the emergency was, Kadir asked, "Is everything okay?"

Abrianna shook her head and then pointed at the news broadcast on the screen.

Federal Judge Katherine J. Sanders will be sworn in tomorrow as the eighteenth chief justice of the United States Supreme Court, enabling President Daniel Walker to put his stamp on the court for decades to come. Sanders's nomination had been slow walked, while the Republican Senate members waited to see whether the new speaker would pursue impeachment of the president. But with Speaker Reynolds's death, the Senate majority leader decided to move ahead with the confirmation.

Abrianna stared transfixed at the image in the corner of the screen. "That's her!"

"That's who?" Kadir asked.

She pointed. "That's the other woman from the hotel. That's Kitty!"

"Judge Katherine Sanders?" he thundered. "*She's* the one you think framed you for murder?"

"Yes! I'd know that face anywhere. It's her!"

"But why?" Kadir asked, puzzled.

"Didn't you hear the reporter?" Draya asked. "That speaker guy was going to impeach the president. An impeachment meant no confirmation. No Supreme Court."

Ghost slapped a hand across his forehead and whistled. "Holy shit. The same judge who sent you to the clink," he said. "The *new* chief justice of the Supreme Court. Ha! Good luck taking her down."

"We're going to need more than luck," Kadir grumbled, ripping off his fake mustache. "We're going to need a miracle."

Ghost shook his head. "Yo, Dawg. That road you are on just got as crooked as a muthafucka."

"No shit," Kadir hissed, staring at Judge Sanders's image on the screen until the telecast cut to a commercial.

Defensive, Abrianna glanced around the eclectic group and read doubt and disbelief. "You guys believe me, don't you? I'm not making it up. She's Kitty—the other woman at the hotel that night."

Draya pressed a hand against Abrianna's shoulder. "I believe you."

"Yeah. I believe you, too," Julian added, curling up only one corner of his lips. His eyes, however, avoided her gaze.

Abrianna's jaw hardened.

Julian explained, "It's just that . . . well, this is *huge*, Bree. The fucking *chief justice* of the Supreme Court? What the fuck are we going to do?"

Abrianna's body slumped. "I have no idea."

"Well. How about that?" Ghost said. "We're all on the same page with our heads up our asses. Great!"

Kadir cut his friend a hard look. "Chill."

"What? I'm just stating facts. It's a miracle that every Uncle Sam soldier isn't pouring into this bitch and hauling our asses to jail right now. You're wanted for bombing the damn airport and your new chick here is wanted for killing the third most powerful man in America. Firing squads were made for terrorists like you two." He held up a hand and added, "I'm just telling you how the media *is* going to spin it."

"And don't forget the dead bitch we left back in the van," Draya reminded them.

Shut up, Abrianna mouthed.

"Come again." Ghost cupped his ear and leaned toward Draya. "Dead body? What dead body?" He looked to Kadir. "What the fuck is she talking about?"

Kadir hedged.

"Mutha—come here! Let me holler at you for a moment." Ghost spun his boy by his shoulder and then shoved him out of the door.

Sighing, Kadir went along. Deep down he knew that he was wrong for springing this situation on Ghost. If the roles had been reversed, he would have gone apeshit.

Ghost jostled Kadir to the bunker's break room and slammed the door. It took another minute to calm down and choose his words carefully. "There is no point in my asking whether you've lost your damn mind, because I already know that since you've laid eyes on that suicidal stripper, you've completely checked the fuck out of reality."

"Ghost, calm—"

"Ah, ah, ah." Ghost held up a finger and shook his head. "You've lost any right to tell me to calm down. I'm not the one whose face is plastered on the news as a domestic terrorist."

"Hold up," Kadir interjected. "You're wanted by the federal authorities too for political hacking."

"For *questioning* . . . and for something that they can't prove *and*, more importantly, my mug shot hasn't debuted on a single wanted poster or news broadcast."

Kadir cocked his head. "Are you jealous?"

"Jealous? Who? Me?" He waved the notion off. "Don't be ridiculous."

Kadir squinted and read the truth in his face.

Ghost swung the conversation back to the matter at hand. "Who is the corpse?"

Kadir sighed.

"Please, please tell me it's not *the* President of the United States."

"Don't be ridiculous," Kadir said.

"Then who?"

"Remember the madam we raced across town to *talk* to?"

"You're shitting me," Ghost said. "She killed her?"

"No. Abrianna didn't kill her," Kadir snapped. "We just . . . sort of *kidnapped* her."

"Oh. Well. That makes more sense. What's a little kidnapping every now and then?" Ghost shrugged with a straight face. "What the fuck, man? Snap out it!"

"We didn't have much of a choice since the woman cleared out of her estate. A friend of Abrianna was catering a party for the woman's boyfriend, so her other friend, Draya, created these disguises and we crashed the joint."

"To kidnap the madam?" Ghost clarified, following along.

"Right. Only . . . there was a hiccup."

Ghost crossed his arms. "That tends to happen when committing *federal* crimes."

Kadir glared.

"What happened?" Ghost asked, rolling his hand, wanting to get the end of the story.

"Bruh, I'm still not sure. This guard showed up when we were loading the body up and I think . . ." Kadir glanced at the closed door and then crossed over to stand in front of it, to make sure that no one entered. He lowered his voice. "I think . . . Abrianna threw this four-hundred-pound guy up against the side of the house—*without* laying a finger on him."

Ghost stared.

"You think I'm crazy, don't you?" Kadir tossed up his hands. "I don't blame you. If I hadn't seen the shit for myself, I wouldn't believe it either, but . . . there's no other explanation. I saw what I saw."

"Catering?"

"Yeah. We—"

"Never mind. Finish the story."

"Like I was saying. The guy startled us, and when he approached the van to see for himself what we were doing, Draya slammed the van door into his face and his gun went off."

"So that's how she got shot?"

"Right. But when the gun went off,"—Kadir voice went even lower—"Abrianna screamed and . . . this huge guy *flew* backwards. I mean literally up in the *air* and slammed into the side of the house, knocking him out cold. I've never seen anything like it."

Silence.

Kadir's hands fell to his sides. "You don't believe me."

"Believe what? That your hooker girlfriend out there has super powers? Sure. Of course, I believe you. Why wouldn't I?"

Kadir's gaze leveled on his friend. "I'm not bullshitting you, man."

Ghost evaluated Kadir and then took a deep breath. "Okay."

"Okay? So you believe me?" Kadir checked, surprised.

"I believe that *you* believe what you thought you saw."

Kadir ran that sentence back through his head. "But . . . you don't believe it happened?"

"Is it important that I believe it? Does it change anything?"

Kadir sighed. "I guess not."

A few minutes later, they returned to the cot room where the group waited.

"I'm not crazy," Abrianna Parker insisted.

Ghost folded his meaty arms while his black gaze centered on her. "I've only known you for a few days, I hope you don't take offense, but I personally think you're bat-shit crazy and I don't want anything more to do with this nonsense." His lethal gaze sliced toward Kadir. "Look, bruh. We go *way* back, but this mess right here? I want no parts of it."

Kadir squared his shoulders at the curt tone. Emotions warred across his face and, despite his own visible doubt, he defended Abrianna. "Why don't we just hear her out?"

"Hear her out? She just said that the new chief justice of the Supreme Court . . . and your mortal enemy, I may add, *murdered* the House speaker of the U.S. Congress, the second man in line to the presidency. Do you know how fucking *crazy* that shit sounds?"

"No crazier than half the conspiracy theories that you've entertained over the years. All of which has you huddled down here in this underground bunker, hiding from the feds in the first place. Is what she's saying really that hard to believe?"

Ghost opened his mouth, but the words never tumbled out.

Kadir arched a brow and cocked his head.

Finally, Ghost closed his mouth and then speared Abrianna with a look. "What happened to the madam? Wasn't she supposedly behind the conspiracy theory when y'all left here the last time? Who is it going to be next? The president?"

"Hey!" Kadir shoved Ghost, sending him careening into the nearest wall.

"Yo, dude!"

"Watch it," Kadir warned.

Julian crowded behind Kadir, ready to tag into the fight.

Tension layered the room while everyone else held their breaths.

Ghost backed down. "All right, man. My bad." He clamped his mouth shut.

Kadir glanced back over at Abrianna. "Please. Continue."

Abrianna battled her pride to get the rest of her story out. "Look, you guys already know the rest. It was my first night as an escort working for Madam Nevaeh. That woman showed up and introduced herself as Kitty. My john was happy when she arrived up. They knew each other. We . . . partied . . . and when I woke up my client was missing part of his head and that Kitty bitch was nowhere to be found. I got out of there, but then gunmen showed up at my apartment. My best friend Shawn, who's still laid up in the hospital right now, took a hit, but I kept running until I jumped into your car, Kadir."

"Where they shot up my car and I brought you here the last time," Kadir finished the story for her.

"Right." She huffed. "Now. What are we going to do?"

Everyone's eyeballs ping-ponged around the room again. Clearly, none of them had a clue to what to do next.

Ghost sighed.

"Great," Ghost moaned.

Their gazes shifted around the room again.

Roger, one of Ghost's hackers, cleared his throat and drew everyone's attention.

Ghost's brows climbed to the center of his forehead. "You got something to say? Speak up."

Nervous, Roger cleared his throat. "Well . . . I take it that the media received the image of Abrianna from the Hay-Adams Hotel security surveillance."

Ghost shrugged. "Yeah, and?"

"Then Kitty, er, Judge Sanders should be on surveillance, too," Abrianna said, grinning.

Roger smiled. "Exactly."

Hope, the last emotion in Pandora's box, filled into the room.

"But how are we going to get our hands on their surveillance footage?" Draya asked.

Kadir's handsome grin stretched. "How else? We *hack*."

However, hacking the luxury hotel turned out to be a more difficult job. Ghost and Kadir ascertained that it would require physical access to the hotel's security server.

"How are we going to manage to do that?" Abrianna asked.

"My guess is that someone is going to have to pose as an employee and break into their security department. Once in there, upload a custom malware to give us access to their digital files."

"That sounds simple, which means it's anything but," Abrianna said.

Ghost smiled. "Smart girl. I'd imagine posing as an employee would be difficult. Something as small staffed as a hotel, everyone would know everybody. Don't you think?"

"Well, it's a pretty big hotel with shops and restaurants—but getting near security . . ." Abrianna shook her head.

"Right."

Julian spoke up. "What if someone was applying for a job?" He had everyone's attention and continued, "I worked security once at a hotel, and our security department was near the human resources office. New hires passed by our department every day."

Ghost and Kadir smiled. "You're hired."

Julian blinked. "Me?"

"Yep. You're not on anybody's radar. And you have the expertise to get in the door." Kadir slapped Julian on the back. "First thing tomorrow you're applying for a job."

Julian looked sick.